The Truth is Always Negotiable

Ernie Dorling

Trenton, Georgia

The Truth is Always Negotiable

Print ISBN: 978-1-64719-864-0
Ebook ISBN: 978-1-64719-865-7

Published by BookLocker.com, Inc., Trenton, Georgia.

Printed on acid-free paper.

This book is a work of fiction. As such, great liberty has been taken to shape the story in a way that is intended to entertain the reader. The characters and events in this book are fictitious. Any similarity to real persons, living or dead, is coincidental and not intended by the author.

BookLocker.com, Inc.
2021

First Edition

Library of Congress Cataloguing in Publication Data
Dorling, Ernie
The Truth is Always Negotiable by Ernie Dorling
Library of Congress Control Number: 2021920413

It seems that in today's woke, PC, entitled, non-violent, power-hungry, avaricious society, with companion mindless and draconian political ideas, any opportunity to be an asshole and create dissension, is what many politicians, and criminals, see as a golden opportunity.

Donald Kincaid

Chapter 1

Six weeks after the presidential election

"It's getting late," the man said.

"Yeah, almost midnight," the other man replied, as he glanced at his watch for the third time in as many minutes. Time passed slowly when he had to wait. Waiting was always the most challenging part. The cold winter air sliced through his lungs and sent a chill through his body as he stood outside waiting for the right moment to enter the house. It would not be long, he told himself. Patience. After all, it is one of the traits of his profession. *Take a deep breath and relax,* he thought to himself. He had been taught never to let personal feelings get in the way. There was too much at risk.

A few lights remained on inside the house. He knew that some would stay on throughout the night, especially the hundreds of white ones decorating the outside that signaled the approach of the holiday season. That would not be a problem. Neither would the two men inside. In another hour they would be tired, and their senses diminished. He knew that too. It did not matter that they were part of a rotating shift and that they had slept earlier that afternoon. The mind and body were not designed for being up all night one week, and then working a different shift the following one. It wreaked havoc on the body's internal system, especially on one's circadian rhythm, the internal body clock that is keyed to daylight and darkness. He also knew that shift work often led to depression, high blood pressure, and of course, trouble staying asleep. After several weeks, the constant changing of shift work left you mentally tired and physically exhausted, especially without a day off. He too was tired and needed rest. But not tonight. He was as committed as he was cautious. And while he tried to keep fit, he did not have the energy to continue doing what he was hired and paid to do so many years ago. Every morning while shaving he would notice the ever-increasing gray in his thick brown hair. That and the wrinkles under his eyes painfully reminded him he was aging. The stresses of his profession only contributed to speeding up that process.

This was one of the times her husband had been away while she remained home, safe inside the fenced fortress they called the mansion. Both were often gone for weeks, sometimes together, but more often apart. In a few days, they would both be gone. He knew this would be his last opportunity. In a way, he welcomed it. This would be the last time, he told himself as he tried to keep warm. The risks were becoming too great. He had gone on undetected far too long. Everyone's luck runs out at some point, he reminded himself. This would have to be the last time.

He glanced at his watch again. It was almost one a.m. He wouldn't have much time. He would have to get in and out in just under an hour. After that? He didn't want to think about it. *Should I go in at one or wait until two a.m.* he thought. He convinced himself that waiting the extra hour would be better. The two men inside would be tired and maybe even doze off. Not both. But maybe one. In another hour, they would be less attentive. They were trained to react swiftly when necessary. But that's not what they would do tonight. Patience, he told himself.

It was one minute after two in the morning when he heard the last man on the security detail signal over the secure radio net that everything was in order. It was then that Michael Dionis quietly entered the house through the rear door. One man, no more than thirty years old, was sitting at the kitchen table reading a sports magazine. Something he read caused him to groan. The smell of old coffee permeated the air. He could see the young agent sipping coffee from a plain white cup. From the color of the coffee, Dionis realized that the man had ruined it by adding cream. *The young ones always do that*, he thought.

The man's coat jacket was hung neatly on the back of a kitchen chair revealing the government issued semi-automatic, Glock 19 pistol hanging from his shoulder holster. The young ones liked the shoulder holster. It made them feel like real detectives. But they weren't. They were hired to be guards. And the better one looked in a suit, the better their chances of being hired.

Dionis could see that he was just a kid. Jet black hair. Tall, good looking, just the kind of kid the agency was looking for these days. It didn't matter if they would ever become good investigators; that was secondary at best. Look good, stay alert, and keep your mouth shut, and you would do well in the service.

Dionis wondered where the other man was. In the bathroom perhaps? Maybe napping on the couch as many of them often did on the midnight shift. That would be good, he told himself, as he crept quietly behind the man whose attention was on whatever it was, he was reading. It was always a game with him to see how close he could get to someone before being detected. Sometimes he would quietly walk right on past them, no-one ever knowing he had been there until it was too late. Dionis turned and faced the young agent sitting at the kitchen table, brought his hand up to his mouth, placed his finger next to his lips and whispered, "Brian. Where's Brian?"

The young agent simply pointed to a room adjacent to the kitchen. Curious, the young agent got up and quietly followed Dionis into the next room, making sure to keep enough distance to not disrupt whatever it was Dionis had planned on doing. But the man sitting at the desk in the next room was more alert than the young agent in the kitchen had been. He turned while Dionis was still a few feet away, and said, "Hi boss. Cold outside?"

"Damn cold, Brian," Dionis said. "I'll be glad to see this detail move to D.C. so I can get back to my office."

"Not many bosses work the night shift," the young man said. "Can I get you some coffee?"

"Absolutely," Dionis answered. "Just black, the way you're supposed to drink it." The comment was, of course, lost on the kid.

The two men walked into the kitchen where the young agent poured both Dionis and Brian Olsen a cup of coffee, not suspecting anything more than this being a routine visit by the senior man on the shift. Agents from the local office were always assisting the permanent protection detail of a candidate when the protectee was home or traveling through their area. But most bosses who had to supply agents supplementing the regular security team made sure they caught the day shift. Dionis was quick to put himself on the night tour. It was the shift with the least number of people to deal with. The number of agents providing protection would be reduced and the media would be asleep or someplace writing their stories. The late shift was the only shift he could work if he were to be successful. Getting out without being detected was still going to be a problem. But he was going to take the risk; just this one last time.

Olsen was one of Dionis' senior agents assigned to his office in New Haven, Connecticut. They had been friends for over a dozen years since they first met during the Obama campaign in 08. It would help to have a friend nearby if something went wrong. Olsen might even help give him the few added moments he would need to get out of the house undetected, if necessary. At a minimum, Dionis thought he'd be able to concoct some believable story to momentarily divert attention from what he was doing long enough to confuse everyone involved. Olsen would cover for him long enough to talk to him privately. Dionis was still convinced that wouldn't be necessary.

"So, how's it going?" Dionis asked. "And don't bullshit me."

"Not bad. Can't imagine why you and I couldn't have gotten a better detail than this," Olsen said half laughing.

"What are you complaining about?" Dionis asked. "No big bosses, no press. You just sit here on your ass, read and drink coffee. Besides, I'm the one making the rounds and hanging out in the cold."

"I'm getting too old for this midnight shit," Olsen told Dionis. "Besides, man, you're a boss. You could have cut yourself a better deal than this. This stuff is for the young guys."

"Just because we can retire in a couple of years, doesn't make us old," Dionis said, as he sipped his coffee. "Anyway, I've got to use the head. Then I'm going to take a walk-through. I'll let myself out the other end in a bit. You mind sending the rookie outside for an hour or so? Let me warm up in here?"

Olsen knew the phrase "walk-through" meant "catch a short nap."

"Of course."

"Thanks. Let's not corrupt him just yet. Let the service get a few good years out of him before he figures out just how screwed up the system is and gets disillusioned like the rest of us poor bastards."

"Sure, whatever you say boss," Brian said, not trying to hide the smirk on his face.

Dionis walked into the hallway leading from the large staff kitchen into the bathroom down the hall. He waited a few moments then quietly made his way through the dimly lit formal dining room and then to the staircase leading to the upstairs living quarters. Knowing which room she was in made his travel instinctual. He also knew that no one else was in the house. None of the staff had remained. It was just her upstairs, alone in the bedroom.

Dionis reached down and quietly turned the doorknob. She had left the door unlocked as she had said she would. That was considerate, he told himself. The room was dark. The shades were drawn preventing even the hint of light from shining through. No nightlights. The only illumination came from the digital clock radio on the nightstand. But it was enough. Dionis had been there twice before. The bedroom was large but spartanly furnished. Ann Banks kept things simple. And no matter the night chill, she opened the window just a crack. She knew he liked it that way.

Dionis waited a moment, allowing his eyes to adjust to the darkness so he could see. It was something he had learned in the Marine Corps years ago. His life had depended on it on more than one occasion. It might just depend on it again.

Dionis walked quietly toward the bed. He could hear her breathing as she slept unaware of his presence. He wondered if he could go through with it. Maybe he should just turn and leave the room. Just walk away. But he knew he couldn't. Instead, he stood next to the bed and gazed at her for just a moment before placing his hand on her head.

"Michael; I didn't think you'd make it," she said as she sat up in the bed. "How much time do you have?"

"Not much. Less than an hour," he replied. "Brian thinks I'm taking a short nap downstairs. He'll stay in the kitchen while the kid is outside for an hour or so."

"Then we shouldn't waste time," she told him, as she ran the palm of her hand across his cheek. "I've missed you. I don't know how we're going to keep seeing each other once I move to Washington. But I'm going to expect you to find a way."

Dionis said nothing. Instead, he answered her with his eyes as he stroked her neck.

Dionis knew that continuing the relationship was hopeless. He couldn't tell her this was the last time they could be together. She just didn't understand how protective security worked. There were few opportunities for them to be together during the campaign, and especially after she won the election. But once she took office and moved into the White House, it would make such meetings virtually impossible. The risks were too great, especially after the media frenzy during the Clinton administration and the Lewinsky affair. The press would ruin everyone involved, especially her, an independent candidate that beat the odds by winning the presidency. This was going to be the last time. Dionis knew it and, in time, so would she. Besides, being the governor of a small New England State like Connecticut was one thing. Being the president of the United States was another. He kept reminding himself, this had to be the last time.

"Please don't lie to me," she whispered. "You know this isn't going to be easy."

Hoping to avoid that conversation, he said, in a soft voice, "Can we discuss this later?"

"Of course. I've missed you Michael," Banks told him again. "Please come to bed with me."

"Hush," he said, as he placed his finger over his lips.

Momentarily forgetting the career ending risk he was taking, Dionis quietly undressed, dropping his clothes on the floor. He was careful not to make any noise. He placed his small hand-held radio on the nightstand so that he could hear if anyone tried to contact him. He then slipped into bed with her. Even in the darkness, he could see through the sheer nightgown she was wearing. He gripped her shoulders and pushed her back down on the bed; their gazes met, and his lips found hers in an instant. She leaned into him and felt his arms wrap around her.

Ann Banks had the body of a woman half her age. And she knew it, using her smile, appearance, and spirited personality to win the hearts and minds of many voters. Now, she simply lay down in the bed stroking Dionis' hair. Their love making had to be quiet. Not like the times when they first met when she was a federal prosecutor. It started innocently enough, the two of them working together long hours preparing for a trial. It wasn't just animal lust. They started to have feelings for each other. But Dionis was married at the time. He had had affairs before, but Banks was different. They became friends. And they remained friends after she married Patrick. They quietly resumed their affair when she learned that her husband enjoyed the company of a number of other women, as well as his political career, far more than he enjoyed being with her.

As Banks' popularity grew, she was persuaded by the state's independent party to run for governor. When she won, it shocked the Democratic and Republican political machines who gave her little chance of success. The politicians in Connecticut hadn't had the time to prove to her just how the game was played. They hadn't had time to groom her to their way of thinking and, in the process, make her indebted to them. She was a newcomer, and not simply political window dressing. They knew she was smart, but they never expected her to become governor, at least not just yet. Nor did they think she was up to the job. She was proving them all wrong in that she was truly an independent political operative; the first one the state of

Connecticut had experienced since Lowell Weicker was elected the state's governor in 1991.

The time went by quickly. For a brief moment, Ann felt a sense of timelessness and peace. She wanted nothing more at this moment but to lay there and feel the warmth of his body and his heartbeat against her chest. But time was fading. Dionis dressed and sat on the edge of the bed. For the first time that night, Dionis' fears of being caught did not dominate his mind. His eyes rested on her forehead wishing he could stay and watch her sleep.

Banks' eyes met his. The two lovers didn't speak; they simply stared at each other. Ann Banks wanted nothing more than to be with him and wished the night would not end. She was the first to break the silence. "What are you thinking about? Is there something you want to tell me, Michael?" she whispered, sensing his thoughts were somewhere else.

For a moment Dionis didn't answer. He knew there was no possibility that the two of them had any type of future together. In fact, he had come to realize there was virtually no chance at all of them being together. But he wasn't ready to tell her that, not now; not tonight. He said, "I'll get word to you somehow. You know how to call me. But you'll have to be careful. All the calls from the White House are logged. The more you come back to your home in Connecticut, the better chance I'll have of seeing you." Dionis knew that was a lie. Everybody lies. And he was no different, at least not at that moment. He couldn't tell her the truth. He couldn't tell her that he wouldn't take this chance again. He couldn't leave her with that thought. *What was one more lie*? You can negotiate the truth with wives, lovers, bosses, friends, enemies, defendants, prosecutors and even witnesses. Lies can be manipulated. Lies become truths when it serves one's purpose.

"In the meantime," Dionis continued, "keep using the email account we set up. Remember to never send the message; simply keep the message in the draft folder. We can communicate through that until we see what happens. You're going to be the President of the United

States, Ann. You don't need me to tell you that this is the last thing you want the media finding out."

Banks started to speak. There was a tear in her eye. That was the first time he had ever seen her cry. It had always been friends enjoying each other. He hadn't seen her exhibit this kind of emotion before. Dionis wondered if she had stronger feelings for him than he had thought. Or was she just scared about her new role in life? He quickly dismissed the latter thought; Ann Banks wasn't afraid of much of anything. She was self-assured, determined, and ambitious.

"Michael," she said.

Dionis put his finger to her lips. "Don't talk." He could hear the stress in her voice. "I don't have much time. I have to get back downstairs before the team discovers I'm not napping in the den."

Banks knew she would not have him for very long. He was right; the time for talking was over, at least for now. She wanted to tell him to come with her to Washington. She even envisioned him marrying her. But she kept those feelings to herself. *Another time.*

Dionis finished dressing, clipped his gun holster to his belt on his right side and his radio on his left hip. He bent over the bed and kissed her on the lips.

"I love you," she whispered.

"I love you too," he replied. But Ann Banks sensed it was a conditioned response. Something was bothering him, and she couldn't put her finger on it. Their lovemaking had not been as adventurous as it was prior to the election. It had been more programmed, almost as if they had been married for years and had lost the art of spontaneity and innovation. Dionis opened the bedroom door and quietly walked down the stairs and out the front door. He had one minute to spare before the three-a.m. security check. The cold air did not bother him now. His shift would end in about four hours. He would go home to an empty condo and try to sleep. Thinking of Ann had kept him awake too many nights. *I can't do this anymore. She is going to be the President,* he told himself. They were good friends and he loved her. But he knew he wasn't in love with her. He was painfully aware of the difference between the two feelings. And it would not be long before her every waking moment would be controlled by people she hardly knew. She would not have time to miss him.

A few miles away, Oleg Lomakina listened as the two lovers ended their quiet lovemaking and said good-bye. He turned off the recorder of their conversation. He had been entrusted with the recording device and had successfully had it placed in Ann Banks' bedroom, with the assistance of a maid at the governor's mansion; a maid whose husband's life depended on her ability to do as she was instructed. He would give the recording to Andre Dunayev, convinced he would be pleased. The recordings over the past several days had not produced anything of value as far as Lomakina was concerned. Congressman Patrick Banks rarely shared a bedroom with his wife. But her sharing a bedroom with a Secret Service Agent was more than he could have ever expected. Lomakina was looking forward to watching Dunayev blackmail the new American president and her Secret Service lover into working for their organization. He wondered what Dunayev would do if either of them refused. *Would he reveal the affair, or would he send the incoming president a message by simply killing her lover?* It made no difference to Lomakina. For now, he just wanted another drink; maybe two.

Chapter 2

Ten months before the presidential election

"Explain to me how this is going to work," Andre Dunayev asked the young man. It was more a command than a question.

"We'll use a combination of email leaks, which we'll release after hacking into the candidates' email accounts. We will also take full advantage of the various social media platforms to spread disinformation among its users. Facebook itself has over a billion followers. The information we plant, using a host of different people, many who won't even know they're being used, will, in many cases, be viewed by millions of people, not just in the U.S., but all over the world," the young man replied. "We'll also plant a host of subliminal clues designed to affect people's emotions. Facebook conducted a massive study on emotional contagion. It was designed, in part, to create and use subliminal clues to get more people to vote. They found that they can affect real world behavior and emotions without even triggering people's awareness that they're being manipulated. And of course, we'll rely on a certain amount of propaganda, which has proven itself to work over many decades."

"We have to make sure this doesn't get traced back to us," Dunayev said. "We need, as American politicians like to say, plausible deniability."

"We've become more sophisticated since the last two elections," the young man said convincingly. "There are more social platforms to exploit, including advertising companies and YouTube. We're going to target those users. Facebook also launched something called Custom Audiences and Lookalike Audiences. These platforms pair the characteristics of various advertisers with Facebook's own algorithms."

"What exactly does that mean?" Dunayev asked.

"Essentially, it allows advertisers to target individual users," replied the young man. "We'll also use the propaganda machine to the extent possible by planting fake stories through fake personas that we will create on social media. In some cases, the personas will indeed be fake. In some cases, they'll be spread through actual users that we will recruit."

"You keep using the term users; what do you mean by that?"

"These social platforms are tools, but not like the tools you would use to build something. People use social media, in large part, as it was designed, to get a hit of dopamine by connecting them with friends."

"How does all of this involve drugs?" Dunayev asked.

"Dopamine is a neurotransmitter inside the brain. When triggered, it produces feelings of arousal, motivation, reinforcement, and reward. There are only two industries that use the term *users*: illegal drugs and software. The various social platforms have been perfecting this for years. So much so, that people have become addicted to these dopamine rushes. As a result, they are completely clueless about the fact that they are being manipulated."

"Good," replied Dunayev. "Remember, we want to conquer by dividing the two political parties as much as possible. We must do everything we can to ensure that our independent candidate has every chance of winning the election."

"We will certainly strive to see that as many Americans as possible ultimately accept the reality of the world we hope to present to them. That is why, as you instructed, we will be targeting both major political parties," the young man said. "As you know, it isn't that hard with the Americans; they're already so divided that our work should be easy. When I worked in America my first year here, I remember the division in our office over where to have a Christmas party. Ten people could not agree on where to have it to the point friends began arguing with each other. We don't need to defame an individual candidate; we simply need to exploit these divisions to further this polarization. But we must be careful; the Americans must believe that your candidate is the one person that can prevent a civil war in this country without us actually starting one."

"Won't some of these social media platforms try to stop these attempts?" Dunayev asked.

"They will, to some degree. Most of these social media platforms are run by young idealistic people. They will certainly do what they think they must to stop the spread of disinformation. But keep in mind, they're in the money-making business more than they are in the social media business. And they know very well that Americans are materialistic and vain; that's why it works. We have a word for that, "*nekulturny*."

"So, tell me, what do you need to proceed?" Dunayev asked.

"We've already begun," the young man responded. "We will need money for ads and, of course, money to buy the help of Americans from both political parties."

"Do you anticipate any problems recruiting enough Americans for this?" Dunayev asked.

The young man began to laugh, not realizing that laughter was not part of Dunayev's persona, and said, "You know, there are plenty of Americans motivated by money. But now, it is clear that there are far more Americans motivated by political and social philosophy than ever before. America has never been more divided. And that, too, is in large part due to the various social media platforms. Exploiting these ideologues from both sides should prove easy enough. The worst thing that can happen for us is if the Americans from both political parties become more centrist in their thinking. Their country is far too divided right now to stop us."

"And the Chinese government?" Dunayev asked.

"You needn't worry about the Chinese," the young man said. "The Chinese Communist Party (CCP) will undoubtedly continue their efforts at penetrating the American tech industry and stealing whatever secrets they need. They have become America's greatest national security threat and, yet, their media refuses to report most of it. That can only help us achieve our objectives."

"How so?"

"The American liberal media is soft on China. Since they refuse to report most of the questionable relationships with their elected officials and their business dealings, we can exploit that and release certain information on the various social platforms I talked about. That should, at least temporarily, provide a distraction and some cover if the federal authorities ever decide to act on the disinformation campaign we're about to start. But I can't imagine that happening. The federal authorities have other things to worry about, including spying from Russia, China, Iran, and even several western countries they put too much trust in. The government does have dedicated servants who take their oaths seriously and do their jobs without political influence. Those are the ones we have to worry about. We'll leak just enough accurate information about spying, as necessary to divert those assets away from our efforts. Besides, I've recruited two of the very best hackers from China to help us."

Dunayev had heard enough. He had confidence in this young man. But he had one more question to ask.

"And do you have the other thing we talked about?"

"It's right here," he replied. "This is a voice activated flash drive. It has a battery life of about five days. You simply have to have it planted in the house. I found bedrooms to work best as that is where so many private conversations take place. But of course, that is your call, Andre. Just let me know when and where you have it placed so I can activate the program."

Dunayev liked this young man. He forced a smile, nodded his head in agreement, placed his right arm on the young man's shoulder and said, "*ne podvedi nas*." Don't let us down.

The young man responded, "I will not fail you."

Dunayev nodded, shook the young man's hand, turned, and walked out of the building and to his car.

"How did it go?" the man behind the steering wheel asked.

"As I had hoped," Dunayev responded. "It is clear the Americans are not the only ones who have an abundance of idealistic young people available to exploit. These kids will do us just fine. We should be able to influence the new president, whoever that might be. Hell, according to this young man, we might just be able to start another civil war in America."

Over the next several months, Dunayev watched as the young man and his small team did as they promised. The political discourse in America rose to new levels never seen before. In previous elections, eighty percent of the country dug in their heels and supported their candidate over the other no matter what outrageous conduct they exhibited. However, in this election, enough voters deviated from their party line and voted for the independent candidate. And now, Ann Banks was going to be the next President of the United States.

It was more than Dunayev could have hoped for when, during the summer leading up to the election, the country witnessed several major cities in the U.S. erupt into violent political clashes between radical members of both parties. What Ann Banks' election to the presidency did provide Dunayev, was the perfect time to plant the recording device he had been carrying with him for several months. After all, it was he who helped her get elected governor of Connecticut, even if Ann Banks didn't know it. Dunayev had sought to have her husband, a congressman from Connecticut, on the ticket instead. But Banks' surprising political victory in November shocked many of the pundits. It was time to hear what the two political stooges were talking about in their bedroom.

Chapter 3

36 Days Before the Inauguration

Andre Dunayev had been in the U.S. for almost five years. The demise of the old Soviet Union years ago had offered him and other members of Russia's *vorovsko mir*, the criminal underworld, endless opportunities inside Russia. But Dunayev had exploited those opportunities a bit too much, and, in the process, made more enemies among the *vor* than he did friends. So, with warrants for his arrest, he fled Russia before becoming a casualty of that world. In the capitalist free society of the United States, Dunayev found the modern culture befitting a professional criminal trained in the mother country. He laughed at the laws that restricted the police in this country. He laughed at the courts, especially the federal courts that preferred to give first time offenders probation or restrict violators to their homes for short periods after they had stolen thousands or millions of dollars from some unsuspecting business. He laughed at the politicians who always needed money for their campaigns and, in the process, sold out to the highest bidders through a variety of lobbyists, ensuring that their votes were more often than not, cast in favor of the interests of those providing them with financial support. He laughed at how American politicians loved to be in the spotlight. *Why else would they speak to an empty room on the floor of Congress in the middle of the night*? he thought. They wanted money, power, and their pictures in the paper and, especially, on the evening news. Patrick Banks was no different.

Patrick Banks and Andre Dunayev had both benefited from their relationship since they met almost four years prior. Both had proven to be of equal value to each other. But as a U.S. Congressman, Patrick Banks needed to be careful; his wife was going to be the next president of the United States, and he had bigger plans for himself; plans that did not include Andre Dunayev.

In downtown New Haven, Connecticut, Oleg Lomakina just finished his fourth vodka at the Owl Cigar Bar on Church Street, nestled less than two blocks from Yale University. In the back of the dimly lit bar, frequented chiefly by middle-aged white males, the Owl was one of the few places in the state where a person could smoke while having a drink. Lomakina was smoking his second Dominican cigar after giving Dunayev the flash drive with the recording on it. Dunayev was finishing his second scotch with his colleague before thanking him for his excellent work. He told him to have another and paid the bill for their drinks, along with the next one Lomakina was going to have. Dunayev stood up, wrapped his arms around Lomakina and gave him a hard bear hug. "*Khoroshaya rabota my friend*," he said. Good work indeed. *If only you weren't such a drunk and could be trusted, old friend*, Dunayev thought.

Dunayev exited the bar, pulled up the collar on his coat to help keep the cold off of his neck, and began the short walk to his car. Oleg Lomakina remained behind, and finished his cigar and another vodka, before walking out of the Owl. He never saw the man emerge from the side of building. He never saw the assassin's face or anything else, ever again. The two muffled shots to the back of his head were fired in rapid succession. Lomakina was here one second and gone the next. He never felt a thing. Now, in the early morning hours on this same cold, dark December night, as a light snow fell across Connecticut, Andre Dunayev rode in his black Mercedes south on Interstate 95 toward New York. Inside the car, Dunayev listened to the recording of Ann Banks and Michael Dionis making love. He smiled to himself as he re-played the recording several times. He knew that Patrick Banks, and his wife, Ann, the president-elect, would be in a position to do more for him now than either would ever want to. Revealing the recording of Ann Banks' love affair would destroy both of their careers. If Patrick Banks didn't fully cooperate, and help convince his wife, Ann, to do as he wished, he would see to it that both of their political lives were destroyed. *This is going to be a very good Christmas*, he thought.

***

Patrick Banks' first memories as a child were those of a possessive mother and a father who lacked interest in sports and most anything else a child would find fun. He liked to recall the story of the day he came home upset because the older boys he had been playing baseball with made fun of his lack of ability to throw and catch. They laughed at him and told him to go ask his father to teach him these things. When he did, his father, preferring to work on home projects, drew a large X on the side of their brick home, and gave Patrick a rubber ball, telling him to aim for the mark. When the ball bounced back, he could practice catching it. That was as close as he ever got to playing catch with his father. His mother taught him to clean and cook, often resulting in his friends calling him a mama's boy. The eldest of four children, he was forced to help care for his younger brothers and sisters. His father believed in hard work and paying one's own way. As a child, Patrick didn't appreciate the things his father was trying to teach him. He was determined to leave home at an early age to prove that he could succeed, in spite of his father's lack of support and encouragement. He had been a diligent student in high school, earning a scholarship to the University of Connecticut, and later went on to earn a law degree from that same institution. After several years of working for a small law firm, Patrick Banks joined the U.S. Attorney's Office. That's where he met Ann, a young, ambitious civil prosecutor who focused her energy on prosecuting corrupt defense contractors who cheated the federal taxpayers, and, in the process, often put members of the armed forces at risk by providing inferior products. Both had political ambitions and shared the same political philosophy, at least as much as most people can agree on anything. While the relationship didn't quite start where many relationships often do, where two people can't keep their hands off each other, it did offer the two political aspirants something else; the chance to support each other's ambitions and rise together as a political power couple.

But now, as a U.S. Congressman still languishing in a position he felt was far beneath him, and his wife, the president-elect, Patrick Banks felt left behind. His jealousy started to dominate his every waking thought. He was tired of being second best at almost everything. His father always accepted second best for himself claiming it was enough to do the best you could. For Patrick Banks, second best simply meant you lost. Being a U.S. Congressman and, now the first husband was not a role he cherished. In time, he would be president. He would see to that.

Patrick Banks sat in his office at the Rayburn House Office Building in Washington D.C., wondering if it would snow as the weather predicted. *Maybe, if it snows enough, the airport will close, and I won't have to fly to Connecticut and deal with Ann*, he thought. His wife did not understand just how much political power he now had. Nor did she know just how much he intended to have later.

Patrick Banks' short-lived reverie was interrupted by the quiet vibration of his cell phone. The caller ID told him it was his Chief of Staff, Josh Martin.

"What's so important this early in the morning, Josh?" Banks asked.

"It's our most ardent supporter. He wants to meet. Claims it's important."

"Impossible. He knows to deal with you. Nothing can be that important."

"I told him that. He said, not this time. It had to be the two of you and soon."

"Fuck him. Tell him to wait. And tell him not to try and make any trouble. I'll arrange something in a few days when I'm back in Connecticut," Banks said.

"So, what are you suggesting?"

"Tell him to wait, dammit," Banks yelled. "I will get back to him. And tell him it better be important."

Banks hung up the phone, leaned over his desk and placed his hands over his face and clenched his jaw. He did not need Andre Dunayev calling him so soon. They had agreed on a protocol for contacting each other and Dunayev was violating those rules; something he rarely did. *Something is wrong. But what*? he thought.

Patrick Banks let out a sigh, took a deep breath, and thought to himself that his day had to get better. Dunayev had helped finance his run for Congress and his foolhardy run for his party's nomination for president four years prior. Dunayev also, and without her knowing it, helped finance his wife's run for governor of Connecticut, and later for the presidency. When Patrick Banks failed to get his party's nomination for president, something in truth he had not expected anyway, he felt confident he would be able to position himself on the shortlist for the VP slot. He was, after all, one-half of the most influential power couple in America. What Patrick Banks also failed to realize, however, was that you simply can't run for anything at the national level on the "It's my turn," platform. Hillary Clinton had learned that the hard way. Then his wife ran as an independent, upsetting his plans. Patrick Banks wasn't sure if the country had gone too far with its political correctness attitudes, or if the country had had enough of it, along with the partisan fighting between conservatives and liberals. Either way, both parties seemed to have, at least for the time being, overplayed their hand.

The country responded to an independent candidate who brought a moderate political philosophy to national politics. Political correctness was undoubtedly the new norm in national politics, private industry, and, of course, academia. Failing to pander to the many factions that existed within both national parties would almost certainly result in a candidate's loss. During the nationally telecast debates, the outrageous accusations between the two primary candidates were so hostile, both liberal and conservative news moderators lost all control of the candidates. But Ann Banks stayed out of the fray. She remained the voice of reason, never allowing her opponents to ruffle her on the national stage. But she was not without hostile emotion. She simply refused to put it on public display.

When Ann Banks selected an unknown independent party Congressman from central Florida as her running mate, her husband was livid. When she was elected president, something he never imagined would happen, he decided that if he was going to be forced to parade around Washington D.C. as the First Husband, he was going to position himself both politically and financially for the end of his wife's term, whenever that might be. Patrick Banks not only needed Dunayev's money, but he also needed his "influence." Dunayev could get *things* done for him. Sometimes, getting "*things*" done meant looking the other way. But he didn't care.

***

It had only been two days since Michael Dionis had seen Ann Banks. He tried not thinking about her. But nothing was working. Even in the early morning hours as he drove south on Interstate 91 toward New Haven to the U.S. Attorney's office, he thought about what she might be doing at that hour of the morning. He genuinely cared for her, maybe more than he wanted to admit. He promised himself that he was never going to fall in love again. Not like the first time when he married while still in college. And certainly not like the second time years later when he married a woman whose career came above everything else, especially him. That marriage had been short lived after Dionis found himself spending more time in the company of other women who he felt were more interested in him, even if it was only briefly.

***

Tina Crawford, the Acting U.S. Attorney for the District of Connecticut, did not have to go back to using her maiden name after her divorce from Michael Dionis; she never adopted his last name after the wedding. Crawford was determined to rise to the highest levels of the judicial profession, even imagining a seat on the U.S. Supreme Court. Although the divorce from Dionis might be challenging to overcome from the public perception of just how picture perfect a potential member of the high court must be, it wouldn't be a problem with the judiciary committee, if she ever got that far. Her party would endorse her vigorously regardless of the divorce, while the opposition party would find fault in her every move and decision regardless of her qualifications. And of course, it didn't matter how scandal free a potential nominee might be; the opposing party would make confirmation of the candidate a political spectacle, putting them center stage in what one U.S. Senator liked to call, "*His Spartacus moment*." But all of that was daydreaming on the part of Tina Crawford. She had a long way to go before she'd be a viable candidate for the high court. But like most Americans, she could dream.

The practice of law had been Crawford's only love, until recently when she realized the world of politics might be more to her liking. Dionis, like the witnesses she used and the investigators she worked with, had proven to be nothing more than a prop or a supporting actor in her life.

A cold rain fell as Michael Dionis pulled into the parking garage next to the federal building on Church Street in New Haven. He could deal with the rain. It was the snow he grew to hate. Either way, it signaled the real beginning of winter, the start of four months in New England for those not into winter sports that turned them into prisoners in their own home. It was dark every day when he left for work and dark when he returned home. One did not go out much at night during New England winters except maybe to get more firewood for the fireplace. It would be several months before he could run along the shore of Long Island Sound again. For now, he was a prisoner of his office, health club, and home. That was bad enough, he told himself. The day would only get worse now, he thought. His ex-wife had called a meeting of several of the law enforcement agency heads for eight a.m.

Dionis was greeted in the lobby of the U.S. Attorney's office by Tony Maffuci, the head of the FBI's organized crime squad in New Haven. The two men had become fast friends after first meeting two years ago. Dionis had found Maffuci's honesty about the job refreshing. The FBI had gained a reputation for inviting you to dinner and then stealing your wallet. The Bureau was the most protective agency in government, always taking information from other agencies but reluctant to share theirs. But not Maffuci. He hid little. And what he did hide, was usually the result of some directive from a member of senior management who had continued to politicize the agency that started under former director John Comey. When you worked with Maffuci, you were a full partner. Maffuci and Dionis shared concerns about the job, the bureaucratic restrictions imposed upon them by political appointees whose "cover your asses at all costs" philosophy so often prevented them from actually doing the work they were hired to do. They shared information that could have destroyed both of their careers, but neither man had ever violated the other's trust. Tony Maffuci spoke naturalized Sicilian, one of just a handful of agents in the FBI with the ability to do so. Other agents had been trained in the language, but Maffuci grew up speaking it every day. His success in fighting what the FBI called "traditional organized crime," those involved in one of the five major "families" operating out of New York and New Jersey, was not just because of Maffuci's great investigative skills or street smarts, although he certainly had them. He always found that playing by the rules, catching people legally, and treating them with a degree of respect and courtesy once they were caught, often brought a degree of respect and good will his way. But like Michael Dionis, Maffuci was never afraid to stretch the imagination of agency policy to make a case. The friendship was cemented early in their relationship when Maffuci took Dionis to meet a made member of one of the major organized crime families to obtain information about a counterfeiter who had used bad money to buy heroin. The heroin had been contaminated, resulting in the deaths of several young people. Maffuci made a deal with the man, giving him information about a possible search of one of his warehouses by local police. To Maffuci, a truckload of stolen electronics did not add up to several dead kids.

"You're living on the edge, Tony," Dionis had told him.

"My friend, if you're not living on the edge, you're taking up too much space," Maffuci had responded. Dionis knew he had finally met someone in the business that still had a set of balls.

But as close as they were, Dionis never shared anything about Ann Banks. That would be career and political suicide for both of them. As much as he wanted to talk about it, he couldn't. It would have to remain his secret.

"So, what's this all about?" Dionis asked.

"Something to do with some murder in New Haven. Some guy was shot twice in the back of the head, execution style. That's all I know. I got the call from Tina's secretary just like you did," Maffuci answered.

"What's a murder in New Haven got to do with us?"

"I'm not sure. You now know as much as I do about this. Except, I hear DEA and Customs have been invited to the party."

"That's Tina for you. She'll turn whatever this is into a press field day with her as the star of the show," Dionis said.

"That's what U.S. Attorneys do, my friend," Maffuci responded. They are political animals. She's your ex. Is she more political or more animal?"

"Fuck you, Tony," Dionis said smiling.

"Sounds like we're still a little jealous of her?" Maffuci asked.

"Not at all," replied Dionis. "It didn't take me long to get really tired of that one. She loves nothing but the law and politics and not necessarily in that order. And she loves no-one but herself. And who is the asshole in this? Me. I'm the ex-husband of this wonderful woman who's the new acting U.S. Attorney. I'm of little to no value to her. I'm old, twice divorced, and close to retirement. Her, well, you figure it out. She's certainly running in the right political circles, getting everything, she wants. But I am happy for her. People should do what they want."

"Well, you're right about one thing, my friend," said Maffuci.

"Yeah, what's that?"

"You are the asshole," he said with a sarcastic grin. "I'm calling the bullshit card on you. You're not over her, are you?"

"I am, my friend. More than you can imagine. But fuck you anyway," Dionis replied. *If he only knew about Ann.*

The conversation was interrupted by the arrival of Manny Gonzalez, head of the DEA in Connecticut, and Conner Clark, from the U.S. Customs Service. The four men exchanged handshakes and signed the visitors log before being given a cheap stick-on tag that identified them as just that, visitors. It was just one more way that the prosecutor's office let the visiting agent know that they were not one of them. They were ushered into the large conference room neatly decorated with a fine long redwood table and matching chairs; all bought by the previous U.S. Attorney who had left two vacancies unfilled so that he could use the money in his budget for salaries to decorate his offices. It didn't matter that it caused other prosecutors to carry a heavier caseload or that some cases didn't get accepted for prosecution. The fact that the office looked modern and professional, something that would compete with the private firms, was all that mattered. But there wasn't any fresh fruit, doughnuts, or fine plates from which to eat; that was usually reserved for meetings with the more prestigious law firms.

"You'd think at this hour of the morning, your-ex would at least have coffee here for everyone," Maffuci told Dionis.

"You really think she's going to provide refreshments with me here?" Dionis replied.

From twenty-three flights up, the conference room provided a spectacular view of the city and the Yale University campus. Dionis wondered what it would have been like to attend Yale or Harvard. His thoughts momentarily wandered. *I wonder what other profession I might have followed had I been rich enough or student enough to have had an Ivy League education.*

"An eight-a.m. meeting with anyone in the U.S. Attorney's office is almost unheard of," Maffuci said.

"It's about as rare as rocking horse crap," Dionis replied. "But leave it to my ex-wife to throw a little drama everyone's way."

Dionis and Mafucci brought their own coffee and were glad they did; there wasn't any to be found in the office at that hour of the morning.

Manny Gonzalez and Conner Clark were about to go find a coffee shop when Tina Crawford walked in with a woman Dionis had never seen before. But Maffuci did know her. For a split second, Dionis noticed Maffuci giving her that quick stare men always give a woman when they sense an initial attraction. Dionis would confront Maffuci about this later when the two of them were alone.

"Good morning, gentlemen. I'd like to thank all of you for coming in so early this morning," Crawford said. Everyone knew she didn't mean it. The tone of her voice was clear: she was pleased with herself for having summoned everyone to her office at such an early hour.

Tina Crawford was 43 years old, and attractive. Her colleagues saw her as strong and self-sufficient but without much of a sense of humor. And Crawford was not shy about letting people know that she considered herself the smartest person in the room. She also knew how to use her appearance to get what she wanted, especially when there were men present. Attributes many men, married or not, found interesting. And Crawford knew exactly how to use those attributes on those same men. They were, after all, more often than not, responsible for making the political decisions that interested her most.

"I'd like to introduce you to Sergeant Sandi DeCarlo from the Connecticut State Police Major Crime Squad. She's going to tell you why you've all been asked to come here so early this morning," Crawford began.

Sandi DeCarlo was 37 years-old, medium height, thin but with an athletic look about her. Her short blond cropped hair would have kept her looking young except for the dark circles under her eyes. This wasn't just simply from a lack of sleep; this woman was tired and stressed, Dionis thought. Dressed in a blue blouse and what appeared to be dirty black cargo pants and tennis shoes, it was clear she had been working right up until the time of the meeting. Dionis glanced at her left hand. No wedding ring. *I wonder what Tony is up to.*

"Sandi, would you like some coffee?" Crawford asked.

"Yes, please. Cream and two sugars if you don't mind."

Crawford had no reservations about asking her secretary to get the coffee. "Go ahead, Sandi, the room is yours," Crawford said.

"Good morning," DeCarlo began. "Two days ago, the body of one Robert Moss was found in an alley here in downtown New Haven. He was killed with two shots to the back of the head. It was an execution. We don't think our deceased is who his identification says he is. We're working on that."

"Why is that, Sandi?" Maffuci asked, smiling at her.

"Two things, Tony," DeCarlo answered. "First, he's missing the small finger on his left hand. It had been cut off long ago and crudely done. Plus, the tattoos on his body. They're foreign."

"Russian?" asked Maffuci.

"We think so. But we're not sure. Hopefully, you guys at the Bureau will be able to help with that," DeCarlo said.

"No problem," Maffuci said.

"How does the Secret Service fit into this?" Dionis asked.

"We were able to talk to his neighbors after we checked his apartment. One in particular told us she thought that he was a political activist and a big contributor to our governor and now president elect. We would like to know if he had any relationship or was close in any way to our governor and/or her husband, Congressman Patrick Banks," DeCarlo said.

"How would the neighbor know that?" Dionis asked, concealing his surprise that this murdered guy might have been somehow associated with Ann Banks.

"Good question," replied DeCarlo. "Apparently, this guy liked to drink a bit too much and when he did, got talkative like he was bragging."

"Okay," replied Dionis. "We'll check that out. Should I coordinate directly with you or with Tony at the Bureau?"

"I'd like everyone to coordinate directly with this office and directly through me," Crawford said quickly as she removed her reading glasses. It was her way of letting her ex-husband and everyone else know that she was in charge and that her office would coordinate all of the information that would be shared with the Connecticut State Police and, potentially, with the Connecticut Chief State's Attorney's Office.

"Let's keep a close hold on all of this," Crawford added. "Need to know only. I don't want any political blowback on this."

For a moment, the former married couple exchanged forced smiles.

The only political blowback you want to avoid is that which might be directed at you, Dionis thought.

"Of course. No problem," Dionis answered as he looked directly into Crawford's eyes. Everyone in the room except DeCarlo was aware of the tension between Dionis and his ex-wife. And like fans of stock car racing anticipating a huge smash up to add to the excitement of watching cars go around in a circle, they were always hoping to witness an actual verbal altercation between the two of them. While they both tolerated each other, the two were both careful to avoid a public confrontation. Still, the rumors of their differences and distaste for each other were a matter of common discussion whenever agency heads got together over a few drinks.

"Did your people find anything in his condo?" Maffuci asked, just as Crawford's secretary brought in her coffee.

"You're getting ahead of me," DeCarlo replied. "That was my next point. As you know, we try to work up a 24 to 48-hour timeline on all victims of homicide. A big part of that includes cell phone calls, credit card charges, who the victim may have last seen, even what they may have last eaten, which we can often discover during an autopsy. In this case, when we checked the victim's apartment, it was almost empty. He had very little inside. Almost no food in the refrigerator, no landline phone. Nor did we find a cell phone or computer, although he had the Internet in the house. We did find a Wi-Fi router. It was as if the guy was simply using the place to sleep and shower."

"Are you thinking someone sanitized the place?" Maffuci asked.

Sandi DeCarlo continued, "Forensics is going over it now. Not sure if it was sanitized or not. But I do think there is a missing computer. In addition to the Wi-Fi router, we found some cables that suggest he may have more than one computer and had it hard wired."

The meeting ended a few minutes later. The Connecticut State Police had little more information to offer about the man shot twice in the back of the head. But surprisingly, they had more than Dionis would have suspected so quickly in an investigation. What Dionis knew, but often failed to remember, was that unlike most federal cases that normally take anywhere from one to three years or more to investigate, homicide cases are made within the first 24 to 48 hours, if, they're made at all. After that, the chances of identifying the guilty party diminish rapidly. In many cases, the chances of solving a murder after forty-eight hours drops by fifty percent. City and state homicide cops don't have the luxury of waiting weeks and months for financial records to be subpoenaed or have weeks or months of recordings from wiretaps to help make their case. Nor do they have the time to sit through endless meetings waiting on prosecutors to analyze every investigative step and possible trial scenario in order to avoid losing a case, since losing could jeopardize their career. Homicide investigators have to move quickly and with determination. Homicide cases, at least in the first forty-eight hours, are akin to a wind sprint in a road race. Most federal investigations are more like a long, slow walk along a scenic lake. Both state and local investigators are better at homicides, while the feds are much better at white-collar crimes and fighting organized crime and terrorism, which, after the attacks on the twin trade towers in 2001, became the nation's highest investigative priority. For the first time, federal law enforcement shifted its focus from being reactive to proactive with the expressed intent of preventing another such terrorist attack in the country.

Dionis and Maffuci rode the elevator alone down to the lobby of the federal building.

“So, you know this DeCarlo,” Dionis asked his friend.

“Met her a few times. Don’t know much about her. She’s very private. A loner. Why?”

“Just curious. DeCarlo looks like she knows what she’s doing.”

“She does,” Maffuci said. “She’s a bit hard. I heard she was in an auto accident a few years ago when she was still in uniform. A chase. She got smashed up pretty good. Almost died. That was bad enough, but the car that hit her was driven by a drunk who had his kid in the back seat. The kid was killed. I don’t think she’s gotten over it.”

“That was her? I read about that or saw it on the news.”

“Yeah, that’s her.” Maffuci replied.

As they exited the elevator, they saw DeCarlo in the lobby checking her cell phone. She looked up and said, “Hi, Tony. How’s it going?”

“Good. You know Mike Dionis from Secret Service?”

“Never really met before this morning. Nice to meet you,” she said, extending her hand.

Dionis reached out his hand and felt a firm grip, almost like a man’s.

“I’m late for a meeting on this with the new Special Agent in Charge (SAC),” Maffuci said, as he rolled his eyes towards the back of his head. “She wants briefed on everything,” he groaned. “How about the three of us get together later this afternoon and compare notes?”

“Fine,” DeCarlo said. “Four o’clock?”

“Too early for me,” Maffuci answered. “How about seven-thirty at Water’s Edge in Westbrook. I’ve got to be out that way later and my day has me on a tight schedule.”

"Okay with me," DeCarlo said. "A little out of the way for me, but okay. Hopefully, the bureau will have something worth our time."

"Yea, I know, but it will put me closer to home and I'm out that way this afternoon," Maffuci said.

Dionis just looked at Maffuci and grinned. He knew that Water's Edge was Maffuci's favorite place to meet for drinks. Quiet, out of the way, and virtually never frequented by members of the law enforcement community. And, it was easy to hide one's government car while stopping for a drink on the way home from work. In today's politically correct world, being caught having a drink and driving a government vehicle almost always resulted in dismissal.

"I'll find out what I can," Maffuci added as he hurried off. "See you both tonight."

Dionis and DeCarlo stood for a moment wondering what next to say. Dionis could handle almost any situation, anywhere, anytime. He had seen combat, ordered men to fight, and had seen some die. He had ordered presidential candidates to make decisions about their travel plans after the discussions had gone on too long and had delayed the time necessary to prepare and have people in place for their next event. He had handled the egotistical news reporters when they tried to penetrate a secure perimeter as he was protecting a president or presidential candidate. He was comfortable around CEOs and the dregs of society, both of which he might encounter on the same day. But he couldn't handle that certain smile a woman gives a man. He couldn't handle that feminine charm. He loved women. He loved talking to them. It was refreshing to not have to deal with that macho attitude men often felt they had to display when they were around each other. For now, all he could think of was Ann. And he knew he would have to get those thoughts out of his mind if he were going to mentally survive.

"Mike, are you okay?" DeCarlo asked.

"Yeah," Dionis answered, momentarily embarrassed. "I was just thinking about something."

"Okay, see you tonight then," DeCarlo said as she turned and walked away.

Tony Maffuci walked the three blocks back to his office and placed an urgent request for a fingerprint identification on the deceased. He needed the information instantly and he got it. In less than an hour, the FBI, using its Integrated Automated Fingerprint Identification System (IAFIS) at HQ's in Washington D.C., identified the late Robert Moss as Oleg Lomakina, last known as a member of Russian organized crime. The results sent a chill up Maffuci's spine.

Chapter 4

Congressman Patrick Banks was more than a little agitated. He and Josh Martin, his Chief of Staff, stood in the den of the governor's mansion, each holding tightly to a double shot of Bushmills 21 Irish Whiskey as they watched the local news.

"State Police have identified the body of the man found two days ago in New Haven, shot twice in the head execution style, as Robert Moss. Moss had lived in Connecticut for about four years. Sources tell us that the FBI is assisting the Connecticut State Police in the investigation. Police have no other information about his murder at this time but say the investigation is continuing. We will keep you informed as we learn more about this terrible tragedy. Back to you in the studio," said the news reporter after ending her live report.

Patrick Banks turned off the television. He could care less about any other local news, sports scores, or even the weather. There was no link to him; at least not now.

"This is fucking great," Banks said, as he pounded his fist on the table. He threw off his suit jacket and jerked his tie loose. "This has to be the work of Dunayev. That asshole is going to get us all screwed. And now, the FBI is involved. I want to know everything the State Police has on this. Do you hear me?"

"We shouldn't be making routine inquiries about this, Patrick. That will only bring us unnecessary attention. I don't think we should do anything…."

Waiving his hand in front of him, Banks cut Martin off before he could finish and said, "Then do it quietly. But find out. The last thing I need is for that evil little bastard to screw things up."

"He's not going to do that, Patrick. He's a businessman. He's got too much to lose."

"He's a murdering corrupt Russian thug," Banks said. "What do I do if anyone questions me about this?"

"Why would they? Dunayev has always dealt with me. They can't link him to you."

"You're linked to me. The fucker was at a fundraiser he wasn't invited to. That prick is behind this. He is sending a message. But why? Just because I didn't stop what I was doing and see him. That son-of-a-bitch."

Martin was wary of the idea of Patrick Banks having any direct contact with Dunayev. "I'll make arrangements to see him myself. Let me handle him."

"What are you suggesting?"

There was a short pause before Martin answered. There were questions swarming in his mind. *What was Dunayev really up to? Did he kill Robert Moss? If so, why? If not, then who? Why the rush to speak to Patrick directly?* "I'll let you know. For now, please do nothing. I'll talk to him."

Michael Dionis sat at his desk staring aimlessly out the window. He had placed several telephone calls around the state and to his headquarters in Washington, D.C., all designed to gather whatever information he could about the late Robert Moss and, and if any, his political affiliations. It was amazing, he thought, just how much one could discover these days without ever leaving the office. It was rare that anyone in his profession had to go far to get information. It was all at your fingertips. Just access the Internet or make some phone calls. A seasoned cop or investigator could almost conduct an entire investigation without leaving the safety and comfort of his/her office or cubicle. But it wasn't quite that simple. In the world of instant information at one's fingertips, people had lost the art of personal communication. Young investigators no longer mastered the art of interviewing and interrogating. It was the biggest complaint of supervisors and police chiefs across the country. In a world where a generation of young people grow up thinking texting is the main source of communication, the idea that one-on-one verbal interaction, where you looked a witness or suspect in the eye, was as critical to learning the truth, was lost. Texting and phone calls didn't provide the telltale signs of deceit when seeking the truth. It was the little things, like a suspect covering his/her mouth to prevent disclosing something or repeating the question that had just been posed to them. Dionis knew that all investigations started and ended with an interview, not a text message. Young investigators, like so many people their age, had lost the art of listening, as had just about everyone in this country. One thing Dionis had learned over many years in his profession was that people like to talk, if given the chance. The flip side was that most really didn't like to listen, preferring to transmit and not receive.

Dionis' private thoughts were interrupted by his cell phone ringing. He could see from the caller ID that is was Tony Mafucci.

"Tony," he said as he put the phone to his ear.

"Michael, you're not going to believe this."

"What's that?" Dionis asked.

"Our dead guy's real name is Oleg Lomakina. He's Russian OC. I'm getting some background on him but there isn't much. It appears he was quiet here. Lived a regular life. Really flew under the radar."

"Well, he pissed somebody off," Dionis said, "You don't get two shots to the back of the head by living under the radar," he continued as he turned away from the window.

"You're right about that."

"Have you told Crawford about this?"

"No. We'll tell her later. I want to tell Sandi first. I'll tell Tina later tonight or in the morning after we meet at Water's Edge. If she hears about this, she'll hold a fucking press conference."

"You said it," Dionis replied.

"If she wants to be an investigator, let her join the Bureau," Maffuci said. "You and I investigate. Prosecutors should stick to prosecuting. She's going to have to learn that."

"You realize, she's going to vent her anger out at me."

"Yeah, I know that too. Part of the fun in this is watching you get your balls busted," Maffuci said laughing. "It makes me happier than a seagull with a French fry."

"Thanks, asshole. See you tonight. Try and be on time for a change."

"Have I ever let you down in the past?"

"Many times. Do I need to remind you when..."?

Maffuci interrupted Dionis before he could finish his sentence. "Not that again," Maffuci said. "I didn't know she was married."

"Yeah, right. See you tonight," Dionis said.

Michael Dionis disconnected the call and returned to staring out of the window. His thoughts were now focused on what Maffuci had just told him. *Some Russian mob guy gets hit. Supposedly a political supporter of Ann Banks. Still not sure what that has to do with me or the Secret Service.*

Dionis returned to his personal thoughts as he watched the lights of New Haven begin to come alive. It was December in Connecticut, just days before Christmas. Darkness came early in December and remained late into the early morning hours. The last few days had been the kind that would cause most people to resort to consuming more alcohol than normal, whatever normal was. Drinking on cold, dark, wet wintery nights had, in many circles, become a sport of choice.

His ex-wife had summoned him to the meeting earlier just to bust his balls. It was her way. He thought about leaving Connecticut. Maybe the service would transfer him. With two years to go, he was probably too old to be considered for a permanent protection detail, especially for an incoming president or vice-president. Even if he could get such an assignment, he didn't want to be that close to Ann

Banks; it would be too risky for both of them. And he certainly didn't want to go back to shift work with rotating days off. No, he'd have to wait it out. He wasn't going to run from his ex or to Ann, not just yet.

***

Andre Dunayev turned his black Mercedes into the Marriott Marquis in New York's Times Square in the heart of Manhattan. He smiled as he handed the parking valet his keys. He was a wealthy businessman, he thought to himself. No need to not act like it. New York was the one city where anyone, the rich and famous, the mediocre, the non-relevant, and the poor, could meet most anytime of the day or night, and almost no one cared. New Yorkers didn't care who you were. They didn't impress that easily. Movie stars and other celebrities of every sort could walk through Central Park and not be bothered, except of course, by the occasional tourist. Dunayev loved New York for its openness. An openness that allowed him to prosper at the misery of others. Most importantly, he loved New York for the fact that he could operate under the radar of most law enforcement organizations. Keep a low profile and the cops won't know much of anything about you. Stay off the telephones, and the FBI won't ever be able to make a case against you. That is the easiest way to get caught by the feds; talk on the phone. The new breed of feds don't get their hands dirty very often these days. They face way too much oversight in the politically correct world they work in. The feds, his sources told him, spend way too much time taking online training in their offices, on everything from sexual harassment in the workplace to diversity education. Younger agents, who grew up living on a computer and/or iPad, often tried desperately to make cases by using the Internet and CCTV cameras. If they didn't have you on tape, or on camera, your odds of being arrested and convicted were slim.

Dunayev took the elevator up to the revolving rooftop restaurant. Immediately after walking off the elevator, he could see Josh Martin sitting alone at a table in the corner.

"Hello, Josh," Dunayev said as he extended his hand.

"Andre," was all Martin said as he motioned him to take a seat. "Would you like a drink?"

"So, our friend sends you again," Dunayev said. "I told you I wanted to meet with him."

"Forget about that right now. What in the hell are you thinking of, killing Moss? And leaving identification on him."

"Listen my friend," Dunayev said as he grabbed Martin's wrist. "There are things you must learn. First, you never question my personal business. Second, never accuse me of things of which you know nothing. I did not kill anyone." Dunayev was careful. While he didn't think Martin would ever wear a wire or record their conversation, he was not about to take any chances. "And whoever did kill him, did us a favor. He had information that was a threat to all of us, especially Patrick. You should be grateful, my friend."

"Bullshit," Martin replied, pulling his wrist away from Dunayev's grip. "You were sending a message. What you do is your business. When it affects Patrick Banks and getting him into the White House someday, it is my business. And keep your fucking hands off me. Who the hell do you think you are?"

Dunayev was not used to being talked to in such a manner. He stared at Martin with his cold eyes. "I'm the guy who helped get your stooge's wife elected. That's who I am. I'm the guy who's going to be very unhappy if I don't have access to her as we agreed."

"Sorry, Andre," Martin said, waving his hand, dismissing his demands. "That can't happen, not right now. Ann's going to be the president. She's surrounded by Secret Service Agents. Her schedule is dictated by too many people outside of her immediate control. She's traveling and setting up her office and team in Washington. Patrick is staying close by her side during this transition period. So, meeting with her right now; that's not going to happen. We can't risk it, and neither can you."

Dunayev didn't like what he was hearing. He knew the intricacies of crime but didn't quite understand American politics as much as he'd thought. He hadn't considered this when he helped Ann Banks get elected.

"I want to meet with Patrick," Dunayev demanded. "I will meet with him. You tell him that just because his wife is going to be the new president, he can't shit on his friends."

"He's not shitting on you, Andre. He just can't risk being seen with you. I have to be the only link between the two of you now."

"So, what do I do if something happens to you?" Dunayev asked.

"Are you threatening me now?" Martin said.

"I never threaten, my friend. Nothing is going to happen to you if you do as we agreed," Dunayev replied. "Now tell me, how do I know our mutual friend gets my messages? How do I know you're not deciding for yourself what he needs to know and what he doesn't?"

"That's my job," Martin said. "I've always decided that. What the hell do you think, Andre? You think this idiot idealist is a real player. Business has controlled him and most politicians most of their lives. Their moves are controlled to project an image of progress and reform. Why do you think it takes so long to get any real legislation passed in this country? Business interests, my friend. They control Washington. And they control state governments. And they control it because virtually every elected politician, certainly governors, and those in Congress and the Senate, all want and believe they can be president. When you play to those egos, not much is hard to accomplish. When you learn just how this works, you'll understand. Some of the American people know that but most either don't want to admit it and bury their heads in the sand, while others are simply too stupid to realize it. It's all about the optics."

"What is this optics you talk about?" Dunayev asked.

"It's what the voters see in a candidate. Most of the time, Americans vote along their ideological party line. They don't care what the candidates really stand for. How in the hell do you think this country elected a peanut farmer from Georgia? Or a man who married a librarian who could hardly spell library. Hell, they almost elected a woman who had committed a host of national security violations simply because over half the country despised her opponent. Never mind what policies he espoused. That, my friend, is part of the optics. Think about the list of candidates you've seen from both national parties in recent years; do you think the American people have been excited about any of them? No, they haven't. Instead, we're seeing people vote against a candidate now instead of for a candidate. That is optics, Andre. And what Ann Banks provides the country right now, and us, is good optics. We don't need to fuck that up."

Dunayev listened attentively. "Then getting our sweetheart couple on board shouldn't be a problem," he said.

"It won't, if you let me do my job," Martin told him. "But keep in mind, we have to be careful. We have to play the long game here. And while manipulating the American people can sometimes be rather easy, they don't want their noses rubbed in it either. Patrick Banks has worked most of his life to get to where he is. He knows nothing else. He's never produced a fucking thing in this world. Never really worked. Like most politicians, he panders to his party and his constituents. And like so many politicians, he is blinded by his own private ambitions. He could easily become a member of the opposing party if he thought that would benefit him. The one big difference between him and so many other politicians is that Patrick Banks grew up poor. Now that he's tasted money and power, he doesn't want to lose it. He thought he could be president when he ran for his party's nomination four years ago. He was delusional of course. But he wanted it badly. And the only way he is ever going to get it, is to ascend to it. Or play the role of loyal husband while also holding down an important position in his wife's cabinet."

"What are you thinking?" Dunayev asked.

"Secretary of State, perhaps" Martin replied. "That will give your people access to him without causing much suspicion. You know, open up more dialogue with Russia. Trips back and forth. Establish open communication. Increase trade. All of that bullshit to make the American people think you guys are actually America's friends."

"Will his wife agree to this? A family member in the cabinet?"

"Perhaps. John Kennedy set the precedent. He put his brother Bobby in the cabinet as the Attorney General. The guy never really saw the inside of a courtroom before that. Nobody in the Democratic party really questioned the fact that someone with virtually no prosecutorial trial experience was now the senior law enforcement officer in the country. He was a Kennedy and part of the most powerful political family in the country at the time. Most people didn't care about the appointment. It was all about the optics," Martin added. "So yes, she just *might* do it."

"That all sounds promising," Dunayev said. "And what about Patrick? Will he go along with this?"

"He still thinks he's going to be president. But he'll never be elected on his own merits, no matter how blind the American voter might be. Our corrupt two-party system isn't that hard to exploit, as your countrymen learned just a couple of elections back. But you have to be nominated first and Patrick Banks is never going to get it on his own. This country has never had an independent candidate occupy the White House. Both political parties are still trying to wrap their heads around how this happened. I think they're more shocked that an independent won than they were when Trump got elected. Nobody saw that coming either. After all, if a narcissist who thinks he's still the star of a game show can win the presidency, we should be able to get Patrick Banks elected. But first, we have to convince his wife that appointing him as her Secretary of State is a good idea," Martin said.

"Go on," Dunayev instructed.

"Like so many of our politicians on the national stage, Patrick Banks exhibits an arrogance of power that we'll easily be able to exploit. We're just going to have to figure out how to use his wife, Ann, to further our mutual interests," Martin said. "The new administration is not going to get much of anything passed. Politicians on both sides of the aisle are shocked over her election. They'll actually band together to prevent her from getting her so- called 'middle of the road' agenda and term limit legislation passed. This whole election was a fluke. No one expected an independent to get elected, and Congress is not going to simply go along with it, despite what the American people might want."

"I don't care about that. I have political and business interests that need to be addressed," Dunayev said.

"Stop bullshitting me, Andre. Your political interests as to what goes on in this country are your country's only real priority. Your personal business interests are a side issue that lines your pockets and mine. But both of those interests will be addressed. Financial gain is our only mutual interest. Both of us will be richer at the end of the next four years," Martin replied. "Your country's ability to manipulate people across the globe through social media and whatever other tactics you employ are your business. I'll leave the international politics to you and to whoever you report to. As far as I'm concerned, your country is far more manipulative and corrupt than ours is. There will never be trust between the two countries. And that's too bad. Just imagine what our two countries might accomplish if none of this corrupt bullshit existed."

"So, I asked you once, what are you suggesting?" Dunayev said.

"We have more to do here than just worry about you seeing Patrick. You need to forget about that right now. If we want access to thc White House, we've got to deal with Ann Banks."

Dunayev wasn't sure that he liked what he was hearing. But he did think that Martin had a set of balls to talk to him like that, and, more importantly, to already be thinking about how to exploit Ann Banks. "You would have done well in Russia my friend."

"Well, we're not in Russia, Andre. And here in this country where everyone has a cell phone with a camera stuck up the cheeks of their ass, and the media turns every spoken word into an evening's political analysis, we have to be careful. And in spite of all the bullshit promises most politicians make to them, most people are simply window dressing, character actors and props. Most politicians are more concerned about their celebrity and notoriety. In time, Ann Banks will be no different."

"If Patrick becomes Secretary of State, what happens to you?" Dunayev asked.

"I'm working on that. But I'll probably go with Patrick over at State."

"What if I can help you become the new president's chief of staff?" Dunayev asked.

"No, Andre," Martin said forcefully. "We can't fuck around here with the president-elect."

"We don't have to do that," he said calmly. "But what if there was another way?"

"Okay, I'm listening," replied Martin, simply trying to appease him.

Martin just sat there and listened quietly as Dunayev revealed the content of the recording of Ann Banks and Michael Dionis making love in the governor's mansion just days ago. Dunayev hadn't intended to tell Martin about the recording. He changed his mind after hearing him explain his strategy for using Patrick and Ann Banks.

Martin's eyes widened and his knees began to shake. He couldn't believe what he was hearing. Not because Ann Banks was having an affair, but because Dunayev had a recording of her lovemaking.

"How did you get you get this?" he asked, folding his arms over his stomach as he tried to mask his shock at what he just heard.

"That's not important right now, my friend," Dunayev said, as he waved his hands in the air. "What's important is that your new president is keeping quite the secret. What you should be asking is how do we use this."

Dunayev called the waitress over to the table and said, "I think I'll have a drink now. Scotch please. Macallan's."

"The 12?" the waitress asked.

"No. The 18," Dunayev replied smiling.

"And can I get you anything?" the waitress asked Martin.

"Just my bill please," Martin replied.

Trying to maintain his composure, Martin asked, "Andre, do you have any other recordings of them?"

"Just this one. Why? Do you think we need more?" he said smiling.

"No. We don't. Can you get me a copy of the recording?"

"I thought you might ask," Dunayev replied as he reached into his coat pocket and removed a flash drive with the recording embedded on it. "Be careful with that my friend."

The waitress came by with the scotch and Martin's bill and placed them on the table. Dunayev looked at the menu and said, "Are you sure you won't have something?"

"No."

"Then let me get that," Dunayev said, grabbing the bill. "You look a little pale. I hope you didn't eat anything that didn't agree with you."

"I'm fine," Martin replied. "We'll talk soon. I have a train to catch. Do you have anything special for our representative?"

"I do," Dunayev replied, as he slid two small clear packages just larger than the size of a quarter across the table. "Please tell him to enjoy himself."

The two men simply nodded. Martin stood up, signaling that their meeting was over. He rode the elevator down to the main level of the hotel, consumed in his own thoughts. *How did Andre get that recording and what other recordings does he have*?

Andre Dunayev sat at the table alone, sipping his scotch. *Patrick Banks refuses to see me. He will never be elected president on his own. I can't trust Ann Banks to nominate her husband as Secretary of State. You left me no choice Josh,* he thought.

Chapter 5

Michael Dionis arrived almost exactly on time at Water's Edge, the only timeshare resort in Connecticut on the Long Island shoreline. He would like to have pulled up under the canopy and tossed his keys to the valet, but he was in a government car; leaving the keys with a valet was not an option. The lobby and restaurant were lit up with Christmas decorations. Another reminder of a holiday soon to come where he'd most likely be alone. He walked through the lobby paying no attention to the people standing around the black baby grand piano. He wanted to get to the bar and have a drink. Government car or not, he was having one. But before going into the lounge, he saw Sandi DeCarlo sitting on the opposite side of the lobby checking her cell phone. She waited there choosing not to go into the bar alone.

"Hi. Been here long?" Dionis asked.

"Just a few minutes," she replied, rubbing her hands together quickly.

"Are you okay?"

"I'm freezing. Can't seem to get warm," DeCarlo replied.

"Here, give me your hands," Dionis said.

DeCarlo shot him a dazed look and wide grin and said, "What? Give you, my hands?"

"Please, just trust me for a moment."

DeCarlo's curiosity was heightened as she held out both of her arms. Dionis took her hands in his and held them tight, then rubbed each hand separately.

"My God, your hands are warm," DeCarlo said.

"So, I've been told. My body seems to run hotter than most people's. There, how's that? Any better?"

"Actually, yes," DeCarlo said. "Thank you."

"Is Tony here?" Dionis asked.

"Haven't seen him."

"Well, how about a drink?"

"Absolutely."

The Seaview Bistro bar inside the resort wasn't crowded. It usually wasn't on weeknights in winter when New England days are short, cold, and dreary. Dionis and DeCarlo grabbed a small table in the corner of the lounge near the large stone fireplace, so they could talk without being overheard; both trying to sit with their backs to the wall, as cops are so apt to do. DeCarlo quickly grabbed the seat closest to the fire. Dionis suspected that she might be one of those women who easily got cold and grabbed a sweater the minute the temperature dipped below eighty. In the background, the music of Rick Braun and Peter White played softly on the smooth jazz radio station.

"So, what has the Secret Service found out today?" DeCarlo asked.

"Not much, I'm afraid. It's going to take a bit longer than just today to find out much about this guy's affiliation with the party. Besides, the bureau will have better luck with that."

"I'm still not sure what the Secret Service has to do with any of this," DeCarlo said quietly.

"I'm not sure either. Part of it is my ex-wife. She likes to make a grand production out of everything. Plus, it's a way for her to bust my balls."

"You were married to her?" DeCarlo asked, surprised.

"You didn't know?"

"No. I had no idea."

The waitress arrived and asked what she could get them.

"What kind of beer do you have on tap?" DeCarlo asked. Dionis was surprised. He didn't hear that question asked by many women. When he did, he smiled to himself.

"None," the waitress said. "Only bottled beer."

"Then I'll have your house cab." DeCarlo said.

"And you?" the waitress asked Dionis, her tone dry and not overly friendly.

"The same," said Dionis.

The waitress turned and walked away. When she did, Dionis continued telling DeCarlo about his past relationship with Tina Crawford.

"Been divorced for a couple years. It was a major mistake," he said. "Didn't last long. She is all career, which is fine with me. But there wasn't any time for much of anything or anyone else. I still have no idea how we ended up getting married. I guess the sexual attraction ran its course quicker than most marriages."

DeCarlo grinned, trying not to smile too much.

Dionis continued, saying, "She has political ambitions. If you're not a lawyer, judge, or highly placed political figure, you're of little value to her. Sort of like people who belong to expensive country clubs; you know, the kind that think that if you're not some titan of industry, they look down their noses at you. My ex is a bit like that. Unless of course you're a celebrity news reporter and can get her some face time on the air or in the media."

"Sounds like jealousy."

"Anything but. I wish her well. I've been in this business a long time. I know it's a game. She plays it as well as anyone. She wants far more out of this than I do or ever did. At the end of the day, I want away from this business."

The waitress returned with two glasses of wine, both carefully poured so that no one would think either glass contained an ounce more than necessary.

"So why do you want out of this business?" DeCarlo asked. "You sound cynical."

"You haven't become cynical yet?" Dionis said. "I'd think it would have hit you a good while back with the deaths you see."

"Didn't say I wasn't cynical. Just asking why you want out so badly."

"The business has changed too much. We used to be respected, at least to some degree. When I grew up my father used to tell me that when a police officer stopped or questioned you, you answered and showed respect. People today, just the opposite. Parents tell kids they don't have to tell the police shit. Cities want to defund the police. People can attack you and you're the bad guy. I guess I've had enough."

"We all deal with it," DeCarlo replied.

"And how do you deal with it?"

"As I'm sure you know, most people don't have a clue as to what goes on in this country after dark. They don't want to know, especially those in the wealthier parts of our towns and cities. Certainly, the CEOs in this country, most of whom live in a bubble, along with their minions, don't want to hear or admit that the country has a dark underbelly to it. Besides, I didn't get into this business to amass a fortune and I suspect you didn't either."

"I did not. I got into it to make a difference. But before joining the Service, I was a uniformed cop in south Florida after leaving the Marine Corps. I responded to my share of deaths, overdoses, domestic disturbances, rapes, robberies, and every medical emergency imaginable. It pisses me off when politicians buy into all of this socialist propaganda. We're supposed to remain non-partisan in the service. But politicians on both sides of the aisle seem to be becoming more radicalized these days. We live in such a politically correct and polarized world that your every word is scrutinized and condemned."

DeCarlo leaned back in her chair, took a sip of her wine, smiled at Dionis, and said, "You'll get no argument out of me on that. Saw enough of that when I went to college. I hear it's far worse now."

Dionis said, "Too many people think we're all racists. You know this systemic killing of blacks is bullshit. My own nephew, a socialist in the making, doesn't speak to me because I had the audacity to point out that the data related to cops singling out blacks for killing was totally false. I even cited a DOJ study published by the *New York Times*, of all places, that contradicted the idea that police were engaged in the systemic killing of minorities. That alone labeled me a racist in his eyes."

"I hear the same crap," DeCarlo replied. "People don't want to believe that most cops respond to criminal behavior. Race, creed, color, or one's sexual orientation, has nothing to do with it. But people's own personal perceptions become their reality. Not sure that's ever going to change."

"So," Dionis asked again, "how do you deal with it?"

"I'm still propelled by hope and the desire to help, I guess. I don't see myself sitting in a business office or trying to make a living in sales by dressing in short skirts and flirting with old men who hold the purchase power of whatever I may be hocking."

"Old," Dionis said. "Now you're hitting below the belt. If this conversation is going to continue, you're going to have to define old."

"Relax old man, you're not old," DeCarlo said smiling. "My father is old. Not you. So, what are you going to do when you retire?" she asked.

"Not sure. Maybe sell out for the big bucks. Sell my soul to one of the corporate giants. Maybe just relax, travel, and have conversations about something other than the job, and, of course, play golf. Although I don't think I'm the private club type as I've never been a titan of industry," Dionis continued. "I like quiet get-a-ways or hanging around the marina with friends."

"You have a boat?"

"Sailboat, small 35-footer. I keep it at Pilot's Point marina just a few minutes from here. Actually, thought about getting something ten to fifteen feet bigger when I retire, maybe live on it for a while. Spend five months up here, maybe the rest of the year down south somewhere; maybe Florida. Beats keeping up a house."

"So, you're a minimalist?" DeCarlo asked.

"To some degree, yes."

"I love to sail," DeCarlo said. "Don't know much about it but I love being out on the water. So how did you and Tina ever get married?" she asked.

"That's a long story. The reader's digest version is that I had just come off a tour on presidential protection. I came up here to head this office up when she was just a young prosecutor. I had connections in Washington. But not the type she thought I had. She was intrigued by my access to the President. Mostly, though, she liked the idea of my having had access to White House staffers and people at the Justice Department. And, I had figured on being out of here in a couple of years and back to Washington. I guess she thought this would get her some political exposure outside Connecticut. But truthfully, that's just my speculation. Looking back, I really don't know how or why we ever got married."

"Still sounds like jealousy to me," DeCarlo said with a smirk.

"Not at all. Do you have any idea how exhausting it is being married to someone you're not in love with? How about you? Ever married?" Dionis asked.

"Once. Fifteen years ago. We met when we were going to the University of New Haven. We both majored in criminal justice. We both got lucky right out of college and landed jobs; him with the New Haven P.D. and me with the State Police, DeCarlo said. "It didn't last long. You know, cops."

"I do know cops," replied Dionis. "Seems most end up divorced somewhere along the way."

"Why is that?" DeCarlo asked.

"That's easy," Dionis replied. "Long hours, not being around for holidays, total attachment to the job, believing that only other cops understand the work you do. Cops are notoriously poor communicators. Especially the younger ones, no offense intended."

"None taken," DeCarlo replied.

"Cops want to protect their families from the atrocities they see in their work. Wives and husbands not in the business think they're being shut out. And of course, the access to members of the opposite sex. The sad reality is, cops, at least a lot of male cops, cheat."

"Are you justifying cheating?" DeCarlo asked.

"Not at all," Dionis replied. "It's not an excuse, only an explanation."

"Now you really do sound cynical," DeCarlo said.

"Didn't we already agree that all cops are cynical? I thought it came with the job."

"You may be right," DeCarlo said, smiling and holding her wine up next to him. As they clanged their glasses, Dionis' cell phone vibrated. It was a text message from Tony Maffuci.

Not going to be able to join you. Been detained on other business. Will call tomorrow first thing. Nothing much to report.

"He's not coming," Dionis said.

"What? Did he say why?" DeCarlo asked.

"Tied up on something. He didn't elaborate." Dionis' first thought was that his friend was gambling again at one of the casinos just over thirty minutes away. He suspected that Maffuci had a gambling problem, but he was not about to share it with Sandi DeCarlo.

"I wonder if he was able to find out anything?"

"Tony did find something out. Didn't he reach out to you?"

"No, he didn't."

"He was probably going to tell you tonight. The dead guy's real name is Oleg Lomakina, former Russian organized crime."

“Russian organized crime? Didn’t see that one coming.”

“It might explain the execution type killing,” Dionis said. “But why the alias?”

“Could be almost anything,” DeCarlo replied. “But this changes some things. I really need to get back to the office and follow up on this.”

“Tonight?” Dionis said, looking surprised.

“It’s a murder investigation that’s already over 48 hours old. This information is important. Might be something that helps us. Give me your cell number; I’ll text you later if it’s not too late. Let me see what I can find.”

“It’s never too late,” Dionis replied. “Call if you learn anything.”

“Tony should have called me right away with this,” DeCarlo said, her agitation quite visible.

“Probably. He can be absentminded sometimes.”

“Oh, I know that, only too well.”

Dionis wanted to follow up on that but decided he didn’t know DeCarlo well enough to ask. And since she was in a hurry, he’d let it pass for now.

DeCarlo quickly finished her wine and, before Dionis could say or do anything else, she took out a twenty-dollar bill and laid it on the table. “You get the next one,” she said. “Talk later.”

“Yes, talk later,” Dionis said. Dionis sat alone for a few minutes lost in his thoughts. DeCarlo was good. She kept him on the defensive. She was opinionated and certainly not shy. But she was clearly agitated about Maffuci not showing up.

Dionis finished his drink, got up, and put on his jacket before walking through the light rain to his car in the parking lot. He opened the door, got in and took out his cell phone. He immediately accessed his email account, the one that no one knew about other than Ann Banks, and drafted a short email message.

Russian member of OC murdered in New Haven two days ago. Name was Oleg Lomakina. He was living under the alias of Robert Moss. State police think he was a huge party donor. Have you ever heard of him? Important.

Dionis placed the message in the draft folder of the mail account he and Ann Banks used to communicate. It would never be sent. He only hoped she would read it soon and respond.

As Michael Dionis and Sandi DeCarlo were leaving the lounge at Water's Edge, Tony Maffuci was at the Mohegan Sun Casino in Ledyard, Connecticut. He was having another good day; already up over six thousand dollars playing blackjack.

***

"I think our friend will be quiet for a while," Josh Martin said to Patrick Banks as the two men sat across from each other in Banks' small apartment in Crystal City, just across the river from D.C. Banks poured Martin a glass of Buffalo Trace and said, "He better be quiet."

"He will. I made it clear. He understands the problems we have now," Martin replied. "And what about Ann?"

"Still working on it."

Martin thought hard about how to break the news of Ann Banks' infidelity with a Secret Service Agent. He decided the best way was to be as direct as possible. Trying to sugarcoat it, or even hiding it, would prove to be more of a problem for everyone.

"You might want to pour yourself another one. I have some very unpleasant news to share with you," Martin said to Banks.

Over the next ten minutes, Martin told Patrick Banks about the recording of his wife and Michael Dionis. Patrick Banks was quiet and stared straight through Martin. He was livid with both his wife for having an affair, and Dunayev for having bugged the bedroom at the mansion.

The color from Banks' face faded. He stared at Martin for what seemed like an eternity. With a huge, pained look he said, "It's been a long day. What time is that damn breakfast meeting with those religious rights fanatics in the morning?"

"Eight a.m. And we're going to need those fanatics someday soon."

"Why else do you think I'd agreed to break bread with them so fucking early in the morning?"

"Then we both better get some sleep. We'll need an early start if we're going to beat some of the traffic. I'm going home," Martin said.

"Do whatever you like. I'm going to bed," Banks said, trying not to reveal his anger and pain.

Chapter 6

Michael Dionis sat alone in his small condo watching the late news. He never really cared about the local news in Connecticut. It was the same faces reporting the same events, night after night. Only the victims' names changed. Connecticut was a small television market and the reporters turned over so often he could barely remember their names. The news broadcasts were often dull and boring when compared to Washington or New York. The major networks in those markets broadcast real local news. Of course, it was just as easy to tire of one shooting after another. Daily police chases caught on the news, too, could quickly lose their appeal. The local news outlets weren't of much value to him other than providing the five to seven-day weather forecast he needed in order to decide whether or not to go sailing. And they screwed that up most of the time.

But Dionis wasn't paying attention to the weather report or anything else on the television. His mind was on Ann Banks and what the future held for her; and for him. And they were separate futures, and certainly not one together as she had hoped. Their last time together was filled with the stress of being discovered. He genuinely cared for her, but that was not enough for him, or her. Ann Banks had ambition. Winning the Connecticut gubernatorial race was quite a feat for someone in a state that notoriously elected liberal candidates not only to that office but in virtually all their congressional and senate races as well. For a state that promoted diversity, they certainly didn't display much when it came to their nationally elected politicians. So, when she ran for governor as an independent, few gave her much of a chance of being elected. The voters, who had become numb to the constant fighting between the two major party candidates, elected her in the hopes she would bring some civility back to the state capital. Of course, the one thing it did do was unite Democrats, and the few Republicans who served in the state's legislature, against her. She was beholden to few, if any, and certainly not to either of the state's political machines. The most outspoken of all was one of

Connecticut's U.S. Senators, who had somehow forgotten that he actually had not served as a Marine Corps Officer in Vietnam, after claiming that he actually had done so during a speech to a group of veterans. This same senator found fault with almost everything not endorsed by his party, and he especially found fault with Ann Banks' stance on immigration. Never mind that she supported legal immigration; what she fought against was illegal immigration.

Conservatives were critical of her support for the legalization of marijuana, but what angered them most was her insisting that some sort of gun control targeting automatic weapons be made part of the national conversation in an effort to save lives. But, of course, conservatives and the gun lobby wanted no part of that, as they saw it as the first step toward taking all guns away from people. It didn't matter to gun rights activists that in 2012, a crazed 20-year-old gunman took a semi-automatic weapon and walked into an elementary school in Connecticut and shot and killed 20 children along with six adults. The National Rifle Association (NRA) agreed this was a tragedy but responded by advocating the hiring of armed guards and placing them in American schools all across the country. California Senator Dianne Feinstein later introduced a bill in the Senate that would ban the sale of various weapons and magazines that held more than 10 rounds of ammunition. The proposed legislation was later defeated in a Democratically controlled Senate by a vote of 60 – 40. The NRA, for years, had systematically blocked the Bureau of Alcohol, Tobacco, Firearms and Explosives, (BATF) from modernizing the agency's paper-based weapons-tracing system; just one of their many assaults imposing crippling restrictions on the agency. By doing so, the NRA continued to demonstrate that it is one of the most powerful lobbying groups in the nation, supporting candidates on both sides of the aisle in order to ensure that its members vote the way they want them to vote. Ann Banks' election did, in some ways, unite the two parties, in that both found common ground in criticizing their independent governor.

Dionis was momentarily distracted by the ping of his cell phone telling him he had an email. He tapped the icon on his phone, accessed his email's draft folder and read the message.

Need to see you. Can you come tomorrow night? Important. Please?

Dionis was reading between the lines; she sounded anxious, and he was worried. He wanted to call her, but that was impossible. He had her private number, but it was late. It would have to wait. He'd find a way to stop by on the late shift tomorrow. It wouldn't be that hard to do with most of the agents in his office supplementing the regular protective detail. He tried to sleep but like most nights, sleep eluded him. He had just dozed off when his phone pinged again indicating he had a text message. It was from Sandi DeCarlo.

Nothing really new here on the identity of the Russian. It's late. Going to bed. Talk tomorrow. Sandi.

It was still dark outside the following morning when Tony Maffuci first started yelling. Getting himself worked up so early, seeing his kids off to school, was the price he paid for watching his children enter their teen years. They were his life. His Sicilian heritage taught him many things; the most important of all was family first, everything else be damned. But getting them out of bed in the morning was a chore he would prefer to avoid. Getting his 16-year-old son Anthony out of bed so that he could get to school and continue to do poorly was another frustration in his life. Of course, his daughter, Amber, was yet another young 13-year-old girl who thought she was going on 25. But it was his eight-year-old son, Tommy, who had been born with cleft lip and palate that occupied most of his time and took up most of his energy. Doctors in New York had botched the surgery trying to repair Tommy's birth defect and, now, the boy faced multiple new surgeries to try and fix the problem. Maffuci was slowly going broke with the added expenses associated with Tommy's care and education. And the Bureau had a hard and fast rule prohibiting agents from engaging in any type of outside employment.

Maffuci was just starting his morning ritual of yelling at his kids when the phone rang.

"Michael, what's got you up so early? Is Sandi still with you?"

"Sure, asshole. She's sleeping next to me. That's why I'm whispering," Dionis said sarcastically.

"So how did it go?" Maffuci asked.

"How did what go?"

"You and Sandi."

"Forget that. You stood us up last night. What's the deal?"

"I didn't have anything new to tell you, so I figured I'd let you two spend some time together."

"Bullshit. You were at the casino again."

"No. I was just trying to give you some time with Sandi."

"I don't need you setting me up," Dionis shouted.

"It wasn't a set up. So, how did it go?"

"It went fine, you moron. Quick witted. Interesting. Not caught up in herself. Good kid. All about work I think."

"She's not a kid, Michael. Or didn't you notice?"

"Anyone in their 30's is a kid to me. But that's not the point. You stood us up."

"So, when are you going to see her again?"

"Today."

"That's great. You don't waste any time. I knew you still had it in you."

"Not that kind of today. The kind where we meet with you and all figure out what this shit is about, if anything. I do not need my politically charged ex-wife busting my balls right now. Not with the new president being from Connecticut."

"Okay, my office. 10:30."

"Fine. I'll call Sandi. Just make sure you show up this time, asshole."

Dionis disconnected the call and sat back down on his couch and stared at a blank television. He had no idea what Ann was so concerned about. It had only been three days since they'd been together. The more they saw each other, the greater the chance of being discovered. *This has to stop. I should just stay in Connecticut. Spend my last two years here and retire,* he thought.

Michael Dionis gathered his thoughts and made coffee for himself, a single shot of Blue Mountain roast, in his Keurig coffee maker. Tonight, he was going to make sure he wasn't on Ann's security detail. Instead, he would simply drop by and see several of his agents. It was still part of his Marine training. Make sure your people are okay. Let them know their welfare was one of your main concerns. Dionis could never shake that. It was quietly laughed at more times than he cared to admit by the bureaucrats in the service; bureaucrats who had never served in any of the armed forces. But it was who he was. The people who worked for him appreciated it and that was all that mattered. He would go earlier so as to not cause any undue suspicion. And he simply wanted to talk to Ann. Sleeping with her again was too risky now. She'd be vacating the governor's mansion just after Christmas and moving to D.C. to continue working on her transition. President Robert Boyer, one of her political opponents in the national election, in a gesture symbolic of George H. Bush, when Barack Obama won the presidency, generously offered her, starting on January 1, the use of Blair House, the president's guest house located across the street from the White House. Ann Banks accepted the offer to live there while she worked with her transition team, before moving into the White House. The Lieutenant governor, after being sworn in as the new governor of Connecticut shortly after the election, told Banks she could stay in the mansion until then. Dionis sat down at his kitchen table, took a sip of his coffee, opened his laptop computer, and logged onto his private email account to send Ann Banks a message.

Risky. Will come by between 10 and 11 p.m. to check on my agents. Be downstairs. We can find a way to talk privately, at least for a few minutes. Please confirm.

Five minutes later Ann Banks responded back.

See you then.

Dionis arrived at the FBI Office on State Street in New Haven at ten-thirty that morning. He hated having to wait and then go through a check-in process that resembled going through TSA at an airport. The FBI took security seriously and made everyone, civilian and fellow federal law enforcement agents, adhere to the same policies when it came to entering the offices. The FBI made sure that everyone knew they were a guest when they entered.

When he arrived, he found Sandi DeCarlo sitting in the lobby.

"Been here long?" Dionis asked.

"Five minutes," DeCarlo replied. "They said Tony would be out shortly."

"That's Tony. He's probably waiting to hear that I arrived, so he only has to come out once. I love the guy, but the fucking FBI makes sure to let everyone know that they're the big boys on the block."

"We get the same thing with them all the time. Personal or professional relationships with agents are usually very good. However, the bureau is the epitome of a bureaucracy."

"Learn that at the University of New Haven or through experience?" Dionis asked.

"Both," she said. "Had professors there who retired from the FBI, and from other federal agencies. They all said the same thing. Of course, you don't have any idea what they're really talking about until you experience it firsthand."

"Tony's not that way. He's good. A bit absent minded sometimes, but he's smart as a whip. And politically connected too. Prosecutors love him. I've never had a bad experience working with him."

"My limited experience with him is the same," DeCarlo replied.

Dionis and DeCarlo were distracted when the door opened, and a smiling Tony Maffuci greeted them.

"Sorry for the wait," Maffuci said.

"You're not sorry," Dionis replied. "You know damn well you had us sit out here on purpose."

"Dude, you're killing me. I'd never do that," Maffuci said grinning.

"Bullshit," was all Dionis could say as he smiled at his friend. "I'm just glad you came to work today."

Dionis and DeCarlo followed Maffuci back to his small office. "The conference room is booked right now so get comfortable," he told them both as he ushered them in.

Dionis and DeCarlo sat down across the desk from Maffuci, who asked, "So, what else have the State Police learned?"

"Not much," DeCarlo replied. "I'm curious what the FBI has learned."

"Unfortunately, not much," Maffuci replied. As you know, we did learn that your victim's real name is Oleg Lomakina, a former member of Russian organized crime.

"That's a broad umbrella," Dionis said. "Can you be any more specific?"

"I can and I can't; not because I don't want to, it's just that we don't know much just yet," Maffuci replied. "What I can tell you is that these guys, Russian mafia that is, go by the name *The Odessa*, and in some cases, the *Bratva Mafia*. We know they operate in many of the bigger cities in this country, with New York being where we often find them to be the most active. Lomakina was affiliated with a NY group. And while they certainly are more into drugs and prostitution, especially white slavery, along with extortion, we haven't seen a lot of them engaged in political activism, at least not openly."

"But certainly, political activism behind the scenes, like using social media," Dionis said.

"Of course," Maffuci replied. "They have been known to do everything they can to influence elections at every level of government. The problem, of course, is tying it back to specific individuals when they do. So again, why this guy lived here under an alias and was apparently a political donor, is a mystery to us, at least for now."

"Does this seem strange to you two or is it just me?" DeCarlo asked.

"Again, yes and no," Maffuci replied. "Russian organized crime is one of the most ruthless criminal organizations that exist. As I'm sure you both know, they're big players in Transnational organized crime. What many people don't realize is that they differ in structure from the traditional organized crime groups the public refers to as the Mafia. The five major families in New York, for instance, have a hierarchical structure where one guy is in charge of each family. With the Russians, there isn't really any one single structure under which they function. They often operate in networks and cells, almost like a terrorist organization. They seek only money, power and influence."

"I get the whole seeking power thing," DeCarlo said, "but why kill one of their own?"

"You're the homicide expert," Maffuci said. "They kill for the same reasons everyone else does; love, jealousy, revenge, anger, money, sometimes simply to eliminate an impediment, you know, someone who might be in their way or pose a threat to them."

"Well, we can certainly rule out jealousy and love on this one," Dionis said.

"Probably," DeCarlo said. "But this guy was taken out with two shots to the back of the head, execution style. He made someone very angry."

"That's my guess," Maffuci replied. "Or maybe someone felt he couldn't be trusted. This one is going to be hard to solve with almost no forensic evidence."

"Well, we do have the two slugs recovered his head," DeCarlo said. "That will help if we ever find the gun."

Maffuci looked at his friend and asked, "You find out anything about this guy's political association?"

"Nothing yet. But I've arranged to meet with Ann Banks this evening."

"You called Ann Banks, the governor and president elect?" DeCarlo said, looking surprised.

"I've known her for some time, long before she ran for governor. She's set aside a few minutes for me tonight at the mansion. It will give me a chance to meet with some of my guys supplementing her security detail. I'll ask her tonight if she knows anything about our victim. And, if she knows who the right people are to ask in her organization regarding our dead guy's so-called political donations."

The meeting ended with little more information being shared between the three. They agreed to bring each other up to date the following morning with whatever new information they found. At least that was the plan.

Chapter 7

It was about ten p.m. when Dionis arrived at the make-shift command center, a trailer parked at the governor's mansion. After checking in with the detail supervisor, a friend from D.C., Dionis went into the house to say hello to Brian Olsen.

"How's it going?" Dionis asked.

"This sucks. I have had enough of this night shift, Michael. Don't we have some young guys to cover this?"

"Just a few more days and she'll be in D.C. most all the time. The full-time detail will cover it then and we'll get back to our routines. We won't have to do much of this except when she comes back to Connecticut for the occasional visit."

"So, what are you doing here? Can't sleep again or just out slumming?" Olsen asked.

"No. My ex has me and Tony Maffuci from the Bureau looking into this murder of the Russian guy in New Haven. It's the state's case. I'm not sure what our angle is on this."

"Maybe she's just busting your balls again."

"Maybe. What I am sure of, is that she's still into getting headlines."

"So, what are you really doing here?" Olsen said.

"Actually, just thought I'd stop by and see how you guys were doing."

"We're fine. Just getting tired of these rotating shifts."

"And our soon to be new president; is she retired for the night?" Dionis asked.

"Are you kidding? That woman is up half of the night. She's around here someplace."

No sooner had Olsen said that, than Ann Banks walked into the kitchen.

"Madam president elect. It's good to see you again," Dionis said.

"And you, Michael," she replied. "How have you been?"

"Good, ma'am."

"Are you working tonight?" she asked.

"No ma'am. Just checking up on my agents. Been busy helping your state police with a murder inquiry," Dionis told her.

"What's the Secret Service got to do with a murder?"

"I'm not sure exactly. Just following up some leads for them. Probably nothing."

"Stop by the den in a couple of minutes and bring your coffee," Banks said clearly so that everyone could hear. "I'd like to pick your brain a bit about what my new life is going to be like when I get to Washington, with all this protection stuff that is. Would you mind?"

"Not at all. I'll be right there," Dionis said.

Dionis walked into the room Banks used as her office in the mansion. He left the door ajar just enough so that no one would suspect anything other than what she had said in the kitchen.

Banks tried to reach out and touch him, but Dionis pulled back; he knew it wasn't a good time.

"I've missed you," she said.

"And I've missed you," he replied. "But we can't do this, not just now. You know it's too risky."

"I know. So, tell me, what about this Russian killed in New Haven?"

"Guy's name was Oleg Lomakina. He was Russian organized crime. Are you sure you've never heard of him?" Dionis asked.

"No. Never. Why?"

"Have you ever heard of a guy named Robert Moss?" Dionis asked.

"You mentioned that name in your email. The name is familiar. I think he was a political donor. My husband may have had some contact with him. What about him?"

"As I said in the email, Moss' real name was Oleg Lomakina. He was operating under an alias. He was the one killed several nights ago in New Haven. It was an execution. Two shots to the back of the head."

"That's terrible. But what does that have to do with you or the Secret Service?"

"I'm not sure it has anything to do with me or the Service. I was asked to try and determine if he had any connection to you as governor or as the president-elect."

"With me? How? You might want to check with Patrick."

"I will," Dionis said. "Where are you and Patrick on all of this now?"

"The same. We still live totally separate lives but maintain the image of the perfect power couple. If the people only knew," Banks said as she forced a grin across her face.

"Everyone has their secrets," Dionis said. It was his weak attempt at making her feel better about her sham of a marriage.

"So, what do we do now?" she asked.

"You know exactly what we have to do. You have to go to Washington and be the president. I'm going to ask the Service to leave me here in Connecticut. There is absolutely no way we can continue to see each other like this. You're going to be watched around the clock by your protective detail. The Secret Service will be with you virtually every minute of the day, even when you're on vacation. There is a record kept of where you are at all times. The media will focus almost all of its energy on you. Your every move will be under a microscope and not just by the media. Politicians across both sides of the aisle will be looking for anything to attack an independent new president;

especially the first elected woman president in the history of this country. Neither political party can boast about the fact you're one of them. So, if you think the media hounded Clinton when he lied to the American public after his sex scandal, George W. for his handling of the 9/11 disaster, or Trump's constant twittering, you haven't seen anything yet. Washington isn't Connecticut."

"I know that, Michael," she said looking tired. "I don't need you to remind me. I remember the campaign very well."

"As do I. But I think it's only going to get worse," Dionis told her.

"Maybe. But I think the American people have had enough of politics as usual. The country is clearly divided by extremists on both sides. But I still believe I can help make this country a better place," Banks said.

"I certainly hope you can. But the political extremists are not simply going to go away. You're going to need to continue your broad appeal to the masses. And if they find out about us, that appeal vanishes in an instant," Dionis said as he snapped his fingers. "Maybe you still can make this country a better place. But you're not going to be able to do that if we try to keep seeing each other. Just keep focusing on your fairer and kindhearted approach to all things political. You're going to do great things, Ann. I do wish I could be there with you."

"I know," she replied. "So, is this goodbye?"

"It has to be for now," Dionis said. "You can't risk it. You're going to be the president. If they discover me, us, that is, your presidency is over."

"Bill Clinton survived it," Banks said.

"Bill Clinton had the support of a Democratically controlled Senate. You don't. You're an independent who is considered a threat to many on both sides of the aisle. Don't give your enemies the ammunition they need to take you down. In Washington, they'll create their own story; don't help their cause."

Dionis and Banks embraced. She kissed him on the lips knowing it might be the last time they saw each other like this. "All my life, there is nothing I wanted more than to be loved by someone like you, Michael," she said as she stared directly into his eyes. "Tell me what you're thinking about."

Dionis paused for just a moment, trying to gather his thoughts, not sure exactly what to tell her. He knew they couldn't continue seeing each other, not now. Dionis put his hand on her back, then pushed her hair back and whispered, "Do you really want to know?"

"Of course, I do," she said just a bit anxiously.

Dionis responded to her passion and held her tightly for just a moment. Then he heard a sound, turned, and instantly wished he had closed the door to the study. Standing there, just a few feet away, was Congressman Patrick Banks.

"Don't let me stop you," Patrick Banks said. "Please, just pretend I'm not here."

"Patrick," Ann said, relaxing her embrace from Dionis. "I didn't know you were coming home today."

"That's clear to see," he replied.

"You know I've always hated surprises," she said.

"And how about you, Agent Dionis, do you like surprises?" Patrick Banks asked.

"Not in my business, Congressman, no."

Patrick Banks was grinning. "Well, it seems we have a situation here that can cause all of us some unnecessary aggravation."

"What do you want, Patrick?" Ann asked. "I'm not sure what you think is going on here, but it isn't what you imagine."

"Oh really," he replied, the naked grin on his face getting even wider. "Well then, what exactly is going on?"

"Nothing," she said. "Just two old friends saying good-bye."

"Good-bye, is it? So, which one of you is ending the affair?" he asked.

"What affair are you referring to Patrick?" she demanded to know.

"Really, Ann! You want to play it like this? Deny it if you like, but Josh has a copy of a recording of the two of you having an affair right here in the mansion, in your bedroom," he said, now smiling from ear to ear.

"You bugged my bedroom," she screamed.

"Not me, love," he replied. "And I didn't ask Josh how he got the recording. But he has it. So, don't deny it. I've heard part of it."

Dionis turned back to Ann and could see the shocked look on her face. There was no immediate way for him to leave, he couldn't abandon her, not now. "Congressman," Dionis said, trying to maintain his composure, "whatever you think was happening wasn't."

"Well, Agent Dionis, why don't you tell me what I'm thinking."

"Congressman, I came here tonight on another matter and, to say good-bye to the president-elect."

"And what matter is that?" he asked.

"A simple inquiry about a man named Oleg Lomakina. He was murdered a few nights ago. He went by the name of Robert Moss. He was apparently a political activist and supporter of both you and your wife."

"What makes you think either of us know anything about him?" Patrick Banks demanded to know.

"I don't think that at all. I'm just assisting the Connecticut State Police in their investigation by following up a lead. We also want to make sure this guy wasn't a threat to either of you."

"You know this guy, Ann?" Patrick demanded.

"No," she replied.

"Well then, Agent Dionis, you have your answer. Do you need anything else tonight?"

"No Congressman, I don't. I can show myself out."

"Yes, I'm sure you know the way," Patrick Banks said. "And stay away from my wife," he shouted, making sure anyone within listening range heard him.

Dionis momentarily glanced at Ann Banks and said, "goodnight, ma'am." He turned and walked out of the den and into the kitchen.

"What in the hell was that all about, Mike. Everything all right in there?" Olsen asked.

"It's fine," Dionis replied. "Politicians, you know."

"Do I ever," Olsen replied.

"Goodnight, guys," he said to the two agents standing post inside the mansion. "See you later. Stay warm."

Dionis walked outside into the dark, overcast night. The weather was cold, sullen, and gray, but he didn't feel the slightest chill in the air. He unlocked the door of his car with the remote key, got in, and started the engine. He knew he had to remain calm; there was always someone watching or a security camera nearby. The time of his leaving would certainly be recorded as was the time of his arrival. He didn't trust Patrick Banks. There was no telling what he might do or what story he might concoct. Dionis knew that the only thing for him to do right now was to go home. At least there, he would be safe. In a few hours, however, he would quickly realize just how wrong he was.

Chapter 8

33 Days Before the Inauguration

It was five-forty a.m. when Sandi DeCarlo was awakened from a dead sleep. She knew from the special ring tone she created for her department's emergency call out number, that she had no choice but to take the call.

"Yes," was all she said when she answered the phone.

"Sandi, there has been a death at the governor's mansion. You need to get there now. We need the whole team there," Lieutenant Mark Rice, the commander of the State Police, Central District Major Crime Squad said.

"Who? The president elect?" DeCarlo asked, trying to grasp what she just heard.

"No, her husband, Congressman Patrick Banks."

"He was murdered?" DeCarlo struggled to ask.

"No idea. That's what I want you to figure out. He died in bed. Appeared healthy. Apparently, he'd had an argument last night with his wife and some Secret Service Agent named Michael Dionis. The Lt. Governor, or should I say the new governor, it's hard to keep track these days, is all over the State Police commissioner. Find out if it's a homicide or not. And be careful. This is a political nightmare already. I'll meet you there as soon as I can."

DeCarlo sat up on the side of the bed, her bare feet touching the cold floor, and took a moment to gather her thoughts. She then called Michael Dionis. He picked up on the third ring.

"That was quick," DeCarlo said.

"Not sleeping much," Dionis replied. "What's up at this hour of the morning?"

“You haven’t heard? Congressman Banks is dead. I’m on my way there now.”

“Dead? How?” Dionis probed.

“They want me to find out. Heard you were there last night and had an argument with the Congressman. What can you tell me?”

“Not much. Not really an argument. It’s a long story but has nothing to do with his death.”

“Michael, you have to give me something, long story or not. What the hell happened last night?” she asked, her voice clearly revealing her irritation.

“The Congressman walked in on Ann and I embracing. Thought it was something more than it was. He got agitated, that’s all.”

“Embracing? Why?” DeCarlo asked.

“We’re old friends. We were simply saying good-bye not knowing when we might see each other again. Patrick Banks is an asshole. Was an asshole. How did he die?”

“I’m not sure. On my way there now,” DeCarlo said. “I’m probably going to need a statement from you. Can we talk later?”

“Of course. Just call when you’re ready.”

“Will do. Stay close.”

Dionis hung up the phone, got up from the bed and walked mechanically to his kitchen. His knees shook with each step that he took. The argument with Patrick Banks and his catching him and Ann in an embrace, had occupied his every waking moment that night. He could feel the ache in his head. Every time he tried closing his eyes, he could feel the tremor that was beginning in the pit of his stomach. In spite of the early morning hour, he reached into his freezer and pulled out a chilled bottle of Ouzo. He didn’t bother to pour a shot into a glass; he simply took two large swallows directly from the cold bottle. *Let’s hope the Greeks are right about this stuff helping to relieve an upset stomach and headache,* he thought.

DeCarlo hung up the phone, got dressed and raced to the governor's mansion. When she arrived, there were only a few state police cars on the scene. *Thank God the media isn't here yet,* she thought.

"In here," the Secret Service Agent said. "A couple of your people have already arrived."

"Can you tell me where the body is?" DeCarlo asked as she slipped on her protective gloves designed to prevent her from contaminating the crime scene.

"Upstairs in his bedroom. Please follow me."

DeCarlo followed the agent up the staircase and into the private bedroom of Patrick Banks. Banks was lying on his back, his eyes wide open. Standing next to the bed studying the body was Kimiko Matsui, the forensics examiner from the Connecticut Office of the Chief Medical Examiner. Matsui had arrived several minutes before DeCarlo, giving her just enough time to start recording her initial impressions of the scene. Matsui was good at her job. She knew the scene would talk to her if she took the time to stop, look, and analyze everything she saw. Crime scenes will often talk to you, she would tell students whenever she gave a lecture. Her favorite line was, "You can talk to the dead all you want, they'll just never talk back to you, with one exception; that being those times when you are examining them at a crime scene."

"What have we got so far?" DeCarlo asked Matsui.

"Just got here a few minutes ago," Matsui said. "Not sure yet. However, you see that white powder on the nightstand; my guess is that it's coke."

"I wouldn't be surprised. I could run a quick test here if I had more of it, but the small trace amount of powder really isn't enough for me to do that. I take it no one has conducted any type of search yet?" DeCarlo asked.

"Not as far as I know," replied Matsui.

"Hold on," DeCarlo said. "Let's see if we can find his suit jacket." DeCarlo opened the closet and quickly located the jacket hanging alone that appeared to match the pants thrown over a chair in the bedroom. DeCarlo rummaged through the jacket pockets, and as she anticipated, found a small clear package containing a powdery substance.

"Ninety-five percent of the time, we find something in the jacket pockets," DeCarlo said with a grin.

DeCarlo reached into her bag and removed a small vial that allowed her to conduct an instant check on the powder to determine if it was cocaine. She removed a small sample, placed it in the vile, and almost instantly it tested positive for cocaine. But the test was not foolproof. The lab technicians would have to conduct the more technical and forensic examination, especially if someone were ever needed to testify in court that the substance was in fact cocaine.

"I'll get this tested and confirmed as quickly as possible," DeCarlo told Matsui. "Anything else just yet?"

"Seemed like a healthy male. Age 52. No sign of gunshot, stabbing, or blunt force trauma. No blood visible anywhere; just this froth around his mouth. But way too early to tell."

"What's your way too early guess?" DeCarlo asked.

"Well, again, based on the froth around the mouth, my first guess would be poison," Matsui said, "We call that a foam cone."

"Foam cone?" DeCarlo asked.

"Yes, a foam cone. We see it in a lot of OD's, especially in fentanyl cases. See this bubbly foam around the mouth that continues to seep out," Matsui said as she pointed her finger at Patrick Banks' lips. "In such cases, the lungs and heart slow their functioning. When that happens, the brain fails to manage what it's designed to do, causing this foam to seep from the nose and mouth. The brain essentially becomes starved for oxygen. It's like drowning on dry land."

"I've never worked a case involving possible fentanyl contaminated cocaine," DeCarlo replied. "This is new to me."

"I'm only speculating here," Matsui said. "It could also simply be bad coke. Poison. Take your pick. Won't know until we do an autopsy and run the toxicology tests. In the meantime, let me run another quick test of the coke with this fentanyl test strip."

Matsui reached into her bag and removed a fentanyl test strip, or FTS. The FTS, she explained, was an inexpensive drug testing technology that people use to detect the presence of fentanyl prior to ingesting a drug. Matsui also removed a small glass and added water to it, along with a small amount of the suspected cocaine. She placed the FTS in the glass for fifteen seconds, and then set the strip on the flat surface of the nightstand. Five minutes later, the test strip revealed the presence of fentanyl.

"This test is not one-hundred percent accurate," Matsui told DeCarlo. "For court purposes, the lab will have to confirm this test. But right now, I'm confident we're looking at cocaine that was contaminated with fentanyl."

"This is really going to complicate things," DeCarlo said. "Any idea who called this in?"

"Our new president herself. Said her husband didn't come downstairs this morning. He had to leave very early for D.C. She knocked on the door and didn't get a response. That's when she found him lying in the bed."

Turning toward a Secret Service Agent and State Trooper just outside the room, DeCarlo said, "From this point on, the president-elect doesn't enter this room. Anyone else that comes in from our team is logged in and out. Until we know what happened here, I'm treating this like a homicide."

"Smart," Matsui said. "So, who is going to tell our president-elect she can't come in here?"

"I will. The last thing I need is to have this scene contaminated any more than it already might be," DeCarlo told Matsui. "We're both going to end up under the microscope on this one. And you know if anything gets screwed up, the political hacks will sacrifice the both of us to save their asses."

"You're way ahead of me, as usual," Matsui replied. "No screwups."

DeCarlo instructed her team to secure the scene, take samples of the powder on the nightstand, dust the room for prints, and take photographs of the body as well as shots from every conceivable angle of the bedroom. Since there weren't any blood spatters, knife wounds, or evidence of gun shots, securing the bedroom was easy. She then turned and spoke to the junior member of her team, Mark Detty. Detty had only been with the major crime squad for three weeks and was still learning the nuances of a homicide investigation.

"Mark, I want you to go with me to meet Ms. Banks. Take notes but don't ask any questions. Right after that, I want you to start working up a timeline. Start reconstructing this guy's last forty-eight hours. I want to know his travel itinerary, who he spoke to, and if possible, what they spoke about. Get a dump of his cell phone calls. And find out anything you can about his possible drug use."

"Anything else?" Detty asked.

"Yes. Check the refrigerator downstairs. Inventory the contents."

"The refrigerator?"

"Yes, the refrigerator. Let's make sure this wasn't anything he ate. Maybe something was contaminated. See what's in there. It might help identify what he last ate when they conduct the autopsy. And find his personal computer. It doesn't appear to be here. If you don't find it get a warrant for it right after we're done here. It's probably in his apartment back in D.C. or in his office. If it's in his office, see if you can get the Capital police in D.C. to seize it for us," DeCarlo said. "If they'll do that for us, send the warrant down to them ASAP."

"Will do."

DeCarlo turned to Matsui and said, “I’m going downstairs to speak with Ann Banks.”

“Now?” Matsui asked.

“The sooner the better. President-elect or not, Ann Banks is going to need to trust the person running this case. The sooner I establish a rapport with her the better.”

“Focus on the drug angle. I know you don’t need me saying so, but I’d want to know if she knew he was using and where he was getting his supply.”

“Way ahead of you Kimiko. Wish me luck.”

***

The national morning news shows, including each of the local networks, all led with the story of the death of Congressman Patrick Banks.

From his condo in Old Town Alexandria, Josh Martin watched, in disbelief, the CNN report. The front of the governor’s mansion was like the set of a Hollywood movie. Trucks with large satellite dishes from every major and local news networks were parked on the streets surrounding the house. Cars from the Connecticut State Police with their flashing red and blue lights took up most of the space directly in front of the governor’s mansion. Yellow tape sealing off the mansion restricted those who could come and go inside the house.

“This morning, around seven a.m., Secret Service Agents assigned to the protective detail of former Connecticut Governor and President-elect Ann Banks, confirmed that her husband, Connecticut Congressman Patrick Banks, was found dead in his bedroom in the Governor’s mansion in Hartford. We know very little about how Congressman Banks died other than he appeared to have died sometime during the night. Sources have told CNN that President-elect Banks is in shock over the loss of her husband. Her press secretary told CNN that Ms. Banks is awaiting the report of the State Medical Examiner’s office to provide an

explanation as to the exact cause of his death. Ms. Banks asked that the public provide her some privacy at this difficult time in order for her to grieve the loss of her husband."

The in-studio commentator asked the reporter broadcasting from in front of the governor's mansion if there was anything else she could tell them.

"We have unconfirmed reports that a Secret Service Agent, Michael Dionis, the supervisor in charge of the Connecticut Office, visited Ann Banks last night. Sources tell us that at one point, they heard shouting between the late Congressman and his wife, while Agent Dionis was in the room with them. According to our sources, Agent Dionis left moments after this alleged altercation. Another source claims that Congressman Banks told a member of his wife's security detail to make sure that Agent Dionis kept away from his wife. We have no other details about this alleged incident."

Martin turned off the television. The last thing he needed right now was to listen to conservative and liberal pundits' opinions on what caused the death of Patrick Banks. Everyone had a predisposed opinion of what the incoming president should do; and to get validation of their personal predisposed thoughts, they simply had to tune in to one of the major news networks that shared those thoughts and philosophy, without ever having to go to the effort of forming their own independent opinion. And the pundits would certainly be offering every fantasy imaginable as to what transpired in the den between Patrick Banks and Dionis once the media learned of their altercation.

The major news networks knew exactly how to exploit people's predilections, those same biases that became their own reality. Whether that reality was based on proof or speculation didn't matter. And Martin had used their ability to exploit people to his advantage more times than he could remember. Now, he was going to have to use those same news networks again. This time, however, he would have to find a way to get both the liberal and conservative networks to actually agree on what he wanted the American people to support.

What the hell did you do now, Andre? You stupid bastard, he thought.

Martin quickly showered, shaved, put on a suit, and walked outside his condo while he waited for his Uber to arrive.

"Please get me to Washington National Airport as quickly as possible," he told the driver. "I have a plane to catch. It's an emergency."

Andre Dunayev sat in his plush New York city apartment watching the same news story Martin and the rest of the country were tuned in to. He switched off the TV, picked up his cell phone, and called Martin.

"Where are you?" Dunayev asked, dispensing with the usual greeting.

"Heading to National Airport to catch a plane to Connecticut. I can't talk now," Martin replied.

"Call me when you land," Dunayev ordered. "You have to control this."

"Talk later," Martin said as he disconnected the call. *I have to control what you did? You miserable prick,* he thought.

Chapter 9

At eleven-twenty that morning, Michael Dionis was sitting in the small conference room in his office across the table from his boss, Andy Ward, the Special Agent in Charge of the Secret Service Boston Field Office. Ward and had driven to New Haven after being awakened with the news of Congressman Banks' passing. The death of a United States Congressman would not normally require Ward's attention. The fact that one of his agents, the supervisor of his office in Connecticut, was there hours before the Congressman's death, had supposedly been caught in the embrace of the president- elect, and had been overheard having a loud verbal exchange with the deceased, did require his immediate attention.

Also in the conference room were two agents from the Boston Field Office.

"I wondered how long it would take for you to get here," Dionis said, looking directly at Ward. "But I didn't expect you to bring these two guys with you."

"We have to talk about what happened last night, Michael. You're all over the news," Ward said. "We need to ask you some questions, but before we do, we want to advise you of your Kalkines rights."

Kalkines warnings are similar to Miranda warnings that inform a suspect of their right to remain silent, if they can't afford an attorney, one will be appointed for them and, anything they say can be used against them. Kalkines warnings go a step further. They compel federal employees to cooperate in internal investigations or face disciplinary action. In some cases, a federal employee can be dismissed for failing to cooperate or for not answering questions in an internal inquiry.

"Kalkines requires a prosecutorial declination," Dionis said. "I'm not sure where you're going with this, but until you have the U.S. Attorney's Office and the Connecticut Chief State's Attorney's Office both issue a criminal declination, I'm not answering anything."

"Michael, please," Ward said. "We just need to ask you a few questions."

"Then ask. But I may not answer. So, let's dispense with Kalkines. What do you want to know?"

"Let's start with what happened last night at the mansion." Ward said. "Why did you go there?"

"I was asked by the U.S. Attorney to assist the state police in the murder of a Russian mobster. The state believes the victim was a close supporter of the president- elect. I thought I would check on my people supplementing the security detail and ask her about this guy," Dionis replied.

"Okay. Did you at some point embrace her while you were in the mansion, specifically, in her study?" Ward asked.

"I did."

"And why did you do that?"

"We are old friends, as you know."

"Okay. And was there an altercation last night with Congressman Banks?"

"A small one, yes. He no doubt misinterpreted what he thought he saw and started making some accusatory allegations. I tried to calm him down and told him I was there to ask about the murder of a Russian mobster and alleged political supporter of theirs. Neither of them claimed to know the man."

"Then what happened?"

"I left and drove home."

Ward waived his hands at the two agents sitting quietly in the conference room motioning for them to leave. The moment they were gone, Ward looked directly at Dionis and asked, "Were you having an affair with her, Michael?"

"No," Dionis lied. "I was not."

"Some in the media are speculating that you were. The fact that the president-elect, an independent, might have been engaged in an extra marital affair with a Secret Service Agent, and whose husband has died under suspicious circumstances, has created a situation that is uniting conservatives and liberals unlike anything this country has experienced since the Japanese attack on Pearl Harbor. The Secret Service is exceptionally good at its job, Michael, and for a variety of reasons. Sleeping with protectees is not one of them. Whether you were or weren't, the optics are very bad. You know the drill, you don't get too close to your security detail, and they don't get too close to you. You must maintain an emotional separation. You failed to do that. What you've done instead, is put yourself and the Secret Service right in the bullseye of this fucking media circus."

"The media, and everyone else for that matter, can fucking speculate all they want. I've done nothing wrong, Andy. This is all bullshit."

"Really," Ward replied. "Who would have ever thought that CNN and MSNBC would be espousing the same political take on this as FOX news is? And it's all in an effort to undermine the incoming president."

"Jesus, Andy, you're worried about the news now? For Christ sake. Depending on your political views, each will report the same event differently, just the way the media reported Lincoln being carried off the stage in jubilation after a debate with Douglas. One reported he was carried off the stage triumphantly while his adversaries reported him being carried off the stage due to exhaustion. And you're worried about the fucking manipulative media?"

"In this case, the media is all on the same page with regard to you," Ward replied. "Do you really want to ruin your career with this massive goat fuck shit storm you created?"

"Andy, I didn't do anything wrong here," Dionis stressed again. "I have no idea what caused Congressman Banks' death. As far as Ann Banks is concerned, we have a friendship that goes back a number of years. She asked me to join her in the den. She wanted to ask some advice on dealing with the Secret Service after she was sworn in as president. You know very well how independent minded most of these politicians are. How was I supposed to say no? And why would I even want to? We were saying good-bye as she prepares to move to D.C. That's it."

Ward didn't want to argue any more. Changing the subject, and in a more calming voice, he asked, "What can you tell me about this dead Russian? What was his name?"

"Oleg Lomakina. He went by the name of Robert Moss."

"And you say neither the president-elect nor her husband knew this guy?" Ward pressed.

"She heard the name he was using as an alias. Thought he was a political donor. But that's all she knew. Her husband denied knowing him. I know he was lying because she told me just prior to him walking in on us, that her husband, Patrick, was aware of him."

"Why would Patrick Banks lie about that?"

"Good question. He's certainly not going to be able to tell us now."

"Okay, I'm going to ask you one more time, were you having an affair with Ann Banks?"

"I told you, Andy, no," Dionis said again. Dionis was also painfully aware that Ward knew he was lying.

"Then why were you seen coming out of her bedroom a few nights ago?"

The question stunned Dionis. *How could he know? Fucking Brian Olsen?* he thought.

"I don't know what you're talking about."

Ward rolled his eyes and said, "Okay, Michael. We'll play it your way for now. Effective immediately, you're on administrative leave. Go home. Stay out of the limelight. Stay away from the media. This isn't going to blow over quickly. Right now, you're a liability."

Dionis just sat there, stunned. “What the hell, Andy? This isn’t you.”

“I have no choice, Michael. This decision was made way above both of our pay grades. You think for one minute this is an aspect of the job I enjoy?”

“And you went along with this?”

“What choice do I have, Michael? You’re lying to me about your relationship with the president-elect. You get into an altercation with the protectee’s husband, you’re seen coming out of her bedroom three nights ago, and you’re looking into the death of a Russian mobster that you didn’t bother to tell me about. What am I missing here?”

“The Russian mobster thing isn’t my doing. And since when do I tell you everything I’m doing here?” Dionis said, his voice now raised.

“Michael, I trusted you. But I find it interesting that your response to all of this centered solely around the dead Russian. You’re not outraged over the accusation of your relationship with our new president.”

Dionis quickly realized the tactical error of his response. Andy Ward was nobody’s fool. They weren’t close friends, but they enjoyed a good working relationship with each other. Dionis always suspected that Ward saw his job only as a vocation, nothing he neither liked nor hated. Besides, Ward supported most everything he did as it pertained to running the office in Connecticut. Ward and Dionis had a mutual respect for each other but that was where the relationship ended. Dionis also knew that his boss was doing exactly what he had to do under the circumstances.

“One more thing, Michael, I’d like you to allow the two agents I brought with me to take you home, collect your computer, and simply conduct a light search. Would you agree to that?”

“You want to search my place? Fuck you.”

"Please Michael, we don't want to conduct a search per se. Just let them look around. Can you do that? There is a warrant available if you want to go that way."

"A warrant available? Whose idea is this? My ex-wife's," Dionis said, answering his own question. "Exactly what do you suspect me of?"

"I don't suspect you of doing anything criminal. We just want to make sure you're eliminated as a suspect in either the death of this Russian or Congressman Banks' death."

Dionis jumped up from his chair and yelled, "Murder? You think I killed those two fuckers? Are you out of your mind?"

"Please, Michael, sit back down. As I said, I don't think that at all. Let's just make sure nobody else suspects it," Ward said.

Dionis was raging inside. He nodded reluctantly, sat back down, and said, "Fine. But they're not going to find anything because there isn't anything to find."

"I would hope not."

"*Hope*?"

"Poor choice of words. I would think not," Ward replied.

Dionis got up from his chair again. This time, he had no intention of sitting back down. He looked at Ward, shook his head from side to side and said, "I'm done here. You know how to find me when this bullshit is over." Dionis walked out of the conference room, and out the front door of the office, careful not to make eye contact with anyone. He got into his car, started the engine, and turned on the heater to take out the chill. Before backing out of his parking space, he took out his personal cell phone and accessed his private email account. He opened the draft folder praying there was a message from Ann Banks. But there was nothing. Dionis drafted a short message that he hoped she would read sooner than later.

WTF happened? I'm basically suspended until further notice. What can you tell me?

***

The Next Morning

"You wanted to see me, boss," Maffuci said as he poked his head into the office of FBI Special Agent in Charge (SAC), Leah Riggs.

"Yes, Tony. Please come in and sit down."

Her classmates at Quantico had always expected Leah Riggs to rise to the highest levels of the agency, not because she was an African American, but because she was good at what she did, not the best, but good. What Riggs brought to the table was a degree of style that most of her classmates, especially the younger ones, failed to exhibit. Riggs had been a Lieutenant in the Air Force, serving four years on active duty as an air warfare officer. She relayed coordinates to pilots for air strikes in Iraq. The most dangerous part of her job in the secure operations building, she had told her mother, was spilling her coffee on the computer keyboard. Still, she had been an Air Force Officer, and served in a combat environment; something most Americans have never done. That made Leah Riggs an attractive candidate for whatever her ambitions were. And she decided to join the FBI.

After a short assignment in New York, where she mostly worked undercover as many new agents are asked to do, Riggs was promoted to first line supervisor of the white-collar crime squad in Baltimore. After two years, she transferred to FBI Headquarters in Washington D.C. Two years later, she was sent to Atlanta as the Assistant Special Agent in Charge, before being promoted to SAC in Connecticut. In the FBI, as it is in so many government agencies, it's very often style and not substance that results in someone's rapid rise to the top. Being responsible for heading up high profile criminal cases will take you only so far. A tour in Headquarters or, being part of the inspection process, and being willing to move and uproot one's family several times over, usually resulted in a rapid rise up the bureaucratic ladder. But moving wasn't a problem for Riggs; she didn't have a family to uproot each time she was transferred. Of course, being a woman of color in the Obama administration didn't hurt either. Clinton and Gore's reinvention of government certainly contributed to many less qualified minorities being promoted ahead of their time, as had always been the case for well-connected white men. It was, in part, the government's effort to make amends for past indiscretions when highly qualified minorities were passed over for promotion because of their skin color. In Riggs' case, it wasn't so much that she wasn't qualified; she was. There were, however, more qualified people for the job. But in the federal bureaucracy, that didn't matter. Agency heads who can check the right boxes demonstrating diversity in the workplace, reap the appropriate rewards and ensure the safety of their jobs. Riggs knew she was qualified and did what she was advised to do years ago by one of her professors in college, that is: play the cards you're dealt. That's exactly what Riggs was doing when she ordered Tony Maffuci to close the door.

"What's up boss?" Maffuci asked.

"You know Tina Crawford, the acting U.S. Attorney?"

"Of course, I do. How are you, Tina?"

"I've been better," Crawford replied.

"And you know Andy Ward, the Secret Service SAC from Boston?" Riggs asked.

"We've met a few times. Mostly on the rubber chicken circuit when we have to give a plaque to someone retiring who usually hasn't done a day's work in years." Maffuci said. It was his way of poking a light jab at senior management.

"Good to see you, Tony," Ward said, extending his hand.

"Please, Tony, sit down," Riggs said. The tone of her voice made it clear that it was an order, not a request.

"You've heard about Michael and the death of Congressman Banks?" Riggs asked.

"Of course. We've all heard about it," Maffuci replied.

"Tony, we've got to know, have you heard from Michael?" Riggs asked.

"No, I haven't. Why?"

"It's important that we find him fast. You understand that?" Ward said.

"I would think so," Maffuci answered. "But why do you think he'd call me?"

"Because you're his best friend," Crawford said sarcastically. "He'd call you before he would call anyone. If he hasn't already."

"I'm not sure I like what you're insinuating, Tina. I told you I haven't heard from him."

"Let's stay focused here," Riggs said. "Nobody's accusing you of anything."

"Stop right there boss," Maffuci said, his voice now raised. "Accusing? I don't like that word. If you suspect me of something, spit it out. All I know about this is what I heard on the news. That's it."

"Tony, we just want to find him. We need your help," Ward said calmly.

"What's going on here?" Maffuci asked. "Have you tried calling him?"

"We have. He isn't answering. In fact, we found his cell phone with the battery removed when we went to his home. That suggests to me that he doesn't want to be tracked. None of his agents in the office have heard from him either." Ward said.

"He could be shacked up someplace with a hangover. Have you thought about that?" Maffuci said. "If what the media is reporting is half-true, I'd get drunk and hide somewhere myself."

"It's worse than that I'm afraid," Ward said. "Congressman Banks told the supervisory agent in charge of his wife's security detail that night that his wife and Michael had been having an affair. Apparently, he has a recording of their tryst from just a few days ago. As you can see, the optics of such an allegation, if true, are bad for Mike, the Service, and of course, and more importantly, the president-elect."

"The media is going to have a field day with this," Crawford added. "We've got to find him."

Maffuci looked directly at Ward and asked, "How many people know about Congressman Banks' accusation?"

"Just us in this room and the agent in charge of Ann Banks' security detail."

"Has anyone heard this recording?" Maffuci asked.

"Not yet," Ward said. "The Congressman died before he was able to produce it."

"So, you don't know if what Patrick Banks said is true or not?"

"We don't," Ward replied. "But the Congressman did tell the agent in charge of the security detail the night he died that he caught his wife and Dionis in an emotional embrace when he walked in on them in the den, something Dionis admitted to when I spoke to him yesterday. We also know Michael and the Congressman exchanged some heated words. One of the agents inside the mansion heard a loud altercation coming from the study where Michael was. Of course, he was unable to make out exactly what was being said."

"We were also wondering if you know whether or not the Connecticut State police have developed anything new on the murder investigation of Oleg Lomakina?" Crawford asked.

"Not much. Michael was supposed to ask our former governor if she knew anything about him. But I never heard back from him," Maffuci replied.

"So, you don't know if the state has any suspects?" Ward asked.

"No, I don't. I can reach out to Sandi DeCarlo."

Ward's eyes shifted from Maffuci to Crawford. It was clear to Maffuci that the two were not sharing everything they knew about the death of Congressman Patrick Banks, or the allegation of Ann Banks and Dionis having an affair. Maffuci suspected that Andy Ward and Dionis' ex-wife, were concerned about something far more important than whether or not his friend had had an affair with the president-elect.

"Yes," Riggs said. "Reach out to her. But be very careful not to share any more information with her than absolutely necessary. We have to keep a tight lid on this."

"I don't like where this is going," Maffuci told Riggs and Ward. "You're thinking Michael had something to do with Congressman Banks' death. Do you even know how he died?" Maffuci asked.

"Under suspicious circumstances is all we know. The autopsy will hopefully tell us more," Riggs said. "I'm assigning an agent to assist the state. I want you to focus solely on trying to locate your friend. Am I clear?"

"Clear."

"Andy and I will be personally heading up the search for Michael Dionis," Riggs said. "You'll stay out of this investigation. But I do want everything you know about Michael on my desk in one hour. I want to know his other friends, hangouts, everything you know. You'll keep me apprised. You will report directly to me with any information that you have. You'll have no discussions with anyone about Michael Dionis other than me. Do you understand that?"

"I understand," Maffuci said. "Now, I guess I better get moving on Michael's bio for you." Maffuci's eyes locked directly on Crawford's. "Tina, even you know, of course, that Michael could never have done this."

"I hope you're right Tony," Crawford said. "One more thing: do you know, or have you ever suspected Michael of using any drugs? Coke for instance?"

"Drugs? Michael? You can't be serious," Maffuci erupted, his voice loud enough for everyone in the room to understand that he was clearly outraged by the question.

"Calm down, Tony. Just please answer the question," Riggs demanded.

Maffuci turned his head back towards Crawford and said, "No, I don't. If he did, it would be news to me. But I don't know. What the hell is going on here? You know something and you're not telling me. Remember, Michael wouldn't have even been at the mansion the other night had you not asked him to look into Lomakina's murder."

"That's not fair, Tony," Crawford shot back.

"Maybe, but I haven't heard much of anything in this room the past few minutes that borders on fair," Maffuci said.

"We found cocaine in Michael's home," Ward said. "We didn't want to tell you. Nothing to do with trust, we just want to keep a tight lid on this."

"Cocaine? Impossible. Not Michael," Maffuci said.

"I'm afraid it's true," Ward said. "Agents found a white powdery substance in his bathroom. We're having it analyzed. And now, we can't find him."

"How did you come to search Michael's place?"

"I sent two agents to check on him after he stormed out of the office. There was genuine concern for his safety, so I sent the agents inside to see if he was okay," Ward lied.

"Don't you find it odd that if he had coke in his place, he'd have left it there like that?"

"In some respects, yes," Ward said. "Right now, we just need to find him."

"Well, if he doesn't want to be found, good luck finding him," Maffuci said.

"We need your help Tony," Ward said.

Tony Maffuci nodded, turned, and left the room, avoiding eye contact with everyone except Tina Crawford. He wasn't going to give her the satisfaction of thinking he was doing any of this to help her.

Maffuci knew his friend was in trouble. How much trouble, he wasn't sure? Dionis had been in trouble before, especially in Iraq. He knew escape and evasion and Maffuci was sure of one thing: if Michael Dionis didn't want to be found, finding him was going to be almost impossible. And Tina Crawford and Andy Ward were not going to find him. That much was certain. *Jesus, Michael what have you gotten yourself into?* Maffuci thought.

***

Andre Dunayev picked up his cell phone on the second ring. "Yes, comrade," was all he said.

"You have good news for us?" the caller asked.

"All is going according to plan," Dunayev replied. "We should have our man, Martin, in the White House working for the new president very shortly. I'm working on our personal selection for Secretary of State. And soon, the Secret Service Agent should be identified as the murderer of Patrick Banks."

"And Patrick Banks' death was necessary?" the caller asked.

"It was. He was too weak. And ambitious to a point where he could cause us harm. His own chief of staff said he could never get elected on his own. Now, his wife is free of his interference and will eventually do as we say."

"Good. We're counting on you," the caller said as he disconnected the call.

Jian Wie, of the Ministry of State Security (MSS) of the People's Republic of China (PRC) hung up the phone, looked at his associate, shook his head and grinned. "Americans," was all he said.

"And Russians?" his associate asked.

"Even more corrupt and power hungry than the Americans. That's what makes much of this so easy," Wie replied.

***

Michael Dionis checked into the Gramercy Park on Lexington Avenue in New York, under the name of Sean Cameron. In New York, nobody gives a damn about your business. New Yorkers are unfazed about who you are, criminal or celebrity. Dionis needed a big city to hide in, and New York served that purpose. A person could hide in plain sight in NY. He also needed to get to and from Connecticut quickly, and New York offered him that. His biggest obstacle at the moment was avoiding being spotted on the endless number of closed-circuit video cameras that covered almost every inch of Manhattan. He could overcome that problem. It was the threat of being terminated from the Service and having his relationship with Ann Banks exposed that dominated his thoughts. *Think, Michael. There has to be more to this. What am I missing here?* he thought.

Chapter 10

Josh Martin identified himself to the officer standing just outside the front door of the governor's mansion. After confirming Martin's identity, the officer pointed him to the inside.

"I'm looking for the president-elect," he told another officer. Before the officer could answer, he saw Ann Banks walking into the living room alongside her chief of staff, Jason Palmer.

"Ann, I'm so sorry," he said, extending his arms.

"Hello Josh," Ann replied, offering him a conditioned hug. "How are you?"

"Never mind me, how are you doing?"

"As well as can be expected. You know Jason, my chief of staff?" Ann said.

"Of course. We've met a number of times," Martin said, extending his hand to Palmer.

The two men shook hands and put on a display of cordiality, although there was little between them. It wasn't from a natural dislike for each other, but more out of the competitiveness between the two who were both charged with looking out for the best interests of whatever political animal they served at any particular time.

"Do you have any idea what happened? What can you tell me?" asked Martin.

"He didn't come downstairs this morning. I went to wake him and found him dead. That's all I know. The police are investigating his death," Banks replied.

"Why? Do they suspect something?" Martin asked.

"I don't know. I don't think so. My guess is that they're just covering the bases," she said. "I had no idea Patrick was coming to Connecticut yesterday evening. Do you know why he came up without telling me?"

"No. Not really. Can we talk about that later? I need to talk to you privately."

"I'd prefer to have Jason with us if you don't mind."

Jason Palmer, in addition to being Ann Banks' chief of staff, was currently heading her transition team. Everyone expected Palmer to be officially named as the White House Chief of Staff. The only reason he hadn't yet been named was because Patrick had asked his wife to wait.

"I really think we should talk privately," Martin insisted. "If after a few minutes, you still want Jason to join us, then fine. But we should speak first. It's personal and it involves Patrick. Please," Martin begged.

Banks nodded to Palmer and said, "I'll just be a moment." She pointed Martin toward the study where she and Patrick had argued the night before.

"You might want to close the door," Martin suggested.

Banks closed the door, turned, and asked, "Would you like some coffee?"

"Yes, just some sugar, please."

Banks poured them both a cup of coffee from the pot sitting on the hutch in her office. "So, what's this all about?" she asked.

Over the next several minutes, Martin told Ann Banks about her late husband's involvement with Dunayev.

"And exactly how does this impact me?" she asked.

"Dunayev helped finance your run for president."

"But I've never met this guy," Banks grumbled.

"No, you probably wouldn't have. The money was funneled through a guy named Robert Moss who funneled it through a variety of other donors. Moss' real name was Oleg Lomakina. Lomakina was a member of Russian Organized Crime."

"He was the guy killed in New Haven a few days ago?"

"One and the same I'm afraid. Patrick got into it with Dunayev over that. Dunayev, of course, denied any involvement in the man's death, but Patrick was convinced Dunayev was behind it."

"But a handful of donors couldn't have had that much influence on the election."

"It masked a lot of money. But there is far more. Dunayev was behind a huge social media campaign designed to influence voters. Those false stories about your opponents were planted all across the various social media platforms. It was all designed to paint you as the candidate of reason."

"Just how did Patrick get involved with these people?"

"Usual way; money. He needed it. Plus, he wanted more power. And of course, he wanted to be president. They saw a weakness in him. He thought it would buy him a shot at the Oval Office. How many Congressmen and Senators do you know that don't imagine themselves in the role you're about to take on?"

"That miserable son of bitch. How can you spin this to keep me out of it and place this relationship all on Patrick?"

"That might be a little difficult right now," Martin said.

"And why is that?" Ann snapped.

"Dunayev had your bedroom bugged. He knows about your affair with the Secret Service Agent."

Banks' heart stopped and her eyes widened. *So, it's true*, she thought. With barely moving a muscle on her face, she said, "How is that possible?"

"I'm not exactly sure. I can only surmise he was trying to get information about you and Patrick. How he had your bedroom bugged is unclear to me."

"Could Patrick have had anything to do with this?" Banks demanded, her voice now audibly higher.

"I'm not sure. If he did, he wouldn't share that with me."

"So, what happens now?"

"Dunayev wants to meet with you. I told him that's impossible right now but he's not one to take no for an answer."

"What does he want?" Banks insisted.

"He wants access to the Oval Office."

"Tell him to go fuck himself," Banks said through clenched teeth. "He's not going to blackmail me. I'll see that son-of-bitch in prison first."

"Ann, please, let's think this through."

"There's nothing to think through," she snapped.

"Dunayev can destroy your presidency before you even get started. Everything you ran on will be instantly destroyed by your opponents and of course, the media. The fact that you, the president-elect, had an affair, will be the focus of every major news outlet in the country and overseas. They will paint you as an adulterer. A woman who cheated on her husband. Some will label you a traitor. They'll ask how anyone can trust such a woman in the Oval Office; the first woman ever to be elected to the presidency. He has you and this Dionis on tape. Dunayev will release it. He'll also connect you to the late Oleg Lomakina through his donations to you and Patrick. And if you don't cooperate with him, he'll make sure Agent Dionis is set up for Patrick's death."

"You miserable mother fucker," Banks yelled. "You're in on this. You conspired with Dunayev to do this. You despicable piece of shit."

Martin could see that Banks knew he was involved, but to what extent, he couldn't be sure. He suspected Banks to be a bit naïve in matters of the heart, but she was nobody's fool. She was politically astute enough to win the presidency. That astuteness helped her to quickly figure out that he was involved with Dunayev more than he was willing to admit. Martin knew he had to act fast.

Looking Banks straight in the eye, he said, "You're wrong. I didn't conspire with Dunayev to kill anyone, or to try to persuade you or Patrick to do anything. I didn't know about your bedroom being bugged, and I certainly didn't have anything to do with you sleeping with a Secret Service Agent. Dunayev always thought Patrick would be on the ticket, certainly not as the nominee for the presidency, but maybe the VP slot. Dunayev is a businessman. His only concern is making money. He and Patrick had certain business interests that intersected with each other."

For what seemed like an eternity, there was nothing, just a tense silence between the two of them. Banks wasn't buying any of it. Her discomfort with Martin grew as did the intensity of her voice. "That's what you say, but let's not bullshit each other," she said, shaking her head. "I know who you are and what your reputation is. You sell out to the highest bidder. You're not loyal to any cause."

Martin thought for a moment before answering. "Maybe you're right about me working for the highest bidder. But that's where it ends. Political causes, like politicians, come and go. People like me who work behind the scenes for people like you and Patrick get left behind more often than you'll ever admit. If not for us, most politicians would fall flat on their asses. I protected that power hungry husband of yours the best I could. He brought Dunayev into the picture without me knowing it. And he left me to clean up his shit." Martin knew he had to pile it on thick if he had any chance of convincing Banks that he was not as involved with Dunayev as she suspected, or at the very minimum, create some reasonable doubt.

Banks said nothing in response. She just stared at him, hoping he'd take some responsibility for bringing Dunayev into her life. There was an uncomfortable silence between the two of them that lasted for almost a minute.

"What business interests?" Banks asked, breaking the silence. "If Patrick had any business interests that crossed paths with a Russian thug, I would have known about it."

"Would you? Did you and Patrick know everything about each other? Did Patrick know about your affair?"

"The affair is none of your damn business," Banks barked.

"Well, it would be my business if I were advising you."

"But you're not advising me," Banks hissed.

"Well, we should talk about that, too," Martin said.

"What do you mean by that?" Banks demanded.

"You're going to need me if you have any hope of saving your presidency, and Michael Dionis."

"What does Michael have to do with any of this?

"Well, for starters, he's a Secret Service Agent who was charged with protecting the president-elect. He jeopardized your safety when he went to bed with you."

"You have no idea what you're talking about," Banks yelled.

"I heard the recording, Ann. I don't care about your love life. What you do in your bedroom is not mine or anyone else's concern. Unfortunately, however, half of the American people, along with your political adversaries in this country, are not going to see it that way. Plus, Dunayev has manipulated just enough of these events to point the authorities in Dionis' direction as a person of interest in Patrick's death."

"But they don't even know what Patrick died of yet. How can anyone be looking at Michael for his death?" Banks fumed.

"Come on, Ann, you've been in this game a long time. It's all about the optics. Demanding husband of the president-elect. Some will say you saw him as a liability and not an asset. You, having an affair with a Secret Service Agent who became jealous of Patrick. Shall I go on?"

"Are you now accusing me of having something to do with Patrick's death?" Banks yelled.

"Of course not," Martin replied. "But it's not me you have to concern yourself with. Think it through, Ann. Patrick got himself involved with the Russians. While I can't prove it, I'm sure Dunayev had one of your straw financial benefactors killed. I also think he had something to do with Patrick's death. Right now, he can walk away and let the media destroy you, which they will certainly do. And all this will start before you're even sworn in as president. Or you can buy some time. Let me become your chief of staff. I can keep Dunayev at bay."

"Out of the question," Banks said. "I don't trust you."

"Right now, you're going to have to. Dunayev has us both by the balls. I know it. And if we don't act fast, you'll soon know it too."

"That certainly sounds like a threat. And you will not threaten me."

"Dammit, Ann, it's not a threat. I've seen how this guy and his people work. Work with me and together, let's buy your presidency some time to do the things you ran on. It's your call."

"And Michael?" Banks asked.

Martin was expecting that question. "He might be the sacrificial lamb in this; at least for the time being."

"What do you mean by that? You're not having him implicated in Patrick's death," Banks insisted.

"No. Together, we can keep Dunayev at bay on that. Your agent, however, will probably be dismissed from the Service. We'll have to make sure he keeps his mouth shut about the affair."

"His job is his life. But Michael won't say a word to anyone."

"Dunayev will have constructed enough evidence to have the death of Lomakina pointed directly at Agent Dionis, which, he'll sit on. But your agent's bosses know about him being here last night and that he and Patrick got into an argument. Other agents heard Patrick tell him to stay away from you. That has already leaked."

"You have to keep Michael out of this," Banks demanded.

"I can. We'll have to spin this in such a manner that he and Patrick's altercation had nothing to do with the two of you having an affair."

"How will you spin that?" Banks asked.

"You know Americans; they have the worst impulses. They draw quick conclusions. Political campaigns encourage short-term thinking. This will be old news in forty-eight hours. I'll have something for you and your press secretary shortly. In the meantime, have your people start preparing a statement naming me your incoming Chief of Staff. Once Dunayev hears the announcement he'll back off. But he needs to hear it soon. In time for the evening news tomorrow, at the latest."

"If anything happens to Michael, I'll see you and this fucker Dunayev in prison. The presidency be damned."

"I'm not going to let that happen, Ann. I'm going to help you get through this. I know you don't trust me and rightfully so. But Patrick fucked us both. And so has Dunayev. Let's take this one step at a time," Martin said.

"Then go now and prepare something to spin this away from me and Michael. Do that and we'll see where this trust bullshit of yours goes."

Martin turned and walked out of the den and out of the governor's mansion. He got into his rental car, and drove north to Bradley International Airport for a flight back to D.C. Sitting in the rear of the airport shuttle van on the way to the terminal, he took out his burner phone and sent a short text message.

COS Done. News release soon.

Dunayev read the message and smiled.

Ann Banks told Palmer, her chief of staff, that she didn't want to be disturbed for the next fifteen minutes. She closed the door to her office, pulled out her cell phone, and opened the email account she and

Dionis shared. She immediately opened the draft folder and read Dionis' message. Her response was short and direct.

Russians behind this. Blackmailing me. Setting you up. Be careful. Say nothing. Patrick's COS dirty. Let me work this on my end.

Michael Dionis sat in his chair inside of his room at the Gramercy Park Hotel reading Banks' message for the tenth time.

WTF, he thought.

Chapter 11

It was almost noon before Patrick Banks was placed inside a black plastic bag and rolled out of the governor's mansion on a gurney. Reporters from every major network, both local and national, tried desperately to get pictures and video of the paramedics wheeling the late Congressman into the back of a medical van. News reporters fought for whatever prime piece of real estate they could find that would give them the best angle to capture both the governor's mansion and the transfer of Patrick Banks' body to the waiting ambulance. One local reporter for CNN went on the air live and said:

"As you can see in the background, medical personnel are moving what we believe to be the body of Congressman Patrick Banks into an ambulance. From what we have learned, the body will be taken to the Office of the Medical Examiner. We do not know what the cause of death is, only that he passed away sometime last night. We do know, however, that the Connecticut State Police, along with the Secret Service, and now the FBI, have been here since the early morning hours. So far, the Office of President-elect Ann Banks has not issued any type of statement. So, whatever is happening inside, is still being kept on close hold. We have learned that outgoing President, Robert Boyer, has issued a statement offering his condolences to Ann Banks and her family."

It was mid-afternoon when Sandi DeCarlo met Kimiko Matsui at the office of the Chief Medical Examiner in Farmington, CT. Laid out in front of them on a stainless-steel table was the naked body of Patrick Banks; the evidence tag still attached to his toe. On the side of one wall was a hose and a bucket. At one end of the table was a drainage tray. The only sound at the time came from the humming of a fluorescent light that hung over the table to help Matsui perform her autopsy. A small microphone was attached to her smock. This, of course, would allow her to record the examination process and any findings she might have during the procedure. DeCarlo removed a small vial from her purse containing mint jelly which she rubbed under her nose just before putting on her face mask. She had learned long ago that the jelly helped conceal the smell associated with death. She offered some to Matsui, but she declined. "The smell is part of the process. There really isn't anything we can do to block the smell of the body; we simply have to get used to it," Matsui said.

After Patrick Banks' body was weighed and photographed, Matsui began speaking slowly and without reservation. "File number PB 233413," she said into the microphone. "The embalmed body is that of Patrick Banks, a Caucasian male. Age 52. Height 5'11". Weight 202 pounds. Dark brown hair and blue eyes. There is what appears to be a scar left from knee surgery. There are no visible tattoos."

Matsui continued with the basic technical findings of the autopsy, reporting those things that were fundamental to most every examination she conducted. But Matsui, from having been to the crime scene, already suspected that the cause of death might be related to the use of cocaine. She picked up a scalpel and made a Y-shaped incision opening the chest and abdominal cavities. She then began removing the internal organs in order to examine each of them. The foul smell resembling something between that of rotting fish and spoiled eggs began to permeate the room. DeCarlo could never get used to the smell during an autopsy. She couldn't understand how Matsui could stand it. She rubbed a little more jelly under her nose. As Matsui continued her examination of Patrick Banks, she asked DeCarlo, "How soon do you think the lab will be able to confirm that the powder is in fact cocaine?"

"It's their number one priority right now. We use a private lab for this type of testing, and it usually takes a few weeks to get results. However, based on the high profile of the deceased, it's their main focus today. I hope to hear from them soon."

"Good. Let me know as soon as you do."

"What are you thinking?" DeCarlo asked.

Matsui turned off the recorder so she could speak freely, and said, "I'm really not thinking anything, or at least I'm trying not to. I want to make sure this examination is conducted without any predispositions in mind."

"Do I hear a but in there?" DeCarlo said.

"Maybe. But I do think cocaine is involved. This was an otherwise healthy male."

"So, what are you really thinking?"

"Well, I have little doubt that the lab is going to find that the substance you recovered is in fact cocaine. I'm also guessing that they are going to find that the cocaine was laced with some type of poison."

"Fentanyl?"

"Yes. Everyone reacts to chemicals and toxins differently. How one reacts, is, of course, associated with their age, sex, size, and weight. We also look at a person's overall health. Our deceased was, for all practical purposes, a healthy male, especially for his age. I don't think this was a simple drug overdose. You should ask his wife and co-workers if he's been sick lately."

"I will. What are you looking for?"

"If he was poisoned, you're going to want to know if it was acute or fast acting, or if it was chronic. If chronic, the poison would have been administered in very small amounts over a period of time. My initial guess is it was acute."

Matsui grabbed a pair of scissors from the tray next to the steel slab Patrick Banks was laying on and cut several pieces of his hair. "I'll test this. It will help determine if the poisoning was acute or chronic," she told DeCarlo.

As Matsui was cutting pieces of Patrick Banks' hair, DeCarlo's cell phone rang. The call was from the private crime lab conducting the test on the substance found in Patrick Banks' coat pocket. Matsui couldn't hear what the caller was saying, only that DeCarlo was nodding her head up and down as if to signal she was affirming something.

"Are you positively sure?" DeCarlo said into the phone. "Son of a bitch. Okay, I'll be there in about an hour." DeCarlo disconnected the call and pocketed her cell phone. She took a moment to compose herself from the shock of the news she'd just received. She returned her gaze to Matsui and said, "Your suspicions are correct. It is in fact cocaine. And it was laced with fentanyl. But not just any fentanyl. It was laced with carfentanil, a very potent form of fentanyl. It's used to tranquilize large animals like elephants."

"Yes," Matsui replied. "I'm aware of it. It's very potent indeed. And not easy to come by."

"No, it isn't," replied DeCarlo.

"Your guy here died as a result of some highly contaminated coke," Matsui said. "Whether or not he was purposely singled out or is just the victim of having gotten his hands on some very bad shit, is for you to figure out. Either way, if there is more of this stuff out there, it has to get off the street fast or we're going to have more victims on this slab."

DeCarlo nodded her head in agreement, and said, "I don't need this shit."

"Well, so much for this death being a ground ball for you," Matsui added, referring to those homicides that are simply obvious and often easy to solve like those where the murderer is at the scene of the crime holding a bloody knife or has a gun in their hand.

"No, this one is not a ground ball at all. For now, it's a real mystery. If he was actually murdered, it's a real who-done-it for sure. Give me a moment, Kimiko, I have to make a quick telephone call."

DeCarlo stepped outside the room, pulled out her cell phone and called Mike Dionis. After the fourth ring, the call went straight to voicemail.

"Michael, it's Sandi. I need to speak to you ASAP. Please call me as soon as you can." DeCarlo ended the message and sent Dionis a text with the same request to call her as quickly as possible. She stepped back into the room where Matsui was continuing her autopsy of Patrick Banks.

"I have to go. Anything you need from me right now?

"No," Matsui said. "I'm wrapping this up. If I find anything else, I'll let you know."

At the same time Patrick Banks was being disemboweled, Michael Dionis sat in his hotel room reading the text message he had received moments earlier from DeCarlo, and how he was going to answer her. He was also thinking of how to respond to Ann Banks' email about her husband's death and the involvement of the Russians. At that moment, he had no idea how to respond to either of those questions.

Chapter 12

On the morning after the death of Patrick Banks, the major news story covered on all the cable outlets, the conservative and liberal networks alike, was Ann Banks' announcement that Josh Martin, her late husband's chief of staff, would now join her in the White House as her chief of staff. The announcement, read by Kiara Howard, Ann Banks' newly appointed White House press secretary stated:

"President-elect Ann Banks would like to announce that Josh Martin, her late husband, Congressman Patrick Banks' chief of staff, has agreed to join her as her new chief of staff. Mr. Martin has been a trusted colleague to not only her late husband but to the president-elect as well. Mr. Martin will be assuming his duties this coming week and will help in the days ahead with the transition team. For now, President-elect Banks has asked for privacy for the next few days as she deals with the passing of her husband. I will not be answering any questions regarding this latest appointment. I'll have more on this after the funeral of Patrick Banks. Thank you." After reading the statement, Howard left the podium and refused to answer any questions.

The CNN anchor was quick to note that the announcement was untimely in that Patrick Banks' funeral hadn't yet occurred.

"Why is President-elect Banks making this announcement now?" he muttered. "It seems a bit early to me to be making any announcements other than what her late husband's funeral arrangements might be. While the country waits for the first ever elected woman to the presidency, and the first ever elected independent president, we hear the announcement of Josh Martin as her new Chief of Staff. She hasn't even buried her husband yet. While some might find it commendable that she is continuing her work during this transition period, one might ask if she's so hardened, and insensitive, that she might actually lean more to the conservative side than she would like us to believe. And what about Jason Palmer, her current chief of staff that was believed by everyone to be going to the White House with her. Kiara Howard

never mentioned him in her press statement. It might cause one to ask, 'What's going on behind the scenes."

Over at FOX, the evening anchors had their own take on the press secretary's statement.

"President-elect Ann Banks announced today that Josh Martin, her late husband's chief of staff would now become her chief of staff, debunking everyone's expectation, including this anchor's, that Jason Palmer, who helped her win the election, would be assuming that position. According to Kiara Howard, the incoming White-House press secretary, Josh Martin, will be assuming his new duties this week, after the funeral of former Congressman Patrick Banks. It's unclear why Banks is making this statement now. Is she more liberal elitist than we've been led to believe? At a time when most people have just lost a spouse, you'd think she would be focused on her personal affairs. But Ann Banks is clearly putting her presidency first. And, of course, some would argue that in spite of her husband's death, she's pushing forward. But an announcement such as this could easily have waited until after the funeral. We've yet to hear anything about the alleged altercation between the late Patrick Banks and Secret Service Agent Michael Dionis. Exactly what did Patrick Banks mean when he was overheard saying, 'stay away from my wife?' Efforts to find and ask this question of Michael Dionis have all met with negative results. We've contacted the Secret Service for comment but, so far, they have not returned our calls."

The liberal and conservative news networks were both having a field day with the announcement of Josh Martin being named as Ann Banks' new chief of staff. There was an endless array of paid talking heads on every network to support whatever personal position a viewer took of Ann Banks' sudden announcement. And if viewers hadn't formed their own opinions, based on their ideological political views, the network talking heads worked hard to convince the undecided exactly what they were supposed to think. For the first time in most everyone's recollection, the major news outlets seemed to be sharing the same position with regard to the incoming president. What they appeared unsure of was what exactly the independent incoming president was going to do next. They all suspected that she was going to implement policies that she took the middle ground on. Conservatives were already skeptical about her position on gun control. Ann Banks believed that additional gun control laws were necessary to reduce gun violence. She clearly wanted to limit the ability of criminals to obtain guns and was insisting that some form of new gun control become part of the national conversation. She had no patience for the NRA's position that any type of new gun legislation was the country's embarking upon the slippery slope road of taking people's guns away. Intelligent people knew better, and she would never allow that to happen on her watch.

Conservatives were also critical of her position on same-sex marriage. Banks supported the union of people who loved each other. "All people; gay, lesbian, bisexual, and transgender have the right to marry," Banks said during her candidacy for the president. And while the Supreme Court legalized same-sex marriage, conservatives continued to fight the ruling, often holding the bible in one hand and the court's opinion in the other to demonstrate their religious opposition to the government's decision. Banks was not afraid to fight that particular culture war. Of course, the religious right had other ideas.

Liberals were vocal in their criticism of her view on health care. She clearly believed all Americans should have access to health care but believed in a free-market healthcare system. Liberals were also critical of her position on Homeland Security issues. Banks believed that profiling was a good intelligence strategy. She didn't care that people were offended by profiling. Preventing a major terroristic attack on the U.S. was more important to her. She knew that the terrorists had only gotten more efficient since 9/11, and she was afraid of the numerous dangers they posed, especially after the foreign policy disaster in Afghanistan. Her liberal critics believed such profiling, especially at airports, was discriminatory and offensive. Yet Banks advocated for a more common-sense approach which, for her, meant increasing intelligence gathering in every way possible. If that meant profiling, so be it. She advocated securing the borders as a means to prevent terrorists and criminals from entering the country and interdicting the flow of illegal drugs.

Liberals and conservatives alike had something to be politically afraid of, while each side clearly supported many of the issues she stood for. With Ann Banks, it was not a one position fits all. She was a free thinker and believed most Americans were too. Banks was convinced that most Americans wanted the same thing: freedom, and a chance for prosperity with as little suffering as possible. Most also wanted a safe, healthy, and crime-free environment for everyone, especially for children. And in spite of the failed policies of liberal politicians in cities like Chicago, to stem the flow of gun related killings, the attacks by the NRA continued. When she advocated making some form of gun control part of the national conversation, the hard-core conservatives attacked her. And try as the liberal and conservative news outlets did to influence the election, the American people, for the first time in history, sent a message loud and clear: the corrupt two-party system wasn't working.

After years of constant political fighting between the country's two opposing political factions, each doing everything possible to prevent one side or the other from claiming any type of social or economic victory that might benefit the American people, the voters had had enough. During the past three presidencies, both parties believed a major jobs program aimed at rebuilding the nation's infrastructure was desperately needed. Neither side, however, could agree on how to move forward, afraid one side or the other might get most of the credit for its passage. And after four years of one of the crudest, most foul-mouthed presidents this country had ever had, who was impeached twice by the House of Representatives, one strictly for in-your-face political reasons, the people appeared to be exhausted from the political infighting. This presidency was followed by a president associated with political correctness, and who pled for unity and cooperation. While pleading for unity, his first day in office was highlighted by signing away through his executive orders many of his predecessors' policies, a number of which were designed to keep the country independent of foreign oil. The voters, demonstrating that they were smarter than the die-hard politicians in Washington ever gave them credit for, sent a message loud and clear: It was time for a third party. And Ann Banks offered that change. And while it surprised the traditional candidates and the ideologue news pundits pandering to their networks and declining viewers, the voters had spoken. What many in both Houses of Congress feared most, was Banks' promise to the American people to introduce legislation imposing 12-year term limits on members of both the House and Senate, and her commitment to ending the use of "dark money" donations toward a candidate's election bid. Even die-hard conservatives and liberals found common ground on the subject of fighting term limits. Both Republicans and Democrats alike had argued and rallied against anonymous campaign contributions, citing it as a corrupting political force.

"The voters should know who's funding a candidate's political campaign. Dark money is one of the most toxic forces in politics and should be stopped immediately," Banks told her enthusiastic audience in front of a rally in Orlando, Florida. Attacking both the Republicans and Democrats, Banks told the cheering crowd, "Mitt Romney had allegedly received somewhere in the neighborhood of $113 million in dark money when he ran for president in 2012. Joe Biden, by the best figures available, and reported by Bloomberg News, suggests that he took in about $145 million in donations from anonymous donors. Now we, the American people, have no idea where this money is coming from. And why? Because neither party has acted to stop it. Sure, both sides talk a big game, but what's been done to stop it? Virtually nothing. When you elect me as your president, you will see term limit legislation introduced in Congress. And you will see me introduce legislation to halt the flow of dark money."

And that was Ann Banks' winning strategy: find as much common ground as possible between conservative and liberal voters, and the independent, non-political ideologues, and begin building the foundation of something better for the American people.

Now, members of Congress and the Senate shared a common fear of an independent movement all across the country. Many of them, of course, refused to accept her as their new president and were already planning on how to prevent her from implementing the legislation she had advocated. And it wasn't only the members of Congress and the Senate that Banks ran afoul of with her proposal to end dark money contributions, she ran afoul of both Republican and Democratic Super PACs who argued that the donors of this money did not need to be disclosed.

Sitting in the office of Susan Welsh, the liberal Speaker of the House of Representatives, was the majority leader of the Senate, Alan Hessler, and his minority counterpart, Jonathan Prince.

Susan Welsh had been in Congress for over thirty years. She ruled with an iron fist and believed almost all of the nation's social problems could be solved simply by throwing money at them. Working with conservatives on most any subject was virtually out of the question, unless, of course, it involved the expenditure of large sums of money for which her party could take the credit. If the country had a problem, her solution was simple: throw money at it. But this evening, she had only one agenda. She handed both Alan Hessler, who was guided by the principle of not spending a dime that the government didn't have regardless of the plight of its citizens, and Jonathan Prince, Welsh's yes man in the Senate, a well poured glass of Green Spot.

"What are we going to do about Ann Banks?" Welsh asked, taking the first sip of her Irish whiskey.

"I'm open to suggestions," Hessler replied. "If she gets term limits introduced in the House, can you stop it?" he asked Welsh.

"I can. But it will be political suicide for all of us. What I'm really asking is what do we do about her now? Her husband just died. She announces that Josh Martin will be her new Chief of Staff just hours after Patrick's death and her meeting with him. And what about this alleged altercation between Patrick Banks and this Secret Service Agent? Am I the only one here that suspects something? This doesn't pass the smell test, gentlemen."

“I agree,” Hessler said. “I propose we each put our teams on this. There’s more here than what we’re being told. Let’s find out before the media does.”

Senator Prince simply nodded. He’d meet privately later with Welsh and get his marching orders. No doubt, they would include discrediting Ann Banks. And if possible, Alan Hessler in the process. But going after Banks was the priority.

“I agree,” Welsh replied. “Let’s find that damn Secret Service Agent. Who do we know at Homeland Security?”

“I’ll make a call,” Hessler replied.

“And Jonathan, can you get a copy of the autopsy report?”

“That shouldn’t be a problem,” Prince added.

“Good,” Welsh replied. “Unfortunately, the election of Ann Banks clearly proves that Clarence Darrow was right when he said, ‘anybody can become president.’ Let’s meet here again tomorrow evening at seven. We need to stay on top of this before that bitch is sworn in. She can go fuck herself if she thinks she’s going to impose term-limits on me.”

“And any type of gun control,” remarked Hessler.

“We just need to be careful that our meetings are not discovered, especially by the media,” Prince said.

“Yes,” Hesler replied. “But then again, we all know how difficult it is to track the shadow of truth through the fog of political conflict,” he added laughingly.

All three of the seasoned politicians smiled as they looked at each other. Welsh raised her glass and said, “To plausible deniability.”

“To keeping the American people from learning the truth,” added Hessler raising his right hand and his glass of whiskey.

“The truth is always negotiable, Jonathan,” Welsh said convincingly. “Don’t ever forget that.”

The three career politicians raised their glasses in a toast, smiled at each other and finished off their drinks. "Happy hunting, boys," Welsh added.

"And to dark money," added Jonathan Prince.

"Till tomorrow then," Welsh said.

***

Dionis flipped the news channels back and forth trying to pick up any bit of news regarding Ann Banks. Her last message to him in the email draft folder left him nauseous. He needed to talk to somebody, but not just anyone. He picked up the burner phone he had purchased and called Tony Maffuci.

Chapter 13

Maffuci was just finishing dinner with his family when his cell phone rang. As a matter of routine, he seldom, if ever, answered a call from anyone whose name didn't appear from his contact list. And even though he didn't recognize the number, something about this call caught his attention. It had been over twenty-four hours since he'd heard from Michael Dionis. *Just maybe*, he thought.

"Hello," he said as he hit the answer button.

"Tony, it's Michael."

"I was hoping it was you. You are using a burner, I presume?"

"Nothing gets by you Bureau boys," Dionis replied.

"Where are you?"

"New York. Thought I'd lay low for a few days in the city. You know, enjoy one of the few restaurants that survived the shutdown during the COVID crisis."

"Yeah, how's that working out for you?"

"Just great. Not sure this city will ever be the same again."

"The question is, will you ever be the same?" Maffuci asked.

"Bosses feel I really fucked up and are not offering much support," Dionis said.

"What the hell did you do, my boy?"

"Nothing."

"It isn't nothing. You're all over the news. DeCarlo is looking for you. If you don't get in touch with her soon, it won't be pretty. Talk to me."

"Not sure I can right now. Other people are involved, and it could cause them irreparable harm," Dionis said.

"Then I'm not sure how I can help."

Dionis asked, “What can you tell me about Patrick Banks’ death?”

Maffuci spent the next few minutes telling Dionis what he had heard earlier in the day from DeCarlo.

“Cocaine, laced with fentanyl?” Dionis said, his voice clearly shaken.

“And not just any fentanyl, but carfentanil, extremely powerful and deadly. And your people found coke in your place,” he added.

“You have to be fucking shitting me,” Dionis said, shocked. “That’s bullshit. Who found this, and how?”

“When your people couldn’t find you, they went to your condo. Allegedly, they were concerned for your safety, so they went inside and found the remnants of coke in your bathroom.”

“This is a set-up, Tony.”

Maffuci could tell that Dionis’ blood was beginning to boil. “Who would want to set you up? And what are they setting you up for?” Maffuci asked.

“For starters, Patrick Banks’ death. I had nothing to do with that. And I certainly don’t use coke.”

“Then tell me what the hell is going on,” Maffuci insisted.

Dionis paused, took a deep breath and said, “I want to tell you. But the moment of truth will have to come later. I’m going to have to defend my conduct in another forum sooner than later. Right now, it will have to wait. Just know that I did nothing wrong, or nothing that is criminal at least. Not even close. But I’m going to need your help finding the people who are setting me up to look as though I had something to do with Banks’ death.”

“You know I’m here for you. Whatever you need. But understand this, *Amico*, my SAC is not one of us. She’s part of this new politically correct woke group of bureaucrats. And, your ex appears to have my SAC’s ear. Your ex will make you the scapegoat in all of this more so than the media made Trump the scapegoat for everything that went wrong in this country, even if he did deserve his share of the blame. The media just wants their sound bites and you're giving them theirs right now. I can only guess who you're protecting. But know this, *Amico*, your ex and my SAC are watching me too. They're both insisting on knowing if I have any contact with you. So, no more calls on this cell. I'll send you a burner number shortly."

"Thank you," Dionis said.

"And call DeCarlo now. Don't let her looking for you add to your problems."

"I'll do it now."

As soon as the two men disconnected the call, Maffuci picked up a burner cell and pressed the number one on the keypad. The party on the other end simply said, "yes."

"He's in New York City. Where exactly, I have no idea. That's all I know right now."

"And?"

"He knows he's being set up."

"I'm sure he does." And without another word, the call ended.

Tony Maffuci sat in his den staring out the window into the cold, gray, Connecticut night, watching the snowflakes begin to fall. A careful frown crossed his face. *What have you gotten yourself into, Amico? Fuck*, he thought.

Two hours away, lying on the bed of his darkened hotel room at the Gramercy Park Hotel, Michael Dionis, with his phone next to him, looked at his watch. It was almost eight p.m. In spite of being mentally exhausted, he called Sandi DeCarlo. And in an instant, he changed his mind and hung up just before the first ring. Without another thought of calling her, at least not yet, he laid back on his bed, and fell asleep.

It was almost midnight when Dionis woke up to the constant noise of police and fire sirens, a staple sound the residents who make their home in the city have long grown accustomed to and think little of. To the casual visitor, it takes some time to get comfortable with this never-ending din. Dionis assumed that his bosses, his ex-wife, and the FBI SAC, all had questions for him. His immediate concern, however, was Ann Banks. *What have I done? This could destroy her presidency before she even gets started. I have to fix this. Reach out, Ann; I have to hear from you*, Dionis thought.

Ten minutes after midnight, Dionis picked up his burner cell and called Sandi DeCarlo.

"Michael, is that you?" DeCarlo asked.

"Good guess. Did I wake you?"

"I wish," DeCarlo replied. "I was wondering when you were going to call."

"Well, I'm here now."

"So, you are. Looks like you have some enemies," DeCarlo said.

"Are you one of them?" Dionis asked.

"I'm just investigating a very suspicious death of a man who you apparently had an altercation with hours before he died. An altercation where he told you to stay away from his wife. Of course, she's not just anyone's wife, she's the president-elect."

"I know that."

DeCarlo said, "Did you know he died of an overdose of cocaine laced with a very powerful and deadly type of fentanyl."

"Yes, I heard."

"And did you know a couple of your friends at the Secret Service found coke in the bathroom of your condo? My guess, it's going to test positive for the same type of fentanyl."

"I heard that too. This is bullshit. I've never used coke in my life."

"Well then, let me ask you same question: are we enemies or not?"

"We certainly are not. But it's clear I have some."

"So, it would appear. And until I can find them, you are a person of interest."

"Are you buying into any of this bullshit?" Dionis asked.

"Well, which part is bullshit?"

"What do you mean?"

"Let's start with why you were in the den with Ann Banks that night?"

"I Went to see her to ask about your dead Russian just like I told you I would earlier that day. And to say good-bye. She is moving to D.C. in a few days. We've been friends for a very long time. Plus, I had agents on post out there supplementing her new permanent detail. I wanted to check on them."

"Okay, that's an easy sell. What about the altercation?"

"People are making it out to be more than it was. Patrick Banks was a dickhead. He and Ann had no real relationship. He always accused her of things that weren't true. Plus, he'd been drinking."

"Did he tell you to stay away from her?"

"He did."

"Why?"

"He thought we were having an affair."

"And were you?"

"No," Dionis lied.

DeCarlo knew she couldn't prove Dionis, and Ann Banks were having an affair. How could she? She couldn't even see the expression on his face. But Dionis hadn't acted offended when confronted with the question or made any outrageous denials.

"I'm not completely sure I believe you Michael so let's table this for now. Where's your laptop?"

"With me, why?"

"You know why. We need to examine it."

"Do you have a warrant?"

"Not yet. How long do you think it would take for me to get one?"

"If you call my ex-wife, she probably already has it ready and would personally deliver it to you tonight," Dionis replied.

DeCarlo was happy that Dionis couldn't see the silly smile on her face when he mentioned his ex-wife. "Well, you seem to piss off not only ex-wives, but husbands as well."

"So, it seems," Dionis replied, trying without success to suppress a small laugh. "But none of them have ever come up dead."

"Where are you, Michael?"

"A couple of hours away. Why?"

"Can we meet?"

"Not sure that's a good idea right now."

"So, then we are enemies," DeCarlo said. Her tone made it sound more like a question than a statement.

"I certainly hope not. I just need a little time. I'm being set up. I think you know that."

"I'm not sure what I think, Michael. I know you only by reputation, which is a good one. I've met you three times, briefly, and shared one wine with you. So, I'm not sure that I know you're being set up. I'd like to think I know you, but I really don't. At the end of the day, we only think we know other people. I'm sure you realize that."

"I do. But I didn't have anything to do with Patrick's death. And I don't use coke or any other illicit drugs. I'm going to find out who is behind this. I think whoever it is, is also coming after Ann Banks."

"Well, finally we're getting somewhere," DeCarlo said. "I guess you're going to have to find a way to trust me too."

"I guess I just might. But as you said, who do we really know?"

“I’ll give you this, Michael, this whole thing reeks of political corruption and a setup. It’s too neat a package. I think the media frenzy that is just getting started is going to be bad for you and Ann Banks.”

“I need to hear from someone first, then we’ll talk more.”

“Ann Banks?” DeCarlo asked.

“Yes. There is far more at stake here than my being set up for something I didn’t do.”

“Stay close, Michael. Let me hear from you soon.”

With that, Dionis ended the call. He laid back on his bed, closed his eyes, and plunged himself into darkness.

DeCarlo poured herself a glass of red wine and sat down on the couch in her living room, losing herself in her private thoughts. *Who have you pissed off, Agent Dionis? Or are you just one unlucky bastard? Either way, someone has it in for you, or you’re about to be made one hell of a scapegoat. But whoever the hell is doing this, is not going to play me too.*

Chapter 14

It was just after ten p.m. when Josh Martin sat across the table from Andre Dunayev in the dark corner of the Campbell Bar at Grand Central Station. Martin had taken a late train into New York for the single purpose of meeting with Dunayev. Both men had much to discuss; most of which centered around the two of them remaining on the same page with regard to moving forward in the Banks administration.

"Tomorrow morning, the *New York Times* is going to run a story about my being named Banks' new Chief of Staff," Martin said. "There will be editorials, of course, some asking questions as to why the abrupt change and announcement immediately after Patrick's death."

"CNN has already announced that. So how is that a problem for us?" Dunayev asked.

"It depends," Martin replied. "The *Times* reporters are good. Even though they are most often one-sided politically, they do know how to investigate. And while real investigative reporting appears to be a dying art, the *Times* will dig deeper than most, especially the liberal reporters from CNN and MSNBC, as well as the conservative ideologues from FOX."

"Then we need to be careful. We still want Banks to be the president, especially now that you're her new Chief of Staff. We can control much of what she does with the information we have on her, yes?" Dunayev said looking for a positive reply from Martin.

"I would think so, especially in the short-term," Martin offered. "But let me explain something, Ann Banks didn't get to where she is by being stupid. She's smarter than many give her credit for. She pulled off something no other politician has ever done; she won the presidency as an independent. So, let's not fool ourselves. If we, you, for that matter, go after her now, you will stir up a lot of shit."

Martin leaned in closer, and speaking in a whisper, said, "I'm probably not telling you anything you don't already know but moving quickly, like you seem to want to do, will only cause us harm. Ann Banks knows of your existence and what you have on her. She doesn't trust me now and might not ever. She appointed me as her Chief of Staff to buy herself some time. I'll be close enough to her to control many of her activities. If she thinks I'm trying to protect her, and that you have me compromised as much as her, I'll be in a better position to move some of her decisions our way. Her current selection for Secretary of State will have to be compromised enough that she will resign her nomination even before she is confirmed."

"We're working on that now. And her lover, this Secret Service Agent," Dunayev replied, "what do we do with him?"

"For now, nothing," Martin replied forcefully. "The coke they found in his condo, along with the so-called altercation he had with Patrick the night of his untimely passing, is causing him all the grief he can stand. Federal and state prosecutors are looking at him as a person of interest in Patrick's death. Some are already speculating that there was something between him and Ann Banks. The last thing either of them want revealed is their affair. So, we do nothing. Let the system deal with him for now. They certainly don't have enough evidence to arrest him for anything, at least not yet. If anything happens to him, it will only cause more speculation. I think it best we let him experience the pangs of the investigative process, both into the death of Patrick, and the internal investigation his agency will conduct based on his conduct with the president-elect. We don't have to do anything more to Michael Dionis, not now anyway. Besides, his altercation with Patrick the night he died was a godsend. Let's not look a gift-horse in the mouth."

"A gift-horse?" Dunayev asked.

"An American expression. When you're handed an unexpected gift, don't find fault with it. Take it, be happy, and keep your mouth shut."

Dunayev knew that Martin made sense. While many, if not most Americans, sought instant gratification in most everything they did and often moved forward on a host of things without adequate preparation or thinking the potential for problems through, Martin was looking to play the long game. Dunayev, the sociopath that he was, had rarely played the long game, opting instead for immediate results and returns on whatever criminal activity he was currently engaged in. Playing all sides at once was his forte. And he played the game well. He had stared down many men who operated within the Russian underworld, most of whom were far more dangerous than any American criminals he encountered. Dunayev was convinced he was the best at what he did. His arrogance knew no bounds.

"I'll run your thoughts by my associates," Dunayev told Martin. "In the meantime, nothing will happen to your Secret Service Agent. We can always deal with him later. What is next for you and Ann Banks?"

"We're just days away from the inauguration," Martin said. "I'm going to be reviewing her inaugural address to the nation. I'll make sure her speech writers put something in there offering an olive branch to the Russian government. We'll probably offer the same olive branch to China."

"And why China?" Dunayev asked, surprised that Martin would mention the country.

"Because China presents a host of other opportunities for us. Need I get into those now?"

"No. Let's not waste time on that right now," Dunayev insisted.

"Of course, it will then be incumbent on both governments to embrace this gesture and move toward a more conciliatory relationship. That should be the impetus for discussions to reduce many of the trade barriers imposed during the Trump administration. Once that is done, we should have better control of things coming in and going out of the country. Banks ran mostly on domestic issues hoping to get the country on track economically and socially. In the process, she's making a lot of people happy. Ideologues in Congress, of course, are not included in that group of happy people, especially with her commitment to getting legislation passed regarding term limits and excluding dark money for future presidential candidates. To many Democrats and Republicans, she is a clear and present danger. It wouldn't surprise me if the power-hungry Speaker of the House isn't already looking for ways to have her impeached. It seems to be her political strategy these days. And now, she might just pull it off since Banks is not really a friend of either of the two political parties."

"And if that happens?" Dunayev asked.

"We'll cross that bridge when the time comes. Suffice to say, Banks does have the will of the people behind her. At least for now. If I were contemplating running for the House or Senate in the next election, I'd certainly consider doing so as an Independent."

"And you think this is enough to protect her from her political adversaries?"

"I do for now. The American people have demonstrated that they've had their fill of partisan politics. Of course, if the affair is leaked, all bets are off. She'll certainly lose more than the religious right as she did over her position on abortion."

"Then she will want her secret protected," Dunayev said.

"She will. And remember, she had little to say about foreign policy during her campaign. I should be able to guide her in the direction we both want. But I'll require a few quick victories in order to win her heart and mind. I need to convince her that you are simply a businessman, nothing more. And, that I can keep you from causing her political harm."

"But she knows I had her bedroom bugged. She's not going to be quick to simply see me as a businessman."

"Let me deal with that. Patrick is dead. We can blame just about everything on him. We can start with convincing her that it was him who bugged the bedroom as he was suspicious of her relationship with the Secret Service Agent."

"And my having the recording?"

"I'll tell her Patrick gave it to you to help him take her down politically, if he ever needed to do so."

"Then a couple of quick victories you will have my friend," Dunayev said. "As long as you don't forget that I can cause you both a lot of political harm. In the meantime, tell your new president that I have withdrawn my demand for who should be her nomination for Secretary of State. And offer her my condolences for the loss of her husband. I hope his death was quick and that he didn't suffer," Dunayev said, taking the last sip of his scotch.

Martin looked at his watch and said, "I have to go. This is the last train back to New Haven tonight."

Dunayev stood and gave Martin a new burner cell. "Keep this close. When I call, make sure you pick it up."

"That's not going to happen, Andre. Once I'm in the White-House, my movements are tracked. You can't call during the day. If you need to reach me, make sure the calls are between ten p.m. and five a.m. Otherwise, I might actually be with the president or other members of her senior staff."

"So be it," Dunayev said. An irritated look washed across his face. "Just make sure you still pick up the phone when I call."

"Seriously, Andre," Martin said, his voice laced with frustration. "This is how you want to play this now?"

Martin took the burner cell from Dunayev and placed it in his coat pocket. The two men parted without saying another word to each other. Martin walked to the tracks inside the terminal and found his train on the Metro North line for his trip back to New Haven. As soon as he sat down, he reached into his backpack and removed a bottle of Xanax. He took out one pill, swallowed it and flushed it down with a small bottle of Poland Spring water that he just purchased for three dollars. *You might think you have me by the balls, Andre, but you're about to find out otherwise,* he thought.

Dunayev walked out of the main entrance to Grand Central Station and onto 42nd Street. A black Mercedes pulled up and he immediately got into the back seat.

"Lusardi's on 2nd Avenue, Dunayev told the driver. The driver knew exactly where to go as it was Dunayev's favorite Italian restaurant. Lusardi's is a neighborhood fine Italian dining restaurant that caters to both locals as well those visiting New York who want to escape the tourist traps of Times Square. When you enter, even as first-time diners, you're greeted by a member of the staff as if you're family. A small redwood bar on the left as you enter, seats only six patrons but adds a degree of intimacy found in the best of restaurants. Behind the bar, of course, is a wide selection of spirits that will satisfy everyone's wishes. The dining area is small and discerning, long, and narrow, with hardwood floors and tables, each covered in an immaculate white tablecloth. The menu is diverse, consisting mostly of gourmet Italian pasta and fish dishes from the Parma region of Italy known for its Parmigiano Reggiano cheese and Prosciutto di Parma. A small table in the rear of the restaurant provides privacy for those wishing to be left alone.

Dunayev picked up his cell phone, punched a button, and on the second ring, heard the word, "yes."

"I'm here."

"I'm on my way," the man replied. Both lines went dead almost simultaneously. Dunayev summoned the waiter over to his table and ordered a scotch with one ice cube. Five minutes later, Dunayev was seated across from Jian Wie, a senior member of the Chinese Ministry of State Security, or the MSS. The MSS operates both in China and abroad exercising the functions of espionage, counterespionage, and cyber snooping; functions that the U.S. dedicates three separate agencies to, including the CIA, FBI, and NSA. The MSS doesn't have a public website and it doesn't have a press office. But it does require Chinese tech giants to cooperate with them.

Wie was in his late 50s, medium height, thin, and muscular. His face was hardened and his eyes dark. "I hope you don't mind, but I ordered myself a scotch. Can I get you anything?" Dunayev asked Wie.

"A club soda would be nice."

The waiter arrived and handed Dunayev his glass of scotch. "Bring me the appetizer of risotto with the truffles, and a club soda for my friend," he instructed the waiter.

"Right away, sir," the waiter replied as he hurried to the kitchen.

Knowing Wie was a man of few words and deplored small talk, Dunayev said, "Josh Martin has just been named the new president's chief of staff."

"That is old news. Your corporate run twenty-four-hour news stations have already reported that. What about the nomination for Secretary of State?" Wie asked. "I see she's already named someone that doesn't fit into our plans."

"In due course. We will get our man the nomination. It will come."

Wie didn't like what he was hearing. "I thought her husband was going to be named Secretary of State. His untimely death is most disappointing. And now her selection of this woman is not what we'd hoped for. It's most upsetting."

"Drugs. It's a terrible habit my friend. We had no idea Patrick was using," Dunayev said, smiling. "Besides, Ann Banks was never going to name him as her Secretary of State. He was becoming uncontrollable. So maybe his death can work to our advantage."

"How so?"

"As soon as the new president is sworn in, she will discover that her selection for Secretary of State, who she has already announced, will have to withdraw from consideration for health reasons. That will allow us to have our man nominated for the position."

"You understand how important it is that we have someone in that position who understands our needs?"

"Your and my country's both."

“Yes, but for different reasons. U.S. relations with my country have deteriorated dramatically since the COVID pandemic. It has brought adverse attention to my country.”

“Adverse attention from most every country in the world as well. Had your country been more transparent in combating the virus, we might not be in this position.”

“China does not welcome accusations or outside interference in its affairs,” Wie said sternly.

“Nor does any country. But even Mother Russia cooperates on a variety of issues such as terrorism, space exploration, and even climate change. And while the relationship with my country and the U.S. has indeed deteriorated in recent years, our government has found ways to compartmentalize our relationship when cooperation is necessary.”

“But no country rivals us for economic superiority like the U.S. does,” Wie said.

“Too many people in the U.S. are never going to believe that the virus was an accident. That goes for many people around the world. Not opening up full cooperation with the U.S. and other nations was a diplomatic blunder on your country’s part.”

“Maybe so, but it was in fact an accident. And there was no working with the last two U.S. presidents who sought only to keep us from growing economically.”

“Perhaps. But the COVID crisis and your careless approach to intelligence gathering hasn’t served you well. Plus, the world is always watching your host of human rights violations,” Dunayev reminded Wie.

“Russia, and certainly you, have no right to point fingers at anyone for human rights violations,” Wie countered.

“Again, maybe so, but we don’t flaunt them any more than necessary. And, if truth be told, Russia knows it will never be an economic threat to the U.S. America fears us more politically and militarily.”

"We prefer to take over economically," Wie said. "You and I both know that an all-out war with the U.S. and their allies would be devastating for everyone involved. The world would cease to exist as we know it."

"Yes, Russia knows that all too well."

Both the U.S. and Russia have known it all too well ever since the concept of mutual assured destruction, or MAD was introduced during the Kennedy administration.

"You don't care about Russia being a major player in foreign relations," Wie said. "You are simply motivated by money, my friend."

"Maybe so. But having the political forces of my mother country in my good graces, will no doubt pay other dividends that are not always measured in cash," Dunayev replied.

The waiter brought Dunayev his risotto and sprinkled a very generous portion of shaved truffles on the top of it. Dunayev swirled his glass in his hand, looked up, and told the waiter, "Another please."

As soon as the waiter left, Dunayev told Wie, "Things are moving along nicely. We have a new president coming into office very soon. And very soon, she will see the benefit of having a Secretary of State who will work on our behalf."

"Good," Wie replied. "We need to reestablish American access to our telecommunications industry. Once we do that, we can get back on track to catching up with America's economic dominance."

"America is so divided; it will be easy enough to convince their politicians to open up talks with your country. Many of them know that in spite of your military, economic and technological expansions, they still have to do business with you."

"Indeed, they do," Wie said.

"Might I suggest that over the next two months, China maintains a low profile with regard to its human rights issues."

"What exactly do you mean?" Wie asked.

"Give the new president time to adjust, just a few weeks. Keep, what their FBI Director calls your 'Fox Hunt', your country's search for dissidents and political rivals in the U.S., to a minimum. The more transparency the new president sees, the better our chances for success are."

"Why should we do this? The Americans, and you Russians for that matter, are not known for acting patiently. The U.S. governs based on emotions. And Russia governs based on fear and financial corruption. Exactly what will Russia be doing during this period of détente you suggest?"

Dunayev sat across from him, sipping his drink, carefully considering his response in the hopes of not antagonizing Wie further. "As soon as our man is in place as Secretary of State, China can move forward with its efforts to rival the U.S. economically. As you pointed out, Americans don't behave patiently. So, if Russia simply wants to rival them politically and militarily, we need to give them a little rope in which to hang themselves. Both of our countries need to let the civil discourse in the U.S. continue to grow, at least in the short term. Let the conservatives and liberals go at each other just a bit longer. As Khrushchev said back in 1956, 'we will take America without firing a shot. …we will destroy you from within.'"

"That is our only objective," Wie replied.

"As is mine," countered Dunayev. "We can then let the U.S. go back to doing the one thing they do best."

"And what is that?" Wie asked.

"Making movies," replied Dunayev, hoping to elicit a smile out of Wie. But Wie didn't smile.

"And the Speaker of the House?" Wie asked, sticking to business.

"Half of America sees her as a despicable nut case. She's coming after the new president for her opposition to dark money and for proposing term limits."

"And the other half of America; how do they see her?"

"Most tolerate her because she's a socialist. She loves giving away other people's money while she lives in luxury. As long as low paid or unemployed Americans receive their checks, they will support her."

"Then let's make sure we are ready to expose the Speaker if she starts screaming impeachment again."

"Not if, Wie; but when."

The two men smiled at each other. Dunayev raised his glass of scotch, and Wie raised his glass of club soda.

"To détente," Wie said.

"To détente," replied Dunayev.

Chapter 15

29 Days Before the Inauguration

The funeral of Patrick Banks took place two days before Christmas. It was held in Old Saybrook, Connecticut, a shoreline community that served as Patrick's summer home when he was a kid. Located on the Connecticut River and the Long Island Sound, Old Saybrook enjoyed the distinction of being the first home to Yale University. Yale subsequently moved to New Haven when it became clear that a major city could not develop at the mouth of the Connecticut River due to constantly shifting sandbars that hindered navigation. Because of these shifting sandbars, the Connecticut River is the only major river in the country without a large city at its mouth.

The service itself was a quiet affair. Banks, dressed in a conservative black dress, carried herself with style and grace into the church. She had restricted the number of people who could attend the service to family and a select few close friends and staff. There was little family available since Patrick and Ann had no children. Patrick's one brother had died several years prior in a car accident and his parents had died years ago. He had few, if any, loved ones in his life. When Ann Banks entered the church, she was both shocked and outraged to see Susan Welsh, the Speaker of the House, sitting in a pew near the altar.

That manipulative bitch will do anything to be in the spotlight, Banks thought.

Banks' request for privacy also went unanswered by the media hounds who insisted on the people's right to know everything there is to know about the life of the incoming president. And after the autopsy report of Patrick's death had been leaked, revealing that he had died from an overdose of contaminated cocaine, there was even more incentive for the news hounds of the major networks to shout an endless array of questions at Ann Banks as she exited the church on Main Street. But Banks wasn't answering any questions. And since she wasn't answering their questions, they resorted to what they so often do best; they made themselves part of the story.

Being the former governor of Connecticut and the president-elect, Banks did enjoy added security. Between the Connecticut State Police and U.S. Secret Service, none of the reporters were able to get close to her. There were several Secret Service Agents and three large State Troopers that protected her while she greeted the few invited worshipers as they exited the church.

"I'm so sorry for your loss," Susan Welsh said to Banks. "As you know, we all respected Patrick. He will be missed in the House."

"It's very kind of you to make this long trip up here for Patrick," Banks replied. "I know you're very busy, especially with the holidays quickly approaching."

"It was no trouble at all," Welsh said, brandishing a phony look of concern. "We all loved Patrick, in spite of our occasional political differences. I do hope the police are able to find out who supplied him with those contaminated drugs. Drugs are such a terrible plague on our society. We should take a look at strengthening the laws surrounding illegal drugs once you're sworn in next month."

"Yes, we should take a look at that; right after we get legislation passed dealing with term limits. Together, we can help put an end to the constant abuse of power demonstrated by career politicians in both the House and the Senate. I hope I can count on your support with that, Madam Speaker."

"Well, there are no guarantees in Washington, madam president-elect. But I do look forward to working with you on a number of issues of mutual interest and concern," Welsh said, smiling so that the media could get her on film for the early edition of the evening news. "Perhaps we can also discuss policy changes related to the Secret Service and its security measures. Nothing can be more important than the safety of the president."

"Who could possibly ask anything more from you, Madam Speaker," Banks replied, her sarcasm clearly noticeable. "Now, if you'll excuse me, I must get back to Hartford. As you might imagine, this has been a difficult day and I have much work to do. Hopefully, there won't be too many more surprises today."

"I understand. Nobody likes surprises. Unfortunately, Washington is usually overrun with them. I pray the rest of your day is quiet and uneventful. I look forward to talking to you later on these and other important issues."

"Well, we both know how politicians love to talk," Banks replied, trying to force a smile. "It's following up on the promises they talk about that career politicians seem to have challenges with. And of course, keeping secrets."

"Sometimes, keeping secrets from the public is the better course of action."

"All the people really want is to be told the truth," Banks insisted.

"Well, Madam President-elect, you'll find that in Washington, the truth is always negotiable."

"I'll certainly keep that in mind, Madam Speaker, Banks replied, as she nodded and raised her eyes. With that, Banks turned, and walked away.

A shiny new Escalade was parked directly in front of the church, while a Secret Service Agent in a dark suit and black overcoat, stood next to the vehicle with his hands clasped in front of him. Another agent, dressed almost identically, stood next to the rear door of the car. As Banks approached the car, the agent opened the door allowing her and Jason Palmer, to get into the back of her bullet proof vehicle. Moments later, they were headed back to the Governor's Mansion. As they pulled away from the church, Banks instructed the Secret Service Agent driving the car to raise the security window, separating him and his partner from being able to hear her conversation with Palmer.

"I can't fucking believe she showed up here un-invited and unannounced," Palmer said. "That woman is beyond redemption."

"Jason, I need to tell you something and I want you to listen very closely," Banks said as she moved closer to Palmer. Whispering, she said, "I'm being blackmailed by Josh Martin."

Palmer was dumbfounded. He had suspected something when Banks named Josh Martin her Chief of Staff the day after Patrick died, but not this. For the next twenty minutes as they rode back to the governor's mansion in Hartford, Banks told Palmer about Martin's relationship with Dunayev, the death of Oleg Lomakina, also known as Robert Moss, and Dunayev's insistence that Martin be named Chief of Staff.

Shaking his head, Palmer asked, "Why didn't you just say no and tell Martin and this Dunayev to fuck off?"

"Because Dunayev has a recording of me and Michael Dionis in bed together," Banks said. And there it was, Ann Banks had just confessed her infidelity to the one person she trusted almost as much as she trusted Michael Dionis.

There was an uncomfortable silence between them. Palmer just stared at Banks for what appeared to be a lifetime. Neither of them were ever at a loss for words. Now, however, instead of political confidants, they were more like two strangers on a train. Disappointment glinted in Palmer's deep blue eyes. Banks stared out the side window unable to look directly at her longtime political partner. "How did this happen?" he asked, finally breaking the silence.

"The sex, or the recording of it?" Banks asked.

"Both. But let's start with the sex first. For how long?"

"On and off for a couple of years. We'd been friends for some time. After I was elected governor, and things went south with Patrick, we renewed that friendship."

"And the recording?"

"That's a bit unclear. I'm not sure if Patrick himself had it done, or Dunayev got to one of the staff. But I know Dunayev has the recording and Josh has heard it. Hell, he might even have a copy for all I know."

"And what exactly do those two want?"

"Josh claims Dunayev is a businessman, which, I know to be utter bullshit. Claims he wants access to me and forced me into naming Josh my Chief of Staff."

"You can't let this all happen."

"I know. And I'm not. But I'm going to need your help."

"Of course. Anything. Just name it."

"I'm going to have to trust someone other than you. But I need to strike back at Josh and this Dunayev quickly."

"Where is Michael Dionis in all of this? I understand they found cocaine in his home."

"How did you hear about that?" Banks asked.

"I got a call earlier this morning from one of my contacts in the Speaker's Office. Apparently, one of her staff got the information from someone in the Secret Service's Headquarters."

"That bitch," Banks said, no longer able to control her anger. "Susan Welch isn't wasting any time."

"No, she isn't," Palmer replied. "You knew she was going to be trouble from the start. You know how she is when she feels threatened or doesn't get her way."

"Oh, I certainly do."

"And what about Patrick dying of cocaine, did you know he was using?" Palmer asked.

"No," Banks replied, no longer able to conceal her frustration. "But then again, we'd been like ships passing in the night for several years. You know, remaining married for political advantage."

"That's very Hillary Clintonian of you," Palmer said.

"What do you want me to say, Jason? Divorcees don't usually get too far politically."

"Maybe," Palmer replied. "But how did staying married to Bill work out for Hillary Clinton?"

Banks was momentarily silent. Palmer looked at her sad face and realized that she looked older and far more tired than he had ever remembered.

"Susan Welsh will release all of the information to the press the minute she has it. We need to start preparing a response," Palmer said.

"Of course."

"And Michael Dionis?"

"He's been lying low for a few days. Maybe too low. His office is looking for him."

"Do you know where he is, Ann?" Palmer was one of the few people who addressed Banks by her first name, and only did so when they were alone.

"Yes, and no. He's close by. My guess, New York, Boston, maybe Vermont. Someplace where he can hide from the press. Michael is very good at this whole cloak and dagger bullshit. He always liked to say that it's easy to hide in plain sight."

"That is probably good for him right now. And maybe good for us too. Just how far are you prepared to go to protect your upcoming presidency?" Palmer asked.

"If I can guess what you're thinking," Banks said, "you can forget it. I will not sacrifice Michael in all of this. He did absolutely nothing wrong. I will not allow him to take the fall for any of this."

"You might not have a choice, Ann."

"Don't you understand? They killed one of their own in New Haven. Dunayev is a murderer. For all I know, he and Josh had Patrick killed. How do you think the cocaine got contaminated? Michael is a dead man if I walk away from them now. The tape ultimately gets released and Michael ends up dead. Have you forgotten how many bullshit murders FOX news tried to connect to the Clintons? Millions of American conspiracy theorists, hell, from all over the world for that matter, will download the recording of the incoming President of the United States having sex with someone on her protective detail. The conspiracy theorists will have a field day with it more than they did trying to associate the Clintons with killing a dozen people who had crossed them. The truth or facts mean nothing to those people. You know that."

Palmer knew that Banks' frustration was reaching a boiling point. And she was right on all accounts. The situation she was in could be politically disastrous. Looking to ease the tension, Palmer lowered his voice and said, "We need to get your new Attorney General briefed in on this, and now. We need serious FBI help. And we're going to need the Director of Homeland Security. Have you thought about who you're going to appoint that position?" Palmer asked.

"Not yet," Banks replied. "I've been a bit preoccupied."

"Well, I'd urge you to think about it fast."

"Get me some names today. But I don't want to bring a cast of thousands in on this just yet. The more people who know, the harder it will be to control. Besides, the new Attorney General doesn't have jurisdiction in this matter, not yet."

"You're right of course. For the sake of discussion, what if…"

Ann Banks raised her hand and cut him off in mid-sentence. "I know exactly what you're thinking. Let me allow that to percolate for a day or so. In the meantime, find me some people with balls who aren't afraid to get their hands dirty. Don't bring me a bunch of thirty somethings who worry more about this whole woke political correctness bullshit or hurting people's feelings. Find me some people that had to actually win at something to get a damn trophy."

Palmer simply nodded. He knew exactly what Banks wanted done. He didn't waste time. He pulled out his cell phone and started making calls.

Ann Banks pulled out her cell phone too. She punched in her personal code and accessed the email account she shared with Michael Dionis. She went straight to her draft folder and backspaced over the last message she left him. In its place she wrote:

We need some help. Who is the one person you can trust outside of the FBI?

Almost instantly, she received a response.

DeCarlo. Connecticut State Police.

Ann instantly responded.

I've met with her. And where are you?

Dionis fired back.

Close. Why?

Banks quickly responded.

You need to come in today. Report back to your agency. But say nothing. You have a leak inside SS. Someone reporting information to the Speaker.

And the recording? Dionis replied back.

Don't think they have that yet. They're keeping that quiet as long as I cooperate with them.

And the media?

They'll be all over it if it's released. Probably later today if I don't cooperate. Deny everything, for now. Then get ready to communicate through Detective DeCarlo after six p.m. today. Got to go now.

Dionis knew that was Ann's way of telling him that she was no longer in a position to communicate with him.

What in the hell is she up to? Dionis thought.

Banks put down her phone, looked at Palmer, and said, "Get me that State Police investigator, Sandi DeCarlo. Have her come to the mansion. I want to see her today, the sooner the better."

Again, Palmer simply nodded.

***

President Robert Boyer had only four weeks left in office. His four years as president were riddled with allegations of misconduct, abuse of power, and incompetence. In other words, a typical presidency, at least in the eyes of the opposing political party and the major news outlets that didn't support his party. What President Boyer had learned, or actually knew but didn't want to admit, was that because the presidency had grown not only in power, but in scope and complexity, it had become too much for one person, and virtually impossible to adequately represent the many competing interests of over 320 million people. And since placating that many people was beyond impossible, the only way to win the support of the masses was to appeal directly to them. Still, he tried to work with both parties. But civility in national politics had lost all meaning. Boyer tried political correctness, in direct contrast to President Trump's approach. And while Trump saw himself as a man of courage and self-reliance, he was a paradox, often being both ruthless and generous. Boyer wanted to instill a degree of "niceness" in his approach to governing and decision making but that, too, was met with political attacks from the opposition, who, like most all political opponents, were afraid of ever giving a political adversary in the White House a victory of any kind.

Boyer also lacked humor. Nor did he possess that bold defiance and spirit that made people want to risk their lives for him. Simply put, Boyer was no one's idea of an action hero. And that contributed to his inability to get much, if any, real legislation passed. It also contributed to the American voters' rejection of his bid for a second term.

Boyer was almost relieved to be leaving an office that was overburdened and unrelenting in its demands. He privately shared many of his thoughts and observations with President-elect Ann Banks when they met for a breakfast meeting shortly after the election.

"I'll share everything with you, Ann, in order to help with the transition. You simply have to tell me what you need," Boyer told her.

Now, Ann Banks was calling in that offer and promise. But first, she wanted to meet with Sandi DeCarlo.

Michael Dionis couldn't get close to Ann Banks at the funeral service for her late husband, Patrick. The Secret Service and Connecticut State Police had the small shoreline town of Old Saybrook sealed off all along Main Street and all the way to the entrance to highway nine that led them back to Hartford. Instead, after returning to Connecticut from NY, he sat in a motel on the Berlin Turnpike in Newington, just outside of Hartford, reading her last message over and over, hoping to find some hidden meaning in it. But there was no hidden meaning. So, he did what Banks had instructed him to do; he telephoned Sandi DeCarlo.

"So, are you back in Connecticut?" DeCarlo asked the moment she picked up the phone.

"You have an uncanny way of knowing it's me when I call," Dionis replied.

"Maybe you need a new burner," DeCarlo said.

"Yes, to both questions," Dionis told her. "I'm in Connecticut and I'll probably get a new burner later today. That is, if the stores haven't sold out of all of them for Christmas."

"Are you ready to meet?" DeCarlo asked.

"Just say where and when."

"What are you doing Christmas Eve?"

"Tomorrow night?" Dionis asked, surprised. "Who works on Christmas Eve when they don't have to?"

"I do. I don't have anything else to do that night. Besides, Ann Banks is worried about you. She wants me to make sure you're safe."

"What could she possibly be so concerned about?" Dionis asked, his sarcasm clearly audible.

"We can talk about that later," DeCarlo replied. "So, tomorrow night then?"

"Why not?"

"Good. I'll text you the time and place. White or Red?"

"What are you talking about?" Dionis asked.

"The wine, dummy, white or red?"

"You pick," Dionis replied.

Dionis disconnected the call. Sixty seconds later, he received a text message from DeCarlo with an address that appeared to be a residence. The text also said to be there at eight p.m. Dionis would drive by the residence later to make sure of the address. *De Carlo can't be having this meeting at her house. WTF is Ann up to?* He thought.

As soon as DeCarlo hung up the phone, she sent a message to Jason Palmer.

Tomorrow night at eight. My house.

The reply came almost instantly.

I'll be there.

Palmer turned and looked at Ann Banks. "He's meeting DeCarlo at her place tomorrow night at eight. I'll see him then."

"Good," Banks replied. "Make sure he understands not to trust anyone. And to deny everything. Tell him that no matter what happens in the short-term, to let the system run its course. Michael will fight you. He's good at what he does. He'll want to kill the people behind all of this. Make sure he understands that anything he does in that regard will make everything worse. You have to make him understand that there is far more to this than him or me simply being blackmailed.

The political forces involved here are far more dangerous than anything he ever encountered in Iraq. Michael will be very frustrated and defiant. It's imperative you make him understand."

"I'll make him understand," Palmer told Banks.

"We'll see. But good luck with that anyway. Just do your best."

The same time that Ann Banks was instructing Jason Palmer on how to deal with Michael Dionis, Andre Dunayev was sending a text message.

I think it's time we got an update on our new president's boyfriend. It would be good to know where he's at. Take care of that and get back to me.

Chapter 16

28 Days Before the Inauguration

Ann Banks had General John Sherry escorted into her office at the governor's mansion in Hartford. Sherry was President Robert Boyer's national security advisor. A retired Marine three-star General, Sherry had been in the intelligence community for years, and was considered one of the country's foremost authorities on intelligence matters. During his tenure as Boyer's national security advisor, Sherry was careful to avoid becoming a highly visible figure. He knew that had he sought a higher level of visibility, he no doubt would have created an environment of competition. Such an environment only resulted in bruised egos, especially among career and appointed bureaucrats, as well as egotistical politicians who would no doubt accuse him of having his own agenda. Sherry strove for political anonymity, which garnered him the respect of politicians on both sides of the aisle; something rarely found in Washington. Now, at the direction of President Boyer, he was meeting the president-elect for the first time; a meeting he knew was eventually coming and had prepared for.

Sherry was surprised that the meeting hadn't taken place earlier. When he was escorted into Banks' study, he was more surprised to see that she was the only one present. He was sure there would have been others in attendance, especially whoever she was considering taking over his job.

"General," Banks said, extending her hand. "Thank you so much for coming up this Christmas eve morning."

"Madam president-elect," replied Sherry, taking Banks' hand.

"Would you like anything? Coffee?"

"Coffee, black, would be most welcome."

"My apologies for taking you away from your family. I promise to have you out of here and on a plane back to D.C. as quickly as possible," Banks said.

"My time is your time, ma'am."

"For the purpose of our meeting here this morning, would you please humor me and dispense with the formalities, General. I'd appreciate it if, while it's just you and I here together today, you call me Ann."

Sherry was momentarily taken aback. In his entire military and government career, he had never encountered any newly elected national political figure who had made such a request.

"That might be a bit difficult for me at this stage," Sherry replied. "Would governor suffice this morning?"

"Well, technically, I'm not the governor right now. But for the sake of this conversation, governor it is. But I'd prefer Ann," she said, smiling. A member of her household staff brought in a silver pot of hot coffee and cups with the state seal of the Connecticut Governor on them. Banks instructed the staff member to simply set the tray on the table. "I'll take it from here, thank you."

Banks poured two cups of coffee. Sherry noticed that she, too, drank hers black.

"So General, can I have your word that everything discussed here stays in this room and between us?"

"Yes ma'am, you have my word."

"As I'm sure you know, my campaign for the presidency was focused far more on domestic issues facing this country than foreign policy issues; something my critics continue to point out whenever, and as often as they can."

"A common issue governor, especially when anyone wins the presidency that has had little to no real experience interacting in foreign affairs. I have found, however, that astute politicians are often quick learners. Bill Clinton learned quickly, as did Barack Obama. They too, were both governors with little to no foreign policy experience when they were sworn in as president."

"I noticed you didn't mention Donald Trump with that group," Banks said.

"Well, Governor, former President Trump, while certainly doing a number of positive things for this country, wasn't what many would refer to as an astute politician."

"Politically well said, General," Banks replied, forcing a slight grin.

"Who knows, had he learned to play the game just a little and not be so self-absorbed, he might have actually gotten re-elected," Sherry said.

General Sherry took a sip of his coffee and added, "Even his most ardent supporters had enough of him. Most agreed he was his own worst enemy."

"And if you had been in a position to advise President Trump, what would you have done?"

"Good politicians, and especially presidents, listen, and make informed decisions based on what they feel is the right thing to do. President Trump didn't listen, he simply made his own decisions. He could not manage expectations."

"Meaning what, General?"

"Everyone has expectations of themselves and others. His opponents expected him to embarrass himself, and he did so, playing right into their hands. If he had only listened and put down that damn phone and ceased his incessant messaging on twitter, he could have managed those expectations. Foreign governments had expectations and he failed them and many of our allies. Pissing off China was no way to get them to maintain trade policies with us; trade that was good for the American people. His chief of staff and Secretary of Defense had expectations to be kept informed, and he failed to manage those expectations. It became difficult for those around him to keep him focused. As I'm sure you're aware, or soon will be, the presidency is too big a job for one person. No sane person can expect one individual to be an expert on everything the president must deal with. That was one of Donald Trump's biggest problems, he thought he was an expert in all things big and small."

"So, in your opinion, Clinton and Obama were good students of foreign policy, while Trump was a failure?"

"That all depends on how you measure success. Clinton and Obama both had wins and losses. I know the military was no fan of Obama. But they were very vocal in their support of him and his policy when he authorized the capture and subsequent killing of Osama Bin Laden, in spite of his vice-president's opposition to it. His biggest military critics praised his decision to go into Pakistan and execute the assault on Bin Laden's compound. But he had many failures as well. Obama will tell you himself that his intervention in Libya was not handled properly. He has said that he did not organize enough support of the international community to help manage the political fallout after Gaddafi was ousted. Obama has gone so far to say that he underestimated our European allies in their willingness to assist in this.

"Trump did stand up to foreign leaders and tried desperately to stem the possibility of committing our troops and this country into a new war by dealing with despots like Kim in North Korea. At the beginning of his presidency, many foreign leaders expressed their fear that Trump would get us into a war with North Korea. Then, he meets with Kim, they shake hands, get to know each other, on some personal level, all in an effort to convince that megalomaniac to stop testing nuclear weapons, which Kim does. Then, these same foreign leaders, as well as his political opponents, attack Trump for giving Kim a forum on the national stage. President Trump made great strides with the North Koreans. In the four years of his presidency, Trump was successful in that he did not get the U.S. engaged in any new foreign wars unlike most of his predecessors the last fifty years. So, how do you measure success you ask? I'm not sure one measurement fits all. My point here, ma'am, is that presidents are not mystical, all-knowing creatures. They are men, and now women, who are human, and make mistakes. All anyone can do, or people should expect, is for a president to listen to the experts on any given subject, digest the information and data offered by opposing views, then make informed decisions that best benefit the people of this nation. When the decision is found to be wrong, take ownership of it. Trump never took ownership for anything that went wrong. Clinton lied to the American people over his tryst with an intern in the Oval Office. Obama sent pallets of money to the Iraqis. Bush One should have been easily re-elected after the overwhelming and quick victory in the first Iraqi war. But he had no idea what the common man was going through and, of course, his 'read my lips, no new taxes,' didn't help his cause. Presidents make bad decisions. But they're human. The trick is keeping the mistakes to a minimum and, certainly, not making the same mistake twice. So, tell me how I can help?"

Banks had sat patiently listening to what General Sherry had to say. Now it was her turn.

"I want to know what country you think is the biggest threat to our nation, and why. And what can we do about it?"

"It's not quite that simple, governor. There are many threats to our nation's security. Korea could pose a nuclear threat to us, especially now that no one is stroking the ego of Kim Jong un like Trump did. Iran is a problem as they move toward having a nuclear capability. Russia and China are huge political and economic adversaries. And, of course, the endless number of terrorist organizations that operate in small cells around the world keep the intelligence community working 24/7. Each of these countries, and terrorist organizations, pose a unique set of problems for us. Are you looking for something particular?"

"It's you who may be the most astute politician in the room," Banks said. "Who would have an interest in seeing me become president, then blackmailing me once I was elected?"

Sherry was silent and just stared at Banks. *Where is she going with this?* he thought. Sherry took a sip of his coffee, laid the cup down and said, "Governor, if that is indeed happening, I may not be the first person you should be talking to. If that's true, perhaps you should have the FBI here."

"I don't want the FBI here just yet, general. Would you please just answer the question."

Without hesitation, Sherry said just one word, "China."

"Tell me about them," Banks instructed.

"If I may be blunt, governor, we are at war with the Chinese Communist Party, commonly referred to as the CCP."

"War?"

"Yes ma'am. The People's Republic of China (PRC) has a population of roughly 1.4 billion. They are governed by the Chinese Communist Party. The CCP has about 90 million members and operates a massive global intelligence network that is overseen by its Ministry of State Security."

"And how does this intelligence network operate?" Banks asked.

"It operates in a number of ways, most often designed to assist Chinese businesses by engaging in industrial espionage, cyber warfare, and economic coercion. Are you aware that the PRC has a military of two million men and currently has the world's largest navy?"

"No, I was not."

"In the last five-years, our naval war game simulations with China have put us on the losing end. Absent our use of nuclear weapons, we would probably lose a naval confrontation with them."

"Do you honestly believe war with China is inevitable?" Banks asked.

"The Chinese do. But for now, they appear to be focusing on economic, political, and biological warfare."

"Can you give me an example?" Banks asked.

"One area of huge concern is Taiwan. They are at the center of chip manufacturing. China and the U.S. are both falling behind Taiwan in that market. These chips, as you know, go into everything from computers to cell phones, to automobiles. More importantly, they go into virtually every type of weaponry employed by our military. By not dominating the chip market, we are at a huge technological disadvantage. China also sees controlling Taiwan as essential to their ambitions to becoming a leader in the field of technology. Some think that if China falls behind in this effort, they might actually get more aggressive with the idea of taking back Taiwan. And if that happens, we could easily end up in a shooting war."

"And the COVID crisis?" Banks asked.

"There are those in the State Department that think the virus was part of a bioweapons program that went awry. That might actually be a stretch since it's hard to prove. Of course, their lack of transparency didn't help their cause. And the fact that the virus took somewhere between 15 – 20 percent of the global Gross Domestic Product, and killed millions of people worldwide, you certainly have to consider it a possibility. Especially since the Chinese population was nowhere near as affected as the rest of the world."

"So, you think China did this on purpose?"

"Personally, no. Again, that would be too difficult to prove. It might have been an accident. But we do know that China has stepped up its bioresearch in an effort to weaponize viruses. Whether they did this intentionally or not, we may never know. What we do know, is that the virus did set in motion a reorientation of American society; one that had grave economic consequences for not only many Americans but for people all over the world; and, of course, grave political consequences for former president Trump."

"How are the Chinese able to get so much inside information on our country's businesses?" Banks asked.

"It's pretty easy actually. The CCP has corrupted many American businesses and financial elites who prefer the economic benefits they can reap by doing business with China. Those businesses see their economic interests as outweighing America's national security interests.

"China also sends over 350,000 students each year to our universities. Every one of those students is required by Chinese law to assist and cooperate with the CCP and their intelligence gathering. This means that all students must, when so instructed, meet with handlers in the Chinese consulates and embassies to report on any research they may be working on and so forth. We believe, based on our best estimates, that Chinese cyber criminals have stolen over $500 billion in intellectual property; much of it coming from Silicon Valley."

"Could the Chinese influence voters through social media?" Banks asked.

"Of course. And so could the Russians. That would be child's play for them," Sherry replied. "Your bigger concern would be what they might do, or might already have the ability to do, with regard to attacking our electrical grid."

"What do you mean?"

"If they, or any terrorist organization, are able to attack and shut down our electrical grid, the country could be thrown back into the dark ages. Nothing would work. No electricity; no gas pumps, no ATM machines; refrigeration units will stop running; hospitals won't be able to monitor patients; air traffic will be shut down. Credit cards won't work, making cash king. Our best estimates are that millions of Americans will die in the first 30 days of such an event. Why do you ask?"

"In a minute, General. Are the Chinese interests aligned with Russia with regard to the U.S.?"

"In some respects, yes. Russia sees China as a business partner. Both countries want to surpass the U.S. on the world stage. But both countries are also cautious and suspicious of each other. Russia wants to be seen, especially by the U.S., as a great power to be reckoned with."

"Would they work together to blackmail the incoming president?" Banks asked.

"I doubt it. Russia isn't looking for that kind of recognition. They might try to influence voters during an election, which has yet to be proven, but conspiring at the highest levels to blackmail an incoming president, very unlikely."

"Individuals, then, of one or both governments?" Banks asked.

"Yes, that is possible. But my guess would be that the CCP would be spearheading such an attack. If the Russians are involved, it's probably without the sanction or even knowledge of Russia's Foreign Intelligence Service, the SVR. However, if the Russian government is involved, they'll exploit any problems that arise between the U.S. and China if it is advantageous for them to do so."

"General, I have something to tell you that simply cannot leave this room," Banks said.

"Madam president-elect," Sherry said, reverting back to a more formal acknowledgement of who he was seated across from, "you have my word. However, I still work for President Boyer. I cannot lie to him."

"I'm not asking you to lie," Banks said. "If he asks specifically, do what you must. In the meantime, let me ask you this: Would you consider staying on as National Security Advisor? I know you're ready for private life and you have certainly earned it. At least consider staying on for a year until I get my sea legs, as they say."

"You put me in a difficult position. I certainly had not expected this. If I agree, at least for the next four weeks, you want me to serve two masters?"

"Yes, General, that's exactly what I'm asking you to do. But know this; both masters have a common goal. I hope you can trust me on that. However, I'd urge you to run it by President Boyer to be sure. Just one year, if you want to leave after that, then go. But right now, your new president needs you."

"President Boyer instructed me to hold nothing back in today's briefing. He also told me to listen closely to what you had to say and to help you in any way I can. So, madam president-elect, it will be my privilege to stay on. Now, please tell me what this is really all about and what you need me to do."

"From this point on, you can start by calling me Ann when it's only you and I in the room. I insist."

"Okay, but please call me John. So, Ann, what's really going on here?"

Ann Banks spent the next thirty minutes giving Sherry as much background information as she could as it related to Dunayev, the death of Oleg Lomakina, the death of her husband, Patrick Banks, and of course, the recording of her and Dionis' night together, which, Martin was using to force her into naming him her Chief of Staff.

"And what of this Secret Service Agent Michael Dionis?" Sherry asked.

"That's a bit complicated, John. I'd ask that you understand it might be best for both of us if you don't know all the details of this relationship. Suffice to say, Dunayev has a recording of the two of us together. For all I know, Josh also has a copy. He certainly has intimate knowledge of what's on it."

"And where is the agent now?"

"In Connecticut is all I know. However, I know where he'll be tonight. Jason Palmer, who will for now, be my assistant chief of staff, and who is coordinating my transition team, is meeting with him and a Connecticut State Police detective, later this evening."

"I'm going to need to talk to Mr. Palmer before he meets with him tonight. I'll have some instructions for him to pass along to your agent."

"Instructions?" Banks' asked.

"Yes, if he wants to survive this."

"You mean they'd kill him?"

"The Russians? Most definitely. But surviving this also means him being set up for the death of your husband. They have the means to do that as well. As I understand it, he's already a person of interest in this matter."

"How can we stop this?" Banks asked.

"There's no question that his life will certainly be in danger if Dunayev gets wind of this, or if we, I mean you, don't in the short-term, do as he wishes. If he's acting alone, that will certainly be to our advantage. But, if the Chinese are involved, your agent's life won't be worth much. The Chinese will kill him and leave enough evidence behind that points to his being involved in Patrick's and Oleg Lomakina's death. And the recording of the two of you will play on every TV station around the world and will appear in print in every newspaper and website there is."

"What do you propose?" Banks asked, praying for a response that would offer her some hope of salvaging the dilemma she had gotten herself into.

"With your permission, Ann, I'd like to contact my sources in both ours and the foreign intelligence community. What I tell them will be minimal, of course. But I need to find out if Dunayev is working alone, with the Russian government, or with the Chinese. It will help us know what we're up against."

"Ah.... the intelligence community," Banks said with a smirk. There are those who would like to see the CIA dismantled. We do, after all, spend billions of dollars a year on intelligence gathering. What do we actually get for it?"

"I'd be lying if I said the CIA hasn't had its share of failures. And there are those in Congress who do think of Langley as a black hole. And yes, there are those in Defense, State, and the CIA who are constantly fighting over resources, trying to increase their budgets, and are afraid of losing their jobs. But the enemy, and I'm not just talking about those countries we talked about earlier, but many of our so-called friends, like Israel, are constantly trying to penetrate and steal much of our proprietary property and our defense technology, by blurring the lines of diplomacy and spying. More often than not, countries like Israel, and they are not alone, will gather intelligence they deem supportive to their own interests, and share that information with our elected officials in order to help kill or pass a piece of legislation. Not all spying deals with stealing state secrets and advances in military technology. Much of it deals with political influence as well. Without a strong intelligence community, the president, very soon to be you ma'am, would have to rely on intelligence gathered by the various cabinets, all of whom have their own interests at heart. The president needs a strong intelligence gathering agency that is not colored by biases. And dealing with human intelligence sources requires special skills and handling."

"I hear what you're saying, John. But the costs seem exceptionally high."

"They can be. For now, I think you may find you need some of those resources."

"Of course. Do what you think is best."

"Thank you, Ann. In the meantime, play nice with Josh Martin. I'll deal with him later."

"And John, you should know that Michael Dionis was a Marine Captain. He served in Iraq. I don't know all the details, but he was some kind of special ops guy."

"Well, if that's the case, we trained him well. Let's hope he retained some of those skills. He may need to use them."

"Jason asked if I was willing to make him a sacrificial lamb in all of this; if Michael went along with it, that is."

"And are you willing to do that?"

"Michael would offer himself up to protect me and the presidency. But I can't allow him to do that, especially not for a murder he didn't commit. If Patrick was indeed murdered. Either way, I won't let that happen. I'll resign the presidency first."

"Then you and I are going to get along just fine," Sherry said, as he did his best to suppress a grin. "And, Ann, one more thing."

"Yes, John."

"Washington is probably the most political town in the world. And most politicians looking to further their careers in Washington have something in their past that they too want to keep quiet. Your secret would certainly cause you some embarrassment and political capital. But rest assured, the issue you want kept quiet pales in comparison to much of what is out there. If you understand anything about Washington, understand that most politicians have secrets, and they are first and foremost concerned about the next election. They'll throw you and their mothers under the bus if they think that will ensure their re-election."

"So, John, am I to assume I'll have no friends in Washington?"

"Well ma'am, as President Truman once said, 'if you want a friend in Washington, get a dog.' And remember, getting into Congress doesn't take any skills. And many of our elected officials without any skills at all, stay in Congress by providing a steady diet of fear."

Ann Banks smiled and nodded. "And just what kind of dog are you, John?"

It was Sherry's turn to smile. He looked into Banks' eyes and said, "I can be as friendly as a Golden Retriever or as deadly as a Doberman, ma'am. It all depends on the adversary. I like to let them decide."

"Good," Banks replied. "I think I'm going to need that Doberman over the next few days and weeks."

"Then Doberman it is," Sherry replied. "It might get a little ugly before it's over."

"I can handle ugly, John. One more thing, I'm just curious; what does General Sherry do in his free time?"

"I have very little, ma'am. But when I do, it's golf or puzzles."

"Puzzles?" Ann asked.

"I like the solitude of it. I can do it alone, exercise my brain, and not put up with other people's bullshit."

Banks smiled and said, "Well, I'll try to keep the level of bullshit in your life to a minimum. As for golf, are you any good?"

"No ma'am, not worth a damn. But if you allow me to do my job, especially with regard to you being blackmailed, you'll see the one thing I am good at."

"Oh, I'm counting on it, John. I'm counting on it."

Chapter 17

Andre Dunayev heard his cell phone ping telling him that he had a text message.

He's meeting with the state police detective later tonight. I'm sure they have some questions they want to clear up with him about the death of Patrick Banks. That's all I know right now.

Dunayev's suspicions were aroused. He'd learned that government bureaucrats, especially investigators, didn't work on Christmas eve unless it was absolutely necessary, such as dealing with a natural disaster or a mass killing. And this didn't meet the threshold. Dunayev took out his cell phone and typed a message.

Send me the cell number for this detective as well as the number Michael Dionis is using.

Dunayev got in his car and made the thirty-minute drive through traffic across Manhattan to meet Ivan, the young man who helped manipulate the various social media outlets that helped convince voters to elect Ann Banks to the presidency. Ivan, whose name in Russian means "a gift from God" had certainly proven to be so, at least as far as Dunayev was concerned. Ivan was expecting Dunayev, who had called earlier telling him that it was imperative they meet. Ivan knew better than to give Dunayev any excuse that he was unavailable. Christmas eve or not, you simply didn't say no to Andre Dunayev.

Dunayev rang the buzzer on the building letting Ivan know he was downstairs. "Come on up," Ivan said.

Ivan had the front door open waiting for Dunayev and greeted him with a soft hug and standard greeting, saying, "Good to see you, my friend."

"And you, my young friend," Dunayev replied.

"What brings you out on Christmas eve, in this freezing weather?" Ivan asked.

“I need your help locating someone. I have two numbers here. I’m confident one is a standard cell number. The other number belongs to a burner phone. Can you help me locate the man using the burner?”

“That shouldn’t be difficult,” Ivan replied. “Do you have the burner number?”

Dunayev gave him the number he’d received. “Can you explain to me how this might work?” Dunayev asked.

“If your man is connecting to a standard cellular network, his location is as traceable as any mobile phone. The trick is to see which network he’s using. But first, let’s see if we can locate where the standard cell phone is right now.”

Dunayev gave him the cell number. “I’m also sure he’s communicated with the person owning the standard cell phone.”

It only took a few minutes, but Ivan was able to hack into DeCarlo’s cell phone account. He quickly saw that the number of the burner cell Dionis was using appeared on the incoming call log the day prior. “Here, look,” Ivan said, pointing to the computer screen. “You can see that the burner phone contacted this cell number yesterday. It also appears here, two days before that.”

“Can you locate where either of the phones are right now?” Dunayev asked.

It took several more minutes before Ivan was able to provide Dunayev with DeCarlo’s home address in Farmington, Connecticut.

So that’s where you two are going to be tonight, he thought.

Dunayev thanked Ivan and wished him a Merry Christmas. As he started to leave, he turned to Ivan and said, “You may now tell your young lady that she can come out of the bedroom. And next time, simply ask her to leave when I show up.”

Ivan simply nodded indicating that he understood.

“And make sure you monitor Michael Dionis’ phone. I want to know where he is at all times.”

"Of course," Ivan replied.

As soon as Dunayev got back inside his car, he called one of his contacts in Connecticut.

"I'm going to text you an address. I simply want to know who comes and goes from the house, the times, and nothing more. Do nothing else to him or anyone else inside the house. Put your two best men on it. The people inside are cops. One's a fed. Do not, under any circumstances, let them discover your presence. Do you understand?"

"I understand," the man replied.

"It's imperative the police do not identify you. Is that clear?"

The man indicated that he understood the order, knowing very well what would happen to him if he did otherwise.

"Good," Dunayev continued. "Do you have an available tracking device?"

"Of course," the man replied.

"I'm going to send you a picture of the man who should be arriving there around eight tonight. Have your men place the tracking device on his vehicle. Can you do that?"

"Of course."

"Good. Call me the minute you have something worth reporting. If I don't hear from you, I'll assume the two parties are still inside and that nothing else has occurred."

The man told Dunayev once again that he understood. He would handle this assignment himself, along with one of his most trusted men.

***

Christmas eve and Christmas day are usually slow news cycle days, unless of course, there is a major disaster somewhere. Barring that, the major networks and twenty-four-hour cable networks usually bring in the B and sometimes even the C teams to anchor the reporting desks to report what little news there is. Even the most hardened political news junkies looking for a fix to support their own political views, often take 24 – 36 hours off from TV news over Christmas eve and day. And it was, in fact, a very slow news day. But there was one piece of political news that cable networks had received, quietly given to them by one of Speaker Susan Welsh's staffers. The leaked story was big enough that several of the networks scrambled to bring in their A teams. CNN was first to report it at seven p.m. Christmas eve.

"CNN has learned this afternoon that Patrick Banks, the late husband of President-elect Ann Banks, died from an overdose of cocaine that had been contaminated with a very dangerous form of fentanyl. Our sources have confirmed that the autopsy conducted on Patrick Banks revealed this information. How Patrick Banks got the contaminated drugs is unknown. Nor do we know how long former Congressman Banks might have been using cocaine. Congressional colleagues have expressed their concern that Patrick Banks, who sat on the foreign intelligence committee, may have been compromised in some fashion. For more on this, let's go to the nation's capital where the Speaker of the House, Susan Welsh, is standing by. Madam Speaker, thank you for taking the time out of your busy schedule this Christmas Eve to join us."

"Thank you, Wolf, for having me. I'm sorry that this information is being discussed on Christmas Eve. As you know, I'm remaining in D.C. over the holidays to help get the continuing resolution passed. The last thing people need at this time of the year is for its government to shut down."

"Madam Speaker, tell us, this news about Congressman Banks' death, how did you learn about it?"

"From the news media. One of my staffers was notified a couple of hours ago that you folks had uncovered this information. Of course, when I first heard it, I thought for sure the information couldn't be true."

"CNN has obtained a copy of the autopsy report and the medical examiner's findings into the cause of the death. Does that cause you concern, Madam Speaker?"

"Right now, I'm concerned about providing the incoming president some privacy to deal with her husband's death. We're all saddened by it. As for whatever Patrick may or may not have been involved in with regard to using illegal drugs, that is something for the incoming president to deal with. As for whether or not it compromised his work on the intelligence committee in the House in any way, well that's something we'll deal with after the holidays, and, of course, after we get the continuing resolution passed. I know the president-elect would appreciate all of us giving her the time necessary to grieve the loss of her husband. And I want her to know that, while we may not agree on many issues, this Christmas, she and her family are in our prayers."

"That's very compassionate of you Madam Speaker. I'm sure President-elect Banks appreciates your kind words and show of support during this difficult time."

"Let me just say, Wolf, that we're all reminded, especially during this time of the year, that many families have members that suffer from any number of addictions. No family is immune to this type of suffering. I would urge all families who suspect that a loved one who might be experiencing any sort of addiction to get them the help they so desperately need."

"Words well spoken, Madam Speaker. From everyone here at CNN, we wish you a very Happy Holiday."

"Thank you, Wolf, and Happy Holiday to you and your family."

Susan Welsh took off her microphone and handed it to the CNN intern standing next to the cameraman. Without so much as a word expressing any appreciation for her help or a quick holiday greeting, the aging Speaker, exhibiting a "fuck you grin," simply turned and walked back to her office. Once inside, she turned to her junior staffer, who had lost any and all hope of getting home early for a quiet Christmas eve dinner with her boyfriend, and said, “Pour me a drink.” Minutes later, Minority Leader Jonathan Prince appeared in her office.

“Got one of those for me?” he asked.

“You know where it is. Pour it yourself,” Welsh said.

Prince did just that. And he wasn’t shy about pouring himself a double shot of Oban 18.

“You may go,” Welsh said to her young staffer, dismissing her like someone telling a dog that was underfoot to go. “But make sure you can get back here quickly if I need you.”

“Of course, Madam Speaker,” was the staffer’s only response.

“And close the door behind you.”

“You’re in a fine mood this Christmas eve,” Prince said as he sat cross-legged on the sofa across from the Speaker’s desk.

“I’m in a very good mood. Did you catch my appearance on CNN?” Welsh asked, as she rummaged through some papers on her desk.

“I did indeed,” Prince boasted.

“You think that bitch got my message?”

“I can’t imagine it being lost on her,” Prince remarked, smiling, as if congratulating the Speaker on her performance.

“That medical examiner’s report was quite helpful, Jonathan. Any chance it gets traced back to you?” Welsh probed.

“Absolutely none. We have plenty of friends in Connecticut. Not all of them are supporters of Ann Banks.”

“Good,” Welsh said. “Let’s make sure that bitch knows what’s waiting for her when she’s sworn in.”

“No grace period, I take it,” Prince inquired.

“The usual 100 days, maybe. No need to piss the masses off right out of the gate. She shouldn’t have any trouble doing that on her own. Then, we’ll get into the fray,” Welsh fumed. “I think I’ll get the hell out of here for a couple of days.”

“And the continuing resolution that’s set to expire four days after Christmas?” Prince asked.

“Fuck it; let it expire. Let that be part of Boyer’s legacy. He was a weak asshole. It’s no wonder the people voted him out of office.”

With that, Welsh told Ward to drink up; she was going home.

Chapter 18

An early winter night had descended on Farmington, Connecticut. The outside of DeCarlo's home would have been cloaked in darkness had it not been for the handful of her neighbors' homes that were decorated with a variety of colored lights in celebration of the Christmas season, and the light snow that had started falling. The two men ordered to watch her home parked two houses down the street at precisely seven-twenty p.m. They'd brought plenty of hot coffee but had not had time to get food, as most places had closed early for Christmas eve. They sat quietly in their plain dark van, watching the snow fall in front of DeCarlo's home, and waiting for Dionis to arrive.

Jason Palmer arrived at seven-thirty p.m., as he had been instructed to do by General Sherry. He parked across the street from DeCarlo's ranch home, only one of the two single story homes that existed in the neighborhood. All of the other homes were the two-story colonial type most commonly found in Connecticut where the rooms are usually compact, serving individual purposes, like a formal dining room that people might use twice a year. DeCarlo preferred a more open concept that the single-story home provided, because, without a family and kids to take care of, the smaller ranch style fit her better.

"That has to be him," the man sitting behind the steering wheel in the van said just as Palmer pulled up. The man in the passenger seat, using a pair of Bosch and Lomb binoculars, replied, "That doesn't look at all like the man in this picture."

"I wonder who the fuck this guy is then," the first man replied.

The man in the passenger seat immediately telephoned Dunayev.

"You have news?" Dunayev asked.

"I'm at the cop's home now. Another man just arrived. I don't think he's the man you're looking for."

"So, you decided to do this yourself," Dunayev said.

"I did," the man replied.

"That is good, my friend. Did you get a picture of this man?" Dunayev asked.

"It wasn't possible. We're too far away and it's snowing up here. But I got a good look at him, and it's not the man in the picture you sent."

"Okay," Dunayev replied, his voice clearly revealing his frustration. "Get the tag number. But when the other man arrives, the one in the photo, place the tracking device on his car."

"Of course," the man replied.

Dunayev hung up the phone without saying another word. His mind started to wonder. *Who in the hell is this guy and what is Dionis up too?* He thought.

DeCarlo was expecting Jason Palmer to arrive before Dionis, so it wasn't a surprise when her doorbell rang.

"You're right on time," DeCarlo said as she opened the front door to her home. "Come in, it's freezing outside."

"Thank you," Palmer replied. "Hell of a way for us to spend Christmas eve."

"I've had worse. Can I get you something to drink?"

"Coffee would be nice."

"Want anything stronger?" DeCarlo asked.

"Well, since you're offering."

"Wine, bourbon, beer?"

"Whatever you're having," Palmer replied.

DeCarlo poured them both a glass of Pinot and told Palmer to make himself comfortable.

Not looking to waste time with small talk, DeCarlos said, "Michael should be here soon. So, tell me, what is the governor's plan?"

Palmer thanked her for the wine and DeCarlo pointed to the sofa, letting Palmer know to take a seat.

"That's a good question," Palmer replied as he sat down. "I know she's concerned about his safety. Exactly what her overall plan is, I think she's still working through the details."

"That sounds a bit disconcerting," DeCarlo replied.

"We've only had one real conversation about this," Palmer said. "She knows he's being set up for Patrick's death."

"And do you believe that Agent Dionis had something to do with Patrick's death?" DeCarlo asked.

"No, I don't. But then again, I don't know Michael Dionis."

"Fair enough. But you know about his relationship with the governor?"

DeCarlo knew about Dionis' and Ann Banks' relationship. Her question was designed to elicit additional information. And there was no way to know what information Palmer had that she didn't.

"She told me. She's concerned, of course, about the recording of the two of them."

"And you didn't know, being her chief of staff and all?"

"No idea at all. That would not be something, as I'm sure you might understand, that she would share with me or anyone else."

"I can certainly understand that," DeCarlo said.

"Their relationship is of concern to me as well. As you well know, a lover's triangle is not an uncommon motive for murder," Palmer said.

"I do know. But in this case, killing the husband of the president-elect? Doesn't make sense. He would have nothing to gain from it."

"Maybe he would. Wait a year or eighteen months, give the president time to mourn, and allow her to engage in a new relationship.

The media would eat it up. There wouldn't be anything else on any of the news outlets," Palmer said.

"That's assuming he was actually involved in Patrick's death. Plus, Ann Banks would certainly have her suspicions."

"About what?" Palmer asked.

"About who really was involved in her husband's death. The coke that killed him was cut with a very powerful and deadly drug."

"So, I've been led to believe."

DeCarlo said, "That's absolutely true. A form of fentanyl that is extremely deadly."

"But how would Patrick Banks get that coke? And how would Michael Dionis be able to spike it with fentanyl?" Palmer asked.

"Good questions. Maybe you're in the wrong business. Ever think of a career in law enforcement?"

"No. Politics is dirty enough. I deal with enough hostile and self-absorbed people in my business. I don't need any more in my life," Palmer said as he took a sip of his wine.

"Well, the money certainly has to be better in your line of work."

"Don't be so surprised," Palmer replied. "The hours are longer than any cops I know. The constant travel. And living in D.C. isn't cheap. Besides, everything can't simply be about money."

"Then why do you do it?" DeCarlo asked.

"Part of it is the rush. You're close to the power. But most importantly, some of us actually think we can help make a difference. Isn't that why so many of you get into your line of work?"

"At first, yes. But we quickly realize that the world can be a very cruel and cynical place."

"And why is that?" Palmer asked.

"Most cops come from middle-class families. Most have never seen a dead body, never dealt with life-threatening injuries, or seen a family disturbance that resulted in a woman or a child being severely beaten or killed. Basically, they've never seen man's inhumanity to man. It's all new to them."

"I can only imagine. I can probably count on one hand the number of politicians in D.C. who have witnessed these things firsthand. You should try working among the egotistical politicians there."

"Now who's sounding cynical?"

"I'm just saying. In D.C., it's all about power politics. One upmanship. When was the last time you saw the opposing parties do much of anything together that was in the best interests of the country?"

"I try not to spend much time following what politicians in D.C. are doing or not doing. I have enough to deal with here in Connecticut with our own head-up-their-ass politicians."

"What have you got against them?" Palmer asked.

"Absolutely nothing, until of course, they pass legislation like the Police Accountability Act that makes our job even more difficult than it already is."

"What have you got against police being held accountable for their actions?" Palmer asked.

"Not a thing. But when they pass legislation as part of a knee jerk reaction in order to appease a part of society that falsely believes cops are racists, then I have a real problem. This new legislation allows the state to revoke our certification if they, whoever they are now, believe we've engaged in discriminatory conduct. Sure, there should be repercussions, if that is proven, but to revoke your certification which, in essence, ends your career."

"Sounds a little harsh I guess."

"Harsh… It's draconian to say the least. The worst part of this legislation is that it changes the language of our qualified immunity. This new legislation makes it very easy for anyone to file lawsuits against us. I'm not sure why anyone would want to enter this profession today."

"What can you do about it?"

"Virtually nothing. It was passed before Banks was elected governor. Being an independent, she didn't have the juice to get it changed. Plus, I'm sure she had bigger fish to fry."

"She is a strong proponent of law enforcement."

"I know. But I'm sure she is going to have far more important things to attend to once she is sworn in as president."

"Why do you think your legislature passed this bill?"

"To appease a minority portion of the public that believes too many police officers willfully violate people's civil rights."

"And do they?"

"It happens. But it's rare. The media would like you to believe it's commonplace. But it isn't. Cops are not out to kill anyone. We're not out to violate people's rights. We see the dregs of society and the harm they cause every day. Do some cops cross a line, absolutely. But we've gone a bit too far with all of this politically correct woke bullshit."

"I'm afraid political correctness has reared its ugly head into every aspect of our lives," Palmer said.

"It's why so many cops today are looking to bail out of the job or ride out their time looking forward only to retirement and a pension."

"Sounds like a sad way to live."

"It does on some levels. Cops have to look for ways to survive the constant changes imposed on them by the ever-changing political landscape. They learn who they can trust and not trust. Most of us have few friends outside the job and the legal system."

"Sounds like cops take things personally more than they should."

"It all becomes personal. It's the nature of the job. We have to be careful with every encounter we have, especially with criminals.

Everyone out there today has a camera shoved up their ass and they don't hesitate to video you when you're fighting for your life."

"So, it sounds like law enforcement and the political arena in D.C. have more in common than most people know."

"Probably so. So, tell me, how does anything ever get done in Washington?"

"Slowly for sure. But with lots of patience, conniving, and, of course, compromise," Palmer said smiling.

Both DeCarlo and Palmer smiled, raised their glasses, and took a good sip of wine. Jason looked at his watch and saw that it was almost eight-ten. "I thought Dionis was supposed to be here at eight," he said.

"He's probably running a bit late. I'm sure the roads aren't great with the snow coming down. So, tell me, Jason, the recording of Michael and Ann; have you heard it?"

"I haven't. And neither has Ann."

"Then how does she know that it really exists?"

"She's convinced of it. Patrick's Chief of Staff, Josh Martin, told her exactly what was on it. She knows that the only way Martin would know that is if he'd actually heard it."

"Does the governor have any idea as to how her room got bugged?"

"She suspects someone on her staff that is no longer there placed it in the bedroom. Or, that Patrick himself did it. What did she tell you when you two spoke?"

"Enough to convince me that Michael had nothing to do with Patrick's death. So, you think Martin has a copy of the recording?" DeCarlo asked.

"I can only assume that to be the case. He's in bed with some very bad people. Josh is using that information to blackmail her."

"How so?"

"Josh is claiming that Dunayev will release the recording of her and Dionis if she doesn't give him access to her. He also wanted to hand pick her Secretary of State if you can believe that."

"The guy certainly has some balls," DeCarlo remarked.

"She put a stop to that immediately. But she was forced to name Martin her chief of staff, at least for the time being."

"A strategy to buy herself some time. Smart," DeCarlo said.

"Yes, to buy some time. Her concern is for Michael's safety and, of course, to keep the recording, if it actually exists, from being released."

"And to keep Michael Dionis from taking the fall for Patrick Banks' death," DeCarlo said.

"It would appear so."

"Appear? You still have your doubts?"

"Not really. But my job is to protect the president-elect. And my job here tonight is to meet Michael Dionis and convey a message and instructions to him. That's my area of responsibility. As to who might be responsible for Patrick Banks death, I'll leave that to you. Any idea where he may have gotten his contaminated drugs?"

"So far, we haven't a clue," DeCarlo replied. "Can you share the message and instructions with me?"

"Ann instructed me to fully cooperate with you and leave nothing out tonight as it pertains to keeping Michael safe. So yes, I can."

"And that message is?"

"Ann is aware of the fact that Josh is working with a member of Russia's organized crime to force her into having him named her Chief of Staff and god knows what else. She is also confident that it was the Russians who had her home, in this case, her bedroom, bugged. And, she is painfully aware that her husband was killed by consuming contaminated cocaine. She knows that there are forces, again, this Russian, that are creating a scenario where Dionis will be implicated in Patrick Banks' murder if she doesn't comply with their demands. And, if she doesn't comply, the recording of her tryst with Dionis, again, if it exists, will be made public. Have I left out anything, and have I provided you enough information that you can now trust me, and Ann Banks?"

DeCarlo was silent for a moment. She wanted to be careful with her response. She raised her glass and took a long sip of wine thinking to herself.

This guy might be smarter than he looks.

DeCarlo looked at Palmer, drew a deep breath and said, "You're doing great. And the message to Dionis?"

"The message is simple; she wants him to return to his home and office. Keep quiet about everything that doesn't pertain to his job. Do not talk to the press. Don't talk to the FBI or his senior management in D.C. Someone from the Bureau and/or the Secret Service is leaking information to the Speaker of the House. With Ann's promise to the American people to get term limits passed, the Speaker and her cohorts are already digging in and gunning for her. And, if and when he needs to communicate with her, to do so through you and me."

"Why me?" DeCarlo probed, as she kept her eyes fixed on Palmer.

"After your meeting with Ann, she had you checked out."

"By whom?" DeCarlo grumbled.

"Me," Palmer conceded as he offered a slight smile.

"You? Why?" DeCarlo demanded.

"She felt she could trust you. And she needs to trust somebody outside her inner circle," Palmer explained.

"Well then, I better not let her down."

Palmer was sure that DeCarlo's reaction was all that he could hope for. "I doubt you will, detective," he replied, as his small smile spread ear to ear and he raised his glass of wine yet again. "There's one more thing; and this is most important."

"And what is that?"

"Dionis is going to be contacted by General John Sherry, the National Security Advisor."

"The National Security Advisor? What for?"

"Right now, I really don't know all the details. But as soon as we see Dionis, I have a Sat phone for him. General Sherry thinks he might be in more danger than any of us realize. So, it's imperative we hear from him soon."

DeCarlo knew better than to ask any more questions about General Sherry. She knew little about him and less as to what he might want to tell Michael. *Sometimes knowing less is better,* she thought.

It was now eight-forty p.m. Palmer looked at DeCarlo and asked, "So what do you think is holding up Michael now?"

"I don't know. He assured me he'd be here at eight sharp."

"Do you know how to contact him?"

"He's using burner phones. He said he'd contact me. But I can certainly try the last number he called from." DeCarlo took out her cell phone and dialed the last number she had spoken to Michael on when he called her. After seven rings, DeCarlo hung up. "He's not answering," she told Palmer. It took her a moment to gain her composure. When she did, she looked at Palmer and said, "I'm starting to worry. I don't know Michael very well at all, but this isn't him."

"Something is certainly a little off here," Palmer said.

"Yes, it is."

Michael Dionis was less than a block away from DeCarlo's home. He had been parked down the street almost an hour before he was scheduled to meet with her. As a Secret Service Agent, and former Marine, Dionis had spent most of his life looking for danger before it found him. That instinct had never left him, and he was sure it never would. Dionis watched when Jason Palmer entered DeCarlo's home. He had met Palmer once, just briefly. He didn't know much about him other than Ann Banks had always trusted him. He had been shocked when the news reported that Josh Martin would be Ann's new Chief of Staff and that Palmer would be his assistant. That announcement by Ann Banks was a clear signal to him that something in Ann's life was severely out of place.

Dionis then saw a man get out of a van and walk up to Palmer's car, which was parked across the street from DeCarlo's home. The man appeared to take a photo of the car and tag number with his cell phone. The snow was continuing to fall a bit heavier now, and Dionis knew the roads would soon be difficult to drive on. But the snow was a welcome shield for him to keep from being discovered. He got the tag number of the van and waited, watching as the two men inside the van continued to focus their attention on the entrance to DeCarlo's home.

At ten p.m., Palmer said, "It's getting late. I'm going to go. You have my cell number if he ever arrives, or you hear from him."

Palmer stood up, and DeCarlo followed suit. "I have no idea what might have happened," DeCarlo said. "If I hear from him, you'll certainly hear from me."

Palmer thanked DeCarlo for the wine and hospitality. "Try to enjoy whatever is left of this Christmas eve," he told her. Palmer left the Sat phone with DeCarlo and drove back to the governor's mansion.

The two men parked in the van watched as Palmer walked out of DeCarlo's home, got into his car, and drove away.

"What shall we do now?" the driver of the van asked.

"Exactly as we were instructed; wait for the other man to arrive and place this tracking device on his car. Nothing has changed," said the man in the passenger seat.

Michael Dionis watched Palmer pull away, thinking the men in the van might follow him. But they didn't. At ten-fifteen p.m. Dionis took out his new burner phone and called the Farmington Police. He gave them a fake name, of course, and used an address two doors down from DeCarlo's.

"Sorry to bother you tonight, but there are two guys sitting in a dark van across the street from me. They've been there for almost two hours. It's very suspicious and it's bothering my sister and her kids. Is it possible you might send a car to check it out?"

Four minutes later, a police car with one man inside arrived. The officer immediately saw the van that had been reported parked in front of the home across from DeCarlo's. With the snow falling heavier now, the officer only noticed one man in the van. Before exiting the cruiser, the young officer radioed his dispatcher informing her that he was out with the van, providing the color, make and model of the vehicle, as well as the tag number. From several houses down the street, Dionis could see the man in the passenger seat quietly exit the van and walk to the side of it, outside the approaching officer's view. As the officer approached the driver, the man who had exited the van came around the back of the vehicle and fired one shot into the back of the officer. It all happened within seconds. Dionis had virtually no time to react.

The officer was on the ground. Dionis could see the man from the van raising his weapon to fire again. Dionis hit the horn and turned on the lights to the car. All of it was just enough to startle the shooter. Dionis floored the gas pedal of his car, racing less than a hundred feet towards the man when the shooter raised his gun and fired into the windshield of his car.

Dionis swerved his car sideways, providing himself some cover from the gunman. Three more shots rang out, hitting the passenger side of Dionis' car. The man in the driver's seat of the van slid across the front seats and exited through the passenger front door. He positioned himself behind the hood of the van and fired two more shots at Dionis. Dionis was pinned down. He fired two rapid shots at the first shooter and one at the man behind the hood of the van. The first shot found its target and the man who had shot the officer was down but not out of the fight.

DeCarlo, who immediately recognized the sound of gunfire, went to her front window, and could see Dionis pinned behind the driver's side door of his car and firing at a van. She grabbed her off-duty Glock 9 mm from the table and ran outside her front door, not bothering to find her shoes. Barefoot, DeCarlo was able to maneuver herself behind a large oak tree. The snow had helped lighten the area up just enough that DeCarlo could see the man behind the hood of the van, but barely.

Dionis hadn't noticed DeCarlo come out of her house; he was busy with the shooter behind the hood of the van. The other man, hit once in the shoulder by Dionis' first shot, had crawled behind the rear of the van, taking cover. Two more shots rang out. Dionis could see the man behind the hood of the van rising up to shoot. The man's shots were wild. He was now simply shooting indiscriminately in Dionis' direction. DeCarlo could see the man rise up, fire, and lower himself down. Holding her weapon with two hands, her arms locked straight in front of her, she took careful aim at the shooter. The next time the man rose, DeCarlo fired a single shot in his direction. In an instant, the man's head exploded against the windshield, spewing parts of his brain onto the hood of the van. Dionis heard the shot behind him, turned and saw DeCarlo standing behind a tree. Dionis locked eyes on her, held up one finger and pointed to the rear of the van. DeCarlo knew that the message meant there was one other shooter. She looked at Dionis, waved her left arm signaling him to maneuver around his vehicle to the right. She would work her way around the front of the van. Dionis nodded that he understood.

The two moved in unison, their weapons held in two hands as they had been trained to do to the point where it was instinctive. But they weren't on the range where the targets didn't fire back. This was real, and at least one man was already dead. Dionis had been shot at before, but that was in Iraq. This was different. There wasn't a squad of trained men with him, along with enough firepower and support, to overwhelm the enemy. But his training and instincts kicked in telling him to move forward and advance. And so, he did. And so did Sandi DeCarlo.

Dionis moved slowly, taking cover behind another car as he inched closer to finding the second man behind the van. The remaining shooter fired two more shots, this time, in DeCarlo's direction.

Dionis turned back around and looked for DeCarlo. But he had lost eye contact with her.

"Fuck."

Dionis quickly ran toward the back of the van firing three shots directly at the shooter. Two shots found their target. The man was down but still breathing.

Dionis kicked the gun away and noticed that the man was losing a lot of blood, and quickly. He wouldn't live long.

"Who are you?" Dionis screamed. "Who sent you?"

There was no response. "I'm not calling the paramedics for you, mother fucker, until you tell me who you are and who sent you," Dionis screamed.

"*Trakhat' tebya*," the man uttered quietly.

"What did you say?"

"Fuck you." Those were the last words the man spoke.

Dionis looked up and yelled, "Sandi, where are you? Sandi, are you okay?"

There was no response. Again, he yelled, "Sandi, talk to me. Where are you?"

"Michael…. " DeCarlo cried.

Dionis followed her voice and found DeCarlo several feet away lying in the snow next to a large bush. A bullet had found its way into the upper left side of DeCarlo's chest. Dionis placed his hand over the wound to stop the bleeding.

"Stay with me. I need you to press here as hard as you can," Dionis told her as he placed her hand over the puncture wound. Dionis could also hear another cry for help; it was the officer shot in the back. The bulletproof vest he was wearing prevented the bullet from entering his body. He was alive but in shock and a lot of pain. Dionis ran to him, knelt down, and said, "stay calm. You're going to be okay. Help is on the way."

Dionis grabbed the officer's portable radio, pressed the receiver, and yelled, "Two officers down. Send rescue, code 3."

"Who is this," replied the dispatcher.

"Michael Dionis, United States Secret Service. I have two officers down and need emergency medical assistance now. I also have two suspects down, both dead. Hurry," he said as he gave the dispatcher DeCarlo's home address.

Dionis returned to DeCarlo and noticed she was starting to fade. "Don't you dare die on me. Don't you dare," he yelled.

Help began to arrive two minutes later. The first officer on the scene went immediately to her colleague on the ground. Eight minutes later, the first emergency rescue unit arrived. As soon as the paramedics arrived, they took over, working to stabilize DeCarlo. Just minutes later, there were six more police cars on the scene and two more emergency rescue units.

In all of the confusion, Dionis walked over to the dead shooter who had told him to go fuck himself before dying and searched his pockets. But there was nothing, no wallet, no identification of any kind. Before he could check the clothes of the other shooter, a police lieutenant escorted him outside the area of the crime scene.

"You need to come over here, Agent Dionis." the lieutenant told him. "This is a crime scene now."

Dionis did as he was instructed. He knew all eyes were focused on him. He also knew that it was only a matter of time before the FBI and Secret Service arrived.

"I think I need some medical attention," he told the lieutenant. Dionis didn't require medical attention, he simply wanted away from the scene and time to avoid questioning.

"I would think so," the Lt. replied.

The lieutenant sent over a paramedic who checked Dionis out for any apparent wounds. Finding none, or any other life-threatening injuries, he walked Dionis to the back of an emergency rescue van. Minutes later, he was headed to the hospital.

DeCarlo was whisked away from the scene with two paramedics attending to her as they raced to the hospital. The young officer shot in the back was regaining some composure as he, too, was taken away to a hospital. In less than an hour into Christmas, the entire middle and western teams of the Connecticut State Police major crime squads had descended on the scene. An hour after that, the scene was crowded with cops, bosses, and crime scene investigators. The entire block was lit up like a night shoot on a Hollywood backlot. Flood lights lit up the night sky. Blue and red flashing lights from emergency vehicles flashed up and down the street. Yellow police tape was hung around an expanded area, well beyond where the two vehicles shot up during the exchange of gunfire still sat with holes in their sides, and where the window of Dionis' car had been shot out. It would be almost nine-thirty Christmas morning before the first FBI agent arrived on the scene.

Michael Dionis laid on a bed at the University of Connecticut John Dempsey Hospital in Farmington, just a few miles from where he had escaped with his life after an exchange of gunfire with two men. He had been brought there after emergency medical personnel thought he might be in shock. A nurse had inserted an IV into Dionis' left arm with a fluid to combat dehydration. He could hear the people talking in low voices just outside his room. Dionis could also hear the crackle of the hospital PA system calling out the names of doctors and nurses, while the smell of antiseptic and bleach from the hospital cleaning crew mixed with the smell of cheap perfume from other patients. The smell of burnt coffee also permeated through the air.

Doctors were observing Dionis while running several tests on him, mostly standard procedure after an officer involved shooting. He was giving a very brief statement of the incident to one of the members of the major crime squad when he asked about DeCarlo.

"She's upstairs in emergency surgery," the detective replied. "I don't have any information as to her condition, not just now."

Dionis needed time to gather his thoughts and consider his next move. He asked for a short break telling the detective that he was experiencing a severe headache and starting to feel nauseous. The detective had no choice but to honor Dionis' request for a psychological break, to which all officers involved in a shooting are entitled. Dionis, of course, did not have a headache; what he had, was a big problem. And he didn't like big problems. He assessed his situation and knew what was coming: questions that he dreaded, and questions knew he couldn't answer, not now anyway.

Dionis also knew that the longer he remained in the hospital, the more danger he was in. Someone had told the Russians of his meeting with DeCarlo. The only people who knew of the meeting were DeCarlo herself; his best friend, Tony Maffuci, and Ann Banks. Since DeCarlo was in surgery, possibly fighting for her life after having helped save his, that left Tony Maffuci and Ann Banks as the two people who could have betrayed him. He also realized that Ann Banks had apparently told her recently demoted chief of staff, Jason Palmer, of the meeting. *Why else would he have been at DeCarlo's that evening*? he thought. He realized that his immediate need was to find a way out of the hospital.

Dionis had little time to spare. It wouldn't be long before he'd be taken into protective custody, or even arrested. He removed the IV from his arm, got up from the hospital bed in the emergency room, walked quietly down the hall and out the exit, as if he had simply been an early morning visitor. Dionis waved a cab, got in and told the driver to take him to Bradley Airport. At the airport, he flagged down an Enterprise car rental van. At the rental counter, he handed the agent behind the desk his fake ID and credit card. Moments after renting a car under the alias Sean Cameron, Dionis was driving across Interstate 84 on his way to New York.

Chapter 19

27 Days Before the Inauguration

On Christmas morning, all the morning news shows in Connecticut all led with the shootout involving state trooper Sandi DeCarlo.

“Last night, in Farmington, Connecticut, just after ten p.m., Sergeant Sandi DeCarlo, a detective with the Connecticut State Police’s major crime squad, was wounded in what appears to be a major shootout with two men directly in front of her home. As you heard here just days ago, Detective DeCarlo is the lead investigator looking into the death of former Congressman Patrick Banks. For more on this story, let’s go to Tami Roche on the scene in Farmington. Good morning, Tami, and happy holiday to you. What can you tell us?”

“Well, it was anything but a happy holiday for the people on this quiet street in Farmington last night. Shortly after ten p.m., gunfire erupted on the street resulting in the death of two men whose identities have yet to be revealed to us. It has also led to one officer of the Farmington Police Department being shot; his condition seems to be stable. However, as you mentioned, Detective Sandi DeCarlo, who lives in this house behind me, is undergoing surgery at this hour at the University of Connecticut’s John Dempsey Hospital. Her condition at this time is unknown.

“Also involved in the shooting last night, was Secret Service Agent Michael Dionis. We have little information as to what Agent Dionis was doing there last night. This is the same Michael Dionis, a U.S. Secret Service Agent, that allegedly had a verbal altercation with the late Congressman Patrick Banks, just a few nights ago. We do know that he was also taken to John Dempsey Hospital. But we have no further information as to his status.

“As you can see, there is a large contingency of police officers here on the scene. We have not been told much more than this and

are awaiting a news briefing from the Commissioner of the State Police. As soon as that happens, we'll know more. For now, this is Tami Roche, live for WFSB Channel 3 news in Hartford."

Outside of the governor's mansion, it was a media circus. There were news vans from all the local television stations. It would only be a matter of time before the cable networks arrived. Ann Banks watched in silence from inside the mansion. She turned off the TV, looked directly at Jason Palmer and said, "What the hell happened?"

"I have no idea. As I told you last night, I waited two hours, he never showed. DeCarlo tried contacting him, but he never picked up. She suspected he may have blown her off for some reason."

Banks shouted, "But he didn't blow her off. He was there when the shooting started. He had no reason to not make the meeting," her voice making it clear she was angry.

"I wouldn't be so quick to suggest he didn't have any reason," Palmer replied.

"What are you implying?" Banks demanded.

"We have no idea what Dionis is going through or what may have caused him to not take the meeting last night. He knows he's a person of interest in Patrick's death, and you told him the Russians are involved in blackmailing you. He's smart enough to connect the dots, Ann. He knows he's in danger. All I'm suggesting is that maybe, just maybe, he's more cautious than any of us might appreciate. Or, he's working his own angle on all of this."

"You're right; Michael is cautious. But it's something else. But what? And why haven't the police contacted you yet?"

"I don't know. My guess: Detective DeCarlo hasn't told them about my having been there."

"Why wouldn't she do that?" Banks asked.

"Well, she is in surgery. They probably haven't had time to question her yet. And, my guess; she trusts you and is trying to protect both you and Michael. Either way, we sure as hell better find out where Michael is, and fast. Do you have any way of contacting him?"

"As a matter of fact, I do," Banks said. "In the meantime, you better start preparing something in case the police do want to question you."

"I'm already on it," Palmer replied.

***

Andre Dunayev sat in his apartment in New York, sipping his morning coffee while watching a national news story of the shootout that Ann Banks had just watched. He was even more infuriated by the story than she was.

You incompetent, stupid mother fuckers. What have you done? Be glad the police killed you last night, for had you lived, you would have begged for a quick death.

The moment the story ended, Dunayev stood up and started pacing in his living room. He'd only taken a few steps when his cell phone rang. It was not a call he could avoid.

"Of course. I understand. I'll take care of it," Dunayev said. Then the line went dead.

Like Michael Dionis, Dunayev was a man with his own set of big problems. But unlike Dionis, Dunayev had no reservations about eliminating the people who created such problems for him.

Dunayev picked up his cell phone and sent a text message to Josh Martin.

We need to meet today.

Moments later, Dunayev's phone pinged.

Can't. Heading to Hartford in the wake of the shooting.

Dunayev's response was only three words.

Ensure no connection.

Dunayev sat back down in his leather chair and realized what he had to do next.

***

Shortly before noon, Dionis found himself just outside Scranton, Pennsylvania. He'd had enough for one day. Tired and depressed, he checked into a small hotel telling the desk clerk that he had decided to surprise his family for Christmas. The clerk could have cared less why Dionis was checking in; she didn't want to be there on Christmas and wanted only to get back to her cell phone so she could continue texting her friends, watching TikTok videos that made little sense, and complaining about having to work.

The minute Dionis entered his room, he turned on the television, looking for any news of the shooting the night before. Of course, the media was reporting the shocking events with plenty of dramatic visuals, and just enough sensationalism to prey on people's insatiable appetite for violence, and of course, to achieve higher ratings. But Dionis looked beyond that. As soon as he heard the reporter say that DeCarlo was out of surgery and expected to make a full recovery, he turned off the TV.

What Dionis was most concerned about, was the news about his having been involved in the shooting. *Fuck me*, he thought. He then checked the email draft folder he shared with Banks and was surprised to see a message.

Need to know where you are. Can send help.

Dionis was sure he could trust her. He simply wasn't sure if he could trust those around her. He laid his head on the pillow telling himself he'd respond to her later. His immediate need was to hide until he could figure out exactly what in the hell to do next. Exhausted, he closed his eyes and fell immediately to sleep, having no idea what his next move was.

Chapter 20

Tony Maffuci arrived at the site of the shooting just after 10 a.m. Christmas morning. The scene was still lit up as the State Police crime scene investigators searched every part of the van, along with the car that belonged to Michael Dionis. The bodies of the two men that Dionis and DeCarlo shot and killed had already been removed and sent to the Medical Examiner's Office. Leah Riggs, the SAC of the FBI Office in New Haven, had learned of the shooting by Acting United States Attorney Tina Crawford, who had been awakened by the Commissioner of the Connecticut State Police. Riggs woke up two duty agents and sent them to Farmington with instructions to assist in any way possible.

"If any of this comes back to the president-elect, we're taking the case over," she told both agents. "Until then, observe and assist. But call me immediately if anything, and I mean anything, points to any involvement whatsoever with Ann Banks."

It was only after watching the morning news and hearing of the shooting involving Sandi DeCarlo, that Tony Maffuci took it upon himself to drive to Farmington. Maffuci knew that Dionis had been involved in the shooting and wanted desperately to talk to his friend before the state police investigators did. He had to get to him first. Maffuci drove from his home in Hamden, up Interstate 91, as fast as the newly plowed roads would allow. The moment he arrived, he stepped out of his car and displayed his badge and credentials to the officer charged with making sure no unauthorized person entered the taped area of the crime scene. The officer gave a quick cursory glance at Maffuci's federal identification and asked if he was looking for the other FBI agents who had arrived earlier.

"I am, yes," Maffuci told the officer, trying to conceal his surprise that two agents from his office were already there.

The officer recorded Maffuci's name on the log that listed the identity of everyone, no matter what rank or position they held, when they stepped inside the cordoned crime scene. The officer then pointed to his right and Maffuci immediately recognized the two agents from his office in New Haven.

"What brings you here?" the first agent asked.

"You know me, nothing better to do on a cold, wintery, Christmas morning than hang around the scene of a shooting," Maffuci said sarcastically.

"You're good friends with Michael Dionis, the Secret Service RAC, aren't you?" the second agent asked.

"I am. Is he around here?" Maffuci asked.

"Taken to the hospital several hours ago," the first agent replied.

"You know which one?"

"John Dempsey, just up the road."

"Thanks. I think I'll head over there to check on him," Maffuci said to the agents.

"Don't rush; he's gone," said one of the agents.

"Gone? What do you mean gone?"

"Snuck out of the ER sometime early this morning," was all the agent said. "We're just hearing this ourselves."

"Who is in charge here?" Maffuci asked.

"Over there," the agent said, pointing his finger at Lieutenant Mark Rice.

Maffuci nodded, turned, and walked the twenty feet separating him and the man in charge. He introduced himself to Connecticut State Police Lieutenant Mark Rice, the commander of the Central District Major Crime Squad.

"Sorry to have to meet like this on Christmas morning," Maffuci said, extending his hand to Rice.

"Never a good time to meet when it involves one of your own being shot. How can I help you?" Rice asked, his voice letting Maffuci know that he was in no mood for idle chat, or to spend much time briefing the FBI this morning.

"I can certainly understand," Maffuci replied. "I know Sandi rather well. We've worked together. Can you tell me how she's doing?"

"She's out of surgery and in recovery. Doctors removed the slug. She lost a lot of blood but she's very lucky; the bullet didn't hit any vital organs. She's expected to make a full recovery. That's all I know right now."

"And the Secret Service Agent that was with her last night?" Maffuci asked.

"Supposedly saved her life. Still gathering information on that."

"Have you spoken to him?"

"Was planning to, but he checked, or snuck himself out of the hospital a few hours ago. I have no idea where he is."

"Checked himself out? How?"

"Apparently just walked out of the place while one of our troopers was on a bathroom break."

"Must have been a long bathroom break. Did the security cameras pick up anything when he left?"

"Our people are checking CCTV footage now. Hope to know more later. You know this Dionis guy?"

"A little," Maffuci replied.

"Any idea why he'd leave like that?"

"No idea. But the Bureau might be able to help you find him."

"That's the kind of help we could use right now," Rice said. "I hear he's been suspended?"

"On administrative duty. An internal matter. Nothing of any consequence, I can assure you. You know how bureaucratic agencies can be with their bullshit."

"That is certainly one thing we do have in common with you feds, bureaucratic bullshit. Connecticut seems to thrive on it."

"Try working for the feds. I promise you, it's much worse. Give me your cell number," Maffuci said. "I'll call you if we learn anything. Michael is a good man. If he left the hospital, my guess, he's onto something."

"This isn't a damn James Bond movie," Rice said, his voice clearly letting Maffuci know he was more than just a little irritated. "We have two dead Russians here and a shot-up trooper. Tell your friend we need to have a long talk, and now."

"Well, Lieutenant, it certainly sounds like a James Bond movie to me," Maffuci said with a smirk on his face. "But I'll do what I can to find Special Agent Dionis. The Bureau would like to talk to him too."

The head of the search team, along with Kimiko Matsui, walked up to the two men. "Lieutenant, can I talk to you for a moment?" the search leader asked.

"I was just leaving," Maffuci said to Rice. "I'll let you know if I find anything."

The two men shook hands again, and Maffuci got into his car, and drove to the hospital. He'd check on DeCarlo's condition, talk briefly with the state police investigators there, and learn whatever he could. He had no illusions of being able to talk to DeCarlo, at least not just yet.

***

"What is it?" Rice asked.

"My team has been going over the van. There wasn't much inside. No registration, or any other type of paperwork. However, we did find a Spytec GPS. It was still in the box."

"Interesting to say the least. But how does that help us right now?" Rice asked.

"That's for you and your detectives to find out. But we also found two packets of what I believe is cocaine. I'm having it sent right now to the lab for testing."

"It's Christmas. There isn't going to be anyone there today."

"Oh yes there is," Matsui interjected. "I've already contacted the Commissioner. He's waking people up. I hope to have an answer early this afternoon."

"Why the rush on this coke?" Rice asked.

"I'm sure it's coke," Matsui said. "I want to see if it's contaminated."

"You think this is connected to the death of Patrick Banks?"

"Again, Lieutenant, I'll leave that to you and your detectives. Have your men run the VIN on the van yet?" Matsui asked.

"Yes. Stolen of course."

"My people and yours are finishing up here. Loan me a trooper to maintain chain of custody and we'll take these packets of powder to the lab and wait for the test results. You'll be the first to know."

Rice grabbed a young, uniformed trooper and did as Matsui instructed. He thanked her and watched as she drove away. He had always liked her style and decisive manner. He also wondered, to himself of course, what she might look like in something other than medical scrubs, or in crime scene coveralls. What he really imagined, but could never dare share with anyone, was what she looked like naked. But in this insane politically correct magical world, full of people easily offended by most anything, Mark Rice was afraid to ask her out. One minor misinterpretation of his interest in her would no doubt end in some draconian form of discipline, up to and including dismissal. For now, he'd have to be content with hiding his thoughts in his own reverie.

***

An hour later, when Maffuci left the hospital and got into his car, he pulled out his burner cell phone and sent a text message.

Cop out of surgery. Expected to live. MD left hospital early this morning. No idea where he went. Police looking for him. No further details.

***

It was about two p.m. when Leah Riggs and Tina Crawford arrived at the hospital to meet with Sandi DeCarlo. Lieutenant Mark Rice greeted them outside DeCarlo's recovery room. Neither Riggs, nor Crawford had ever met Rice before. After brief introductions, Rice asked, "So, what brings the U.S. Attorney and the head of the FBI here on Christmas day? You guys don't normally respond to officer-involved shootings."

"We do when it involves a Secret Service Agent," Crawford replied sarcastically. "Is your detective available to answer a few questions?"

"She's awake and in recovery," Rice replied. "But we haven't interviewed her ourselves yet. Can it wait?"

"I'm afraid not," Riggs replied, trying to de-escalate the tension she sensed was developing between Crawford and Lieutenant Rice. "The FBI is looking for Michael Dionis. We're hoping Detective DeCarlo can help us find him. We just want to ask a few questions, not conduct a debriefing of the shooting last night."

"And just where is your Secret Service Agent?" Rice asked. "He snuck out of here early this morning. What's he running from?"

"We're trying to discover that ourselves," Riggs replied.

"I'll ask her," Rice said. Rice told the two women to wait outside the room while he went in to talk to DeCarlo.

Several minutes later, he opened the door and motioned for them both to come in. "She's asked me to stay with her while you're here. I hope that won't be a problem."

“No problem at all,” Riggs replied.

DeCarlo was lying in her hospital bed, IV bags hanging from two separate stands were connected to both of her arms. Lying next to her was an emergency remote call panel about twice the size of a television remote control. Riggs stepped in close, grabbed the cold metal bed rail, and said, “Dumb question, but how are you feeling?”

Still groggy from the surgery and the meds, DeCarlo whispered, “I have a deep burning pain in my left chest and shoulder. Other than that, tired, but fine.”

“Hell of a way to spend Christmas.”

“Is it Christmas? The days seem to run together these days.”

“We don’t want to keep you,” Crawford interjected. “Can you tell us about the shooting last night? Any idea why those two guys were outside your house? And more specifically, why was Michael Dionis there when it happened?”

DeCarlo immediately realized that the inquiry was more about Dionis and less about the shoot-out. He had warned her of his ex-wife’s antagonistic feelings directed toward him. She didn’t know why, but she didn’t trust the prosecutor to have Michael’s best interests at heart. DeCarlo could also sense treachery and it was plainly evident in Crawford’s tone and line of questioning. She wanted to believe her suspicions were all in her head. But she couldn’t shake the feeling.

“I have no idea why the two men were outside my home last night,” DeCarlo replied. “Michael was going to come by and discuss the murder of Oleg Lomakina and the death of Patrick Banks. I was curious if there might be a connection.”

“And you two were going to do this on Christmas Eve?” Crawford asked.

DeCarlo chose not to respond to Crawford’s remark. Instead, she said, “Michael was late showing up. The next thing I know, I hear gunshots outside my home. I looked outside and could see a police officer on the ground and Michael firing back at a van.”

"And you went outside to help?" she asked.

"I did. Next thing I remember, Michael is standing over me trying to stop the bleeding in my chest. After that, nothing. Not until a couple of hours ago when I woke up in this room."

"Any idea who those men were?" Riggs asked.

"No idea," DeCarlo replied.

"Any idea, detective, why they were there?"

"None. If they were staking out my house, then Michael may have saved my life."

"I hear it was the other way around," Crawford replied. "I hear Michael may have placed you in danger and that you actually saved his life."

"That's not the way it happened. I was there, you weren't."

"What does that mean?" Crawford asked.

"It means, I have no idea."

"No idea of what?"

"They were either after him, or me, I don't know."

"And Michael stumbled upon them?"

"Maybe."

"And you believe in coincidence, detective?"

"No. But either way, I'm glad he was there."

"We could really use your help detective. But we just keep getting these short answers."

DeCarlo asked, "Where is Michael now?" Have you tried asking him those questions?"

"We're trying to find that out," Riggs said in a calm voice. "Any idea why he would have left the hospital this morning before your colleagues could talk to him?"

"I had no idea he was here, much less why he left," DeCarlo replied. "Sorry, but I can't help you there."

"Is there anything you can think of that might help us locate him? Where might he have gone? Where might he go to feel safe?" Crawford asked as she leaned forward, eyeing DeCarlo shrewdly.

"You would know better than I would," DeCarlo replied, clearly letting Crawford know that she, too, could be irreverent and cold. The difference being, DeCarlo had to do it deliberately. For Tina Crawford, it seemed to come naturally.

"Can we finish this later?" DeCarlo asked. "I'm getting tired."

"Of course, detective," Riggs replied. "Please get better quickly. If there is anything we can do for you, please simply ask."

Tina Crawford and Leah Riggs said their goodbyes to DeCarlo and Lieutenant Rice and walked out of the room. The moment they were gone, Rice looked at DeCarlo and said, "Detective, you didn't tell them everything you know, did you?"

"Why would I tell them anything of substance before I even told you?" DeCarlo replied.

"Because if you did, I'd have your ass hung out to dry," Rice said with a large grin on his face.

"You know, lieutenant, that's a very politically incorrect remark you just made," DeCarlo said, as she tried to smile.

"I'd deny it," Rice said. "I'd say you were imagining it and misunderstood me and blame it on the quasi-delirious state you're in as a result of the medication you're on."

Just then, Rice's cell phone rang. It was Kimiko Matsui telling him that her suspicions were correct; the powder was in fact cocaine.

"Thanks for the quick response," Rice said.

"There's more," Matsui added.

"I'm listening."

"The coke was contaminated with carfentanil, a highly toxic substance. It's the same stuff that was found in the coke that resulted in Patrick Banks' death. DeCarlo is going to want to hear this."

"She's right here," Rice said as he handed the phone to DeCarlo.

"Are you sure it's the same stuff?" DeCarlo asked.

"All I can tell you is, the coke we recovered from the van outside your house is, in fact, contaminated with the same type of fentanyl that killed Patrick Banks. Any other connection will require you and your people to piece together," Kimiko said.

"Thanks, Kimiko. We'll talk soon," DeCarlo said as she passed the phone back to Rice.

"Tell me what you're thinking, detective?" Rice asked.

"Right now, I'm thinking about how you're going to help me get out of this hospital," DeCarlo replied.

"I don't think that's a good idea, detective. If I do that, they'll have my ass hung out to dry."

"Lieutenant, with all due respect, I didn't ask you if that was a good idea or not; I asked how you were going to help me get out of this hospital," DeCarlo said. "The two guys outside my home last night are connected with Patrick Banks' death."

"There's more," Rice said. "They found a GPS magnetic tracker in the van. The tracker was still in the box."

"They were looking to track Michael's car. That's what they were there for," DeCarlo said. "They're after him. They want to silence him."

"Why?" Rice demanded to know.

DeCarlo was not ready to share what Ann Banks had told her, nor the fact that Jason Palmer had been to her house earlier that evening hoping to talk to Michael. Ann Banks had shared certain intimate information with her that DeCarlo had promised not to reveal until the president-elect had okayed it. DeCarlo was still in a position to keep that information confidential. But her promise was contingent upon protecting the personal safety of those involved. Once that line was crossed, DeCarlo would let Banks know so she could prepare for the onslaught of media coverage that was sure to follow.

"I don't know why, not just yet," DeCarlo lied. "But I need to find out. I have to get out of here and contact Michael Dionis."

"No promises, detective. First, let me see what they say about your condition. I'll see what I can do after that," Rice said. "But first, you're not telling me everything."

"What do you mean?" DeCarlo replied.

"You want to tell me about the other car in your driveway last night? And the man who was driving it?"

"Car? Man? What are you talking about?"

"The man that left your house shortly before the gunfire started. The one we found recorded on your Ring doorbell."

DeCarlo was speechless, but just for a moment. "Can we talk about him later lieutenant? I'd like to keep him out of it for personal reasons. I can assure you, he had nothing to do with what happened."

"You're hiding something, detective," Rice said. "I don't like being kept in the dark."

"Have you ever been involved with someone whose identity you'd like kept a secret?" DeCarlo asked.

"Okay. For now, we'll table this. But we may have to circle back to this later."

"Still using that ridiculous 'circle back' comment, I see."

"Ridiculous as it is, we're going to have this conversation later."

"I understand. Now please lieutenant, get me out of here."

As they walked toward the front door to exit the hospital, Leah Riggs turned to Tina Crawford and said, "Do you hate your ex that much or are you always such an asshole?"

"Excuse me?" Crawford replied.

"You heard me. I don't give a damn if you're the Acting U.S. Attorney or not. Or, if you get the full appointment you think you're entitled to, don't ever let your personal feelings get in the way of an investigation. Not with me."

"How dare you talk to me that way," Crawford replied, her face clearly revealing her indignation.

"How dare YOU? I'm trying to discover what the hell is going on here. You take your shit up with your ex on your own time. As far as I'm concerned, a Secret Service Agent, one of our brothers, is being set up for a crime he didn't commit. And I'm going to use the full force of the Bureau in Connecticut to help this guy in any way we can."

"The decision to prosecute cases is mine, not yours."

"And the decision to investigate is mine. The Bureau investigates; you prosecute. Right now, I don't give a shit whether you prosecute or not. And when I want to play good cop, bad cop with someone, I'll bring along a trained investigator, not a lawyer whose main priority is promoting her own political agenda and screwing over her ex-husband."

"You don't know him. He cuts corners. Doesn't play by the rules. He can be an asshole."

"I don't care. Neither you, nor I, have the time and manpower to deal with every asshole out there. Hell, if that were the case, we'd be doing nothing but investigating each other. I'm only concerned with whether or not he committed a federal offense. And I sure as hell don't think he's done that. He saved that detective's life in there. That has to count for something, even to you."

"I can see they can take the girl out of the hood, but they can't take the hood out of the girl," Crawford said.

Leah Riggs stepped into Crawford's personal space and said, "Counselor, you wouldn't last a day in the hood. I'm not sure you could even find the hood anywhere in this state, even if they dropped you in the middle of fucking Bridgeport."

Riggs turned and walked away from Crawford as quickly as she could. *Fucking bitch,* she thought.

Chapter 21

It was just after two p.m. on Christmas day when Josh Martin arrived at the governor's mansion in Connecticut. Waiting for him in Ann Banks' study, was Jason Palmer and General John Sherry. Ann Banks had done everything possible to create an atmosphere that would put Martin in as much of a relaxed mood as possible, including starting a fire in the fireplace.

"Josh, thanks for coming up so quickly," Banks said. "Sorry we have to do this on Christmas day."

"Not a problem ma'am."

"I've asked Jason to join us."

"Of course." Martin nodded at Palmer, but the two men made no effort to shake hands.

"And do you know General John Sherry, the National Security Advisor?"

"We met once, albeit briefly. I'm sure the General doesn't remember," Martin replied.

Martin walked over to Sherry and the two men shook hands.

"So, what brings out President Boyer's National Security Advisor on Christmas morning?" Martin asked.

"The General has agreed to remain in that position, for at least a year, as we transition into the White House," Banks said.

"An excellent idea," Martin replied. "But you didn't call this meeting just to tell me that."

"No, I did not. We need your help," Banks said.

"Of course. Anything. What can I do?"

"General," Banks said, glancing over her shoulder giving Sherry the signal to take over the meeting.

"Josh, as you know, there was quite the shootout last night in Farmington, not far from here. Two men were killed and a young state trooper, a woman looking into Patrick's death was wounded and is currently in the hospital."

"Yes, I heard," Martin said, as his face twisted into a confused glare.

Without beating around the bush, Sherry asked, "Can you tell us anything about that, specifically, about the two men who were killed?"

Martin was caught off guard by both the question and the tone. He threw Sherry a curt look and said, "General, how would I know anything about that?" his voice clearly revealed his irritation with the question.

"I'm only asking if you know. I'm not accusing you of anything."

"It certainly appears that way."

"Not at all. However, we believe that Michael Dionis was involved in the shooting last night." Of course, Sherry and Ann Banks knew very well that Michael Dionis was involved in the deaths of the two men in Farmington.

"What makes you say that?" Martin asked.

"Detective DeCarlo let the governor know that Dionis was meeting with her last night. We also know that the two dead men involved in last night's shooting are Russian. The police are still trying to confirm it, but they highly suspect that both men have ties to Russian organized crime."

"And what makes the police think that?" Martin asked.

"Cops are just guessing right now, but the tattoos on both men suggest Russian organized crime affiliation," Sherry replied.

"Okay. But how does this involve me, you, and the president-elect?"

"As far as we know, the only people who knew Michael was meeting with DeCarlo last night were me, Jason Palmer, and Ms. Banks."

"And why you, General; if I may ask?"

"The president-elect thinks that Michael Dionis is being set up for the death of her late husband, Patrick. No one wants to see that happen. I had hoped to talk to Agent Dionis myself; see what, if any, involvement he might actually have had in Patrick's death, as I'm not as convinced of his involvement or lack thereof, for that matter, as some are."

"I understand," Martin said. "So how can I help?"

I'll bet you do understand, she thought.

"I understand a Russian by the name of Andre Dunayev was trying to gain access to the president-elect through her late husband, Patrick. And, that Dunayev may have somehow compromised her, and you. I'm hoping you can help me find him."

Martin was shocked by the question. He couldn't believe that Banks had briefed Sherry on his relationship with Dunayev. He glanced briefly at Banks then turned to Sherry and said, "Sir, I don't know what the president-elect has told you. What I've shared with her, is that her late husband was in bed with a Russian by the name of Andre Dunayev. Dunayev had compromised Patrick, and, in the process me, to a degree. What I know about him is that he's a businessman, no doubt corrupt, as he's motivated by power and money, but mostly money. He also wanted Patrick to be president; short of that, in Ann's cabinet. Wishful thinking on his part of course. But from what I could see, Dunayev hoped to use whatever political influence he might gain from Patrick to his business advantage. Anything else he may be involved in is unknown to me."

"Do you think you can help us find him? We think he's responsible for Patrick's death and is involved in the shooting last night."

Sherry could see that Martin looked uncomfortable. He was also curious as to how he would answer the question.

"I'll do what I can, but Dunayev usually finds me," Josh said. "He uses a variety of burner phones. He's very cautious and overly suspicious. But he does contact me every few days. As I told Ann, excuse me, the president-elect, Dunayev is very manipulative. He doesn't take no for an answer. He's motivated by the business of making money. But murder? I have no information that he's involved in anything like this."

"Nonetheless, we want to find him. We think he's put Michael Dionis in extreme danger. Ms. Banks is quite concerned for his safety. Once his safety is ensured, we can get on with the orderly transition of power."

"What would you like me to do?" Martin asked.

"I have a phone for you. It has but one number in it: mine. I'd like you to contact me the minute Dunayev contacts you. Turn the phone on and place it next to your cell phone. I'll be able to record the call. And I want you to set up a meeting with Dunayev. Then let me know when and where that meeting is going to take place. Can you do that?"

"You're asking me to engage in domestic spying," Martin said.

"Domestic spying? That might be a bit of a stretch. No, Josh, what I'm asking you, as the Chief of Staff to the president-elect, is to help us find Andre Dunayev," General Sherry replied.

"I understand. But it still hinges on domestic spying. You're asking me to put my own safety and freedom at risk."

"I suppose I am," Sherry said. "Can we count on you?"

"I'll certainly let you know the minute Dunayev contacts me. You can count on me for that."

"Good," Sherry replied, straining to keep his temper under control.

Sherry stood, grabbed his briefcase, reached inside, and removed a cell phone. He handed it to Martin and said, "remember, there is only one number on this cell phone: mine. Use it to call me and no one else. Is that clear?"

Martin nodded that he understood.

"Good." Shifting his focus to Ann Banks, Sherry said, "Now, madam president-elect, if there's nothing else, there is a plane waiting for me. I can be back in D.C. in 90 minutes if that's alright with you."

"By all means, General."

General Sherry showed himself out, leaving only Ann Banks, Josh Martin, and Jason Palmer in the study.

The moment Sherry left the mansion, Banks' cell phone rang.

"Excuse me gentlemen, I need to answer this," Ann said as she turned her back on both Palmer and Martin. Ten seconds later she placed the phone face down on her desk. "Now, where were we?"

The dissension started immediately.

"What are you doing bringing Sherry into this?" Martin screamed at Banks. "Dunayev will retaliate in every way possible. We agreed you'd let me handle him."

Banks was seething. She pounded her fist down on her desk and yelled, "Watch your tone with me. I told you I'd think about it. Now, two Russians tried to kill a state trooper, and Michael. What the hell is going on?" she demanded to know.

Martin shook his head. "I have no idea. Whatever Dunayev may or may not have done, I am not privy to it. I haven't heard from him in several days," he said angrily.

"Well, you better damn well find out," Ann commanded. "This stops now. Do you understand me?" The anger on her face said it all.

"I understand. But you must understand, he'll destroy us all," Martin said.

"The hell with him and the tape," Banks shouted. "Yes, Jason knows about the tape," she added, shifting her eyes toward Jason Palmer.

"If the recording goes public, it will only give your adversaries more ammunition to destroy your presidency before it even gets started," Martin explained.

"The president-elect will not be blackmailed into covering up anything, Josh, especially murder," Palmer finally said, joining the conversation.

"Neither of you seem to fully grasp what Dunayev is capable of. If either of you think for one minute that I had anything to do with this, or even knew about it, you're both wrong. Even Dunayev wouldn't do this; this is not his style."

"I don't believe you for one minute, Josh. But for the sake of this conversation, let's assume you're right. Who would do this?" Palmer asked heatedly.

"That's the real question here. I have no idea," Martin replied. "But let me do what I can to find out. If not Dunayev, and I don't believe it is, then someone else has factored into your affairs; someone far more dangerous than Andre Dunayev."

Ann gave him a suspicious look and said, "Then get on it. And bring me something I can use to defuse this. Do you think you can do that, Josh?" Banks demanded to know.

"Of course," he replied. Martin had thought about telling Banks to calm down but thought better of it, especially in front of Jason Palmer.

"Good. I've taken the liberty of getting you a room at the Hilton Hotel in downtown Hartford. Meet me back here at eight tomorrow morning. We have work to do," Banks said with clear irritation in her voice.

Josh Martin told Ann Banks that he'd do whatever he could to learn who was behind the attack on Michael Dionis and Sandi

DeCarlo. He also told her and Palmer to prepare themselves for the release of the recording of Ann and Michael's intimacy. There was a brief silence in the room while Martin and Banks stared at each other.

Martin was the first to break the silence. He looked directly at Ann Banks and said, "If Dunayev believes things are deteriorating too much, he'll cut his losses and move on, but not before releasing the tape and causing as much political damage as possible. He'll want to send a message and releasing the tape will do that."

"Then we all better prepare ourselves," Banks said, her voice now much calmer.

Martin nodded and started to leave but turned back and looked at Banks. "The man can be dangerous. I really don't think either of you fully appreciate how dangerous he can be, to all of us." Martin then turned and walked out of the room and out of the governor's mansion. The moment he left the mansion, Banks turned off the recording function of her cell phone.

"Did you get it?" Palmer asked.

Walking over and standing next to the fireplace, Banks said, "I did. It worked exactly like General Sherry had predicted."

Martin got into his rental car and drove to the Hilton Hotel on Trumbull Street in downtown Hartford. He self-parked, went to the front desk and collected his digital room key. He took the elevator up to the fourth floor, walked to his room and held up the digital key to the keypad and unlocked the door. He entered the room, turned on the light, threw his overnight bag on the chair, removed his coat and suit jacket, and threw himself on the bed. Seconds later, he picked up the house phone from the nightstand, hit zero for the front desk and told the clerk to send up a bottle of 12-year-old scotch and a bucket of ice as quickly as possible.

Four floors above Martin, General John Sherry and three of his closest and most trusted people sat in a suite on the top floor of the hotel.

"We have good video and audio," Aaliyah Minor said, as she adjusted the monitor she had set up on the table in the living room of the suite. Minor was a 28-year-old computer whiz who had still yet to discover what she couldn't do or who she couldn't hack with her laptop. She had known since she was sixteen what she wanted to do with computers, immediately after reading *The Girl with the Dragon Tattoo* by Stieg Larsson. She could have made a fortune selling her skills to various criminal organizations but opted instead to work for the government and, specifically, for General Sherry. It didn't hurt that Minor was the daughter of Sherry's late sister who had alienated most members of their extended family by entering into a bi-racial marriage; something that had absolutely no impact on the General. When his sister passed away, Sherry took Minor under his wing. As soon as she graduated from MIT, she was quietly whisked away to work for her uncle and the intelligence community. Now, Minor risked her career and possible freedom if she were ever caught participating in Sherry's off-the-book secret operation.

Sherry poured himself a cup of coffee, loosened his tie, sat down, crossed his legs, let out a sigh of relief and asked his niece, "And the phones?"

"Getting locks on the cell phone now," Minor replied.

"Good. I want everything said and done in that room recorded," Sherry added.

The other two men in the room were pulled from the Special Activities Division (SAD) of the CIA. Both men had been members of the special operations units; one a former Navy Seal, the other, a member of the Marine Force Recon. While SAD members typically carry out covert operations, such as kidnapping, hostage rescue, and counter terrorism on foreign soil, Sherry, who knew the two men well, had personally recruited them. He also knew that each man would fall on his own sword for him. Neither man revealed a hint of concern or hesitation when Sherry briefed them and asked them to participate in this operation, an operation on American soil and in violation of federal law. Both men had killed enemies of their government and neither of them, nor Sherry himself, was hesitant to do so again, if necessary, American soil or not.

"I want the two of you to get in position outside. If our target leaves, follow him. I want to know where he goes, who he sees, everything this asshole does, I want to know," Sherry told the two operatives. "I want a picture of everyone he meets. Send it here the second you have it. Are there any questions?"

Neither man had a question. They'd done this countless times and knew exactly what was expected of them. "Good," Sherry said. "Dig in. It could be a long night."

Josh Martin had sent Dunayev a text using his burner phone. As the minutes slid by, Martin laid on his bed in his room sipping his scotch, waiting for Dunayev' response. He would, of course, ask Dunayev about last night's shooting. Deep down, Martin knew Dunayev was somehow involved. He also knew he'd never get a straight answer from him. Whatever Dunayev had ordered done, it was poorly planned and incompetently executed. *Why would he do this? This goes against all our plans. There was nothing to be gained from this. Maybe Dunayev isn't behind this. If not, then who?* he thought.

Martin also knew that people like Dunayev, and himself, didn't survive in either the level of crime Dunayev was engaged in, or in national politics, by accepting common reasoning. You survived by planning for contingencies, because, after all, things always went wrong. And something had gone terribly wrong last night. And now, he had to wait for Dunayev's response. Martin poured himself another glass of scotch hoping it would help him sleep. It didn't. He began to realize the inevitable and the inevitable didn't look good for him at the moment. He could try telling Ann Banks the truth but rejected it out of hand as it was not an option, at least not yet. The truth was, he had gotten greedy and power hungry. But he had never signed on to murder. The truth also included his firm belief that Andre Dunayev had Patrick killed and would kill him if things didn't go his way. Martin laid there, thinking about his own contingency plan. It would prove to be the end of his political association with anyone in Washington, but it might just save his life, and allow him to flee the country, if there was enough money involved.

Maybe it's time to call Susan Welsh, the Speaker of the House, Martin thought. Martin's eyes were tired, and he felt the weight of the world on his chest; a weight that he had placed there himself. He took one more large swallow of the 12-year-old Balvenie the hotel had sent up to his room and laid his head on the pillow and fell asleep.

***

When Dionis woke up, he looked at his watch and was surprised to see that it was just before five p.m. He looked out of the window of his room and could see the heavy clouds eating away at whatever sunlight had existed earlier in the day. Outside, it was dark and dreary. The inside of his room wasn't much better. Dionis was frustrated, angry, and tired. And he had a splitting headache. He fought feelings of desperation. He needed something to get his mind back on track. The one-shot coffee pod in the room would have to suffice. After several sips of terrible coffee, Dionis decided it was time to contact Ann Banks. Instead of sending another cryptic message through the draft folder of the email account he had set up, he decided to call her. She answered on the second ring.

"Michael, are you alright?"

"I've been better, but I'm okay. And you?"

"Fighting on several fronts here. Where are you?"

"A couple of hours away," Michael said.

"You need to come in. Everyone is looking for you. Staying hidden isn't helping."

"I'm only hiding from people trying to kill me. Until I identify who they are, I have to do this my way."

"I have people trying to help you right now, Michael. Do you trust me?"

"Of course, I trust you. It's the people around you that I'm unsure of. What the hell was Jason Palmer doing at DeCarlo's last night?" Dionis asked.

"I sent him there. He had instructions for you," Ann replied.

"Instructions? Instructions to do what?"

"Not over the phone Michael. I'm going to send you a message, the usual way. Please, Michael, do as this man says."

"What man?"

"It will all be spelled out for you in the message."

"I just want to find out who is behind all of this," Dionis said. "Who else did you tell I was meeting DeCarlo last night?"

"No one, Michael. Why?"

"And just how much do you trust this, Jason Palmer?"

"As much as I trust you. He's been with me for years. Why are you asking me this, Michael?"

"Those guys had to know I was meeting DeCarlo last night. Their being there wasn't a coincidence. If Palmer didn't reveal it, and whoever this 'other guy' is you're talking about, didn't, that leaves only one person."

"And who is that?"

"My friend at the FBI, Tony Maffuci. He's the only one I told yesterday that I was meeting with DeCarlo last night. I even told him the time. I was there when the two shooters showed up thirty minutes prior to the time I was set to arrive. The only reason I didn't go in right away was because Palmer showed up."

"I don't like what I'm hearing here, Michael. Are you suggesting the FBI is involved in this?"

"Not the FBI, just one agent; Tony Maffuci. I need to find out who is behind this," Dionis stressed.

"As do I," Ann said. "What I do know is that some very powerful and dangerous people are behind Patrick's death. I suspect they're also responsible for the death of the Russian killed in New Haven several days ago."

"Why Russians?" Dionis asked.

"They want to get to me, Michael. It has nothing to do with you. You were just in the wrong place at the right time for them."

"What does that mean exactly; wrong place at the right time?"

"The last time you visited me upstairs. They have a recording of it."

Dionis felt like he had just been sucker punched in the stomach. The air in his lungs appeared gone and he couldn't breathe. "So, Patrick was telling the truth that night in the den. But how?"

"They had someone plant a bug; that's all I know. We're still unsure who planted it. Might have been Patrick himself for all I know. The point is, they have a recording of it and are threatening to release it."

"Unless?" Dionis said.

"Unless I cooperate with them and let them have access to the Oval Office."

"You can't let that happen, Ann."

"I won't. But for now, I need you to follow the instructions I'm about to send. Do what this man says. Can you do that for me?" Banks asked.

"Send the instructions," Michael said.

"Doing it now. And Michael, one more thing,"

"Yes."

"I'm sorry about all of this. I'd say Merry Christmas, but it certainly isn't, is it?"

"This isn't your fault, Ann. It's mine. All mine. You deny everything. I can take the hit for all of this."

"I know you will, Michael. But for now, let's see if we can get us both through this," Banks said as she wiped a tear from her eye.

Dionis hung up without saying another word. He felt the knot in his stomach tighten as he was trying to figure out who had betrayed him. There were only four people who knew he was meeting with DeCarlo last night: Ann Banks, her Chief of Staff, Jason Palmer, Tony Maffuci, and DeCarlo herself. DeCarlo had saved his life and took a bullet for her trouble. Ann was going to be the president in three weeks and had nothing to gain by revealing his meeting with DeCarlo last night. And according to Ann, she sent Jason Palmer to DeCarlo's to give him instructions. If he trusted Ann, then he almost had to trust Palmer. The process of elimination left only one person: Tony Maffuci. Dionis didn't want to believe it. *There has to be another answer*, he thought.

***

From his apartment in New York, Ivan checked his computer to see if he was still able to track Michael Dionis through his cell phone. Dionis had made a grave tactical error calling Ann Banks and remaining on the phone for so long. Ivan locked on to his location with little trouble.

"He's at a small hotel in Scranton, Pennsylvania," Ivan said over the phone. "He just got off the phone with Ann Banks."

"Very well done my young friend," Dunayev said. "Please text me the address."

Immediately after ending the call with Ivan, Dunayev telephoned one of his built like a football linebacker associates and began the two hour plus drive to Scranton, Pennsylvania.

***

On the top floor of the Hilton Hotel in Hartford, Aaliyah Minor looked away from her keyboard, turned toward General Sherry and said, "He just called the president-elect. We have a location for him."

"Where?" Sherry asked.

"He's in Scranton, Pennsylvania."

"That wasn't very smart of him," Sherry said.

"No, it wasn't," Minor replied. "If I have his location, you can bet whoever has him in their crosshairs, also knows where he's at."

"This guy is smarter than that," Sherry replied.

"Meaning?"

"What if he wants to be found?" Sherry said.

"Then calling the president-elect, and staying on the line for so long, is certainly one way to do it," Minor replied.

"The question is, who does he want to find him?" Sherry asked. "This is either the act of a desperate man, or a man with a plan. *What are you planning to do Agent Dionis*? Sherry thought.

"I have his number. Should I get him on the phone?"

"In a moment. Do we have any assets near Scranton?" Sherry wanted to know.

Minor knew what to do. She punched in the information on her computer that would give General Sherry the answer to his question in a matter of moments.

"We have one. She's visiting family just outside of Philly. But she's not on your short list of dark operatives. She'll want to know why she's being called out to do this on Christmas day. No doubt she'll run it by her superiors."

This created a huge problem for Sherry who looked exasperated. "What's her name?"

Minor gave her uncle the name and contact number for Chrissie Chan, a CIA operative. But Chan wasn't one of his trusted confidants. Sherry decided not to call her; not just yet anyway.

***

Dionis opened his cell phone and called up the email account he shared with Ann Banks. In the draft folder was Ann's message.

Russian by the name of Andre Dunayev is trying to blackmail me. Also setting you up for Patrick's death if I don't cooperate by giving him access to Oval. Josh Martin in bed with Dunayev. He's not to be trusted. You have to trust Jason Palmer. He knows everything. Also, General John Sherry is helping hunt Dunayev. He wants to talk to you. He's agreed to remain as National Security Advisor. He's trying to reach out to you. Please do as he instructs.

Dionis read the message three times and thought to himself, *she's told people about us. National Security advisor involved. She's jeopardizing her presidency far more with this operation than her and I sleeping together. Why, Ann?*

Dionis decided to let Ann's comment pass and tapped out a quick response to her message.

So that's who has been trying to contact me. I'll be in touch with him soon.

Minutes later, Ann sent a message to Dionis with Sherry's number, just to be sure he had the right one. Dionis immediately replied with a question.

Any news on Sandi DeCarlo?

Ann's reply was quick and to the point.

Doing better. Wound was clean. Nothing vital hit. Full recovery expected. Contact Sherry, please. Now.

Dionis didn't respond to Ann's last message. He was tired and depressed. And, he knew he didn't have much time. Whoever was looking for him was no doubt on the way. As Dionis prepared for the

Russian's arrival, his cell phone rang. He looked at the caller ID and although it said "Restricted," he knew it had to be Sherry. He answered on the third ring.

"Yes," Dionis said.

"You know who this is?" Sherry asked.

"Why don't you tell me?"

"We both are trying to help save the president-elect," Sherry said.

"How can I help you, General?"

"I don't think you can, Agent Dionis. However, I think I can help you."

"And how is that?" Dionis asked.

"I don't think you have much time," Sherry replied.

"Nor do I, General. My guess is that they're on their way now." But Dionis wasn't worried about something as trivial as his own safety. He had a plan. It wasn't a very good plan. And he wasn't sure it would work; but he had a plan.

"I don't think I can get people there to intervene in time," Sherry said.

"You mean this isn't like the movies where the CIA has teams of agents ready to respond to any international crisis on a minutes' notice," Dionis said.

"Well, for one thing, I don't work for the CIA. And second, this isn't an international crisis, at least not yet. But you're right, this isn't like the movies at all."

So, then you really can't help me, can you?"

"Well, for starters, you can get out of there now. Leave your cell in the room and get back to Hartford. Can you do that, Captain?" Sherry said, appealing to Dionis' former rank when he was in the Marine Corps.

"I can leave the cell in the room, but I'm not heading back to Hartford until I identify who is behind this."

"We're working on that here, Michael. Let us do that."

"I'll have their identity soon enough. At least their photo. Once I have it, I'll send it to you. Consider it a Christmas present," Dionis said as he disconnected the call. *Sherry is operating in the dark. His actions aren't sanctioned. That's why he doesn't have the manpower*, Dionis thought.

John Sherry stared at the dead phone. He was taken aback for a moment, as he was used to getting his way. It had been some time since anyone so junior to him, like a GS 14 Secret Service Agent, went toe-to-toe with him. He turned to his niece, revealing his infuriation, and said, "Aaliyah, get me Chrissie Chan on the phone. Right away please."

The intelligence and law enforcement communities are two totally different animals. Since 9/11, however, those two communities have had an ever-increasing amount of contact, mostly due to overlapping interests, especially in the area of drug trafficking and terrorism. Intelligence agencies collect political and military intelligence through human sources for policy makers, usually in ways that would never be admissible in a court of law. The law enforcement community collects information in order to prosecute criminals. But they must adhere to the guidelines and legal constraints of the Constitution. The one thing both communities do have in common is that it's about people. At the end of the day, law enforcement and intelligence gathering is about human interaction. Sherry was hoping that Chrissie Chan, someone he had never met, would understand the need for this human interaction and would act quickly and quietly. He prayed that calling her would not prove to be a colossal mistake. He was putting his career and that of the president-elect at risk if Chan denied his request. He was taking a chance that Chan would help and not be guided by the strict rules of the bureaucracy known as the federal government.

The call started off well enough. Chrissie Chan knew who General Sherry was; everyone in the intelligence community did. Half of the people in the community loved him, the other half tolerated him. Sherry didn't care if people liked him or not, but he damned well wanted their respect. Sherry began the conversation with just enough talk to try to get a sense of who Chrissie Chan was. Before he would ask her to get involved, he'd have to rely on his gut. A few minutes of discussion told him that the woman would do as he asked. Over the next few minutes, Sherry provided Chan with just enough information to gain her trust and participation in aiding Michael Dionis without her notifying her superiors.

"I know this is highly out of the ordinary, and especially on Christmas day, but this needs to happen quickly, and with the utmost secrecy. Can I count on you?" Sherry asked.

Chan was happy to help. It would get her away from her bickering family for a few hours. She could always follow up with her bosses later, if necessary.

"Text me the address, General. I can be there in about an hour," Chan said.

"The agent doesn't know you're coming. He's rented a blue Toyota Camry. I'll text you the tag number as well. Remember, his life may very well be in danger. The people we believe that are coming for him are Russian OC figures. Do not intervene unless absolutely necessary. But make damn sure he isn't harmed. Am I clear?" Sherry said.

"Clear, General. Text me the information. I'm leaving now."

"Thank you," Sherry said. "I'm also texting Dionis your name and vehicle description. If he checks his phone, he'll know about you. But I can't promise that he'll access the information. So be careful. Call this number when you have anything."

Chrissie Chan tried to conceal a small smile and thought to herself, *the old man wants me to be careful. Just like a protective father*. She had to work at removing the smile and forced a grimace on her face when she told her family that a work emergency just occurred, and that she would have to leave for a few hours. It would also get her away from the single guy her brother had invited to dinner in an effort to fill what he believed to be a void in his sister's life after her divorce.

"Please don't wait dinner for me. I'll be back as quickly as I can. Hopefully, this won't take long," she said as she grabbed her coat and purse; inside of which was her gun and walked out the front door. Despite the unknown danger she might be facing, Chan was glad to be out of the house.

***

Dionis went into the bathroom, threw cold water on his face, and checked himself in the mirror. It was clear to him that he was exhausted. He was also feeling overwhelmed, and anxious. He'd seen that look on the faces of Marines he had commanded in battle. And he had seen it on his own face while in a war zone. Now, he was seeing it again. Frustrated and dismayed, he sought to focus on his next move. Dionis knew that when someone feels threatened, their survival instincts can result in impulsive decisions. He knew he was being threatened by a dangerous enemy looking to destroy him and Ann Banks if necessary. Dionis also knew that he was being threatened by someone he considered a friend. He couldn't allow for his fatigue and fear to undermine his plans. He walked back into the bedroom, sat on the floor, crossed his legs, closed his eyes, and began to breathe in through his nose and out of his mouth. Dionis needed a few minutes of quiet meditation to gather his thoughts as he considered his next move. Five minutes later, he heard his phone ping. It was a text message from Sherry.

Have an asset coming your way to assist if necessary. She'll hang back and observe.

Sherry also texted the make and model of Chan's car.

Dionis' reply was short.

Got it.

Dionis dropped his burner cell phone on the bed and left the room. He wasn't coming back.

Just over an hour later, Chrissie Chan was parked across the street from the small motel where Michael Dionis was registered as Sean Cameron. It was as close as she could get without being discovered. The fact that it was cold and dark, helped conceal her presence. Chan didn't see the car that Sherry told her Dionis was driving. The parking lot was sparsely populated so his car should have been easy to locate. Chan sat alone, drinking a cup of coffee with way too much sugar in it. Thirty minutes later, she saw a car pull up in front of the motel and watched as two men, dressed in dark suits, got out and walked into the lobby.

Andre Dunayev looked around and saw what he believed to be just one security camera mounted on the wall behind the check-in counter. He would deal with that later.

"Can I help you?" the girl behind the counter asked.

"Yes," Dunayev said. "I'm looking for a friend, Michael Dionis. He called and asked me to meet him here, but he didn't give me his room number and I can't seem to locate him."

"We're not allowed to give out room numbers, sir, but I can ring his room for you."

"Yes, please," Dunayev replied.

The girl looked at her computer screen but couldn't find anyone registered under the name Michael Dionis.

"I'm sorry sir, but I don't see anyone here registered under that name."

"He would have arrived here just a few hours ago. Are you sure?"

"Yes sir. No one by the name of Michael Dionis."

Dunayev described Dionis, and the girl thought he was describing Sean Cameron, but said nothing.

"I'm sure he's here," Dunayev said, doing his best to appear congenial. "Perhaps he registered under a different name. Who may have checked in here in the last few hours?"

"I'm afraid I can't give out that information."

The young girl never saw it coming. Dunayev's associate, with one swift move, grabbed the girl by the throat and squeezed it just enough to stop her from breathing. Dunayev looked directly into the girl's eyes, and asked, "Are you feeling in the Christmas spirit of giving today?"

The girl's eyes were bulging.

"My friend is going to let go. You are not going to scream. Do you understand?" Dunayev asked. "Blink once for yes."

The girl blinked once, and the man let go of her throat. Tears began to fall from the girl's eyes as she struggled to regain her breathing.

"Take a deep breath, young lady. You're going to be fine. What is your name?"

"Carley," the girl said as she continued to cry.

"Stop crying, Carley. Now, check again for me please."

Carley was lazy but she wasn't stupid. She knew this wasn't just some random robbery. Thirty seconds later, Carley gave Dunayev the information he was looking for.

Her breathing still labored, Carley said, "He's in room 148, just down the hall. He's registered under the name of Sean Cameron."

"I'll need a key for the room, please."

Carley entered a blank card into the machine, coded a room key for Dunayev, and handed it to him. As she did, she was able to trigger the hotel's silent alarm.

"Now, where do you keep the recordings of that camera up there?" Dunayev asked, pointing to the camera on the ceiling behind the desk.

"Just back here in the office," Carley replied.

"Thank you. And Merry Christmas to you," Dunayev said.

They were the last words Carley heard that day. The man with Dunayev removed a gun, with a silencer attached, from his jacket and fired two shots directly into Carley's chest. Sitting outside in her car, Chan never heard the gunshots. But she did see the girl behind the counter go down. Dionis never heard the shots either. But he did see Chan get out of the car with a gun in her hand and walk up to the front door of the motel. Dionis walked out from behind a secluded area and followed Chan as she approached the front door. Chan caught Dionis out of the corner of her eye, turned and gave him a quick stare. Dionis nodded, letting her know that he saw her. The two, who were just five yards apart outside the front door, waited. They would confront Dunayev and his hired help once they were outside.

Dunayev walked into the small office behind the desk. He was happy to see that the one security camera was hard wired and not digital, making it easy for him to rip out the wires and cord. There was a thumb drive in the computer as well. Dunayev grabbed it and put it in his pocket. He and the muscle walked quickly down the hall and stopped at the door to room 148. Dunayev put his ear to the door and listened as patiently as he could. He heard nothing. No television, not a sound. He then called Dionis' cell number and could hear the phone ringing inside. But the phone went directly to voicemail. Dunayev then knocked on the door. There was no answer. He knocked again. Still, there was no response. He then slid the pass key in the electronic lock and threw open the door. His associate, of course, was the first to enter. The room was dark. Dunayev found a light and switched it on. Except for Dionis' cell phone lying on the bed, the room was empty.

Dunayev was beside himself. *Where are you?* he thought.

"This is a set up," the man said. "He's watching us."

"I think you're right," Dunayev replied. "But where is he?"

"My guess, outside waiting for us."

Dunayev then heard the sound of sirens. "That son-of-bitch called the police," Dunayev said. Nothing was going according to plan. Dunayev grabbed Dionis' cell phone, put it in his pocket, and ran from the room in time to see a man walking down the hall with an ice bucket. The muscle grabbed the man and put the barrel of the gun with a silencer attached to the man's head.

"What room are you in?" Dunayev asked.

"151," the man struggled to say.

"Quickly, let's go," Dunayev instructed.

The muscle shoved the man inside the room and locked the door.

"Your car; where is it?" Dunayev demanded.

"Out back."

"Which one is it?"

The man, too scared to do anything but comply, surrendered his keys.

Dunayev then looked at the muscle and said, "You know what to do."

He nodded that he understood. He would buy Dunayev as much time as he could.

"Good luck, my friend," Dunayev said, giving his colleague a bear hug before walking out the sliding doors of the room and into the man's car.

Dunayev started the car and quickly, but without calling attention to anyone, drove out of the back parking lot and onto the road taking him back to New York.

Three police officers arrived at the front of the motel within seconds of each other after receiving the silent alarm call. Dionis and Chan backed away after first hearing the sirens. Dionis had hoped to confront Dunayev when he exited the motel but that still hadn't happened. For now, he had little choice other than to let the police handle it.

The first officer on the scene waited for a moment, then signaled the other two officers that he was going in. The other two followed close behind. The lead officer noticed that there wasn't anyone behind the check-in counter. As he approached the desk, he could see blood spattered on the wall. Then he saw the girl on the floor. He checked for a pulse and yelled, "She's still alive." A second officer quickly radioed for medical help asking that EMT's be dispatched code 3. The third officer knelt down beside Carley and placed his hands over her one wound that seemed to be the cause of most of her blood loss.

The lead officer radioed again asking for additional backup. As soon as he ended his transmission, he and another officer checked the lobby of the motel. They found nothing.

Just down the hall, the muscle ordered the room's occupant to hand over his wallet. He then told the man to get into the bathtub, where he then fired two shots into the man's chest before closing the shower curtain. He then took off his coat and shoes and laid flat on the bed with his gun concealed beneath his body.

Five minutes later, the motel was covered with uniformed police officers. Detectives on call were still being rousted from their holiday dinners and had yet to arrive.

"Start knocking on doors," the sergeant commanded. "Two men to a room. Let's see who may have heard or seen anything. If there is no answer, use the passkey to enter."

The officers started searching on the first floor going room to room. Many of the rooms were empty. With each door they opened, the first officer entered with his gun held in both hands, pointed straight in front of him. Their hearts pounded, fear narrowing their vision and tightening their chests as they went to each room, not knowing what awaited them behind each door. When they got to room 151, they knocked and announced their identity. But the Russian muscle simply laid in the bed refusing to answer the door. As the officers entered, the muscle fired two quick shots, hitting the first officer in the chest, knocking him backwards against the wall. The second officer returned fire with three quick shots hitting the big Russian twice. One shot caught the muscle just below the right eye killing him instantly.

Outside, just over a block away, Chan looked at Dionis and said, "You might want to get in." He knew she was right. And since Sherry sent her, he had little choice but to trust her.

"Chrissie Chan," she said, extending her hand. "Michael Dionis, I presume?"

"Yes. Who sent you?" he asked, hoping to confirm it was the National Security Advisor.

"A friend of yours named Sherry. Known him long?"

"Never had the pleasure," Dionis replied. "You get the tag number of the car those two goons drove up in?"

"I did; same as you. New York tags."

"So, where are we going?" Chan asked.

"Ever been to Hartford, Connecticut?"

"Spent a week there one night a few years ago," Chan said with a smirk on her face.

"Sounds about right," Dionis replied.

"Whatever you were doing, sounds like your plan went south."

"Not all of it. Got good photos of the two guys looking for me. I believe one of them is the mastermind behind this nightmare."

"Then we better keep going," Chan said looking at her watch. "It's about a three-hour drive."

"Do you mind letting me drive? I can get us there quicker than that," Dionis said.

"Chauvinist Pig," Chan said with a grin.

"Not at all. The Secret Service is known for its skilled pursuit and escape driving. Please," Dionis said, "let me drive."

Chan pulled over, got out, and walked around to the passenger side of her own car, and got in.

"Okay there Jason Bourne, show me what you got."

"Jason who?"

"Really? Never mind."

It was all Dionis could do to rein in his emotions. He wanted nothing more this instant than to find a way to make his nightmare go away. His stomach was in turmoil. He didn't like feeling vulnerable and certainly couldn't let Chan see just how scared he was becoming. He turned his head to the right and said, with the confidence of a Marine drill instructor, "buckle up. We're on a very tight schedule."

On the way to Hartford, Dionis had Chan send the photos of Dunayev and the muscle to Sherry from yet another of his burner phones. Dionis was praying that Sherry would be able to discover the identity of the men at the motel through facial recognition.

By the time the police identified the body of the man in the bathtub in room 152, Andre Dunayev was back in New York. When the police were finally able to get a description and tag number of the dead man's car, Dunayev had abandoned it in a New York City parking garage.

Careful to avoid looking directly at any of the security cameras covering most every inch of Manhattan, Dunayev walked outside of the garage, lit a cigar, and telephoned Josh Martin.

"Where are you?" Dunayev demanded to know.

"The Hilton Hotel in Hartford," Martin replied.

"I want Michael Dionis. Find him now. Do you understand?"

"How am I supposed to find him?" Martin asked.

"I don't care. You find him, or your life is nothing to me. Do you understand?" Dunayev shouted. "I'll release the tape and make sure the media knows that you're the one who planted the bug."

"You're not going to intimidate me any longer Andre. You do this, then we're both done. But give me some time. I'll see what I can do."

"Be quick, my friend. My patience has run out," Dunayev said as he disconnected the call while hailing a cab.

The next call Dunayev made was to Tony Maffuci. But Maffuci never answered the call. So, Dunayev sent a text.

Find your friend Dionis, now. Text me when you have his location.

Josh Martin realized that Dunayev was panicking and that their plan was rapidly falling apart. *The man is a loose cannon. He truly is a sociopath. He cares about nothing,* Josh thought. Dunayev simply couldn't understand that there were both opportunities and obstacles to most everything in life, especially for the things they were involved in. Dunayev was fine when the opportunities looked good. The obstacles were a totally different thing. He was tiring when the slightest obstacle presented itself. Now, he was totally unmanageable, and more dangerous than ever. Martin picked up his burner cell and called Susan Welsh, the Speaker of the House. He knew that the Speaker wouldn't recognize the phone number and would not pick up the call. As he had anticipated, the call went directly to her voice mail.

"Madam Speaker. This is Josh Martin, Patrick Banks' former chief of staff. I have a matter of great interest to discuss with you concerning the president-elect. If you're interested in hearing what I have to say, please call me at your earliest convenience."

Martin ended the call and laid back down on his bed. He took another sip of scotch and dozed off.

"Did you get all that?" Sherry asked.

"Both calls and conversations have been recorded," Minor said with a smile. "Still trying to identify who telephoned him. It was from a burner phone."

"Keep working on it."

"Any idea what he wants to talk to the Speaker about?" she asked.

"Yes," Sherry replied. "But I'm not at liberty to share that with you right now."

Minor knew better than to ask any further questions. “What about our guys downstairs?” she asked.

“Tell them to stay put. They need to be in place if Martin leaves his room or has visitors.”

Sherry then called Ann Banks and told her about Martin’s call to the Speaker of the House.

“How did you come by this information?” Banks asked.

“It might be best if you don’t know all the particulars ma’am.”

“You’re holding back on me, General.”

“Yes, ma’am, I am. You’ll need plausible deniability. Plus, there are people involved with me whose careers and liberty are at risk. Let me handle this for you.”

Banks seemed to calm down for a moment and said, “Very well, John. Did he specifically mention the recording?”

“He did not. Only that he had information about you that he wanted to discuss.”

“The recording?”

“That would be my first guess.”

“But Josh wouldn’t dare.”

“Oh, I’m afraid he would, and is,” Sherry replied calmly.

“Any news on Michael?” Ann asked.

“He’s on his way here.”

“He is?” Ann asked surprised.

“Yes. Long story. I’ll reach out to you after he and I have had a chance to talk. Important that we keep him safe for now.”

Sherry chose not to tell Ann Banks about the events in Scranton, or the fact that he had sent Chan there to help protect Dionis. He also thought it best that she didn’t know about the fact that there had been a shooting at the motel and that a young girl was fighting for her life.

"Thank you, John. You'll keep me informed?"

"Of course. I'll call you back when I know more."

Banks disconnected the call feeling bad about the situation she had put the General in. She summoned Jason Palmer to the study.

"I just got off the phone with John Sherry," Banks said.

"And?"

"And, he just added to the constant drum beat of bad news I've been receiving lately."

"What do you mean?"

"Josh contacted the Speaker. I think he's getting ready to release the recording to her."

"Why would he do that?"

"My guess, whatever plan he had is starting to fall apart. At least that's how it appears. Maybe he's looking for an exit strategy."

"What do you want me to do?"

"Start preparing a press release for me. I want to be able to beat them both to the punch."

"You know the problems this will create for you?"

"I do," Ann said.

Chapter 22

John Sherry received the two photos Dionis was able to capture of Andre Dunayev and his huge friend as they exited their car in front of the small motel in Scranton. Moments later, on the computer screen in front of her, Minor was running the pictures through a facial identification software program. She and Sherry watched silently as the photos were scanned by millions of facial shots. In just a few moments, the muscle was identified as Igor Volkov. Minor immediately accessed information that revealed Volkov was tied to a Russian gang in Moscow that specialized in extortion. When he wasn't whacked out on coke or vodka, he was one of the gang's most feared enforcers.

The next photo the facial recognition program provided was that of Evsei Balagula, also known as Andre Dunayev.

"Are you sure it's the same guy?" Sherry asked.

"It's him," Minor said, after searching through a variety of records not available to anyone outside of the intelligence community and some, but not all, of federal law enforcement.

"He's Russian mob for sure. Balagula specializes in extortion and selling political influence. He was considered one of the most dangerous crime figures in his country. So much so, even Russian politicians fear him. He's suspected in the killing of two judges in Russia. According to what I'm seeing here, Balagula disappeared off the radar about six years ago."

"How could he have gone so dark for so long?" Sherry asked.

"Not all that hard to do if you plan it properly. You end all your contacts with agencies that might come looking for you such as your electric, creditors, and so forth. You terminate your agreement with a mobile provider and work strictly off unlocked burner phones. Don't use credit cards. Pay everything in cash. Stay completely off all social media. Of course, you also change your name, which is easier than people think. You also have to cut all ties to family and friends.

Changing your appearance doesn't hurt, but that isn't all that necessary."

"Sweetheart," Sherry said to his niece, "I know that. What I don't know is how a sociopath, criminal mastermind like Balagula, could operate under the radar for so long." Sherry called his niece sweetheart when he wanted to make sure he had her full attention or wanted to stress a point. He knew that in this politically correct world, he couldn't use that term with anyone other than her. And she didn't allow anyone other than her uncle and her partner to address her as sweetheart.

Minor smiled and said, "I realize that you know that unco," using the nickname she called him since she was a child. "I'm just pointing out that this guy did a great job removing his digital footprint. That's how he has successfully been able to reinvent himself. He's hiding in plain sight in New York, which of course, makes perfect sense."

"And why do you say that?"

"Because a guy like him would stand out like a fly on a wedding cake if he were to hide in rural Alabama."

"Of course," Sherry replied. "I was just curious as to how you came to that conclusion."

"I hope I'm passing your little impromptu tests."

"For now, you seem to be doing okay," Sherry said, as he did his best to suppress a smile."

Minor frowned and said, "Since Balagula has created a new identity for himself, that has made it difficult for Russian authorities to locate him."

"Or perhaps they're happy he's disappeared because they're afraid of him?"

"What are you implying?"

"I'm saying that if the Russians really wanted him bad enough, they'd find him. Their federal security service is first rate."

"Maybe," Minor replied. "Either way, he had to have a lot of cash when he made the identity change."

"Which means, of course, he had to smuggle the cash into the country. And, that someone is financing him."

"Exactly," Minor said. "And maybe the Russian security service is allowing him to operate just to see what he does in our country."

"I agree. However, a guy like this, stepping up his game in an effort to blackmail an incoming president in order to gain access to the Oval Office, just doesn't add up. Not unless…." Sherry said, as stopped short of finishing his comment.

"The Russians?" Minor asked.

"Maybe. But I doubt it. Too much risk."

"The Chinese?" Minor asked.

"Maybe. But if so, a radical wing. I'd be surprised if this were sanctioned or backed by the Chinese president," Sherry said. "Start learning everything you can about him. I want to know everything about Evsei Balagula."

"Already on it," Minor replied.

While Minor returned to her computer consul, Sherry tapped out a short text to Chan.

Tell Dionis that the Russian is operating under the name of Andre Dunayev. We can't seem to find an address for him in New York just yet. Will give you details when we meet.

Chan's reply was short.

Got it.

***

It was almost nine p.m. when Chan and Dionis approached Danbury, Connecticut, about an hour outside of Hartford on Interstate 84. Dionis, who was still driving, pulled over at a convenience store rest stop for gas and coffee. He needed caffeine; Chan needed the restroom. When she went to the bathroom, she sent John Sherry a short text message.

About an hour away. Have Dionis with me. Be there soon.

Sherry immediately responded.

One shooter and motel guest killed. One cop wounded. Desk clerk in critical condition. Any of this your work or Dionis'? Urgent that I know.

Chan knew there had been shots fired inside the motel but had no idea as to the carnage. She typed out a reply to Sherry.

Not us. No idea of extent of what happened. Cops arrived within minutes of Russians arriving. We left.

When Chan came out of the rest stop with two coffee's she didn't see Dionis or her car. He was gone. Chan was both pissed and impressed at the same time. *You got balls my friend, I have to give you that,* she thought. Chan was also mad at herself for leaving the keys with Dionis while he gassed up the car. That was a rookie mistake. She thought about the crap she'd take from her colleagues for such a foolish act. But she was going to avoid the ribbing that normally accompanied such a mistake. Nobody but Sherry would ever know about her lapse of judgement since her role in the night's events never happened.

Sherry had a difficult time wrapping his mind around what Chan had told him over the phone. Privately, he understood why Dionis fled. But he was sure that Dionis didn't fully appreciate the potential ramifications of his decision. Sherry also knew that every man had his breaking point and prayed that Michael Dionis hadn't reached his.

It was almost eleven p.m. when Sherry told his two operatives outside the hotel to secure for the night. Martin was alone in his room and passed out from drinking over half a bottle of scotch. He wasn't going anywhere tonight.

"I wonder where Dionis is going," Minor said.

"New York city," Sherry replied.

"How do you know that?"

"Because I told him that's where Dunayev was living," Sherry replied. "What I need to know is exactly where he's heading to in New York."

"I hope to be able to tell you that shortly," Minor replied. "I'm getting the VIN on Chan's car now. I should be able to access the GPS."

"Can you track him from his burner phone?"

"I'm working on that too. But first, he'll have to make a call on his new burner to someone we're monitoring."

***

Dionis drove into Brooklyn, and parked Chan's car in front of one of the many Greek restaurants that dominate the Bay Ridge area. He then took a taxi to the Casa Blanca hotel near the Brooklyn Navy Yard. The night clerk was surprised to see anyone at that hour on Christmas night. Dionis looked around for security cameras and found very few. Of course, there was one inside the lobby, but he didn't consider that one to be a problem. Brooklyn wasn't as covered with CCTV's as Manhattan was. He handed the desk clerk a credit card and checked in under the name of Sean Cameron. He took the elevator up to the fourth floor, opened the door to his room, switched on the light, and immediately laid down on the bed. His body demanded rest. He also needed a new plan; one that would allow him to find Andre Dunayev in New York before the Russian could cause him, or Ann Banks, any more harm. But the new plan would have to wait until morning. Exhausted, and with a headache that was killing him, Dionis fell instantly asleep.

Twenty minutes later, Minor had located Chan's car.

"The car is parked in the Bay Ridge area of Brooklyn," she told Sherry.

"By any chance, can you search hotels in the area to see if he's checked in anywhere?" Sherry asked.

"Of course."

"He's probably not using his real name. What I'd like to know is if anyone checked in in the last hour or so."

"On it."

"You're going to have to explain to me sometime just how you do this stuff. I doubt I'd ever get hired in this business today if I had to compete with kids like you," Sherry said.

Chapter 23

26 Days Before the Inauguration

It was almost seven a.m., the day after Christmas, when Susan Welsh accessed her voice mail and heard Josh Martin's message. Sitting in the living room of her small apartment in Crystal City, just across the Potomac River from D.C., she played the message three times. After the third time hearing Martin's message, Welsh got up from her chair, went into the kitchen, and poured herself a cup of coffee. She sat back down, took a long sip of coffee, and started the recording again. Welsh had met Martin on a few occasions through Patrick Banks, but she was having trouble placing him. She'd met so many staff members of different legislator's that she simply couldn't remember them all. Welsh grabbed her cell phone and called the junior staffer she summarily dismissed Christmas Eve and without so much a as good morning greeting, said, "Get me everything you can on Josh Martin, the former Chief of Staff of the late Congressman Patrick Banks. I want to know who he is, where he lives, his likes, dislikes, sexual orientation, does he drink, if so, what, previous employment, everything. And I want it within the hour. Tell no one what you're doing. And call me as soon as you have the information. Do you understand?"

The staffer told Welsh that she understood her instructions, after which, Welsh simply said, "good," and disconnected the call.

***

On the day after Christmas, Josh Martin arrived at the governor's mansion just before eight a.m. Ann Banks had coffee for everyone but deliberately avoided providing any food. Sherry had kept her apprised of Martin's movements, or lack thereof, the previous night. Banks was also aware of Martin's call to the Speaker of the House, and the fact that he was, no doubt, extremely hungover. She fought to conceal her knowledge of Martin's betrayal. He had certainly revealed his greed when he got into bed with Dunayev and her late husband. Banks was also convinced Martin's only loyalty was to money. And now, Dunayev seemed to be acting on his own, without caring what Martin thought or did. Martin appeared to have lost all control of whatever it was he had hoped to accomplish by throwing in with Andre Dunayev and her late husband. Ann Banks could smell political weakness and Martin was beginning to reek of it.

As they were sitting down to discuss the latest events involving Dunayev, Martin's phone pinged telling him he had a text message. He quickly glanced at his Google watch and saw that he had a text message from Susan Welsh that said, "ready to talk now."

***

It was just after nine a.m. when Lieutenant Mark Rice entered DeCarlo's room at the hospital. DeCarlo had had a sleepless night. It wasn't that she couldn't sleep, or didn't want to, she was kept awake most of the night because of the constant interruptions by the staff nurses checking her vital signs, changing IV packs, taking temperature readings, and checking bandages. Of course, the cleaning crews emptying waste baskets and checking the bathroom in the middle of the night didn't help either.

"How are you feeling?" Rice asked.

"Fine. Just tired. Not sure how anyone ever gets well or sleeps in a hospital with all the interruptions every friggin hour all night long."

"I think the insurance companies mandate that the hospitals do that so that the patients will demand to be released sooner. Part of a conspiracy to cut hospital costs I suspect," Rice said.

"You may be right. No wonder health care fraud is so lucrative. Maybe I'll switch over to white-collar crime after this case," DeCarlo said with a smirk.

"Yeah, I can just see you sitting in a room all day scanning through thousands of medical records and pay invoices looking for that one document that would prove a case of medical fraud."

"Doesn't sound that hard. I think I can start building a few cases right here from my bed. Besides, I hear it's like catching fish in a barrel after all the fraud associated with the inflated COVID numbers reported by hospitals."

"Well, do you want to get out of that bed or not?"

"If you can make that happen, you'd have my undying loyalty till the day I take my last breath."

"I thought I had that anyway," Rice replied, grinning.

"Just get me the hell out of here, I'm begging you."

"Sit tight. They're getting the paperwork together now."

"I'm impressed Lt. You apparently have more juice than I thought."

"Actually, it's the president-elect that has the juice. She wants you back on this case if you're healthy enough."

"Ann Banks called you?"

"Oh no, not me, the new governor, who then called the commissioner. For some reason, she trusts you."

"I'm not sure I understand."

"What's to understand? Apparently, something clicked between the two of you when you interviewed her after her husband died."

"The interview was pretty standard; all cut and dry. Nothing unusual. Not sure where she thinks the connection is," DeCarlo said, careful not to tell Rice that Banks' chief of staff was with her at her home just minutes before the shoot-out.

"I'm just the messenger," Rice replied. "But she wants you back on this case involving her late husband and working with the feds to find this Secret Service Agent, if you're up to it that is."

DeCarlo took a sip of the mildly warm hot coffee that was on the breakfast tray the hospital staff had put in front of her. She had no interest in the food.

"I can't eat this crap, Lt. And how hard is it to make a hot cup of coffee. Am I getting out of here or what?" she asked as the coffee spilled down her cheek.

"Relax. You should be out of here in an hour. I'll take you home so you can get some rest and get organized."

"Can we stop somewhere and get some real food first?" DeCarlo asked as she grabbed a napkin from the tray and wiped the spilled coffee from her chin.

"Of course. But first, I've been told to have you call Banks' chief of staff, Jason Palmer. Here's the number. He's waiting on your call. You know this guy."

"We met at the governor's mansion the morning of Patrick Banks' death."

DeCarlo placed the call immediately. Palmer told her about the events of the past twenty-four hours. There were aspects of the case that Palmer didn't reveal. He would let Sherry do that himself if DeCarlo was up to meeting him later.

"Are you alone?" Palmer asked.

"No, my lieutenant is here with me now and told me about Banks asking about me."

"When you get released later today, can you get free?"

"Of course."

"Text me the minute you're alone. I'm going to send you to meet someone. Please trust him. I'm sure he can use your help."

"I'll be in touch soon," DeCarlo replied as she ended the call. She looked at Rice and said, "He basically asked me to call later for an update from Ann Banks. Not really sure what this is all about just yet."

"I'm calling the bullshit card on you detective," Rice replied. "But I'll play along, for now."

DeCarlo was angry with herself for not being totally truthful with Rice. She knew that there was far more to Patrick Banks' death and Michael Dionis' actions then met the eye. But the newly elected president was relying on her confidence and discretion. DeCarlo also knew she had to follow through with whatever Ann Banks was trying to do. "My shoulder hurts. That's it. I can work through that. Just get me out of here," she told Rice.

"On it."

"Good. I really need to get out of here." DeCarlo said.

Chapter 24

Few federal and state employees work the day after Christmas, especially when it falls on a Wednesday or Thursday. Those that do work, often use the relaxed day to catch up on paperwork while engaging in more office chatter than usual. Unless there is some pressing matter, there is rarely any heavy lifting being done. That wasn't the case for Leah Riggs and Tony Maffuci.

Riggs was still fuming over her altercation on Christmas with Tina Crawford. She had no misgivings about how she was perceived by many of the agents in the office. She was young and considered a fast riser because of her skin color. It didn't mean she wasn't qualified for the job; it just meant that a few, mostly the older white male agents close to retirement, knew there were other equally, or more qualified agents, for the job that didn't get the consideration they deserved because they weren't a minority. Fortunately, that was not the view taken by many of the younger agents, the ones that the FBI was now recruiting; those with the skills needed to track the more techno savvy criminals in today's world of instant information and social media. However, the new breed of agents were not as quick to get their hands dirty as their predecessors were in order to put criminals in jail. What the new agents did bring to the table was a more inclusive view of society. More often than not, they viewed race and sexual preference the way older agents looked at someone who was left-handed: with no concern whatsoever.

Riggs was painfully aware that FBI SACs had, in the past, crashed and burned because of a variety of operational and administrative issues. The FBI, often cited as the epitome of a bureaucracy by students of government and political science, was less than forgiving when it came to holding the agent in charge responsible for every aspect of running a field office. Being the SAC was a massive leadership test for any agent with aspirations to rise higher in the Bureau. Having a corrupt or compromised agent in your field office, and not discovering it and dealing with it promptly, could easily end a SAC's career. Minority or not, there would be little chance of walking back from something like that. An open and hostile personal conflict with the United States Attorney, who could easily decline any prosecution brought forward by her office, could certainly prove to be another career killing issue.

Riggs decided to deal with one problem at a time. After ending her short conversation with the president-elect that morning, she knew her most pressing matter was dealing with Maffuci. She had her suspicions but little proof of his covering up Dionis' movements. And now, Banks' suggestion that he might actually be assisting the Russians in finding Dionis, sent a chill down her spine.

It was almost ten in the morning when Riggs summoned Maffuci to her office.

"Tony, please sit down," she said.

Maffuci took a seat directly in front of Riggs' desk. She could have come around and sat next to him signaling a less formal meeting. But Riggs wanted to make sure that Maffuci knew this was not a social call.

"What's up?" Maffuci asked.

"Tony, there are times when I'm not up for a lot of small talk, and this is one of those times. I want to know if you've had any contact the past few days with Michael Dionis?" she asked.

"Is this an official inquiry?"

"It can become one if you want."

"I'm not sure what you're looking for boss, but I haven't had any official contact with him in days."

"Don't go Clintonian on me, Tony. We're not doing the whole 'depends on what your definition of it is.' Official, or unofficial, I want to know, and I want to know now."

"Since when is it the Bureau's business to ask which one of my friends I talk to and when I talk to them?" Maffuci said defensively.

"Tony, I understand you want to protect your friend. I suspect you think you're helping Michael, but you're not."

Maffuci was silent, wanting to gather his thoughts for a moment. He knew that cops and others in his profession were often too quick to answer questions that compromised themselves. His first instinct was to not be one of those people. Instead, he knew he had to craft his answers carefully.

"He called sometime in the afternoon on Christmas Eve. Didn't tell me where he was, or what his plans were. We talked for a couple of minutes, and he said he had to go."

"And that was it?" Riggs asked.

"That was it."

"And why did you go to Farmington on Christmas Morning. You were at the scene of the shooting and at the hospital?"

Maffuci rubbed his chin as he thought about his answer. "I'd heard about it. My interest was in seeing how DeCarlo was doing. That's when I learned Michael had been involved."

"You didn't think to tell me about that?"

"You had agents up there assisting in an official capacity. I figured they'd tell you. I was simply there to check on Sandi. We've worked a good bit together."

Maffuci was literally dancing around every question in an attempt to make it look as if his presence in Farmington was nothing more than his humanitarian effort to check on a colleague who had been shot the night before.

"This is unacceptable, Tony," Riggs said, trying to restrain herself. "You're a supervisor. You know what is expected of you. You're letting your personal relationship with Dionis get in the way of doing what is required of you."

"And what is it, specifically, that I am required to do here?"

Riggs sighed. Maffuci was reacting just as she had feared. She could see the furtive look in his eyes. “You know what you’re required to do,” she said calmly. “He’s technically a suspect in the death of Patrick Banks. While I’d certainly be shocked to learn that he was involved, that’s not the point. His own agency is looking for him. You can’t have contact with him and not report it.”

Maffuci shook his head. He knew that Riggs had a much clearer picture of his relationship with Michael Dionis than he hoped. For now, however, all she had was that; nothing more. His political instincts, and his gut, told him to do everything he could to keep it that way.

“You’re right. He is my friend. And has been so for some time. He’s being set up; I’d stake my career on it. But I’m not helping him in any way. He’s working behind the scenes to try and identify who is behind this. When he called me Christmas Eve, it was simply to hear a friendly voice. He would not tell me where he was, where he was going or what he was doing. I had no idea he was going to DeCarlo’s that night.”

Riggs struggled to avoid looking stunned. Maffuci was lying to her face.

“Okay, Tony. Please keep me informed.”

As soon as Maffuci left the office Riggs told her secretary to hold all of her calls. She got up from behind her desk and closed the door to her office. She sat back down and called Ann Banks. After speaking with Banks, she called the FBI’s Office of Professional Responsibility, the Bureau’s version of internal affairs.

Chapter 25

It was shortly after three p.m. when Sandi DeCarlo, her left arm in a sling, finally arrived at the Hilton Hotel in downtown Hartford. Her instructions had been to go to the lobby, use the house phone, and ask to be connected to Aaliyah Minor. DeCarlo did as she was instructed to do. Moments later, one of Sherry's men appeared and introduced himself as a friend of Minor's.

"Detective DeCarlo?" the man said, extending his hand.

"Depends. Who is asking?" she replied suspiciously.

"I'm asking, on behalf of the General," the man replied.

"Then take me to your leader," she said smiling.

The man never acknowledged DeCarlo's lighthearted comment or inquired about her arm being in a sling. He remained stoic as they rode the elevator to the top floor. The two exited the elevator and walked inside the suite.

Sherry stood, extended his hand and said "Detective DeCarlo. It's a pleasure. I've heard a lot about you."

"General," DeCarlo replied smiling, as she shook Sherry's hand. DeCarlo immediately walked over to the artificial fireplace to warm herself. "You'll have to excuse me, General, it's a little cold outside. I can never resist a warm fire."

"That's quite alright, detective. Please let me introduce you to Aalliyah. She'll be working with us."

Minor nodded then turned back to her computer screen.

"And these two gentlemen?" DeCarlo asked.

"Their names are not important right now," Sherry answered. "What is important, is that we get in contact with Michael Dionis before he does something stupid, or worse yet, gets himself killed."

"And how can I help?" DeCarlo asked, as she rubbed her cold hands together.

General Sherry was, by nature, a man who kept secrets. But he also knew when to reveal information that was necessary to recruit the support he needed to complete a mission or operation. This was one of those times. He briefed DeCarlo into most everything he knew as to Dionis' movements since the night of the shooting, including the events at the motel in Scranton, as well as Dionis stealing another agent's car, and leaving it abandoned in Brooklyn.

"I had no idea," DeCarlo said, surprised. "The last I heard, he simply walked out of the hospital the morning after the shooting."

"We think he was being set up that night, either to be followed, or killed," Sherry said.

"If that's the case, how did the shooters know to look for him at my place?" DeCarlo asked.

"We think Tony Maffuci is responsible for that," Sherry replied.

DeCarlo was stunned by the reply. "You can't be serious. Tony and Michael are friends. I've worked a bit with Tony, I can't see him doing that."

"Agent Dionis told the president-elect the names of everyone who knew he was meeting with you that night. The only people who knew were me, Jason Palmer, Maffuci, and you," Sherry said. "This morning, he lied to his boss, Leah Riggs. I think you know her."

"We've met, yes. He lied how?"

"He told her that he had no idea Dionis was meeting with you on Christmas Eve."

"But why would Tony do that?" DeCarlo asked.

"That is also something we'd like your help with," Sherry said.

"There is more to this than simply saving Michael," DeCarlo said. "What are you not telling me?"

There was a momentary silence in the room. Sherry then asked the two men and his niece to give them some privacy.

"Aaliyah, why don't you go downstairs and get us all some of that good Starbucks coffee. I'm sure it will take you about fifteen minutes or so. I'll take mine black. And you?" Sherry asked DeCarlo.

"Cream and two sugars please," DeCarlo said.

Sherry didn't see any point in briefing any of the other people in the room about Banks and Dionis' relationship. The fewer who knew, the better. Sherry wanted to keep the fact that their intimacy had been recorded and was being used to blackmail Banks, as quiet as possible. He also knew that Banks had broached the subject with DeCarlo but had not given her the details of the matter.

"So, you're telling me that there is a recording of Michael and Ann Banks having sex," DeCarlo said, not wanting to reveal that on Christmas Eve, Jason Palmer had told her about the tape.

"That is correct. But you already knew that, detective. I don't really have time for all of this cloak and dagger, back and forth, question and answer business. Or, for this whole political correctness bullshit the young generation seems to be consumed with. I find that we end up spending too much time on the inconsequential while issues of real importance get pushed to the side. So, let's play straight with each other, detective. Can we do that?" Sherry asked.

"Absolutely," DeCarlo replied, a bit surprised at Sherry's change in tone but certainly happy to hear that he wanted to get down to the facts and not beat around the bush. She was only too happy to play it Sherry's way, and asked, "Then tell me, General, have you heard the recording?"

"I have not."

"So, we don't know for a fact that there is a tape. No one seems to have heard it."

"I'm confident it exists. And it could destroy Ann Banks' presidency before it even gets started."

"And Russians are allegedly behind this?" DeCarlo asked.

"Not allegedly, detective, they are."

"And they're setting Michael up for the killing of Patrick Banks in order to get to the incoming president."

"You catch on quick. We also know that Josh Martin, Patrick's former chief of staff, is in bed with these very Russians. We have a recording of his last conversation with an Andre Dunayev, the man we believe is responsible for killing Oleg Lomakina, a murder case you're working, along with providing Patrick Banks with contaminated cocaine."

"And you can prove this?"

"We have information to corroborate this, yes."

"So, you have a wire on this case?" DeCarlo asked, looking surprised.

"Yes and no," Sherry replied.

"Meaning?"

"Meaning we have certain techniques available to us that not everyone can appreciate."

"So, you've bugged Martin's phone and you don't have a wire authorization?"

"Yes."

"I know you realize that whatever you're getting from this illegal wire will be inadmissible in court."

"You're right, detective, it is inadmissible. But we don't want this to go to trial," Sherry said.

"But I'm investigating two murders that WILL hopefully go to court. So far, everything you're telling me is either speculation, or contains contaminated evidence that I can't use. Exactly what is it that you expect me to do?"

"We'd like you to treat this like you would any other homicide investigation. You'll simply be given a certain amount of support that you would not normally receive in such cases. Think in terms of solving the case, not necessarily having it prosecuted."

"And why would I not want it prosecuted?"

"Because there is far more at stake here than simply bringing Andre Dunayev to trial. If we all do our jobs, the justice he'll receive will be far beyond anything he'd have to deal with in your state courts."

"I won't be a part of you having him killed," DeCarlo warned.

"No, no, detective. You're watching too many movies. We just think justice will be better served if he answers for his crimes somewhere other than a court in Connecticut."

"Connecticut isn't afraid to deal harshly with convicted murderers, General. Just ask Beth Carpenter; she's still serving life in prison."

"Beth Carpenter?"

"She had her brother-in-law, a young man named Buzz Clinton, murdered over a child custody issue. Connecticut isn't afraid to send people away for life. There's a great book on it called, *Lethal Guardian,* by M. William Phelps. I can get you a copy of it. Seems to me, that's a good place to send Dunayev."

"That may be true, detective, but life in an American prison would mean nothing to a man like Dunayev. If you can trust me on this, the justice he will experience, if we're successful, will be far harsher. My job is to protect the president-elect. And, I will, if necessary, sacrifice Michael Dionis to do that. But I don't want to do that. And neither does Ann Banks. And frankly, I don't think you do either."

"You're right about that, General. I don't think for one minute that Michael Dionis is guilty of anything other than thinking with the wrong part of his anatomy as many men so often do. You have to be asleep under a rock to not realize he's being set up."

Sherry liked what he was hearing. “With your help, we might just be able to save her presidency, and Dionis at the same time.”

“And if Michael finds Dunayev first?” DeCarlo asked.

“If Michael finds him before we do and does something stupid, there’s going to be serious political blowback on Ms. Banks. Dunayev will try to kill him and if he does, he’ll make it look like self-defense, after he releases the tape of course. She’ll be ruined. If Michael hurts or kills him, the end result might not be much different for her.”

“Where is Michael now?”

“He’s checked into a hotel in Brooklyn. He’s registered under the name of Sean Cameron.”

“He’s using an alias, hiding in plain sight but flying under the radar,” DeCarlo said smiling. “How did you discover this?”

“Aaliyah. There’s no one better at hacking into computers than she is. She compared the names of people checked into the hotel in Scranton along with people who checked into various hotels in the Brooklyn area. What are the chances of two Sean Cameron’s checking into those places on Christmas day?”

“I’d say almost zero. Especially since I don’t believe in coincidences in my business.”

“Neither do I,” Sherry said “So, detective, can we count on you?”

“General, I was in the moment you folks got me released from the hospital. I just needed to hear your sales pitch.”

Sherry smiled, something he almost never did. “Young lady, when this is over, we need to have a long talk. I think you and I are going to be good friends. What do you suggest we do first?”

“For one thing, do you have the resources to have someone sit on Michael?”

“Yes and no.”

“Meaning?”

"This operation is not sanctioned by the intelligence community, for obvious reasons. The people working with me here are doing so out of loyalty to me. If this operation is discovered, their careers, and mine, are over. So, this is basically it."

"That's not great news," DeCarlo said.

"There is one more possible asset I could use. But I don't really know her, and she's already been burned by Michael once."

"The woman whose car he stole?"

"The very same, I'm afraid. Chrissie Chan."

"Trust your instincts, General, they've gotten you this far. My guess is she's already in far enough that she's probably more than willing to at least sit on him for a while."

Wanting to hear what DeCarlo thought about the next strategic move they should make with regard to Michael Dionis, he looked directly into her eyes and said, "That's an excellent idea, detective. I made that call right after we learned where Michael was."

"You have any more tests for me, General?" DeCarlo asked.

"Not for now."

"Then if I, were you, I'd send one of your commando's to New York right now to assist her. You don't need them both here. I just need the use of one of them."

"Now that you're fully on board, detective, I can do that. Anything else?"

"First, since we're both sticking our necks out and may eventually find ourselves out of work and possibly in prison, you might start calling me Sandi. Second, can I hear the recording of Josh Martin and Andre Dunayev?" DeCarlo asked.

Sherry sent a quick message to Minor instructing her to come back up to the room. Five minutes later, Minor was sitting behind her laptop. She opened the wiretap software and played the recording for DeCarlo. As soon as the recording ended, DeCarlo looked at Sherry and, stealing a line from *The Godfather*, said, "I think it's time we make Josh Martin an offer he can't refuse. He needs to become a cooperating source, today."

"A cooperating source?" Sherry asked.

"An informant. You would call him an asset."

"And how do you propose to do that?"

"Easy. He needs to believe he's going to prison for a very long time if he doesn't cooperate."

DeCarlo turned to Minor and asked, "How quickly can you make me a copy of that recording?"

Minor simply turned toward DeCarlo, extended her hand, and said, "here."

DeCarlo took the ScanDisk from Minor, placed it in her pocket, and asked Sherry, "Where is Josh Martin now?"

"He's with the president-elect. He has a room downstairs. We'll know the minute he leaves the mansion and of course when he's in his room."

"Good," DeCarlo replied. "I'll confront him tonight. Can one of your men accompany me?"

"Of course," Sherry said.

Sherry had one of the men remain in the suite while ordering the other one to get to New York as quickly as possible and assist Chrissie Chan in watching Michael Dionis.

***

Josh Martin left the governor's mansion at four-thirty p.m. The moment he got in his car, he re-read the message from Susan Welsh. He decided to place the call as he drove back to the Hilton in downtown Hartford. The Speaker picked up on the second ring.

"Josh, how are you? I never had the chance to tell you how sorry I was about Patrick's death. It must have been hard on you. But I see you've bounced back as the president-elect's new chief of staff."

Susan Welsh was talking as if she and Martin were old friends when, in fact, they barely knew each other. Like so many politicians, she was saying the right things to simply make him feel better about himself. But Martin had worked on Capitol Hill for too long to be taken by the phony comments of a seasoned politician like Welsh.

"Thank you, Madam Speaker," Martin said.

"Please Josh, call me Susan. You left quite the message for me. Exactly how can I help you?"

"I have information that might be of value to you regarding the president-elect."

"What kind of information?"

"Personal information concerning her affair with a Secret Service Agent prior to Patrick's death."

"And why would I be interested in such information?"

"Madam Speaker, if you're not interested, then I'm wasting both yours and my time." With that, Martin disconnected the call. Moments later, Welsh called him back.

"I'm not used to being hung up on, Josh. I hope this won't become a habit."

"That depends on you, Madam Speaker," Martin replied.

"This is quite concerning, Josh. Why would you want to share this information with me?"

"That's not important right now. But I can assure you, you'll find the information politically valuable."

"So, you're doing this out of your commitment to serve the best interests of the American people?" Welsh asked.

"Hardly, Madam Speaker. My life will be in grave danger once I make this information available to you. I need to leave the country."

"Ann Banks has threatened you?"

"No. There are other forces at work here that are far more dangerous to me and others than Ann Banks."

"What forces?"

"Again, that's not important right now. I'll tell you more about that later if we reach a deal."

"How much are we talking about Josh?"

"Five million."

"For information? That's outrageous."

Martin told Welsh that his information concerned Ann Banks and a Secret Service Agent having sex just days before Patrick Banks' death. He also told her that he had a copy of the recording.

"If you don't want it, then I'm sure I can find another buyer," Martin replied.

"Let me think about this. But I'm going to need something tangible. A taste of what I'm buying, as some would say."

"When you agree to my terms, you'll get your taste before you buy."

"I'll be in touch soon, Josh. And thank you for calling," Welsh said. She disconnected the call before he could respond.

The moment Martin heard the phone go dead, he felt a morbid sense of fear. There was no turning back now. The call to the Speaker could easily backfire on several fronts. Susan Welsh could decide to report the offer directly to Ann Banks; something he doubted she would do given the Speaker's utter dislike for her. Dunayev could get wind of it and come after him for making such a decision without his approval. Or the Speaker could release the tape before he could make his way out of the country. What Martin did know for certain was that

Ann Banks would fire him the moment she got the chance. And, that Dunayev would kill him if their plan didn't succeed; and it was coming apart by the minute; mostly because of Dunayev. But that wouldn't matter. It was time he looked out for himself. Moments later, Martin pulled into the parking garage of the Hilton Hotel and went up to his room. The fog around his head was growing. He was frustrated and angry; mostly with himself for getting involved with Patrick Banks and Dunayev in the first place. All he wanted was a drink to calm his nerves. But that drink would have to wait; Ann Banks wanted him back at the mansion at eight p.m. for a late-night strategy session. *Maybe just one,* he thought as he poured himself a drink.

***

"He just disconnected with the Speaker," Minor told Sherry. "You're going to want to hear this."

Minor played the recording for Sherry and DeCarlo. There was silence as both took a moment to digest what they had just heard. DeCarlo was the first to speak.

"You're right, General. You do have resources that I normally don't have access to."

"This changes things just a bit with regard to our timetable, detective." Sherry, who was used to thinking about most everything he did like a chess player making his next strategic move, asked DeCarlo, "So detective, how might this alter your approach to Mr. Martin?"

DeCarlo knew from experience that men like Josh Martin had delicate egos. And unlike more traditional and hardened criminals, people like Martin were easy to intimidate, especially when faced with the threat of a long prison sentence.

"General, people like Martin, when faced with the prospect of political or business ruin and the possibility of a long-term prison sentence, are usually quick to give up their own mothers if it might save their own asses. His phone call to the Speaker of the House is only going to make my job easier," she said with a smile. DeCarlo knew that Martin had the potential to become a very useful tool in the search for both Michael Dionis and Andre Dunayev.

Sherry excused himself and told everyone in the room that he needed a few minutes of privacy. He walked into the bedroom of the executive suite, closed the door, and took out his cell phone. He accessed his contact list and scrolled down until he found the name he was looking for. He highlighted the contact and hit the send button. On the third ring Sergi Nikitin answered with a simple greeting. "*Privet*, my old friend."

"Sergi, old friend," Sherry said. "How are you?"

"Well, my friend. And you?"

"Old and getting tired. I think it's time to retire."

"And what would you do? Golf?"

"There are worse things. Maybe I'll fly to Russia and let you take me out on one of your courses in Moscow."

"I'll look forward to it. But you didn't call me to discuss golf."

"No Sergi, I didn't. I have a serious issue here and hope you might be able to help me before the problem proves embarrassing for both of our countries."

"I'm listening."

"You have a fugitive, or at least I think you do, by the name of Evsei Balagula. Are you interested in finding him or would you like me to handle him? Take a moment to check if you like. If you're working with him in this country, simply hang up. I will understand. But he'll be picked up soon," Sherry lied. He had no idea where Balagula was at this very minute.

"Balagula is a problem. He's not working for us. On the contrary, we'd be very interested in having him back in Russia. He's been in hiding for some time."

"Then I think we can help each other. In the spirit of détente, how would you like to collect comrade Balagula?"

"I can have some men available to take him off your hands in a few hours. I just need a geographic location."

"New York city or Washington D.C. But it might be a day or two. Can I get back to you?" Sherry asked.

"Of course. But why are you being so generous?" Nikitin asked.

"We have a new president taking office soon and I'm certain she wants to see a thaw in our two countries' relationship. But if he is working for you, his actions are going to set our two countries back even more than they already are. If he isn't working for you, then his actions are designed to cause us both harm. And then I'm sure justice for him would be better served in Russia than here in the states. That is, if you really want him."

"I can share this, my friend; Moscow would love to have their hands on him. And not because he's a valuable asset. He's a dangerous criminal who has murdered at least two judges and several police."

"Then stay close to your phone for the next couple of days. You'll hear from me one way or the other."

"Tell me, how did you find him?" Nikitin asked.

"Ah…." Sherry sighed. "Let's just say it was almost by accident. But like our friends in law enforcement like to say, 'all criminals make mistakes.' Balagula apparently is no different; he simply made a mistake, a very big mistake."

"Then I shall wait to hear from you, Jonathan."

"Until then," Sherry said as he disconnected the call. He then called his contact at the CIA. "I've just learned of a possible Russian intelligence operation in New York and possibly D.C. Would you please let me know if you see an increase in communication traffic or activity over the next 24 – 48 hours?"

The man at the CIA assured Sherry that he would let him know if there was any increased communication activity. They would also let the FBI's New York and D.C. field offices know so that their counterintelligence units would be put on alert. Sherry had a long-term relationship with Nikitin; one that had benefited both of them over the years. On more than one occasion, it saved the lives of both countries' operatives. Sherry trusted Nikitin to a point. But like all of his adversaries in the intelligence community, that trust went only so far. Sherry always subscribed to Ronald Reagan's philosophy of "trust but verify." He hoped he could verify Nikitin's word that Balagula wasn't operating under Russia's guidance. He wasn't about to simply hand him over to the Russians if he was.

Chapter 26

Jian Wie didn't like being contacted by Andre Dunayev. He saw Dunayev for exactly what he was, a criminal thug who thought he could parlay his way into the good graces of the Chinese and Russian political hierarchy. Dunayev was nothing more to him than a tool, an unwitting source who was as disposable as an unproductive car salesman who fails to make his monthly quota. It was Wie who contacted Dunayev, but only when it was absolutely necessary.

Wie never liked talking on the telephone. He always operated as if he were being monitored by various intelligence sources or the FBI. He knew that if he simply stayed off the phone, the chances of him being caught doing anything, dropped dramatically. Besides, he never understood how Americans could get so bored with their lives that they could spend hours on end talking on the telephone, neither party usually listening to what the other had to say. So, when Dunayev called, Wie answered with just one word, "Yes."

"Can we meet? Important."

"When?" Wie asked.

"Usual place. In an hour?"

"Outside. Not in. We can walk." With that, Wie hung up. The less said, the better. Wie had been following the events of Christmas Eve. He also heard about the Russian shot and killed in the motel in Scranton. Wie knew right away, after seeing the man's picture on the news, that the dead Russian in Scranton was one of Dunayev's men. There was no doubt in his mind that the two Russians shot to death on Christmas Eve, were also associated with Dunayev. Wie's first instinct was that something was wrong and that it might be time to sever his relationship with the Russian thug. First, he'd hear what he had to say. But he didn't like where this was headed.

***

It was almost six p.m. when Michael Dionis left his room. He had tried to sleep but did nothing but toss and turn most of the day. He couldn't shut his mind down. He was craving exercise. His body began to feel run down, as if he were going through withdrawal from a drug. But something as simple as a short run wasn't something he could do right now. He'd have to be satisfied with a brisk walk around the neighborhood. He hoped that just getting some air in his lungs might help clear his head. So, he put on his coat, took the elevator down to the lobby, and went outside into the cold, dark night. He was obsessed with a host of thoughts, including the medical condition of Sandi DeCarlo, and the mental condition and safety of Ann Banks. But the thought that kept him awake most was how to find Andre Dunayev and stop the recording from being released. New York City was far too big for him to simply ask around. He knew the car Dunayev drove up to the motel in Scranton had New York tags on it. He had been able to run the tag, but it came back as a rental to a bogus company. He needed something to help in his search for this Russian. Finding him was his immediate priority. Dionis did not usually fear the worst in most situations, but all he could think of was the tape being released, Ann's presidency being put in jeopardy, and his being set up for at least one, and possibly two murders he had nothing to do with. His ex-wife, Tina Crawford, already suspected him and would happily have him hung if she thought it would advance her own career. When he was a Captain in the Marine Corps, and it came to protecting his men, Michael was never one to shy away from bending the rules, crossing the line, or looking the other way. He maintained the same mind set when he joined the Secret Service. But now, he knew that simply crossing the line was not going to be enough; he'd actually have to break the law to stop the tape from being released. And once he did, there would be no turning back. At the very least, his career would be over. At worst, he'd be killed, and, if he survived, he'd face the wrath of the justice system and his ex-wife, who would love nothing more than prosecuting him. But it was a risk he had to take. Dionis had walked less than ten minutes when it finally sunk in.

***

It was almost seven p.m. when DeCarlo knocked on Josh Martin's hotel door. She and Sherry's commando, as she liked to refer to him, agreed that he would remain quiet during the contact with Martin. And unless Martin became difficult, or posed a threat of any kind, the commando would remain as invisible as possible. Sherry and Minor would remain upstairs in the suite and monitor the meeting on a hidden video feed they had placed in Josh's room earlier in the day. DeCarlo was confident that before the night was through, she was going to turn Josh Martin into an informant and a cooperating source. Of all the reasons one becomes an informant, being threatened by the law or other criminals who seek to do you harm, is considered the most beneficial to police. Josh was certainly motivated by money, but not enough to cooperate with the cops. And he certainly wasn't looking for revenge, another motivating force more often used by a host of people, usually with the prefix "ex" in front of them, like ex-spouses. DeCarlo knew that if she were going to be successful, she needed to capitalize on Martin's fear. If she failed to do so, Sherry would have to resort to plan B; whatever plan B was.

DeCarlo identified herself as a detective with the Connecticut State Police, showing Martin her badge and credentials. She simply pointed to the man with her, and said, "This is my associate. We'd like to talk to you for a few minutes about Patrick Banks."

Martin was so annoyed by the interruption he didn't pick up on the fact that DeCarlo never introduced her associate by name. The last thing he needed right now was to take time out of his schedule and talk to the police.

"I'm really busy right now. Can this wait? Or perhaps you can make an appointment with my assistant."

"Not really, Mr. Martin. This will only take a few minutes. Ann Banks gave us your room number. We spoke to her just a few minutes ago," DeCarlo said. "May we come in? This will be quick, I promise."

Martin relented and let DeCarlo and the man in. DeCarlo noticed the scotch bottle on the table along with a glass containing a healthy pour. *He's been drinking. Good; he's nervous and scared*, DeCarlo thought.

DeCarlo grabbed the back of the desk chair, turned it around and said, "Mind if I sit? It's easier on the shoulder if I do. I'm still healing from a gunshot."

"Of course," Martin replied. "I'm sorry. I didn't realize you were the detective shot on Christmas eve. How are you doing?"

"Better. Thank you for asking," DeCarlo replied.

"Terrible thing. You folks risk your lives every day. I'm sure Ann Banks will be a friend to law enforcement once she takes office," Martin said.

"Oh, I'm sure of it. Do you mind if I call you Josh?"

"Of course. Please. So, how can I help?"

"Well, you can help by telling me about your relationship with Andre Dunayev," DeCarlo said. "And why are you cooperating with him in blackmailing the president-elect with the threat of releasing a recording of her in bed with Michael Dionis?"

DeCarlo wasted no time. She began with an accusation which changed the meeting from an interview to an interrogation. There was dead silence in the room. Martin's heart fell through the floor. He rose up out of his chair and in a loud and accusatory voice shouted, "What the hell are you talking about, detective?"

DeCarlo knew that the power to resist confessing could be overwhelming. After all, it is human nature to resist unpleasant things. Her goal here was to destroy all hope in Martin's mind that he was anything but screwed. To do so, she would have to abandon most every ethical consideration she most always considered when interviewing or interrogating someone. If turning Martin meant making an illegal promise, one she had no authority to make, or using a form of coercion that might get her prosecuted, so be it. This case was never going to trial. DeCarlo sat calmly, looked up directly into Martin's eyes, shook her head, and said, "You know, Josh, lying to me right now isn't a good idea. Why don't you sit the fuck back down before my colleague here forces you to?"

"I think it's time for you to leave," Martin said angrily, as he remained standing.

"Sit down, Josh," DeCarlo said quietly, but with authority. She took her cell phone out of her pocket, opened the recording app and said, "Listen to this. Then, if you still want us to leave, we'll leave."

DeCarlo told Martin that they had tapped his phone and his texts. She then played the recordings of him talking to Dunayev and Susan Welsh.

"You've fallen deep down the fucking rabbit hole, Josh. No matter what you do from this point on, you're done working for Ann Banks. She knows we're meeting with you. You're being fired as we speak. Your credentials are being revoked. If you have any hope of climbing out of the hole you've dug for yourself, you're going to have to work with me. Because right now, I'm your only chance of surviving this. In other words, Josh, you're in a world of shit."

DeCarlo had hoped she hadn't overplayed her hand with that last remark. If Martin asked for a lawyer, she would no longer have much of a chance to convince him to work with her. *So far, so good*, she thought.

Martin sat there quietly, his face pale as a ghost. His political instincts were failing him. He thought about asking for a lawyer, but quickly realized that he was finished in politics no matter what he said or did. The look on his face clearly revealed to DeCarlo that he was scared. "I can't go to prison, detective," he said.

With that simple phrase, DeCarlo knew that she had him. With seasoned or career criminals, the question-and-answer interrogation was always like a dance, each partner feeling the other out before making any disclosures that might reveal more than either wanted the other to know, without first garnering some concessions. But with those who had never faced the likelihood of incarceration, the dance was different. It was usually one-sided with the interrogator controlling each move. DeCarlo knew that Martin was about to break; it was time to set the hook.

After a short period of silence, DeCarlo placed her hand on Martin's knee and said calmly, "I have a proposition for you. Let's see if we can work together to make sure that doesn't happen."

Martin fought back the bile rising in his throat and said, "Andre Dunayev will kill us all if he thinks we're a threat to him. I swear to God, I had no idea how deep Patrick was in with him," he lied. Martin was trying desperately to maintain some sense of self-worth and self-esteem. DeCarlo knew that when suspects introduced the Almighty into the conversation, they were not only being less than honest, but they were also being deceptive.

"Let's keep God out of this for the time being, shall we," she said. "I'm guessing Patrick deceived you as well as he did his wife. Once he got into bed with Dunayev, you had little choice but to go along. Does that sound about right?" DeCarlo asked, hoping that the comment would make Martin more comfortable talking to her.

"Yes," Martin replied. "Patrick was jealous of Ann. He wanted to be president. When he finally accepted the fact that that was never going to happen, he got greedy. Dunayev secretly financed a good bit of Ann's campaign, along with Patrick's campaign for Congress. In return, Patrick convinced Dunayev that his wife would nominate him as her Secretary of State."

"Why was it so important that Patrick be named Secretary of State?" DeCarlo asked.

"Dunayev was convinced it would help eliminate certain trade restrictions with Russia which, in turn, would increase his business opportunities. If he could influence the Secretary of State, he would also ingratiate himself with Russian oligarchy. He's all about making money."

"But he's a murdering thug," DeCarlo said. "He's wanted in Russia for the murder of a couple of judges. Come on, Josh, you really expect me to buy into all this bullshit? You really think you can sit there and sell me the fact that you think all of his business interests are legal."

"I'm telling you that I didn't know that, or the extent of it. Yes, I suspected many of his interests crossed the line. But I certainly didn't know how dangerous he was, not when Patrick first introduced me to him. Yes, I knew he was volatile. I knew he had a threatening manner about him, but it wasn't until after Patrick's death that I realized just how dangerous Dunayev is. I had no idea."

DeCarlo just heard Martin refer to Dunayev in regard to Patrick Banks' death. She decided to store that information for the moment and circle back to it later. She also knew it was never a good idea to back a suspect into a corner, and she didn't want to do that just now. Like a wild animal with no means of escape, they'll attack if they have no means of egress. But DeCarlo also knew Martin was being less than truthful, and she needed him to keep talking. And if that meant giving him enough room to save face, so be it.

"I'm going to want your copy of the recording you have of Ann Banks and Michael Dionis," DeCarlo said.

That was DeCarlo's one mistake. Martin quickly realized he had one bargaining chip and he was prepared to use it.

"And in return?"

"You think you're in a position to bargain?" DeCarlo asked.

"Actually, I do," Martin said. His political instincts were now kicking in. Or so he thought. To DeCarlo, he was nothing more than a criminal seeking to minimize his exposure to the justice system. The first rule of all criminals is to not get caught. The second rule, if caught, do whatever you have to do to minimize the amount of jail time you have to serve. It was more than just Martin's political instincts kicking in, it was his animal survival instincts. He knew that the consequences of his actions ended any hopes of working and operating in the political arena ever again. He was damaged goods, like an actor who had been accused of some politically incorrect remark from years past, whether true or not, the cancel culture would see too it that he would never work again on the political stage. But unlike an actor who may have been falsely accused, Martin was guilty of sins that would forever keep him out of the political mainstream. But what he feared most, now, was prison. Martin was looking for a way out. But DeCarlo knew that he wasn't a sociopath. Had he been, Martin would never have freely admitted his involvement in the blackmail conspiracy. Martin was nothing more than a greedy criminal, and a political thug. But he wasn't a hardened criminal. He hadn't done time, and, from her assessment, he wasn't one who could easily adjust to life behind bars. And those were the kind of people that were most often easily turned into cooperating sources. It made DeCarlo's next move an easy one.

"I know you regret your role in all of this," DeCarlo said, as she placed her right hand on his knee. "Sometimes, we get in over our heads before we realize it's too late." She was giving Martin a way out of the corner he had backed himself into.

"I never thought any of this would go this far," Martin replied. "Patrick let his ego and thirst for power blind him to what was happening."

In the past, DeCarlo had felt bad for criminals who broke down and confessed to their crimes. She did not feel bad for Martin. She saw him on the same plane she viewed child sex offenders: despicable. *This man should be tried for treason*, she thought.

"We can't allow you, or Dunayev, to destroy the incoming president even before she's sworn in. You have to understand that. And blackmailing her is going to get you sent to prison."

"As I said, I can't go to prison."

"Well, Josh, there's also the question of two murders," DeCarlo added. "Those trump blackmail for sure. So, you either cooperate with me, or you can plan on spending a long time in prison. But don't despair, prison will afford you an opportunity to catch up on a lot of recreational reading."

"I don't know anything about any murders," Martin shouted, as he jumped up out of his chair.

"But you gave Patrick Banks the cocaine that resulted in his death," DeCarlo said, fishing for a response to a question she didn't know the answer to.

Martin lashed out and said, "I didn't know it was contaminated. Patrick was getting it directly from Dunayev until Patrick cut off direct contact with him. He then made me his fucking middleman. I got it from Dunayev and gave it to Patrick, that was it."

DeCarlo could see that Martin was terrified. He was trying to come clean, or as clean as any criminal can when they know they're screwed. She also now knew how, and where, Patrick Banks had gotten the contaminated cocaine. She then felt her phone vibrate letting her know that she had a text message.

Tell him you can keep him out of jail and that there might even be some money it for him.

"What if we can find a way around you going to prison? Would that interest you?" DeCarlo asked.

Martin sat back down and said, "Exactly what do you want from me, detective?"

DeCarlo had a good idea where this might be going, and it wasn't a direction that she was used to taking when dealing with suspects. But she needed more information. If her suspicions were correct about Sherry's next move, she would need to discuss it with him personally. *This is well beyond my pay grade and job description,* she thought.

"Stay here Josh. Try to relax," DeCarlo said coolly. "Have yourself another drink. But don't drink too much. And by the way, don't think about leaving; you're being watched. And your phone is being monitored too. Call anyone and we'll know it. Sit tight, I'll be back in a few minutes. Then we'll talk about exactly what I want from you. I'm sure you won't mind if my partner keeps you company for a few minutes."

Martin simply nodded. He got up from his chair, reached over to his bottle of scotch and took a large sip letting it burn down his throat. The peaty taste of the alcohol did nothing to change the nausea, or what had become painfully clear; if a man ever knew he was fucked, it was him.

DeCarlo rode the elevator to the top floor for a short strategy meeting with Sherry. “Do you think he’ll cooperate to the extent we need him to?” Sherry asked.

“They almost always do when you have them by the balls, General. And when you have them by the balls, their hearts and minds usually follow,” DeCarlo said. “Let’s let him walk if he gives us Dunayev and the Speaker.”

Sherry’s response was short and direct. “I like the way you think, detective. Make the deal.”

***

Andre Dunayev was waiting outside the front of Lucardi’s when Jian Wie arrived in a black Cadillac Escalade. The rear passenger side door opened and Wie motioned for Dunayev to get in.

“It’s too cold to walk,” Wie said. “Let’s take a ride.”

Dunayev got into the back seat alongside him. The only other man in the car was the driver. Wie told the man to simply drive around the city for a few minutes but not to get too far from Lucardi’s.

“So, tell me Andre, what is so important that we must meet again so soon?”

Wie’s face was passive. Dunayev could sense a coldness about his tone.

“We had a problem in Scranton, Pennsylvania on Christmas,” Dunayev said. “I lost a good man as we tried to deal with this Secret Service Agent.”

“And how is that my problem?” Wie asked.

“It’s our problem,” Dunayev countered. “He needs to be dealt with and I need your help finding him.”

“You also lost two men on Christmas eve if I recall,” Wie said.

Dunayev had no idea that Wie knew about the shooting in Farmington. “That was not planned. Those two idiots were instructed to watch the man and place a tracking device on his car; nothing more.”

“Still, it has brought you unneeded attention. Surely, the new president must suspect you’re behind this.”

“Josh Martin should be handling that. I don’t see a problem.”

“And your man Martin? Can’t he find this man for you?”

“Martin has been unavailable since the shooting on Christmas eve. I don’t know what he’s doing right now but I’m sure he’s handling things the way he’s supposed to.”

Wie hated listening to excuses. He didn’t tolerate it from those who reported to him, and he certainly wasn’t about to listen to it from Dunayev. When he was informed of problems by his associates, he expected to hear possible solutions at the same time. “It sounds like your plan to get close to the new president is unraveling in front of you, comrade.”

“I need leverage. If I can get to Michael Dionis, the new president will do whatever she must to save him. I’m sure of it,” Dunayev snapped.

“And what if you’re wrong?”

Barely able to restrain himself, Dunayev said angrily, “I’m not wrong. The new president is weak. She’ll do anything to save her lover.”

“Do you have any idea where this man you seek might be?” Wie asked.

“No. But if I were him, I’d be looking for me. So, my guess, he’s somewhere in New York.”

“New York is a big city. Many places to hide. Maybe it’s time for us to reconsider moving forward with your plan.”

Dunayev wasn’t just a sociopath, he was stubborn and not one to usually listen to reason.

"That's why I need your help. Do you have resources that can assist me?" Dunayev asked.

"Perhaps. I'll see what I can do. In the meantime, you should stay out of sight for a few days. I'll be in touch with you when I have something."

Wie told the driver to return to Lucardi's. As soon as the car came to a stop, Dunayev looked directly at Wie and said, "Help me find this man and everything will be back on course."

Wie nodded and Dunayev got out of the car. Wie was a believer in the old saying, "desperate people are dangerous people." And Andre Dunayev was becoming desperate. As Wie drove away, he told the driver, "I think it's time for us to abandon our ties with our Russian friend. But maybe we can establish some good will in the process."

***

Michael Dionis had no idea that Chrissie Chan and one of Sherry's men were parked just down the street from the Casa Blanca hotel. He also had no idea that Sherry had discovered the fact that he was registered in the name of Sean Cameron. Had he known any of this, he might not have called Tony Maffuci and told him that he was going to look for Dunayev but needed to get back to Connecticut first.

"I'm going to check in at Water's Edge late tomorrow night. I could certainly use your help if you get free," Dionis told Maffuci when they spoke briefly on the phone. Maffuci made no promises or guarantees. "I'll do whatever I can *Amico*. Till then, stay safe," Maffuci said.

Dionis laid his head on the pillow and tried to nod off to sleep. But his thoughts, centered on finding Dunayev and confronting Maffuci, kept him awake. One way or another, he was going to find the hole that Dunayev was living in. He'd deal with Maffuci later. He was gambling that Dunayev would find his way to Connecticut. *Let him find me. That will be easier than me looking all over New York for him,* he thought.

Dionis got up from his bed, took a huge drink of water, walked to the door to make sure it was securely locked, then lay back down on the bed, fully dressed, hoping to clear his head. His head was pounding, and he was unable to sleep. He knew that tomorrow would be a long and very dangerous day. No matter the outcome, his way of life, his reputation, and career, were probably going to be lost forever. His mind was racing with way too many thoughts. Dionis had never felt more alone. He actually felt like crying. It was only his anger that kept him from completely breaking down. An hour later he finally closed his eyes and faded off to sleep. His Walther .380 PPK was under his pillow.

***

Several minutes after Dunayev got out of Wie's car, he felt his cell phone vibrate. He looked down and saw that he had a text message.

Dionis will be at the Water's Edge resort in Westbrook, Connecticut tomorrow afternoon.

Dunayev could barely restrain his enthusiasm as he hailed a taxi for the ride back to his apartment.

Chapter 27

DeCarlo's second meeting with Martin picked up where the first one had left off. With Sherry's commando standing the whole time and following the script to not talk during the interview, DeCarlo sat directly across from Martin and said, "Here's what I'm going to need you to do, Josh; you're going to call the Speaker of the House again and tell her you have a recording of the president-elect engaging in what she would consider an embarrassing and possibly career ending act. And, that you're ready to hand the recording over if she meets your price of five-million dollars. Are you ready to do that Josh?"

Martin shook his head no, and said, "I'm not wearing a wire."

"It's not a wire Josh. We'll simply be recording the call."

"Same fucking thing," Martin said grudgingly. "I'm not doing it."

"Then I guess we're done here. You'll be arrested and charged. And trust me, you're going to be convicted and sent to prison."

"And the recording goes viral. Banks will be ruined," Martin shouted.

"Maybe," DeCarlo said. "But you know politics, Josh; people have short memories. And Americans are very forgiving. How forgiving do you think they're going to be when it comes to you blackmailing the president-elect and being in bed with the Russian mob?"

"You're setting me up," Martin said. "There's no way I can recover from this."

"You're listening, Josh, but you're not hearing me. Let me walk you through this. You make the call. You pick up your conversation with the Speaker right where you left off. Then make arrangements for the payoff. Get the money transferred to an account you're comfortable with; someplace offshore if you like. When you're done with the call and I have your copy, and all copies of the recording for that matter, you walk away. I'm sure you can figure out how to survive on five million."

"Dunayev will have me killed," Martin said, shaking his head.

"Dunayev isn't going to be a problem for you. You have to trust me on that. If you want to help yourself here, you'll make the call."

Martin got up from his chair and began to pace around the small room. His head was spinning, and he wasn't thinking straight. But he knew he had backed himself into a corner and the only way out was to cooperate with DeCarlo. He also realized that once he made the call, his life, as he knew it, was over. He sat back down in his chair, put his hands over his face, leaned forward and asked, "So how does this work?"

DeCarlo explained the procedure and laid out the plan instructing Martin as to what to say and do. He would give the Speaker just enough information to convince her that Ann Banks had engaged in an extra marital affair that would cause her political damage to the point she might actually resign her presidency before it ever got started. The key to the conversation was simply to get the Speaker to offer to pay for the information and the recording. If she actually wired the money to Martin's account, all the better.

Martin stood up, poured himself another drink, and began to feel dizzy, dropping his glass to the floor and spilling his scotch. He sat back down, his face reddened and in low voice said, "Okay. Set it up."

Thirty minutes later, Martin was on the phone with Susan Welch. A few floors up from Martin's room, Aaliyah Minor was recording the conversation. Martin was following the script exactly as it was presented to him. And Susan Welch was taking the bait better than DeCarlo and Sherry had hoped. DeCarlo didn't know who she was going to get more satisfaction out of taking down in all of this, Martin, or Welsh. *These politicians, especially Welsh, are more despicable scumbags than any of the real criminals I deal with. If the American people only knew,* she thought.

When the call ended, DeCarlo said, "Now, give me your copy of the recording." Martin handed DeCarlo a flash drive and told her the recording of Ann Banks and Michael Dionis' lovemaking was on it.

"Are there any other copies?" DeCarlo asked.

"As far as I know, just the one Dunayev has," Martin said.

"And you? None hidden away somewhere that might surface later?"

"That's it. I didn't make any other copies. So now what?"

"We'll be in touch, Josh. But if I were you, I'd make plans to relocate, out of the country. And the sooner the better. Your assistance here will keep you out of jail, especially if you disappear. But short of that, I make no promises."

"And my money?"

"That's between you and the Speaker. Hopefully, you trust her enough to wire the money she promised. You know how well politicians keep their promises; I'm sure you'll be fine," she said with a smirk.

The sarcasm wasn't lost on Martin. His only hope now, was that Susan Welsh wired the down payment, half of the five million dollars, to thc account he provided her. He didn't want to think about what might happen to him if she didn't send the money.

"So, I'm free to go?" Martin asked.

DeCarlo knew that Josh Martin was coming as clean as he could; especially for someone not used to exposing himself to the possibility of a long-term prison sentence. To most career criminals, going to prison is considered the price of doing business. To white-collar criminals, the thought of going to prison wasn't something most could deal with. But to ensure Martin's full cooperation, DeCarlo had a few more unpleasant and stern warnings for him.

"Yes, you're free to go. But Josh, let me share this with you: If another copy of this tape surfaces and it's traced back to you, there is no hole you can hide in where you won't be found. And it won't end well for you. Do you understand?"

Martin couldn't speak. All he could do was simply nod. He wanted nothing more than to get back to D.C., grab whatever he could from his condo, and run. Hopefully, to someplace safe, wherever that might be.

Moments later, back in Sherry's suite, DeCarlo asked, "Did you get the call between Martin and Welsh recorded?"

"Got it," Minor replied. "All good."

"Now what?" DeCarlo asked Sherry.

"Now we wait to see if Welsh wires the money."

"What about Michael?" DeCarlo asked.

"We have people on him. It appears he's headed to someplace here in Connecticut called Water's Edge."

"Water's Edge? That's down on the shoreline near Old Saybrook. What's he doing heading there?"

"Trying to lure Andre Dunayev into a confrontation is my guess."

"How do you know this?"

"We have Dunayev's number. We intercepted a text to him."

"Who sent the text?" DeCarlo demanded to know.

"Came from a burner phone. We're still working on it," Minor interjected.

"Michael must have told someone he was headed to Connecticut. And that someone told Dunayev," DeCarlo said.

"Any ideas?" Sherry asked.

"Unfortunately, General, I do."

"Care to share that with me?"

"I pray I'm wrong, but my guess would be Tony Maffuci, one of his closest friends and an FBI Agent."

"Why would an FBI Agent tell Dunayev that?" Sherry asked.

"Your guess is as good as mine, General. But if I'm right, Michael is in more trouble than he knows," DeCarlo whispered, her voice lowered now afraid that her suspicions were true.

"Unless Agent Dionis suspects his friend Maffuci and shared the information with him to confirm his suspicions."

"Michael is smart, of that there is no doubt. If you're right, then maybe he does have the advantage here. You say you have two people following him?"

"I do," Sherry replied.

"Well, I better get down to Water's Edge myself. They're going to need some help. I can get some troopers down there to assist."

"We can't do that right now, detective."

"And why not?"

"This is still a very quiet operation. The objective here is to stop Dunayev, get his copy of the recording, and turn him over to the Russians."

"You'd risk Michael's life trying to do this?" DeCarlo snapped.

"I told you from the start, I would. My goal is to protect the president-elect. This operation is completely off the books. Nothing has changed, detective."

"Then I better get down there now to help keep Michael alive."

"That's a good idea," Sherry replied. "How's the shoulder?"

"Sore as shit. But thank god it's the left side."

Sherry gave DeCarlo the names of the two people following Dionis and how to contact them. "I'll let them know you're on your way. Once you have Dunayev in custody, they're in charge. You stand down and get Agent Dionis as far away from that resort as you can. Understood?"

"That's fine. But tell your people they work for me until that happens. I call the shots until we have Dunayev. Are you good with that?"

"We have a deal, detective. And the recording Martin gave you?" Sherry asked.

"It's right here, General." DeCarlo took the flash drive out of her pocket and tossed it in the fireplace. "That should keep the conversation safe from being released," she said.

The smile on Sherry's face evaporated. He sat back in his chair and said nothing. DeCarlo could see the anger in his veins as his eyes shifted away from her. That's when she knew it was time to leave.

As soon as DeCarlo left, Sherry got up and took a huge sip of Buffalo Trace. He knew he needed to calm down before making his next move. Moments later, he notified Chrissie Chan that Dionis would be leaving soon for Connecticut, and that Detective DeCarlo would meet with her. Sherry then called Sergi Nikitin.

"General. Good to hear from you again. I take it you have news?"

"Some. Are you still interested in Balagula?"

"Of course."

"Can you get an extraction team to Hartford, Connecticut tomorrow?"

"I'm sure I can."

"Then do so. And await my call. I want him out of the U.S. as quickly as possible."

With that, Sherry disconnected his phone.

"Now what?" Minor asked.

"Now we transmit a message that the Russians and Chinese will pick up about Dunayev being at this Water's Edge resort. I want to see who bites and who might be hiding in the wood pile, as my friends in Georgia like to say."

Sherry drafted a short, cryptic, message about Andre Dunayev, a/k/a Evsei Balagula, a member of Russian organized crime operating in Connecticut, and the state police's plan to arrest him the following day. The message also alluded to the fact that Dunayev had information that might be beneficial to the U.S. about Chinese and Russian intelligence. Sherry made sure the message was transmitted in such a manner that both the Russian and Chinese intelligence agencies operating in the U.S. would easily intercept it. He wanted to know what, if any, chatter there might be related to Dunayev and the message he sent.

"It's done," Minor said. "I must admit, DeCarlo did a great job getting Martin to cooperate."

"She employed a classic interrogation technique. Get the subject to believe they have no way out of the shit hole they put themselves in. Then bluff and lie about the evidence you have on them if necessary to get them to cooperate. I've used it many times myself," Sherry said.

"Then why not just do the interrogation yourself and leave DeCarlo out of it?" Minor asked.

"Because if all of this blows up, DeCarlo is expendable and I have plausible deniability," Sherry replied.

Minor was stunned by the response. She sat silent for a moment, then asked, "Now what?"

"Now, my dear niece, we wait."

***

DeCarlo got off the elevator in the parking garage of the hotel and walked quickly to her car. She reached into her purse, found her keys, and hit the unlock button. As soon as she sat down and started the car, she hit the seat warmer button. The second thing she did was telephone Leah Riggs at the FBI.

"I need to talk to you. It's urgent," DeCarlo said the moment Riggs picked up the phone.

"Can you come by the office in the morning," Riggs replied.

"Not your office. Someplace where we can have some privacy; just you and me. And it needs to be now; tonight."

"It's late detective."

"You know I wouldn't call at this hour if it wasn't urgent," DeCarlo replied.

"It's that serious?" Riggs asked.

"It's about Tony Maffuci," DeCarlo said. " And it's not good."

Riggs wasn't surprised by the call, especially when she heard DeCarlo mention Maffuci. Bosses at most every level of any law enforcement agency usually don't want to hear about the minor infractions or illegal steps one of their investigators might take when trying to perfect a criminal case. At the end of the day, supervisors want results; the system is such that careers live or die based on it. Riggs was no different. She too wanted results and she was not so naive to think some of her agents didn't occasionally cross the line; after all, she had done it herself. But Riggs was also from a new breed of agents coming up the line: she might overlook and even support a minor investigative infraction, but she wouldn't tolerate any form of corruption. Maffuci was lying about his involvement with Dionis. She knew it, and now it was clear that DeCarlo did too. It was time for Riggs and the FBI to share what it knew, not something easily done by the FBI.

Forty-five minutes after DeCarlo telephoned Riggs, the two women were sitting in the Playwright Irish pub in Hamden, just north of New Haven.

"What made you pick this place?" Riggs asked.

"An old professor of mine used to play guitar here on Sundays with a pick-up Irish group. Some of us used to come here to listen to him play."

"I didn't take you for a lover of Irish music," Riggs said.

"It's an acquired taste," DeCarlo replied. "I enjoyed his music more than I did his lectures. He is a good guitar player. Plus, I got to bond with his wife, another professor who everyone loved."

"Well, you didn't bring me out at this hour of the night to talk about Irish music," Riggs said.

A waitress came by and took their order. Lisa Riggs ordered a mojito while DeCarlo ordered a Guiness.

"A Guiness?" Riggs said, looking surprised.

"When in Rome," replied DeCarlo.

The two spoke in detail, both women being as honest as necessary about what they knew and suspected. DeCarlo held back from telling Riggs about Sherry's involvement in all of this, or the fact that Dunayev had a recording of Ann Banks and Michael Dionis having sex. That was on a need-to-know basis. Instead, DeCarlo concocted a story that was partially true.

"What I can tell you, is that the president-elect has asked for my help in trying to keep Michael from getting himself killed. The guy he's after, a Russian going by the name of Andre Dunayev, is trying to blackmail Ann Banks. Dunayev is my chief suspect in the murder of Oleg Lomakina in New Haven. He's also my chief suspect in the death of Patrick Banks."

"So, you want the FBI's help in arresting Dunayev?" Riggs asked.

"Yes and no. The Russians want him bad. And a couple of our government's alphabet agencies want him handed over to them. This case is never going to trial."

"And why is that?"

"Because of what Dunayev is capable of doing to the president-elect. It's extremely sensitive. And, because our intelligence agencies have been working on this for several days now. Unfortunately, they've collected information and evidence in such a manner that it could never be used in court."

"What the hell is going on here, detective?" Riggs demanded to know.

"There are people trying to protect the president-elect from some embarrassing information being leaked; information that has nothing to do with her ability to serve as president and is in no way criminal in nature. I'm not going to lie to you. I know what that is. But I've been sworn to secrecy. I'm just asking you to trust me. All I need from you is help with following Maffuci tomorrow. I think he's involved with this Russian and is going to meet him at Water's Edge tomorrow. That's where Michael Dionis is going to be. But I don't believe Maffuci has any knowledge of Dunayev trying to blackmail the president-elect."

"Has any of this been discussed with Tina Crawford?"

"The U.S. Attorney? Hell no. She'd call an all hands meeting and then a press conference if she knew about this."

"You're asking me to put my career on the line," Riggs said. "I'm not used to operating in the dark like this."

"I don't operate this way either. I know exactly what I'm asking you to do. And my career is also at risk. But this isn't like anything I've encountered before. You have plausible deniability for most of this. You're simply helping the State Police determine if your agent is involved in a criminal offense. So, do you want to help me catch a Russian thug screwing with our incoming president or not?"

There was a quiet awkwardness between the two women for what seemed like several long minutes. It was clear to DeCarlo that Riggs was wrestling with how to answer her question. She decided to break the silence. "This is a big ask, I know it. Tell me what your gut is telling you to do?"

Rigg looked DeCarlo in the eye and said, "I've filed a complaint with the FBI's Office of Professional Responsibility (OPR) in

Washington, D.C. Maffuci will be under surveillance starting tomorrow morning," Riggs said.

DeCarlo was momentarily stunned. "So, you suspect him too," she said.

"He lied to me about knowing of Michael's meeting with you on Christmas Eve. That's when I knew. But I had no idea how deep he might be involved in all of this until now."

DeCarlo explained that she was going to meet Dionis the next day at Water's Edge. If her suspicions were correct, Dunayev and Maffuci might be coming for Dionis. She needed Maffuci to think he was in the clear until then.

"I can't allow Maffuci to be part of a potential murder," Riggs said.

"Not asking you to. Can your surveillance team keep an eye on him without him knowing it?"

"Of course, detective; that's what they do. What are you proposing?"

"Let Maffuci go to Water's Edge. Let's see if he meets with Dunayev. Then you can grab him."

"I can do that. Twenty-four hours. Then I notify him he's under an internal investigation."

"That's all I need." DeCarlo said. "Care to join me tomorrow? And in the process, maybe help save Ann Banks' presidency?"

"I don't think I have a real choice, do I?"

"We all have choices Leah; I'm praying you make the right one here."

"In that case, I wouldn't miss it for the world," Riggs replied.

***

"She just called the head of the FBI here in Connecticut, a Leah Riggs," Minor said. "What the hell is she doing?"

"She's doing exactly what I thought she'd do," Sherry replied. "She's doing her job."

Chapter 28

25 Days Before the Inauguration

It was just after ten a.m. when Michael Dionis arrived at Water's Edge. It was two days after Christmas and for the first time in three weeks, there was actually a blue sky covering most of the state of Connecticut. Even though the temperature hung around the freezing mark, the fact that the sky was clear of gray clouds prompted many to go outside and take advantage of the rare winter day of sunlight.

Water's Edge is a large resort on the Long Island Sound. There are no more than four floors to any of the buildings that occupy the large tract of land the resort sits on. A long driveway off of U.S. 1 in Westbrook takes guests to the front of the resort. The back of the property sits on a small but beautiful private white sand beach that guests can use. For those who prefer a pool, a large one sits right next to the beach. The beauty of the resort is concentrated in the back along the Long Island Sound, where there is a large green that reminds one of a quad on a college campus. In the summer, the resort hosts an outside bar with music on most nights. Weekends are usually booked a year in advance for those looking for the most romantic and scenic venue to exchange their vows. Guests, timeshare owners, and locals, all flock to the Water's Edge on warm summer days and cool New England nights to share drinks, stories of boating adventures, and of course, to discuss how lucky they are to be wealthy enough to take advantage of such surroundings. In the dead of winter, the resort is quieter. Locals still frequent the bar and restaurant in spite of the higher than usual prices, if not for anything other than enjoying the warmth of the fireplace and some of the best New England clam chowder in the state. But Michael Dionis wasn't there for the clam chowder. He was there to stop Andre Dunayev from destroying Ann Banks.

Dionis was always careful with those he allowed into his inner circle. He had found that people would turn on you quickly if and when it best suited their personal needs; especially those with whom he had little common interest. Between those who had no experience in either the military, or law enforcement, he had little to talk about. He also found, over the years, that those without any experience in his profession were never hesitant to tell him how much better the job could be done. He especially avoided those whose only goal in life was to accumulate as much money as possible, especially at the misery and expense of others. Dionis also realized, years ago, that maintaining personal relationships required a commitment and a great deal of personal energy; energy that he no longer had the enthusiasm for. So, he kept his circle small, careful not to tell even his closest friends and associates more than they ever needed to know. But he had allowed Maffuci to get close; close enough that he considered him a friend he could rely on. Now, that friendship was dead. The question nagging him most, was why.

There was almost no wind blowing when Dionis stepped out of his car in front of the resort. He walked through the lobby, past the front desk, toward the back door, careful not to make eye contact with anyone, and walked outside toward the Long Island Sound. Looking out at the water, his thoughts centered around Ann, DeCarlo's injuries, and why his friend, Tony Maffuci, had betrayed him. His thoughts, however, primarily centered around how he was going to deal with Dunayev. Dionis ran over all the possibilities for how he might approach him, and how he'd deal with him. It was obvious to Dionis that he was going to need more than simply skill and cunning to survive the day; he was going to have to be extremely lucky. Dionis looked at his watch. It was ten-forty a.m. *Let's see if I can check in early*, he thought.

***

DeCarlo and Leah Riggs met with Sherry's two Special Ops people in the back of their black SUV. It was eleven a.m., and they were parked two miles south of Water's Edge in the lot of Bill's Seafood, a local landmark restaurant that accepts only cash and serves a variety of fried seafood along with traditional hot and cold lobster rolls. In spite of the cash only policy, Bill's has outlasted most of the many restaurants that come and go on the shoreline and packs people in virtually every day, especially during the short summer months in New England.

After brief introductions, Riggs explained that an FBI surveillance team from New York was watching Maffuci. He was currently in his office, but she would keep them apprised of his movements.

Chan explained that she and her partner, who they could call Larry, would take custody of Dunayev the minute Maffuci was in custody. If all went as planned, neither DeCarlo nor Riggs would ever see or hear from Dunayev again.

"I'm fine with that," DeCarlo said.

"And if all of this south? What do we do then?" Riggs asked. "This could easily come back to bite us all in the ass."

"We need to make sure that doesn't happen," DeCarlo replied.

"She's right," Chan said. "No matter what happens, let us take custody of Dunayev and we'll disappear. Like they say in the movies, we were never here."

"I have two people inside Water's Edge," Riggs added. If Maffuci meets with Dunayev, we'll know."

"Do they have eyes on Dionis?" DeCarlo asked.

"They did. He just checked in. Booked two rooms. One under his own name, and one under the name of Sean Cameron," Riggs said.

DeCarlo looked at her watch and told Chan that they should split up. "I'll go to Water's Edge to find Michael. The rest of you should stay close but out of sight." A few moments later, DeCarlo was turning down the long driveway leading to Water's Edge, while Riggs headed over to the Westbrook police department. Riggs knew the chief there. He wouldn't ask any questions if she asked to hang out for a while. She thought that might be the best course of action for a woman of color in order to maintain a low profile on that part of the Connecticut shoreline with an extremely limited black population. Chan and Larry, headed to the Westbrook Outlets, just two miles away. She had checked out the area earlier and thought that she and Larry could blend in as a couple simply by appearing to do some shopping. Twenty minutes later, DeCarlo was knocking on the door to Dionis' room.

When the door opened, DeCarlo saw Dionis sitting in a chair. It happened too fast for her to respond. She felt the gun placed on the side of her head as she was jerked into the room.

"Detective DeCarlo," Sergi Nikitin said. "It's nice to meet you."

Sandi DeCarlo looked at Dionis in stunned silence. A man shoved her to the floor, removed her purse and gun, then grabbed her by the hair, stood her up and threw her onto the bed. "Michael are you okay?" she asked.

DeCarlo could see blood trickling from Dionis' mouth as he sat in a chair with his hands tied behind his back. He'd taken a punch; of that she had no doubt.

Sergi Nikitin was one of those intelligence operatives that still believed in protecting Mother Russia. Many of his colleagues and most every member of the many Russian organized crime groups that operated there had learned long ago that protecting one's own self-interests was more important, and financially beneficial, than supporting the Kremlin and its questionable and constantly shifting political alliances. Most thought that if Vladimir Putin could amass a fortune through a policy of corruption, they should be able to do the same.

Nikitin had played the game well. In the process, he had made friends in the American and British intelligence service trading favors when it benefited him and Russia. In the process, he was rewarded with career advancement and the perks that came with it. But friendships, like the one he had with John Sherry, didn't override his commitment to protect the interests of Russia. And this recording would be well received by his superiors. Nikitin was not about to let Andre Dunayev use it to his advantage, or benefit from having it.

"Agent Dionis is fine," Nikitin interjected. "I'm afraid, however, that we did have to get his attention, just like we had to get yours."

“I’m fine,” Dionis said to DeCarlo. “What are you doing here?”

“Yes, detective. That’s a very good question. What are you doing here?” Nikitin asked.

“Apparently, the same thing you are; looking for Andre Dunayev,” DeCarlo answered.

“And what do you want with Mr. Dunayev?” Nikitin asked.

“He’s the prime suspect in two murders. And he’s trying to set Agent Dionis up for it,” DeCarlo replied.

“And what makes you think Mr. Dunayev would be here today?” Nikitin demanded to know.

“Just a hunch,” DeCarlo replied.

The man with Nikitin slapped DeCarlo across the face just hard enough that it stunned her.

“My friend here is very impatient,” Nikitin told DeCarlo. “And for some reason, his temperament gets more aggressive if he feels someone is not being truthful with me.”

“So, beating up a defenseless woman with her arm in a sling, is your way of getting my attention?” DeCarlo asked.

“It’s unfortunate, I do understand. Not something I enjoy,” Nikitin replied. “Let’s see if you and I can come to some more agreeable means to exchange information, unless of course, you’d like your other arm in a sling as well?”

“Okay, what information do you have for me that you care to share?” DeCarlo asked.

“Well, let me think,” Nikitin replied. “How about this; you tell me everything you know about why Dunayev might be here today and what he’s up to and I’ll tell you how you might survive the day. How does that sound?”

"I don't know whether Dunayev is coming here today or not. I only knew that Agent Dionis would be here. But I know that Dunayev is looking for him, and somehow, he has a way of tracking him."

"Is that right, Agent Dionis?" Nikitin asked.

"She's smarter than she looks," Dionis replied.

DeCarlo shot Dionis a quick glance with a look that could kill.

"And why do you think Andre Dunayev is setting you up for murder?" Nikitin asked Dionis.

"If you're asking the question, you know why," Dionis replied.

"I would still like to hear it from you," Nikitin demanded.

"Dunayev wants to blackmail the president-elect," Dionis replied. "I'm not going to let that happen."

"And how do you intend to stop him from doing that?" Nikitin asked.

"I'm going to kill him," Dionis said in a calm voice that left no doubt of his intention.

DeCarlo shot Dionis a glance that was not lost on Nikitin. "Michael, what the hell?" she said.

Dionis sat in the chair contemplating what to say and do next. He did not have a plan for this. His only hope of delaying what Nikitin might do next, was to try and keep him engaged in some sort of meaningful dialogue.

"I appreciate your forthrightness," Nikitin said. "Isn't killing a little bit out of your league, agent?"

"It wouldn't be my first time. We all do what we have to do at times," Dionis replied.

"Yes, that is true."

"So, humor me, what do you want from us?" Dionis asked.

"I want the recording," Nikitin said.

“Michael, what the hell is he talking about? What recording?” DeCarlo asked.

“It’s a bit complicated,” Dionis replied.

“It really isn’t that complicated, detective. It seems Agent Dionis and Ann Banks have been having an affair. Somehow, Andre Dunayev was able to record one of their love making sessions. I simply want the recording. Get me the recording, and you can have Dunayev, solve your two murders, and your superiors will no doubt reward you with a promotion; just like we would do in Russia. And you get to live. How does that sound?”

DeCarlo wasn’t buying any of what Nikitin was selling. “I don’t care about any recording,” DeCarlo lied. “I want Dunayev for one, and maybe two murders. And I don’t care about your corrupt promotion system in Russia.”

“There is no need to make this personal detective. You Americans are not immune to political corruption. What is it your media accuses your police of, oh yes, systemic racism? And so much corruption covering it up by your police. What is it you Americans like to say, ‘don’t throw stones when you live in a glass house?’”

“You know better than to believe the media and all their bullshit,” DeCarlo said. “The facts don’t support that, and you know it. Besides, we don’t execute our political enemies in this country.”

“Now who is listening to the lies of the media,” Nikitin said.

“If you two are going to have a political debate, can I leave?” asked Dionis.

“It seems you ARE smarter than you look, detective. But I did not come here to engage in political dialogue. I care only about the recording,” Nikitin said. “And if you want my help, you’ll see that I get it.”

“If Dunayev shows up here, I’ll make sure to ask him for it,” DeCarlo said cynically.

"I don't think so," Nikitin replied. "I think we'll keep you here and let Agent Dionis deal with Andre Dunayev."

"I don't know where the recording is. You want me to get it from Dunayev, let her go," Dionis said.

"Here's how this is going to work," Nikitin said, looking directly at DeCarlo. "You're going to tell me everything about Dunayev, the evidence you have on him, who knows you're here, everything. Then I'm going to decide what your next move is. Do you need a moment to let this sink in, detective?"

"And if I don't?" DeCarlo asked.

"As Agent Dionis said earlier, we all do what we have to do sometimes. You understand that I found Agent Dionis here. Do you really think there isn't anything I can't do?"

Dionis knew that he was dealing with a dangerous man who dealt in obtaining information. The man would kill for it, but Dionis was confident he would prefer not to. The Russian tipped his hand just a bit by demanding information on Dunayev, information he didn't have, and wanting to get his hands on the recording. To buy time, Dionis knew that he was going to have to negotiate with the egotistical bastard. He quietly thanked God he'd spent some time on Donald Trump's security detail; there was no better on- the-job-training dealing with egotistical narcissists than being around Trump and many of his inner circle. Dionis' objective now, in addition to buying time for him and DeCarlo, was to make Nikitin think he was prepared to meet his demands.

Dionis took a moment to compose his next thought. His pulse was pounding. He leaned forward, his hands still bound behind his back and, in a voice that sent a clear signal that he wasn't all that rattled, said, "This isn't the first time I've had a gun pointed at me. If I'm dead, you're on your own finding Dunayev and the recording."

"And you don't think I can do that?" Nikitin asked with sneer.

Dionis shook his head and said quietly, "If you could have found him and gotten the recording, you would have already done so.

Apparently, you know who Dunayev is. And it's clear to me, he doesn't work for or with you. He's operating independently and his actions are not sanctioned by you or your government. Otherwise, you'd have what you're looking for."

"You're very astute, Agent Dionis. You're not the only one who might be smarter than they look."

Dionis knew he was putting his and DeCarlo's life at risk. He also knew that as long as the Russian was talking, he had a chance.

"Dunayev is trying to set me up for at least one murder, maybe two. I haven't murdered anyone, and Detective DeCarlo knows it. I can deal with the fallout regarding my past relationship with Ann Banks. But I won't be set up for murder. We both want Dunayev; let's work together to make that happen. What you do with the alleged recording is your business."

DeCarlo picked up on the fact that Dionis was keeping Nikitin engaged in conversation. She decided to join in. "Hold on, Agent Dionis," DeCarlo said, looking directly at him. "I don't know that you had nothing to do with the murder of Lomakina or the death of Patrick Banks. And now that this female abuser here has told me about your affair with Ann Banks, you're back on my persons-of-interest list."

Dionis was sure DeCarlo was playing along, or least he prayed she was.

Nikitin had heard enough of Dionis' and DeCarlo's banter. His patience was wearing thin. Looking directly at DeCarlo he asked, "Who knows you're here, detective?"

"My supervisor. Told him I'd be no more than an hour or so. If he doesn't hear from me after that, he'll get concerned."

"Then you better contact Dunayev now," Nikitin said, looking back at Dionis. "Otherwise, Detective DeCarlo here might just be happy with arresting you for those murders."

"How do you expect me to do that? I don't have his number."

"But I do," said Nikitin. He handed Dionis a cell phone.

***

"Are you getting all of this?" Sherry asked.

"All of it. I have it all. What now?" Minor asked.

"Get me Larry Barnes on the phone," Sherry told his niece, using his operative Larry's last name for the first time. Sherry also told his other operative to get the car ready.

"We're going to someplace called Westbrook," Sherry said. "And we need to get there quickly."

Chapter 29

Andre Dunayev had just crossed into Connecticut on Interstate 95 when his cell phone rang. He didn't recognize the number but decided to answer the call anyway.

"Yes," Dunayev answered. Everyone in the room could hear Dunayev since Nikitin had made sure Dionis' cell was on speaker.

"I hear you're looking for me," Dionis said.

"Who is this?" Dunayev asked.

"The man you're trying to frame for murder," Dionis replied. "I think it's time we talked."

"Indeed. Talking would be good. Where should we do this?"

"You know where I am. How soon can you be here?"

"Give me an hour."

"Meet me in the bar."

"The bar it is. But just us. I don't want to see anyone else."

"Just us, Andre. Just us."

With that, Nikitin, who was controlling the phone, ended the call.

"Okay, he's on his way," Dionis said. "Now what?"

"Nicely done Agent Dionis," Nikitin said. "We have a little time to prepare for his arrival. Now we wait. In the meantime, why don't you order room service; get us all some coffee. And maybe one of those expensive lobster rolls I hear so much about from you New Englanders. And a bottle of Tito's while you're at it."

Dionis shot DeCarlo a quick glance then shifted his gaze to Nikitin and said, "By the way, an FBI friend of mine might show up. His name is Tony. I asked him to meet me here today."

"Sure, you did," Nikitin replied.

“Don’t say I didn’t warn you,” Dionis shot back while making eye contact with DeCarlo.

DeCarlo received the message loud and clear; Maffuci told Dunayev that Dionis would be at Water’s Edge today.

***

Dunayev couldn’t believe his luck. “This fool wants to talk,” he told his driver, a Russian enforcer accompanying him to Connecticut. “Maybe we can negotiate with him. His life for access to Ann Banks.”

Unlike Nikitin, Dunayev was obsessed with his own-self-interests. Being the sociopath that he was, he was acting on impulse and not thinking his next move through. Once again, Dunayev believed that he was smarter than everyone around him. *I can still blackmail this bitch, but now, with the cooperation of her lover*, he thought.

“Does that change our plans?” the driver asked.

“We will see how cooperative our friend is. Then we will decide.”

Dunayev then sent a text to Maffuci.

Dionis called me. Wants to talk. On the way to meet him at Water’s Edge in Westbrook. Meet me in the parking lot there in an hour. Don’t be late.

Maffuci was livid. He hit Dunayev back within seconds.

Not happening. Busy at the office.

Dunayev’s response was short and direct.

Then my man will meet you later. I’m sure you’ll have no problem paying the money you owe from your so-called winnings at the casino.

Exasperated, Maffuci sent back a short message.

On my way, but only if this makes us even. Debt satisfied. Confirm.

Dunayev sent a short text confirming the fact that Maffuci’s debt would be wiped clean if he made the meeting. Of course, he had no intention of honoring that agreement. He was a liar first and foremost. And Dunayev felt no remorse whatsoever for those who foolishly believed him.

Maffuci shut down his computer, reached into his desk drawer, removed his service weapon, holstered it, put on his suit jacket, and told his secretary that he was going to a meeting on the shoreline. He wasn't sure if he'd be back in the office or not. The moment Maffuci pulled out of the parking lot of the FBI building on State Street in New Haven, he was under the eye of a surveillance team. Leah Riggs had asked for a team from the New York Field Office in the hopes of keeping Maffuci from recognizing any of the agents he worked with in Connecticut.

The leader of the surveillance team, FBI Special Agent Steve Bamford sent a short text to Riggs.

Subject just left the office and is heading on I-95 north.

Riggs stood up, grabbed her coat from the back of the chair, and opened her cell phone. She sent a text to DeCarlo and Chan telling them both that Maffuci was heading north on Interstate 95.

"He has to be heading to Water's Edge," Chan turned and said to Larry. She then sent a text back to Riggs that she understood and was heading closer to Water's Edge. Since the only one who might recognize her was Michael Dionis, Chan thought she and her partner, Larry, could sit in the bar and wait to see if Dunayev showed up. As Chan was contemplating her next move, Larry Barnes' cell phone rang. It was General Sherry.

"General," Barnes said.

"Listen closely. The Russians have Dionis and DeCarlo."

"What? Does Dunayev have them? We just now learned that Maffuci is heading this way," Barnes said.

"Not Dunayev. An intelligence operative from Russia by the name of Sergi Nikitin. He was going to take Dunayev once we had him. Nikitin has them both in room 390. From what I can tell, he's roughed up DeCarlo a bit. Just head that way. I don't know how many people Nikitin has with him or where they're all at. I'm on my way there now."

"And Dunayev?" Barnes asked.

"I just learned that he's on his way there as well. He should be there in about an hour. So, you better get into position. Between Dunayev and Nikitin, we might very well be outnumbered. And we have to keep this operation dark. We can't let this get away from us."

"Understood, sir. We're heading there now."

Sherry disconnected the call. He seldom ever second-guessed himself or the decisions he made. But he was now. He had no idea how Nikitin found Dionis. He'd look into that later. What was clear to him was knowing that Nikitin would want the recording of Dionis and Banks. That would be too valuable for him to let slip away.

***

Nikitin could hear DeCarlo's phone pinging several times.

"What's the code?" Nikitin demanded.

DeCarlo placed both hands over her face and stared straight into Nikitin's eyes.

"I'm not going to ask again, detective."

"Give it to him, Sandi," Dionis said.

"You should listen to him," Nikitin said.

DeCarlo frowned and gave Nikitin the code to open her phone.

"Who is Leah Riggs?" Nikitin demanded to know. "And who is this Maffuci heading this way?"

"She is a friend of mine from the FBI. Maffuci works for her. Michael told you that earlier. You don't seem to want to listen, asshole."

"You American women simply don't know when to shut up do you?" Nikitin said.

"I think I have to go with our Russian friend here on this one," Dionis said, trying to instill some levity into the situation, and, hopefully, keep DeCarlo from being hit again. "You're saying what most men in the country think every day, but can't say themselves," Dionis fired back. "You know, this whole fucking woke thing going on over here. Never mind her. You know women; when they don't hear what they want, they tend to fill in the gaps with their own opinions."

DeCarlo shot Dionis a look that said, *if we get through this, I'm going to cut your dick off.*

"What is this "woke thing" you speak of?" Nikitin asked.

Despite all of his military and law enforcement training, Dionis had never engaged in a discussion with an intelligence officer from Russia, or any country for that matter, especially a conversation that his very life depended on. He simply hoped to keep the conversation moving to buy him and DeCarlo time. "Political correctness bullshit," Dionis replied. "I'm sure you don't have those problems in Russia."

Nikitin was losing his patience. He looked directly at DeCarlo, and with his voice clearly raised, said, "I have no time to discuss your anti-Russian attitude. Text them back. Tell them there is nothing here and that you're leaving."

"Okay, give me the phone," DeCarlo said.

Nikitin handed the phone to DeCarlo and said, "I'm watching every word. No tricks detective. Do not send the message until I've seen it. Do you understand?"

DeCarlo took the cell phone in her hand and drafted a reply text that was automatically going to go to both Leah Riggs and Chrissie Chan.

Nothing happening here. Please tell Tony we'll have lunch with Michael another day. I'm heading home early for the day. I'm exhausted.

"There, are you happy?" DeCarlo grumbled.

"Okay, send it. But for your sake, they better not show up here."

Chrissie Chan read the message twice, the second time, out loud so her partner, Larry Barnes, could hear it.

"They definitely have her," Chan said.

"Yes, they do," Barnes replied.

Chan called Leah Riggs and asked if she'd seen the text message.

"I have," Riggs replied. "What the hell is going on?"

She told Riggs about the call she'd just received from Sherry.

"Maffuci is heading this way too. My guess, he's meeting Dunayev at Water's Edge," Riggs said.

"Agreed," replied Chan. "But I don't think Dunayev knows about Nikitin having them held in the room."

"So Dunayev is also heading into a trap," Riggs said.

"It would appear so."

"How many people do you think Nikitin has with him?" Riggs asked.

"Unclear. But probably not many. We just don't know how many or where they are."

"I still have two agents inside the resort," Riggs said.

"Can you contact them quietly and let them know what's going on?"

"Of course."

"Also, can you send DeCarlo a text back and tell her okay and that you're heading back to the office. Tell her you'll talk soon," Chan said. "You stay close to the resort. Larry and I are going in. We'll grab a table in the bar. I'll text when we have something."

***

Sherry wanted to rattle Nikitin's cage. To do so, he needed to make Nikitin think they were going to grab Dunayev at any moment. Nikitin picked up on the third ring.

"General, my friend. How are you?"

"Doing fine, Sergi. How soon can you meet to make the pick-up?"

"You have the package?" Nikitin asked, surprised.

"In the next few minutes. We have eyes on him as we speak. How soon can you get to the airport in Hartford?"

"I'm not sure. Can I call you back in a few minutes?"

"Of course. But please be quick. A lot of wheels are in motion here."

"Give me thirty-minutes," Nikitin said.

"Call me back in five," replied Sherry. With that, he disconnected the call.

Sherry's call had the desired effect on Nikitin. He needed time to meet with Dunayev and get his hands on the recording or get him to say where it was. Nikitin hoped the possibility existed that a sociopath like Dunayev might actually be keeping the recording on him.

"We have a problem," Nikitin said to his man watching Dionis and DeCarlo. "My contact wants us to collect Dunayev at the airport in Hartford. He wants to know in ten minutes how long it will take for us to get there and take him off their hands."

"But he's coming here," the man said.

"I know that. The Americans plan to grab him any minute."

"Won't they want to question him before handing him over to us?" the man asked.

"Normally, yes," Nikitin replied.

"So, what do you want to do?"

Nikitin had one move to get his hands on the recording. It was time to play nice with Dunayev. Nikitin grabbed Dionis' phone and called Dunayev.

"Have you changed your mind Agent Dionis?" Dunayev asked, the moment he answered the call.

"This is not Agent Dionis. This is Sergi Nikitin. Do you know who I am?"

Dunayev was shocked. The last person he was expecting to call him was Nikitin. The silence lasted so long, Nikitin wondered if the call had been disconnected.

"Are you still there?" Nikitin demanded.

"Of course, comrade. I'm a little surprised at this call."

"Listen to me carefully. I have your Agent Dionis and this woman detective that is hunting you. I've just learned that the Americans are following you and are close to arresting you. Their intelligence agents want to question you about the recording."

Dunayev was stunned. "How do you know this?" he asked.

"You need to ask? Just know that my information is correct. If you want to get through this, comrade, you need to listen to me and do exactly as I say. How far are you from this Water's Edge place?"

"Twenty-minutes."

"Are you being followed?"

"No. We've seen no tail."

"My sources tell me you're going to be arrested any minute."

"How is that possible? No one knows where I am right now. I'm not being followed."

"Then get here fast. Meet me in the bar. And be ready to leave here with me quickly. I want you on a plane to Russia this afternoon. And I want that recording. Do you understand?"

"And what's in this for me, comrade?"

"For one thing, your life. Second, a clean slate back in Russia for your efforts here. But only if you can produce the recording of the president-elect."

"I have it with me," Dunayev said, then regretting his comment.

The man really is an idiot, Nikitin thought.

"If you're stopped, find a way to hide it. We'll find a way to get it and you, later. Do you understand?"

"I'm also going to need some money," Dunayev said.

"You're in no position to make demands right now my friend. Just get here and get me the recording. Do that, and you'll be rewarded. Fail, and I can't help you. And you will spend the rest of your miserable life in an American prison." With that, the line went dead. Nikitin threw the cell phone on the table.

"What now?" the Russian man asked.

"Now we wait," Nikitin replied.

Dunayev sat silently in the passenger seat of his car. Now that Nikitin knew about the recording, and had Dionis and DeCarlo, he was going to have to alter his next course of action. Dunayev wanted respect, and a way back into Russia with some political influence. At a minimum, he wanted some good will, which is probably the one reason he let Nikitin's words sink in. Dunayev also knew that if he wanted to regain his former position in Russia's vor or Bravata, he had to do what Nikitin said. While certainly ruthless, Dunayev was also cautious. Being cautious helped him survive longer than most might in his profession. He picked up his cell phone and called Tony Maffuci.

"What is it?" Maffuci answered.

"You have balls setting me up."

"What are you talking about?"

"My sources tell me I'm about to be arrested. The only one who knew where I was going was you."

"I have no idea what you're talking about."

"I do know what I'm talking about. If I'm arrested, you know what will happen to you and your family."

"Don't threaten me, Andre. I didn't set you up. I have more to lose here than you do. So, what the fuck are you talking about?"

"A highly placed source tells me I'm about to be arrested. And this source is in a position to know."

"I have no idea what's going on here. But if you believe this source, abort the meeting. Turn around. They have nothing on you. If you're being followed, that could prove to be a problem."

"That's not an option right now. How far away are you?"

"Less than ten minutes."

"Don't be late." With that, Dunayev ended the call.

Dunayev looked at his driver and said, "Pull over here at this rest stop." The driver did as he was ordered and pulled the car into the service plaza in Madison, just minutes away from Water's Edge. With the usual trappings including a Dunkin Donuts, Panda Express, Subway, and McDonalds, the plaza offered travelers a host of non-healthy, fast-food options as they drove to and from the upper regions of New England.

"Wait here," Dunayev told his driver. "Keep the car running. I'll be right back."

Dunayev walked into the plaza gift shop, purchased some tape, and a blank zip drive. He also asked for a plastic bag. He tore open the plastic container, removed the zip drive, and placed it in his pocket. He then walked back to the car, got in and asked his driver for his knife. Dunayev cut a small piece of the bag and wrapped it around the zip drive. He taped the plastic bag securely around it, opened the car door and walked back outside. He looked around, then quietly bent down as if to tie his shoe, and with his hands, dug a small hole around a shrub and buried the drive. A moment later, he got back into the car, fastened his seat belt, and told the driver to go.

If I'm being followed, they can dig up a blank drive, he thought. Dunayev then quietly took the zip drive with the recording on it out of his pocket and slid it under the front seat of the car and taped it to a piece of metal. *Not the best place to leave it, but it will have to do for now,* he told himself.

***

A million thoughts went through Maffuci's mind. *What was Andre talking about? Who is going to arrest him?* Then it hit him.

Maffuci stopped at the Madison rest stop just minutes after talking to Dunayev. He pulled into the parking lot and was sure he spotted the surveillance team. He went into the men's room, took out the chip from his burner phone and flushed it down the toilet. He then threw the burner into a trash can, walked over to the Dunkin Donuts, and ordered a small coffee to go.

Fuck it, he thought.

***

"I'm going downstairs," Nikitin said to his accomplice. "Stay here with these two. I'll call you if there is a problem."

Nikitin's muscle simply nodded that he understood. Turning to Dionis and DeCarlo, Nikitin said, "Don't give him a reason to kill you. Cooperate and you'll both be home before dinner."

Nikitin walked downstairs, through the lobby, and took a seat at a table in the corner of the Seaview Bistro. Unbeknownst to him, sitting at another table was Chrissie Chan and Larry Barnes.

"Recognize anyone?" Chan whispered to Barnes.

"The place is busy. I have no idea who any of these people are."

"Let's hope Dunayev shows up soon. I'd recognize that son-of-bitch anywhere."

"Just give me one good shot at Nikitin when this is over," Barnes said.

"Why?" Chan asked.

"DeCarlo. There was no need for slapping her around."

Chan grinned and said, "Get in line."

"And what do we do about Agent Dionis?" Barnes asked.

"Let's hope we don't have to do a thing," Chan replied, with a worried look on her face.

Dionis sat back in the chair, his arms still tied behind his back. DeCarlo was on the edge of the bed, her face still stinging from the hard slap across her face. Nikitin's accomplice sat in another chair with his gun on his lap. Dionis knew that Russian intelligence agents would prefer not to kill anyone. But kill they would, if necessary. And with Dunayev arriving almost any minute, he knew he had to do something, and fast. Dionis didn't like sitting around doing nothing when he fought in the Gulf. And he especially didn't like the tedium that accompanied his life as a Secret Service Agent. But sitting around waiting to be shot was irritating him more than anything he'd experienced in war or during protection assignments. What he wanted most right now, was to put a bullet through this Russian's head, then head downstairs and shoot Nikitin and kill Dunayev. But first, he had to get free. He had few options, especially with DeCarlo sitting nearby with her arm in a sling. Anything he did would put her safety at risk. He also knew that he would have to attack quickly. His palms were sweating, and he could feel his heart racing. He quietly started taking deep breaths to help lower his heart rate. What Dionis was also able to do, was quietly twist his wrists to a point that he had loosened the ties just enough to free his hands. *Stay calm and work the problem. You've got one shot at this,* he told himself.

"Any chance of going to the bathroom here?" Dionis asked the man with the gun.

"No," was his only response.

"Really. It's killing me," Dionis added.

"You can piss your pants for all I care."

"That's exactly what I'm going to do if you don't let me go."

"Then piss yourself. What do I care? I'm not untying you."

"Can you at least bring me a towel and place it on top of me?"

The man gave Dionis a stern look. He walked toward him and stopped directly in front of him. "I don't care if you piss your pants," he said, as he tilted his head and eyes back in annoyance.

Neither the Russian nor DeCarlo saw it coming. Dionis lunged at the man with the full force of his body, hitting him like a football lineman moving forward on the snap of the ball, and knocked the man to the floor. Dionis hit him with three quick blows to the face and was able to land an uppercut to the man's chin. But the Russian was not only strong, but he was also an experienced fighter and threw Dionis off of him, landing a quick kick to his midsection in the process. Dionis felt the wind being knocked out of him. As he stumbled backwards, he could see DeCarlo grab a glass vase from the table. She managed to raise her one good arm and smashed it with all the force she could muster across the side of the man's face. The crashing blow caused the Russian to drop the gun and stunned him just long enough for Dionis to land a blow into his neck with his forearm. The Russian was knocked over and blacked out for several moments. Dionis fell to the floor, trying to catch his breath. His heart was racing as he struggled to sit up.

"Nice shot there, double 07," DeCarlo said.

Dionis struggled to recover from having the wind knocked out of him. He took a few deep breaths and gathered his strength. He then asked DeCarlo for her handcuffs. Glass from the vase was protruding from the man's face and he was bleeding profusely. As the Russian regained some level of consciousness while still lying on the floor, Dionis handcuffed the man's hands behind his back, jerked him up onto his feet, and forcefully threw him into the chair he, himself, was just sitting in. He then retrieved the man's gun and stuck it to the side of the Russian's face.

"Give me one reason and you're dead."

The Russian was in pain. He had two pieces of glass stuck in the side of his right cheek and was in no position to argue with anyone.

DeCarlo grabbed a small towel from the bathroom, and told the man to sit still. "Don't move. I'm going to try and get the glass out of your face." She then removed both pieces of glass without much difficulty, although it did cause the big Russian to wince. "Don't you just love Karma, asshole?" DeCarlo scowled. "I think your face is going to sting for a while."

DeCarlo finished her minor bit of triage, wetting another towel and cleaning as much blood from the man's face as she could. She then tied a clean towel around the Russian's cut face. "There, that should hold you until we can get you some medical attention." DeCarlo then turned to Dionis and said, "You're just full of surprises, aren't you?"

"You haven't seen anything yet," Dionis replied. "Nice job with the vase, by the way. How's the shoulder?"

"Hurts like hell. Wasn't planning to engage in a physical altercation today or get slapped around."

"Consider it part of your rehab exercise," Dionis said.

"Funny."

"Humor can help you deal with the worst of situations. At least it works for me," Dionis told her.

"And you think this shit is funny?"

"Anything but, kid," Dionis replied, as he gulped down some water from the non-complimentary bottles in the room.

"So now what?" DeCarlo asked.

"Now I'm going downstairs. Think you can keep this guy under wraps?"

"Not a problem. But there's some things you need to know." DeCarlo quickly briefed Dionis about the FBI placing Maffuci under surveillance, along with the fact that Chrissie Chan and another operative of Sherry's were nearby and possibly already inside the resort. "Be careful. Dunayev will probably try to kill you," she said.

"I'd be disappointed if he didn't try," Dionis said.

DeCarlo retrieved her service weapon from the table across the room and, smiling, sat across from the Russian. Dionis grabbed his own gun, the Walther .380, along with the Russian's, and placed both inside of his pants. He then grabbed his sport coat and quietly opened the door to his room. Looking into the hall, he didn't see anyone. He then turned toward DeCarlo and said, "Can you get him up and come with me?"

"Where are we going?" DeCarlo asked.

"Not far."

DeCarlo followed him and watched as he removed an electronic key card from his pants and opened the door to the room next to the one, they were in.

"Take him in there."

"What's this?"

"I rented a second room in another name."

"Sean Cameron, I presume."

"How did you know?"

"Later. I think I'll shut up now. You know how we women can talk too much," she said.

Dionis just grinned, shook his head, and rolled his eyes backwards. He then motioned her into the room. As soon as DeCarlo had the Russian seated in a chair, Dionis opened the door and glanced down the hallway. Not seeing anyone, he started down the stairs to the lobby. As soon as he left the room, DeCarlo set the security latch on the door, sat down on the edge of the bed, crossed her legs, and chambered a round in her weapon. She stared directly at the Russian and said, "One question there, Ivan, or whatever the hell you call yourself; and just between us: I'm curious as to why your boss sent those two goons to my house to kill me and Michael Dionis on Christmas Eve?"

The Russian remained silent. He had no intention of answering DeCarlo's question.

DeCarlo let out a sigh and said, "Come on, you owe me one answer. After all, I cleaned your cuts and stopped the bleeding. Besides, if we wanted you dead, you'd be dead. What is it you told me, oh yeah, 'relax and you'll be home in time for dinner.'"

The Russian hesitated for a minute, stared back at DeCarlo and said, "It wasn't us. We had no idea that was happening. It was that idiot Dunayev."

"Dunayev?"

"He's a dangerous criminal. Nikitin is working with your General Sherry to help us get him back to Russia."

"So, you're double crossing the General now."

"Your General would do the same under the circumstances."

"Maybe. Is there no honor among you people?"

"Honor is a matter of interpretation. And, of course, with who or whatever the constantly shifting alliances might be."

"So, what are you saying, today's enemies are tomorrow's allies?"

"Or vice versa, depending on the day of the week and the circumstances."

"Is it really that simple for you guys?"

"Well, it's not that simple. But in some respects, yes. It's a very dangerous game, detective. I'm not sure you would understand."

"Try me."

"Our business is required because politicians in every country are afraid. They don't like uncertainty."

"You mean they don't trust each other."

"No, they don't. And they never will. Every nation wants to advance their own interests, especially America."

"And you Russians don't?" DeCarlo asked.

"I said every nation does. You will never live long enough to witness trust between nations."

"But they do work together on many things. That has to mean something."

"Don't be fooled. Countries, like people, operate in their own self-interest. The world is a dangerous place, detective. Even in your small, micro world of solving crimes, you must know that."

"So, this is how you justify all of this cloak and dagger bullshit?"

"I don't justify anything. I do it because it's my job and because I want to protect my country."

"Protect them from what? Who would ever be so stupid as to attack Russia?"

"Well, the Germans did it in WWII and killed about twenty-six million Russian citizens."

"Yeah, and Japan bombed Pearl Harbor. But now, they're one of our largest allies and trading partners. We build their cars in this country, and they ship us baseball players. And Vietnam is now a tourist destination. So how long are you guys going to hang your hat on this WWII business? And how long do we all go before we put the bullshit of our previous politicians behind us?"

"It's more complicated than that, detective. It's about resources, food, oil, territory, and political dominance. It's about protecting the corporations that control the politicians. Your country has not seen a major attack since 9/11. Do you think that is a coincidence? No, your intelligence gathering agencies have helped prevent that. America operates in its own self-interests, just like the rest of the world."

"You don't think countries can put aside their differences and work together?" DeCarlo asked.

"Don't be so naive, detective. How can you ever expect countries with different languages, religions, and ideologies to work together when your own politicians, even within their own party, can't get along?"

"Well, Ivan, you do make a good point there. So why rough up me and Dionis?"

"It's not personal, detective. You Americans are so easily offended."

"Slapping me across the face while my arm is in a sling is personal."

"You were never in any real danger, detective. If I had wanted to hurt you, you'd have known it. I just needed to get your attention."

"Yeah, you had me fooled."

"You think we want an international incident here? Your General Sherry will tell you that we all try to avoid such things."

"Then tell me why."

"It's about the recording. It's more valuable to us than Dunayev. You police think in such small terms. You don't see the bigger picture of geopolitics."

"Funny thing about this recording, no one seems to have heard it. Did you know that?"

The Russian didn't answer.

"I guess I'm just a narrow-minded thinker at that, Ivan. But I'll share this with you; I may just be investigating a couple of murders here, but I'm not going to allow you or anyone else to blackmail the incoming President of the United States; not if I can help it."

"I'm not sure there is much you can do at this point to stop it, detective."

"We'll see about that," DeCarlo said as she shot the Russian a wide smirk. She then picked up her cell phone, punched in a number and said, "Hi Aaliyah, did you get all of that?"

"Got everything so far. Nice job. Are you okay?"

"I'm fine. Just chilling with my man, Ivan, here."

***

Michael Dionis walked quietly into the lobby of the hotel. He didn't see anyone he knew. *So far, so good*, he thought. He then walked into the lounge and made direct eye contact with Nikitin. Nikitin's heart sank. He started to get up from his chair but thought better of it.

If Dionis was able to free himself, he had to have a gun on him, Nikitin thought.

Dionis took three steps toward him when he saw Chrissie Chan out of the corner of his eye. She was sitting at another table with a man he didn't recognize. *What the fuck*, he thought.

Dionis shot her a quick glance but made sure he was focused on Nikitin. He walked to the table, pulled out a chair and sat down.

"Well, Agent Dionis, nice of you to join me."

"Oh, the pleasure is all mine, mother fucker," Dionis replied.

"No need to get ugly, agent. But if I may inquire, how is my associate doing? Still alive I hope."

"For the time being. Although he's going to need a doctor to stitch up his face where the glass cut into him. Detective DeCarlo, against my better wishes, cleaned the wound, and stopped most of the bleeding."

"I hope I get the chance to thank her for that."

"You will."

"So now, what shall we talk about?" Nikitin asked.

"I suspect our conversation will be short. I'm going to get this alleged recording from Dunayev and turn him over to Detective DeCarlo. After that, you can take your enforcer and leave. That's if you don't give us any trouble. If you do, I'm going to turn you over to our intelligence folks."

"You mean General Sherry," Nikitin said.

Dionis was momentarily stunned by the comment. It was clear that he knew who Sherry was.

"I can tell from your silence that you don't know that I'm here because Sherry told me about Dunayev," Nikitin said.

"I don't have many conversations with the General. We run in different circles."

"He promised me Dunayev. He's a killer. I plan to take him back to Russia."

"He's going to stand trial here first."

"No, he isn't, Agent Dionis. General Sherry will never allow that. He's going to do everything he can to keep your relationship with the new president out of the press."

"You don't know what you're talking about."

"If you're going to play dumb, Agent Dionis, then there is nothing for us to talk about."

"Sherry told you that I was here and that Dunayev was coming here as well?" Dionis asked.

"Not exactly. We do have other sources."

"But you spoke to Sherry."

"He called and offered me Dunayev. Nothing more. I do, however, wish he had told me about the recording. That would have changed things."

Just then, Dionis saw Dunayev walk into the bar. Dunayev's eyes locked onto Dionis sitting at a table with Nikitin. He smiled, walked toward the two men, and without waiting for an invitation, sat down. The moment he did, a waitress came over and asked if she could get them anything.

"Your best scotch," he insisted.

"I'll have Tito's on ice," Nikitin added.

"Nothing for me," Dionis said.

As soon as the waitress left, Dionis broke the silence. "I want the recording, Andre. If you actually have it that is. It's the only way you walk out of here alive."

"So dramatic, Agent Dionis. And here I thought you were more of a lover," Dunayev said, sneeringly.

"I think he's right," Nikitin added, looking directly at Dunayev. "Your only hope now is to give me the recording and let me take you back to Russia where you'll be rewarded for your efforts."

"I thought you said I was about to be arrested," Dunayev said to Nikitin.

"You know how fragile some information can be, Evsei. Or should I call you Andre?"

"Well, my source says it's bullshit," Dunayev said.

"Agent Maffuci, you mean," Dionis said.

"Yes, Agent Maffuci. How long did it take you to figure that out?" Dunayev asked, smiling.

"Just now when you confirmed my suspicions. I'd hoped I was wrong."

"No, you're right. It seems your friend's gambling habit got the best of him. Way too many trips to your Indian casinos I'm afraid."

"He wouldn't sell me out for a few dollars."

"Oh, it's not a few dollars. But if it makes you feel any better, he owes more money than you'll make over the next few years."

"I'm curious, just how much did he lose before he got into bed with you?" Dionis asked.

"Lose? Your friend didn't lose Agent Dionis. He won. We made sure of that."

"What are you saying? I don't understand."

"We made sure he won. Terrible thing having a son with expensive medical needs. But rest assured, we kept track of exactly how much he won. We had him targeted from the start. Gotta love the people running the casinos in this country. They know who their friends and enemies are. But you're right, it wasn't about the money. Seems he loves his family more than he cares for you. He was supposed to be here," Dunayev said as he glanced around the bar. "I guess he's not as trustworthy as I'd hoped."

"Well, what is it they say, there's no honor among thieves," Dionis said.

"Gentlemen," Nikitin interrupted, "we seem to have a situation here that requires some negotiation and compromise."

Dionis, looking Dunayev directly in the eye, said, "I would disagree. The solution to this is simple; pheasant dick here turns over the recording, and I hand him over to Detective DeCarlo." Dionis shifted his gaze to Nikitin, and said, "And you take your cut up coward upstairs and get the fuck out of my country before I put a bullet in his head."

"I can see we're at a point where diplomacy might not work as well as I'd hoped," Nikitin said.

Dionis didn't see it coming. A man walked up behind him and stuck a gun in his back.

"Now, Agent Dionis, don't do anything stupid," Dunayev said. "We're going to go quietly upstairs to your room and continue this discussion up there."

"I don't think so," Dionis replied. "You can tell your man to shoot me right here."

"Oh, he'll do that," Dunayev said smiling. "And he'll kill most of the witnesses in here too if he has to. Then, he'll kill Detective DeCarlo. And when I'm done, it will look like you initiated it. Then I'll release the recording of you and Ann Banks fucking. So, what will it be, Agent Dionis?"

Dionis stared at Dunayev. "You better do as he says," Nikitin said.

Dionis stood up just in time to see Maffuci enter the lounge. The moment Dunayev locked eyes on Maffuci, Dionis, moving on instinct, turned quickly, grabbed the barrel of the gun the man had stuck in his back, and shot his elbow upwards and into the man's jaw causing the Russian's brain to bounce around the inside of his skull. Before the Russian could reset, he fell backwards, firing a shot that went high and into the ceiling. As the man was falling, Dionis pulled his Walther from inside his waist band and fired two quick shots into the man's chest. Nikitin was shocked but kept his composure enough to drop to the floor.

The patrons in the lounge began screaming. Two collided with each other trying to get out and fell to the floor. Another tried crawling under a table. The bartender dove behind the bar, leaving the waitress he was talking to seconds prior, standing alone in the open. There wasn't anything he could do for her at the moment. Two members of the kitchen staff raced out to see what was happening, then screamed as they turned and ran back into the kitchen.

Dunayev threw his chair back, stood and fired one shot at Dionis, hitting him in the right side above his abdomen. The shot knocked him over and onto the floor. Dunayev walked over to him, pointed the gun at his head, and said, "You should have listened, Agent Dionis."

Dunayev never felt a thing. Maffuci drew his weapon and fired one shot directly at him. The bullet punched through his neck, shattering his vertebra, creating a gaping hole that caused his blood to spill onto the floor. Dunayev slammed to the ground, clutching his neck while his own blood, spewing from his severed arteries, formed a pool around him. In a few moments, Dunayev choked to death.

Chan was crouched down on one knee behind the table she had tipped over to take cover when the first shot rang out. She pulled her 9 mm from her purse and pointed it directly at Maffuci. Maffuci had no idea who she was, only that she was pointing a gun at him. He fired two more shots; both went wide but one round hit Sherry's man, Barnes, in the upper left shoulder. The force from the shot knocked him backwards and into the wall, causing him to fall onto his knees. Chan, not knowing who Maffuci was, fired two quick shots hitting him once in the chest. Two other patrons in the bar covered their ears from the noise of the gunshots. One of them, a woman, caught a hot shell casing that had been ejected from Chan's gun, which found its way down the front of her blouse causing a slight burn. She screamed and started to stand up. Chan put her hand on the woman's shoulder and pushed her back down onto the floor. "Stay down," she yelled.

Two FBI agents that had been inside the resort when the shooting started, ran into the lounge with their guns held in both hands. One pointed a gun directly at Chan and ordered her to drop her weapon. Chan did exactly as she was ordered. The other agent scanned the lounge looking for anyone else that might be armed and considered a threat.

Neither FBI agent recognized Dionis. As soon as he identified himself and while holding his hand over the bullet hole that entered his body, he walked over to Maffuci and knelt down beside him.

"You're hurt pretty bad there, Tony."

"You don't look so good yourself, *Amico*," he replied.

"I'm fine," Dionis said as he wiped his hand over his cheek and felt the smear of blood. "Stay with us. Help is on the way."

"I'm sorry, Michael. I never suspected it would go this far."

"We can talk about this later, just hang in there."

"I don't think there is going to be a later," Maffuci said. "I got in over my head and they threatened my family."

"So, I've been told. They do that sometimes."

"They sent several messages that convinced me they were serious," Maffuci said as he struggled with each word. "They actually picked up my son once just to let me know they could get to him whenever they wanted. They told me no harm would come to you. At first, it looked like they were keeping their word. But then it all went to hell. I'm sorry, Michael. I really fucked up this time."

Dionis tried to fight back the tears in his eyes but couldn't. He knew that he was watching his friend die.

"I have to know, Tony, how much were you into these guys?"

"A lot."

"I told you that gambling at that casino was going to get you into trouble," Dionis said.

"They let me win. That's how I paid for Tommy's surgeries."

"It's okay. I would have done the same," Dionis lied.

"I'm so sorry, Michael. Please forgive me."

Dionis looked at him hopelessly. "You're going to get through this."

"No, Michael, I'm not," he said. "Tell Tommy…." Then everything stopped for a moment as he gasped for air. They were the last words Tony Maffuci ever spoke. He died before the first ambulance could arrive.

In the confusion, Nikitin slipped out of the bar and quickly made his way back upstairs to Dionis' room. He slipped the key card into the slot and opened the door. Sitting alone in a chair in the corner of the room was General John Sherry. Nikitin tried to turn and leave when a man put a gun in his back and waived him into the room.

"Come in, Sergi. Have a seat." Sergi had little choice but to comply; Sherry's soldier was pointing a gun with an attached silencer, directly at him.

"General. I'd like to say it's good to see you."

"If you said that, you'd be a bigger liar than you already are."

"So now what, my old friend?"

"Now you listen and listen good. I don't have much time. Your colleague is hurt but not that bad. You're going to drive him to the airport in Hartford where I know you have a plane standing by. My man will follow you. A doctor will meet you there and treat your man just enough so that you can get him home. Then you're both going to get on that plane and leave the country immediately. If I find you back here, you'll be arrested. Do you understand?"

"You could have told me about the recording," Nikitin said.

"What recording?"

Ivan smirked and said, "All of this could have been avoided."

"I don't know what you're talking about. Nothing happened here."

"Do you expect your people to believe that?"

"You needn't concern yourself with that. People's perceptions become their own truths. And they'll believe what we tell them. As you well know, the truth is always negotiable."

"You lied to me, my friend. You gave me no choice. You would have done the same."

"Spies lie, Sergi. You know that. You tried to deceive me. My position is clear. You're leaving the country now. But I do have one question."

"Just one question? I would have suspected you'd have several."

"Just one. How did you learn that Agent Dionis would be here today?"

"Dunayev told our mutual adversary, Wie. They were apparently working together up until recently. They turned on him when Dunayev became uncontrollable. They thought they could salvage some good will by telling us what he was up to regarding your new president."

Sherry stood up and offered Nikitin his hand. Nikitin took it, looked Sherry in the eye and said, "Stay safe, my old friend. Till next time."

"Till next time," Sherry replied.

Sherry walked Nikitin out of the room and into the hallway. He knocked on the door next to them. DeCarlo opened the door and handed the Russian over to Nikitin.

"My man here will get you both downstairs and out the back. You'll be in Hartford in just over an hour," Sherry said. He then turned his attention to DeCarlo and said, "You better get downstairs, detective. People are waiting on you."

Chapter 30

There was mass confusion in the lobby and bar lounge. DeCarlo badged her way in and caught Chan's eye. The two women approached each other and nodded.

"Any of this your work?" DeCarlo asked.

"That one," Chan replied, turning her head and eyes at Maffuci.

"Him? He's FBI. Why? What the fuck happened?"

"He shot Dunayev then fired two shots at me and Larry. I had no idea he was FBI."

"That doesn't make sense," DeCarlo said.

"No, it doesn't. But he saved Michael's life. Shot Dunayev in the throat. Just one quick shot."

"This is going to be a huge problem," DeCarlo added. "How is Michael?"

"He's over there being attended to. Took one on the side of his abdomen."

"And your friend, Larry?"

"He'll be okay. On his way to the hospital right now."

"And you?"

"Not good. Not sure how I'm going to explain any of this. Or live with it for that matter."

"Yeah," was all DeCarlo could say as she shook her head.

"So, what now?"

"I'm going to run part of this investigation with my Lt. You were here with your boyfriend having lunch. You heard the shooting, took cover, and when Maffuci fired at you, you returned fire. You carry a gun for protection. Understood? Say nothing more. I'll try to do the interview. But if someone else does, don't say more than that. You don't know why this happened or anything about it. Understood?"

"Easy enough. Have you seen the General?"

"He was upstairs. No idea where he is now."

"Any guess why Maffuci opened up on us?"

"Not really. I'll leave that for the psychologists when they pick this all apart doing their psychological profile of the victims. But if you want my uneducated opinion; maybe he wanted to die or was seeking some sort of redemption. I guess we'll never know."

"So, what now?" Chan asked.

"You leave now, and quietly. I'll tell my Lt. I got your contact info and let you go to the hospital." Chan nodded and quietly walked out of the bar and disappeared.

Leah Riggs was clearly in charge of the scene. She directed the local police to set up security outside and to not, under any circumstances, allow anyone in or out of the resort, except for the FBI and State Police. She was livid when she heard DeCarlo released Chan.

The bartender, waitress, and kitchen staff were all quickly and quietly escorted out of the bar and into separate rooms near the main dining area.

Lieutenant Mark Rice arrived thirty minutes after the shooting, along with several members of the State Police's major crime squad. They would take charge of the killing of Andre Dunayev. The FBI was not relinquishing control of any part of the investigation that involved the death of Special Agent Maffuci. Ten minutes after Rice's arrival, Kimiko Matsui arrived.

"Is this your work, Sandi?" Matsui asked.

"Not this time."

"Okay, we'll talk later."

DeCarlo walked over to Dionis who was being treated by a paramedic.

"How's he doing?" she asked.

"He'll live. But we need to get him to a hospital," the young paramedic replied.

"Can I have a minute with him?"

The two paramedics walked away giving DeCarlo and Dionis some privacy.

"I imagine that hurts like hell," DeCarlo said.

"It does. But this isn't the first time I've been shot."

"Are you telling me this shit gets easier?"

"Just the opposite. Especially the older I get. How's your shoulder doing?"

"Hurts. Got to keep the dressing changed a few times a day. You know the drill. I won't be going to my private Pilates classes anytime soon."

"I wouldn't think so," Dionis replied.

"So, what are you going to do now?" DeCarlo asked.

"Me? I have no idea. I'm pretty much screwed in this district. There's no way I can ever testify in court around here. My ex will see to that. The Service, if they don't try to fire me, will hide me in some D.C. basement counting canteen covers until they can force me out."

"How soon can you go?"

"Just under two years."

"I can stand in a bucket of shit for two years if it means getting my pension," DeCarlo said. "I thought you Marine commando types could do just about anything."

"I can do just about anything, except time travel and give birth, that is. And I'm working on the time travel thing, so stay tuned."

"There's that sense of humor."

"There's nothing funny about today, Sandi. Just my way of coping with this shit. I lost a friend today. Whatever caused Tony to turn on me, it had to be something that scared the shit out of him. He was one of the few I let in. I've lost too many over the years, especially in the Gulf. That's why it's so damn hard to get close to people."

"And Ann Banks?" DeCarlo asked. "You were certainly close to her."

"I take it you've heard the recording?"

"Nope. And as far as I know, neither has anyone involved in this, other than Dunayev and Josh Martin. And I don't see him saying anything about it now," DeCarlo added as she pointed to the dead Russian. "And you don't have to worry about Josh Martin either."

"Tony killed Dunayev before I could even ask him where his copy of the recording was. Now we'll never find it."

"That might be a good thing, don't you think?"

"I don't actually. It could surface anywhere, anytime, and cause her a lot of harm."

"She's a big girl. She can handle it."

"They'll crucify her if it comes out."

"Maybe. But my money is on her, Slick."

The comment caught Dionis off guard. He shot her a look and realized it was all part of her sarcastic approach to life and her profession.

"I not only lost a good friend today, but I also almost lost my life. You've saved my ass twice. Not sure I'm going to be around this business long enough to repay you," Dionis said.

"Remember what Rocky Balboa said to his brother-in-law, Paulie, 'friends don't keep score, friends do because they want to.'"

"You're a Rocky fan?" he asked.

"Who isn't? Especially with that new kid, Michael Jordan, taking over. He's not hard to look at."

"I don't get to the movies much these days. I think I'd rather spend my time sailing."

"What are you going to do about Ann?"

"Nothing. She's going to be president and I'm a huge liability. Plus, I don't want to be in that world any more than I wanted to be in my ex-wife's. They both love power politics. I deplore it. After today, Ann will realize that she and I are not meant to be."

"Well, I have a lot of work to do here. For what it's worth, the media will soon know you're no longer a person of interest in Patrick Banks' death."

"I never thought I really was."

"Yeah, you keep telling yourself that, Slick," DeCarlo said as she winked at him.

"And the recording?" Dionis asked.

"So far, I think we've kept the recording a secret. But I don't think this is over just yet."

"What do you mean?"

"I think that Ann Banks has some political loose ends to tie up."

"Can we help her with that?"

"I'll let you know."

"And the two Russians who roughed us up?"

"The all-powerful General Sherry has dispatched them both back to Russia. They should be on a plane out of the country very soon."

"Have you met this guy, Sherry?" Dionis asked.

"Oh yes, I have. Scary, and not in a fun way. No nonsense. Lots of connections."

"Do you trust him?"

“About as far as I can throw him.”

“Meaning?”

“Like most powerful bureaucrats, they serve their own self-interests. As far as I can tell, your interests, mine, and his, just happened to line up the last few days. If they didn’t, you’d be dead. But for now, he put wheels in motion to help Ann Banks and save your life. Would I trust him tomorrow if things changed? No.”

“Why did he let the Russians go?”

“It served his self-interests to do so is my guess. Still, there’s a lot you need to hear. But not from me. I’m sure someone will be in touch. Just know that as of a couple of days ago, it became clear that Dunayev’s case was never going to trial. One way or another, he was never going to see the inside of a courtroom.”

“And who made that decision?”

“People whose pay grade is a lot higher than yours or mine.”

“I have no idea who to trust anymore,” Dionis said as a tear formed around both of his eyes.

DeCarlo looked at him and saw a fragile man; something she would never have imagined seeing in Michael Dionis. She said, “Man up there, Michael,” as she placed her right arm on his shoulder. “If you haven’t figured out yet that you can trust me, then you’re not as smart as you look. Short of that, I’d watch my back if I were you. Especially with guys like Sherry and his bunch. They’ll shift alliances on you in the middle of the game, all depending on which way the political winds are blowing. You get that wound taken care of. When you do, and if your ex doesn’t have you locked up, and you ever feel like trying to get close to someone again, call me. I hear it’s a lot like riding a bike. Just don’t keep me waiting too long, old man; you’re not getting any younger.” With that, DeCarlo smiled, turned, and walked away. She had no intention of waiting for a response. Nor did she want Michael Dionis to see the tear starting its way down her left cheek.

DeCarlo walked over to Leah Riggs, wiped the tear from her eye and said, "I'm sorry about Tony. You know he saved Michael's life?"

"So, I've heard," Riggs replied.

"Last minute change of heart, I guess."

"Hard to say, detective."

"I certainly had no idea how this was going to play out today," DeCarlo told her.

"Neither did I."

DeCarlo asked, "So how are you going to play this, Leah?"

"Well, let's see; I helped a state police detective take down a Russian organized crime figure without telling my headquarters or anyone in my office. One of my agents, who I reported to the OPR, and was under surveillance today, was shot and killed here by an intelligence operative of our country, after he saved the life of a Secret Service Agent. That operative is now gone because you released her. Another Russian, who was at the table with Dunayev moments before the shooting started, is nowhere to be found. So, you tell me detective, how do you think I should play this?"

"Well, I wouldn't tell the whole truth and nothing but the truth if I were you."

"Funny."

"Sorry. I'm not trying to be. Maybe you want to think about exactly what your version of the truth is here," DeCarlo said.

"Meaning?" Riggs asked.

"The intelligence operative that killed Tony is going to be a citizen traveling in New England with her boyfriend. She was simply protecting herself when the shooting started. When I'm done with her, it will be a case of mistaken identity with regard to Tony. She'll tell your agents the same thing. In fact, you do the interview yourself, if that's possible. Tony will be portrayed as a hero for saving Michael's life. An agent killed in the line of duty as far as I'm concerned."

"My thoughts exactly. I'll have a closed door with the director over this, probably in the morning. Not sure what will happen to me after that."

"Find a way to survive this, at least in the short term."

"Why is that?"

"Ann Banks. She's going to hear from me what you did here."

"I'll let you know if I need help," Riggs said. "I have to go now and meet with Tony's wife and make a death notification."

"Yeah," was all DeCarlo could say as she shook her head and walked away.

Throughout the rest of the day the Connecticut State Police collected shell casings from the blood-soaked redwood floors of the Seacrest lounge. They dug two rounds out of the wall and ceiling and took over three hundred photographs. An FBI forensics team duplicated virtually everything the state police did, thinking, of course, that no forensic team could do anything as well as they could.

Kimiko Matsui bagged the bodies of Andre Dunayev, his Russian accomplice that had no identification on him, as well as the body of Tony Maffuci. All three were transported to the medical examiner's office in Farmington.

It was almost six p.m. before Sandi DeCarlo made her way back to Hartford. Her first stop was the governor's mansion. She was immediately escorted into the study where she had first met Ann Banks. Sitting there was General John Sherry and Jason Palmer. Palmer stood and shook DeCarlo's hand. Sherry remained in his chair and simply nodded as he took a sip of Colonel Taylor bourbon.

"Detective DeCarlo," Ann Banks said, extending her hand. "How's the shoulder?"

"It hurts like hell, ma'am."

"I'm so sorry to have heard about your shooting. Can I get you anything? Coffee perhaps?" Banks asked.

"No ma'am, I'm good."

"The shoulder will heal, detective," Sherry said. "You did an excellent job today."

"I'm not sure how three dead people equates to an excellent job," DeCarlo replied.

"In this case, it does," Sherry said. "So, tell us, what is your next move with regard to Agent Dionis and your investigation?"

"He's at Yale New Haven hospital being attended to. The bullet hit him in the upper part of his abdomen. Grazed it to be more accurate. I'm told he's going to be fine."

"Thank God," Ann Banks said.

"I'm surprised that your people haven't told you that already," DeCarlo said.

"You know we can't make inquiries like that, detective," Palmer said.

"Yes, I'm learning more each day how this works. You don't want to draw yourselves any undue attention."

"It's about protecting the presidency, detective, I told you that," Sherry said.

"Yeah. Everyone else is expendable. I get it."

"Detective, is there a problem?" Ann Banks asked.

"No ma'am, there isn't. Two Russian thugs, one who killed Oleg Lomakina, and made sure your husband was given cocaine laced with fentanyl, were killed today. I have no problem with that. But an FBI agent was killed in the process. He'd been compromised, that's for sure. They threatened his family. But he didn't deserve to die. I think your girl Chan seized the opportunity and killed him to keep him quiet," DeCarlo said, looking directly at Sherry. "And I think she did so under your orders."

"Detective, this is absolutely outrageous. How dare you," Sherry said in a piercing voice.

"How dare you, General," DeCarlo said, clearly revealing her indignation. "You sent her and your man, Larry, down there to actually kill Michael, if necessary. If not Michael, then certainly Tony. They were both liabilities."

DeCarlo then turned her attention to Ann Banks and said, "Ma'am, there's one thing that doesn't make sense; Michael was expendable. The General told me so. What I'd like to know is why?"

Ann Banks turned and looked directly at General Sherry and said, "John?"

Sherry stood up and said, "I did what I had to do to protect the office of the president, nothing more."

"He's right, ma'am. He did what he had to do to protect you and your presidency. Luckily for Michael, he survived it. I just wanted you to know."

"She knows, detective," Palmer said curtly.

"Yes, detective, I know," Banks added more calmly. "Nobody was supposed to die, not even Dunayev. General Sherry was betrayed by his Russian contact. And we were all betrayed by the Chinese."

"The Chinese?" DeCarlo asked.

"Yes, detective," Sherry said. "We learned that the Chinese were playing Dunayev. They wanted the recording. Had they gotten it, they would have blackmailed the president and been more of a threat to her presidency than Dunayev could ever have dreamt of. There are things you don't know, detective. And I kept them from you for a reason."

"You put a lot of people in harm's way, General," DeCarlo said.

Sherry said, unsympathetically, "It's what I do, detective. Unfortunately, I sometimes have to put people in harm's way. The strong get through it just like you did. Now, the recording; have your people located it?"

"They have not. But the forensics team will go through Dunayev's car very carefully. The FBI is also having his apartment in NY searched." DeCarlo was lying. But no one picked up on it.

"Well, I do hope you'll tell me if they find it," Sherry said.

"I certainly don't want it," DeCarlo said. "But there is no telling what Dunayev did with it."

"So where is Josh Martin now?" Banks demanded to know.

"We released him, on the General's authorization. If he had any sense, he's running, and running fast. Martin is too frightened to double-cross us."

"You're far too naïve, detective," Sherry said.

"Maybe. But you have Martin and the Speaker on tape conspiring against Ms. Banks. I'm guessing you can take it from here."

Ann Banks could sense the tension rising in the room. In an attempt to defuse it, she said, "Sandi, it's been a long week. I can't thank you enough for what you've done here. Please tell me, how can I help you?"

"I'm glad you asked, ma'am. The head of the FBI here in Connecticut, Leah Riggs, she put her career on the line for you today," DeCarlo said looking directly at Banks.

"Yes, I know Leah. What about her?"

"We can only keep so much of this under wraps. And trust me, General," DeCarlo said, turning her attention directly at John Sherry, "I know what we need to do here. Leah might actually get fired over what she did and failed to do the last forty-eight hours. I need you to intervene. She's as good as they come and she's not afraid to get her hands dirty when necessary. Today should prove that."

"That's not going to be a problem," Palmer replied, injecting himself into the conversation.

Palmer looked directly at Banks and said, "I'll take care of that immediately."

"Leah will be just fine, detective. You have my word," Banks said.

"And Michael?"

"What about Michael?" Banks asked. The distressed look on her face was clearly noticeable to everyone in the room.

"He's also going to face a lot of problems from the Service. He's going to be cleared by us tonight during a press conference. But that's not going to void all the internal and administrative issues he's facing."

"I'm not sure what you're asking here, detective?" Sherry asked.

"It's simple, General, he can't sit out the next two years fighting administrative battles and pushing paperwork with the Secret Service before he's eligible to retire. Michael is not designed for that."

"What are you proposing?" Sherry asked.

"Well, sir, you either take him with you, let him use his military skills to train people, or find some other productive role for him, or use your considerable sources to have him medically retired as a result of his wound today. Frankly, I don't give a damn which one you do. But he's no longer expendable. And you can't hide him in some black hole until he can collect his pension. Are we all good with that?"

"We will certainly figure out something suitable for Agent Dionis, you have my word," Sherry said.

"Then I guess we're all good here. By the way, the gun that was used to kill Oleg Lomakina, was the same gun used to shoot the desk clerk in Scranton and kill the poor guy in the motel the other day. We were able to verify that through ATF's National Tracing Center. With that, we can close this case and hold Dunayev and his associate accountable for the murder of Lomakina."

Palmer said, "Then it looks like you'll be able to close at least one murder investigation here in Connecticut."

"Yes, but unless you want to recall Josh Martin, I'm afraid the death of your husband, Patrick, will remain unsolved and go down as a drug overdose."

"I guess it will," Banks replied.

DeCarlo nodded in agreement and added, "Yeah, sounds about right. I'd like to say this has been fun, but it hasn't. I think I'll stick to finding killers. I'll leave the political cloak and dagger and manipulating the American people to those of you in Washington."

"Detective," was all Sherry said as he nodded and raised his glass of bourbon.

DeCarlo forced a slight grin and nodded. She then turned and walked out of the den and the mansion and got into her car. She reached into her pocket and pulled out the zip drive she found under the right front passenger seat of Dunayev's car before the forensics team had it loaded on a flatbed truck and transported to the crime lab.

I'll bet I can guess what's on you, she thought.

About the same time DeCarlo was leaving the governor's mansion in Hartford, Sergi Nikitin and his injured comrade were boarding a private Gulfstream jet bound for Russia, one of several that the Russian government kept under contract in the U.S. to shuttle people in and out of the country, as necessary. Nikitin knew he owed Sherry a huge favor for helping him; one the general would no doubt call in sometime soon. Nikitin just hoped he'd be in a position to survive the scrutiny his superiors would certainly give him upon his return. His best hope was to avoid mentioning the recording and simply stick to the story that Dunayev overreacted during a meeting and was killed in the process.

***

Two days after the shooting at the Seacrest lounge inside the Water's Edge resort, President Robert Boyer and Ann Banks' press secretaries issued a joint written press release in concert with the U.S. States Attorney's Office in Connecticut.

"Yesterday, supervisory FBI Agent Tony Maffuci was killed during a joint undercover operation conducted in concert with the

U.S. Secret Service and the Connecticut State Police. During the last two weeks, law enforcement authorities learned President-elect Ann Banks' late husband, Patrick Banks, died as a result of using cocaine laced with fentanyl. The cocaine was allegedly contaminated by members of Russian organized crime, who had tried, unsuccessfully, to convince the late Congressman to provide them access to the president-elect. Exactly what they wanted the access for, is unclear. But it is believed Congressman Banks was killed when he refused to allow these organized crime figures access to his wife, President-elect Ann Banks. In an elaborate undercover operation, the Secret Service and the FBI were able to identify the Russian figures involved, and confronted them at Water's Edge, where FBI Agent Maffuci was killed saving the life of U.S. Secret Service Agent Michael Dionis. Two Russian mobsters were also killed in the shootout at the Water's Edge Resort.

"President Boyer and President-elect Banks are saddened by the death of Agent Maffuci, calling him a hero for his service to his country. They also wish to thank and compliment the FBI, the U.S. Secret Service, along with the Connecticut State Police, for their quick reaction and dedication to this matter during the past two weeks. President Boyer would also like to thank the Russian Federal Security Service, known as the FSB, for assisting in this operation. The extent of their cooperation in identifying those involved, for reasons I'm sure you can appreciate, will not be discussed. Also, this is an ongoing investigation. As such, we will not be answering any questions involving this matter."

After the release of the joint statement, the talking heads on every major twenty-four hour news network, had a field day speculating what was really behind the shooting. But nobody involved in the operation was talking. At least not for now. Everyone knew that Tina Crawford was the unknown wild card. She was waiting to be officially named the U.S. Attorney in Connecticut after the inauguration. When that happened, she too, would remain silent.

Chapter 31

Inauguration Day

January 20, was exceptionally cold in Washington, D.C. At noon, Ann Banks was sworn in by the Chief Justice of the U.S. Supreme Court. Banks took the podium and looked out over the thousands of people who had lined the Capital Mall. In the distance, she could see the Washington Monument and the Lincoln Memorial. Ann Banks kept her inaugural address shorter than previous incoming presidents. She wanted to keep her speech brief and direct, never mentioning how "*she*" was the answer to Americans' hopes and dreams. Instead, she stressed harmony and cooperation and tried the best she could to compliment members of Congress on both sides of the political aisle for the work they had tried to do for the American people. She also appealed to political ideologues on both sides to put their own self-interests aside and join her in a full-fledged effort to work for the American people. When she took to the podium and adjusted the microphone, she began:

"There is a problem in this country. We must stop from seizing every opportunity to verbally assault members of the opposing party over every spoken word or difference in political philosophy. The floor of the House and the Senate is not a stage where you can take the time to espouse your own personal philosophy, and yes, your dramatic presentation of your outrage over something suggested by the political opposition. Just because you differ on a subject, doesn't make people you differ with your sworn enemy. And if you disagree with the position of your party, be strong enough to say so. The days of simply towing the party line just because, must end."

Of course, the crowd watching at the Capital applauded as Ann Banks, the first woman to be elected to the office of the president, talked about unifying America to the extent it could ever be unified. She stressed that she would pursue her promise to seek term limits for members of the House, and Senate. Again, there was more applause, and she had to wait to continue speaking. Of course, members of the

Congressional leadership on both sides remained stoic in their response. Banks also pleaded for the U.S. news agencies to start reporting more actual news instead of dominating the airways with political talking heads whose only goal was to influence voters based on the wishes of the mega, for-profit corporations they worked for. It did, of course, make for good soundbites. But at the end of the day, politicians were not going to change how they conducted the party's business, at least not anytime soon.

Trying to add some levity to her comment, Banks smiled for the cameras and added, "I can't wait for the news outlets, and the late show comedians to attack my comments tonight."

Banks also appealed to the Chinese government to work more closely with the U.S. She invited them to sit down and discuss matters of mutual interest including China joining the U.S. and Russia in space exploration. Her reasoning, she told the American people in her speech, was that the more countries cooperated in such things, the more there was transparency and less chance of armed conflict. She was offering China an olive branch. She had no misguided expectation that they would take it. But it did serve as excellent media fodder.

After the short thirteen-minute speech, one of the shortest inaugural addresses in history, Banks left the podium and was escorted inside the Capital where the temperature was much warmer. Shortly thereafter, she was in the back of the presidential limo surrounded by Secret Service Agents and being paraded down Constitution Avenue.

After the parade, there was a short period of down time before she was to attend a luncheon with the Congressional leadership. Just prior to the luncheon, she arranged for a one-on-one meeting in the Oval Office with the Speaker of the House, Susan Welsh.

"Madam Speaker, so nice of you to join me," Banks said. "Thank you so much for taking the time to come by. Please have a seat," Banks added as she pointed to the sofa.

"This is quite unusual, Madam President," Welsh said as she sat down. "Incoming presidents usually don't have time for personal meetings like this on their inauguration day. To what do I owe this honor?"

"I wanted us to have a few private moments together and ask what you planned to do, now that I'm President?"

"What I plan to do with regard to what, Madam President?"

"Your future, Madam Speaker."

"I still don't understand," Welsh said.

"Paying for a recording in hopes of blackmailing the president," Banks said.

Welsh's smile quickly faded. Madam President, I'm not sure what you're talking about.

"Well, Madam Speaker, let me play a short recording for you and see if that refreshes your memory." Banks hit a button on the phone on her desk and almost immediately, Jason Palmer walked in. He nodded politely, opened an iPad, and hit the play button. For about two minutes, the three of them listened to a recording of Susan Welsh agreeing to pay Josh Martin five-million dollars for the recording of Banks and Dionis in bed. The moment Palmer ended the playback, a morbid silence filled the room.

Susan Welsh was the first to talk. "You think you can get me to resign over this?"

"That's up to you, Madam Speaker. But your role in this blackmail scheme will be made known to the American people very shortly. I'll tell them the recording that Martin played for you was fabricated. Since you don't have a copy of this so-called recording, all the people will hear is your conversation with Martin agreeing to pay for a copy of it in order to blackmail me. And I'm going to give a copy of the recording of you agreeing to pay Martin for it to every media outlet in the country: the liberal ones, and the conservative ones. They can debate it any fucking way they want because that's what they do. And of course, my new Attorney General will use it as evidence in your criminal trial."

"You're no different than the rest of us. You're blackmailing me now."

"I'm not blackmailing you; I'm simply telling you what I'm going to do. Life is a bit like a chess game, Madam Speaker. This is a critical move for you. I suggest you think carefully as to what your next move is. For instance, if you were to resign, let's say by close of business tomorrow, I might have to rethink releasing the recording that implicates you in a criminal conspiracy to blackmail the President of the United States."

Banks nodded at Palmer and said, "We're good Jason. Please leave us for a moment."

Palmer left the Oval Office with the iPad and closed the door behind him.

"We can work together on this. There is no need for us to be adversaries," Welsh said.

"And what do you propose?"

Welsh asked, "What do you want?"

"In the morning, you come out in favor of term-limits. You tell the media you've rethought it and support the idea. Appeal to your colleagues and the American people that it's time for term limits. Let them know that in support of this, you will not be seeking re-election. Let everyone know that you're joining me in getting this legislation passed in the next 100 days."

"Madam President, you know I can spin this recording. I'll make it look like you recorded me illegally. And that the conversation was taken completely out of context."

"Well then, let's see how that plays out for you in the morning. Then you can also explain why you advanced Josh Martin two and a half-million dollars. That's right; we tracked the wire transfer. You think Josh fucking Martin is going to serve time for you? Let's see how the American people and your supportive news networks spin that. I'll be interested in hearing that myself. My new Attorney General is anxious to hear how this meeting goes. What should I tell him?"

"You're going to learn quickly, that no matter what you think you might accomplish during your presidency, that all bureaucracies are corrupt. And you're demonstrating that you are as corrupt as any of us here in Washington."

"No, Madam Speaker, nowhere near as corrupt. But if what you say is true, I'll fight with everything I have to rid Washington of people like you."

"Donald Trump said he was going to rid people like us from Washington; drain the swamp he said. You see how that worked out for him?"

"I see how the people who didn't want him draining the swamp reacted to him. I guess I'll have to make sure I don't make the same mistakes he did."

"What you're asking me to do goes against everything I believe in. And my coming out in favor of term limits is far from the truth."

"The truth is, you paid for a recording that you planned to use against me. But Martin never delivered the tape to you, did he?"

"He played enough of it for me to know you had an affair with one of your Secret Service Agents during the campaign and election. And we both know that is the truth."

"Well, Madam Speaker, what is it you told me at my husband's funeral? Oh yes, 'the truth is always negotiable.'" Ann Banks stared directly at Welsh and in a calm and threatening voice, said, "Madam Speaker, your days of spinning falsehoods into truths are about over."

Welsh rose from her chair and said, "The truth depends on where you sit and who you listen to."

Ann Banks rose from her seat moved to within a few inches of Welsh's face and said, "Madam Speaker, I sit in the Oval Office. And right now, the American people are fucking listening to me."

Epilogue

One day after the inauguration, Speaker of the House, Susan Welsh resigned her position in Congress. She cited health concerns and thought it was time to pass the gavel to someone younger who might find a way to help the new president unite the nation. The liberal media called her a hero and one of the bravest women they'd ever known as a result of her past work and the difficult decision she made to resign. They applauded the fact that she stayed on through the election, putting her party first at the risk of her own personal health. Her bravery was the talk of the news pundits that day, the same day two female police officers were gunned down in Chicago, and a Navy Seal was killed on a rescue mission in the mid-east. Only one news network made mention of them being heroes.

Two months after the inauguration, Leah Riggs moved to the nation's capital after receiving a promotion that catapulted her over a number of more qualified FBI agents. Knowing that she might be in over her head with her new job; one that she wasn't quite ready for, she befriended former Secretary of State, Condoleezza Rice. Rice was generous with her time and counsel, often choosing to discuss national politics with Riggs while the two played golf at the Augusta National club, home of the Master's tournament each April.

Six months after the inauguration, term limit legislation was still being discussed on the floor of the House of Representatives. Many elected officials argued that term limits already existed and were determined by the voters during each election. Ann Banks kept up her appeal to the American voters, urging them to demand to know their representatives' and Senators' position on the topic, and if they failed to support term-limit legislation, to vote for the opponent who did support it in the next election, regardless of party affiliation.

Ann Banks was also fighting with members of the conservative wing to bring about any type of gun legislation that the NRA felt would infringe on their rights: which included virtually any type of legislation at all. In spite of several mass shootings of innocent victims in the country since she took office, the NRA continued to successfully attack and derail any efforts to control the sale and possession of weapons that aided in rapidly shooting multiple people. What Ann Banks was learning most, was that it took real power in Washington for things to not get done. And she was finding herself surrounded by very powerful people, including the powerful lobby groups who wanted little more than to maintain the status quo. Whatever did or didn't get done, was designed to keep the clients of the lobbyists happy; it had little to nothing to do with promoting the good of the American people. Washington, she was learning, could be the cruelest place on the planet.

Banks began video recording meetings with the leadership of both parties, in order for the American people and media giants to see for themselves exactly what was being said by all concerned during discussions relating to foreign affairs, budget legislation, police reform, illegal immigration, gun control, medical care, and civil rights legislation.

Banks also met with the leaders of China and Russia in an effort to open a dialogue that would, at the very least, assure both nations' leaders that issues surrounding trade, scientific advancement, and the exchange of information to combat terrorism, were of common interest to all parties. She had hoped to gather some support from Putin and Xi Jinping on these issues in order to build a foundation from which to build trust. Both leaders provided lip service and told the president that she could count on them to work with her.

When her meetings ended, Putin continued his Cold War-style confrontation with the U.S. According to her intelligence briefings that she received each morning by her national security advisor, John Sherry, and the new FBI Deputy Director for counterterrorism and intelligence, Leah Riggs, the Russians were continuing to deploy cyberattacks against the country's critical infrastructure. Sherry stressed again, as he had in his first meeting with her, that the Russians and the Chinese had, or were close to having, the ability to attack our electrical grids, oil pipelines and water supply. If and when they chose to do so, it would have a catastrophic impact on the country, possibly resulting in the deaths of millions of Americans in just over thirty days.

North Korea was starting up its nuclear missile testing again, posing yet another threat to the U.S. Banks wasn't quite sure how to respond to that just yet. When she consulted General Sherry about it, he reminded her that when Trump was elected, his political opponents and people around the world, especially in Europe, thought Trump's rhetoric would get the U.S. into a nuclear war. When Trump met with the Korean leader, those same critics attacked him for meeting with Kim and giving him a position on the world stage.

"You can't win here, Madam President," Sherry told her. "Your opponents will find fault in most any approach you take. It is, in large part, a personality contest. Trump made it about himself. You need to make it about trying to keep the peace. If that means appeasing that little psychopath, then so be it. Trump could have gotten a lot of mileage out of his meeting with Kim had he just not tried to make it all about himself. For what it's worth, you might consider sending former President Trump over there on a diplomatic mission. The liberals will crucify you for it, but the conservatives will see it as a wise move. But think about it. If your goal here is to get Kim to throttle back on his nuclear missile program, it might be worth it, no matter how distasteful it might be to do."

Banks continued her efforts at finding some common ground between the two political parties that would result in improving the lives of all Americans while keeping them as safe as possible. She was able to claim one small victory when she persuaded legislators on both sides of the aisle to take whatever measures were necessary to stop robocalls. But after six months, she was still learning the meaning of partisan politics.

During her six months in office, she had not seen or heard from Michael Dionis.

Seven months after the inauguration, Josh Martin was sitting at the Banana Beach bar in Costa Rica. He had just ordered his second margarita when a woman walked up to the bar and took the seat next to him. Martin couldn't help but notice her wearing a tank top tee shirt over her bikini. The woman was the first to speak, making small talk about the great beach, weather, and of course the drinks. After forty-five minutes of flirting conversation, she asked Martin if he had a room at the resort. Martin couldn't believe his luck. Never one to fully appreciate the saying that if something is too good to be true, it probably is, he asked her if she wanted to go back to his room with him. As soon as the door opened, Larry Barnes grabbed him by the back of the neck and twisted Martin's head until it snapped. Chrissie Chan wasn't sure if Martin was dead yet or not. If he wasn't, he would be soon. Either way, she looked at Martin and said, "General Sherry sends his regards."

Ten months after Ann Banks was sworn in as president, Michael Dionis pulled his sailboat into Conch Harbor Marina in Key West, Florida. The minute he was able to do so, he had launched his boat from Pilot's Point Marina in Westbrook, just two miles south from Water's Edge. The yard workers at the marina were skeptical, telling him it was too early in the season to launch. But Dionis was adamant. He was sailing south; the weather be damned.

He tied his boat to the slip he'd rented, and walked over to Sloppy Joe's, the bar made famous by Ernest Hemmingway. He sat at the bar alone, listening to one of the many house bands play songs that he'd never heard, or couldn't understand. He'd been traveling down the east coast for months after being medically retired from the Secret Service. Along the way, he only spoke to people that he had to in order to secure a boat slip for a few days or weeks. He had no television on board and avoided the news as much as possible. He did, however, occasionally surf the Internet to see what Ann Banks was doing or was trying to do. He could sense her frustration but could also see that she was not backing down from any political fights. He cared for her, but the feelings he had for her were gone. As much as he might like to talk to her, that was not an option. And he was good with that.

After two beers at Sloppy Joe's, Dionis picked up his cell phone and called Sandi DeCarlo. She picked up on the second ring.

"Took you long enough, Slick. Are you back in Connecticut?" DeCarlo asked.

"Nope. Connecticut will forever remain in my rear-view mirror."

"Sorry to hear that. So, what's happening?"

"How's the weather up there in Connecticut?"

"It's November. How do you think it is? It's cold, rainy, we're expecting some snow this weekend. Tell me you didn't call to discuss the weather."

"Well, yes and no."

"What does that mean?"

"Do you have an interest in getting away from that miserable weather to someplace warmer for a while?"

"That depends. Where and with who?"

"Still funny and sarcastic I see."

"Yes and no. But you haven't answered the question."

"Key West. With me."

"And why would I want to do that?" asked DeCarlo.

"Because we went through some serious stuff together."

"We did. But you've been through serious stuff with lots of people. Are you inviting them to Key West too?"

"No."

"Then you're going to have to do better than that, Slick."

"Because I'm ready to let someone back in, and I'm hoping that someone is going to be you. I miss you, Sandi. I have for quite some time. And I'm betting you miss me."

"Betting? You saw the trouble gambling got Maffuci into?"

"I remember. But he was betting against the house. I am the house."

"I don't know, Michael. I'm not sure this is a great idea."

"If you don't think what we went through together has drawn us closer, then I've misread this," he said.

"I'm not saying you've misread anything. But you left without saying good-bye. You just sailed off into the sunset."

"Yes, I did. But you know why I did that?"

"I suppose I do. Have you heard from our president?"

"Not a word since all of this went down."

"And how are you coping with that?" DeCarlo asked.

"I'm coping just fine. Ann's a fine woman and is trying to do great things. But we move in different circles. I always knew that. And so did she. Any more personal questions?"

"None for now," DeCarlo replied. "But I may have a number of them later."

"Then I have one."

"Okay, I'll give you one, but just one."

"Do you still take your coffee with cream and two sugars?" he asked.

"How in the hell do you know that?"

"The morning we first met; at the U.S. Attorney's Office. You told the secretary how you liked your coffee."

"You remember that?"

"People remember what they want to remember when something is important to them," he replied.

DeCarlo was happy that they weren't having this conversation on FaceTime. She didn't want Dionis to see the smile on her face. "Let me think about it Michael."

"I understand. Take as long as you like. But remember, I'm not getting any younger," Dionis said, trying to elicit a laugh.

But Sandi DeCarlo wasn't laughing. There was a momentary silence prompting Dionis to ask, "Sandi, are you still there?"

"Yeah," she replied. "I'm still here. I'll think about it. Stay safe Michael," she added, as she hung up the phone.

Dionis paid his tab and walked back toward the marina. On the way, he stopped at Dante's Key West Restaurant & Pool Bar. He took a seat at the bar and ordered a cup of She Crab Soup and the grilled mahi tacos. He also ordered a Stella on tap. The moment his food arrived he heard a ping telling him that he had a text message. He opened his phone and punched in his code. It was a text message from Sandi DeCarlo.

Arriving Key West Airport, the day after tomorrow at 1:45 p.m. American Airlines, flight 4237. Don't make me take an Uber to find you old man.

Dionis read the message three times, then laid the phone down in front of him on the bar. He looked up and could see his face in the reflection of the mirror behind the bar. He was smiling for the first time in almost a year.

Acknowledgments

I will forever be grateful to a handful of people who helped with this project. First, former grad student, Jennifer Roberts, of the Office of the Chief Medical Examiner in CT. Jennifer provided valuable information related to how autopsies are performed and as well as how testing is conducted related to contaminated narcotics.

Another former graduate student, Captain Mark Davidson, of the Connecticut State Police, provided valuable background and the accuracy of various police procedures; many of which has changed during the many years since my retirement from that profession. His recent book of poetry, *Another Side of Accountability*, also helped provide insight into the many emotional feelings the men and women who put themselves in harm's way experience every single day for us.

Many thanks to Eric Tyler, yet another former student, who allowed me to bounce questions off of him regarding the bureaucratic nuances of contemporary issues in law enforcement. Nothing pleases an old professor more than when he/she can say, "The student, has become the teacher." Eric is indeed now the teacher, and I am the grateful student.

I want to thank my friend of over 30-years, and golf partner, John Sherry, a Beta Reader for this book. John has been a "first reader" for each of my previous books and has always provided valuable feedback. John has also generously agreed to the use of his name as one of the most integral characters in this story. He is however, a much better golfer than the character by that name in the book.

Another friend and golf partner, retired U.S. Air Force Colonel, Tom Belise, the author of *Raptor Bloom,* and *Taking the Dream Spinner,* read the initial draft and provided honest, and painful, feedback; exactly what an author looks for from a Beta Reader. His comments and suggestions have helped shape this into a more interesting story.

I want to thank my former colleague at the Defense Criminal Investigative Service (DCIS), Henry Mungle, a highly decorated Vietnam combat veteran and the author of *The Apostate*. Henry, too, was a Beta Reader and provided critical feedback and many strong suggestions.

Many thanks to my good friend Bob Geist, a first reader who made sure my descriptions of the various scotch references were accurate. I also want to thank good friends, Gail Sherry, and Susan Pinette for reviewing the early draft and finished product. The fact that the story kept your interest provided valuable input. I appreciate all of you taking the time to read the manuscript.

A special thanks to friends Larry Barnes and Steve Bamford for agreeing to allow me to use their names as characters in this story.

When I started this project, I reached out to my former colleague, mentor, and friend, from the University of New Haven, Lynn Monahan, Ph.D. Now retired, I was hoping that Lynn was looking for something to do. I was right. I've been fortunate to work with some very talented people at the university, but none more so than Lynn. The help and guidance she provided when I wrote my textbook was invaluable. When I went back to the well, Lynn jumped at the chance to help. She painstakingly went through every line, page by page, editing the book as if she were redlining a doctoral thesis resulting in detailed editorial feedback. She will never know how grateful I am for her help, guidance, and perseverance with this project. I hope she is happy with the end result.

Finally, to Linda, my wife for over thirty-four years. There is no way to say thank you enough for all your editorial help, suggestions, and fact checking. Your many questions during this project helped keep the story accurate and the characters true to themselves. I can never imagine taking on another project like this without you by my side.

CPSIA information can be obtained
at www.ICGtesting.com
Printed in the USA
LVHW111340011221
704980LV00016B/762

9 781647 198640